Volume One Of The Last Colony Series

THE
EDGE OF
CASCADIA

S.A. SEBUCHI

2021 Sage's Tower Publishing

Copyright © 2021 by S. A. Sebuchi

Cover Design © Makoto Sebuchi, Carla Buchanan

Published in the United States by Sage's Tower Publishing.

Sage's Tower Publishing is a registered trademark.

Hardcover ISBN 978-1-63706-026-1
Softcover ISBN 978-1-63706-027-8
eBook ISBN 978-1-63706-028-5

www.sagestowerpublishing.com

For my husband—my best friend, my rock, my true love.

Chapter One
Annabelle

The day her grandmother died she burdened Annabelle with a secret. The sun shone brightly that afternoon but Gran didn't permit one ray of its brilliance into her room. She seemed to want to die in the darkness.

"Gran? You awake?" Annabelle waited a few seconds after entering the dim room to let her eyes adjust. Clutching a sketchbook and pencil, Annabelle walked to the bed, leaving the door open to let some light in. Annabelle's shoes tapped as she crossed the cement floor and the cold, musty air made the room feel like a cave in the desert.

"Annabelle?" Gran reached her hand up and Annabelle took it after laying the sketchbook on the nightstand.

"Yes, it's me." She sat on the chair next to the bed.

Gran smiled, but her eyes darted back and forth. Annabelle had intended to draw her portrait but shadows dominated Gran's face. She couldn't bear to let Gran's last sketch be dark when her life had been filled with color and warmth.

Gran closed her eyes and took a few slow breaths. Her lips parted and her face looked relaxed. Had she fallen asleep so quickly? Should she let her sleep? Annabelle watched Gran breathe, waiting.

"Is everything okay?" Annabelle whispered finally. After all, Gran had summoned her to talk privately.

Gran opened her eyes and let out a laugh. "Of course everything isn't okay," she said, this time managing to make eye contact.

Annabelle frowned, but nodded all the same. Gran spoke the truth. How could everything be alright when she was dying?

"I know, I'm sorry," she said, brushing a loose strand of hair from Gran's eye.

"No, it isn't what you think." The spunk and energy Annabelle loved about Gran came back, and her eyes widened as she tried to sit up. Her frail arms shook under her body's weight.

"Gran, what are you doing?"

"Help me up, will ya?"

Annabelle bunched some pillows under Gran's back. Gran's clear and focused eyes made her look years younger. *Is this a good sign, or a bad sign?*

"There, that's better." Gran sighed and looked around. "Now listen, I need your help with something." She leaned forward, dropping her voice into a whisper. "But I don't think you'll like it."

Annabelle furrowed her eyebrows in confusion. "Gran, how can you say that? I'd do anything for you."

Gran stared over the top of Annabelle's head, hesitating.

"Gran, what is it?"

"Annabelle." Gran stared at her now. "I have a secret and I can't let it die with me."

Annabelle slid her chair closer to the bed and took Gran's hand. She'd do anything to relieve Gran's pain. "What is it?"

Gran squeezed Annabelle's hand and looked into her eyes, unblinking. "I need you to get something for me," she said.

"Ok," Annabelle said, giving Gran a reassuring smile. "What is it?"

Gran rubbed Annabelle's hand with her thumb, stalling again. "It's in the old bunkers," she said, looking down.

"What?...Gran...I..." Annabelle couldn't go in the bunkers, and Gran knew it. Danger lurked inside the deteriorating tunnels and the Colony prohibited anyone from entering.

"I said you wouldn't like it." Gran chanced a look back at her and Annabelle didn't know what to say.

"Everyone keeps telling me I've lived a long and wonderful life," Gran said. "That I have much to be proud of. But it isn't true. I've lived a life full of pain and grief. I feel like it's all I've ever known."

"Gran, what are you talking about?" Annabelle shifted in her chair. Everyone in the Colony shared a history of heartache, especially Gran's generation, but no one spoke of it. Gran should feel gratitude toward the Colony for saving the human race. Everyone focused on looking forward instead of back.

"We all thought we were free when we abandoned the bunkers," Gran continued, "but we'll never be free." She widened her eyes and clenched her jaw. She leaned forward until she gripped Annabelle's shoulder and squeezed tight. "Annabelle, you need to retrieve a key. Never let it out of your sight, and don't tell anyone about it." Gran's sharp tone made Annabelle feel like she couldn't ask anything else, but she had so many questions she couldn't focus on one.

"What does this key unlock?" she finally asked. "Why is it so important?"

"It was your grandfather's. Annabelle, please." Gran lowered her voice and her lip quivered. "I just need you to keep this safe. Can you do that for me?"

Annabelle's pulse quickened. "How will I even get into the bunkers?" The intensity became too much for her and she leaned back, forcing Gran to release her.

"Your grandpa built a secret tunnel from our room in the bunker. I left directions to its location and a compass in the nightstand. You should still be able to access it," Gran said.

"How could he do that? Wouldn't it be dangerous?"

"He was curious. We'd been stuck underground our whole lives, and we didn't fully understand the risks involved when he built it." Gran gave a mischievous grin. "The good news is he never got caught."

Annabelle never would've imagined that sweet, law-abiding Gran would have an illegal exit out of the old bunkers. Maybe she didn't really know Gran at all. "Did you ever actually go outside?"

Gran chewed her lip. "Not often," she said under her breath.

"Gran! I can't believe you. What about the radiation?"

"We figured it would've been long gone by the time he started building it. Annabelle, please promise me you'll get it."

Annabelle tilted her head to the side, frowning. She loved her life in the Colony. Working at the Parenthood Association gave her status and continuing there would guarantee her success once she had children. Getting caught could jeopardize everything she'd begun to work toward.

She glanced back to Gran. She looked small in the bed, her eyes big and pleading. After her mother died Gran had taken her place. She'd been the only mother Annabelle had ever known and she couldn't refuse Gran's dying wish.

"Okay." She leaned forward and lowered her voice. "But what does it unlock?"

Gran pursed her lips. "I actually don't know."

"Gran! Why would I need to get the key if you don't even know what it unlocks?"

"I just know it's important. It was your grandfather's, and he got angry with me every time I brought it up. He said it was for my safety that I didn't know what it unlocked. He was very firm on that." Gran started speaking slower, and blinked a few times before continuing. "I know it must uncover something big. He said the Colony would banish him if anyone ever found out he had it. It was supposed to be destroyed. Annabelle, if it falls into the wrong hands its secret might never be revealed. It would be best if you had it, and even better if you could solve its mystery."

"Banished?" Annabelle almost laughed. "Gran do you realize what you're asking me to do?" Gran didn't respond and when Annabelle looked at her for more information, she had her eyes closed. *Oh no.* A tremor jolted through Annabelle and she grabbed Gran's hand. "Gran?"

Gran peeled her eyes open. "Please, Annabelle, I can't go in peace unless you promise me you'll get it." Her words came out quiet and unsteady.

Annabelle blinked back tears. "I will, I promise," she said. She didn't want to think about what agreeing meant.

Gran let out a slow, labored breath. "Thank you," she said.

Annabelle feared more questions would cause Gran stress. "Okay, Gran, okay. Don't worry about anything. Just relax now."

Gran nodded and closed her eyes. Her face became emotionless. Annabelle stared at Gran and her heart pounded in her ears. It couldn't be the end already, she wasn't ready to let go. She watched until she saw the slight rising and falling of Gran's chest, then leaned back in relief.

Annabelle retrieved the compass and note from the drawer, but didn't look at them. Instead she pushed them into her pocket and grabbed her sketchbook. She wanted to enjoy these last moments with Gran doing what she loved most, sketching. She hoped drawing a portrait would comfort Gran.

Annabelle watched Gran's face. As long as she could remember Gran had always greeted her with a warm smile, eyes lighting up and inviting her in. Gran's beauty remained even in these final moments. Her cheekbones stood out, giving her an air of elegance despite the wrinkles, which showed her age. Her shoulder-length white hair had once been dark brown, like Annabelle's. Even though they no longer shared the same hair color, they still possessed the same smoky gray eyes. Her father said Annabelle resembled Gran as a young woman, and she took it as a compliment.

Annabelle lost herself in the sketch, the dim light somehow not impeding her ability to draw. The challenge of capturing Gran's beauty consumed her, and she placed each line with concentration and precision. In the end, Annabelle believed she had a sketch which transcended age. Gran's inquisitive eyes and calm smile radiated warmth, exactly how Annabelle wanted to remember her.

Gran didn't say much more the rest of the day. She opened her eyes and nodded each time one of Annabelle's brothers came to visit and share their love, but struggled to stay engaged. She took her last breath surrounded by loved ones, and in the dark.

***

The next morning Annabelle set out for Gran's secret tunnel early, hoping fewer people would be out to notice her. A dust storm greeted her, distorting the sunrise and casting an eerie amber glow across the sky. She would've thought the unusual color was beautiful if it weren't for her destination. She didn't see any bikes yet, everyone was probably waiting for the dust storm to die down before heading to work. Annabelle didn't blame them, traveling in this weather would be challenging but at least it would provide her some cover. She kept her head down while the wind grabbed at her backpack.

The tunnel to the bunker's entrance lay beyond the Colony's boundary, something Gran had failed to mention. When Annabelle had read that, she'd decided she wouldn't go. The risks put her outside her comfort level.

Everytime she'd closed her eyes the night before, however, she would see Gran staring at her with large, pleading eyes. She'd told Gran she'd get the key, and she couldn't break her promise.

So much could go wrong though. She could get caught outside the boundary without a guide, she could get lost and wander into a radioactive zone, she could get caught inside the bunker… She pushed her fears aside and marched forward. She hoped this would only take a few hours—she'd promised her dad she'd go to his house that afternoon to help sort some of Gran's belongings.

She passed the uniform homes of the Colony, feeling exposed. In order to save water for growing food, the Colony forbade landscaping, and the homes sat a few feet from the sidewalk. Only a line of gravel separated her from every home's sunroom entrance and the endless row of windows stared at her like a million eyes. Colorful doors interrupted the windows and she noticed a thin layer of dust from the storm covered them.

After a few minutes, she reached the pathway behind the homes, where the massive neighborhood biodome towered above. *From the grains exit of biodome #4 follow the compass N.*

Rather than walk around the back to the grains exit, she went through the biodome. She needed a break from the windstorm and with any luck it would look like her final destination.

Uprooted tumbleweeds blocked the door, and it took Annabelle a few minutes to clear the entrance while trying to avoid getting pricked by the thorns. Once inside she took a deep, cleansing breath, then went down the hallway toward the large chamber which grew fruits and berries. When she arrived she pushed a button on the wall, and the pocket door whooshed as it opened. She stepped through and the door closed behind her.

Annabelle didn't linger as she would usually, plodding past the apple and cherry trees toward the grain chamber. The buzzing bees helped relax her, and she took a deep breath of the thick orchard air, tasting its ripeness. She passed by her strawberries, noting how good they looked after hours of her care, and arrived at the grain chamber.

Annabelle opened the door to the grains chamber and a few bees flew past her. She sighed with relief when she saw no one in there and pushed onward. As she walked down the path between the sea of golden wheat, her heart rate increased. At the other end of the wheat, she entered the hallway leading to the outside exit and closed the door behind her. After she made sure no bees had escaped, she took a step. She went at a slow pace as she approached the metal exit door.

She could still turn back but once she went through that door she committed to leaving the Colony and retrieving the key. Even if she didn't get caught, she'd forever carry the secret of breaking many Colony rules. She'd feel like a fraud. She arrived at the exit and stopped, closing her eyes and taking a few deep breaths. Crossing this threshold would make her a different person. She opened her eyes and pushed the door button.

Outside the sky was no longer orange, but the dust still distorted her view. She took the compass from her pocket and positioned herself facing north, straight ahead from where she stood. She understood why Gran had picked this spot as a starting point—no houses were built on this side of the biodome and only empty, scrubby fields separated her from the Colony boundary. She set off north.

Annabelle fought the urge to run as she crossed the scrubland. Instead, she concentrated on feeling small, invisible. She'd worn her tan patchwork pants and top, and she hoped it would help her stay camouflaged. She kept near the largest sagebrush bushes, slinking across the sandy ground. Her heart pounded as she approached the small trench marking the Colony's boundary.

The Colony didn't build the trench to keep people in, but to let everyone know where safety ended and potential danger began. A person leaving needed a permit and a trained guide to make sure they didn't venture into any radioactive zones. Annabelle had neither. She shuddered thinking of all the infants that had died when her people first left the bunkers. She didn't know how to avoid the contaminated land, or how much danger it posed to her now.

She paused and stared into the trench. A gust of wind blew against her back, as if trying to push her across. *Cross the trench.*

14

There should be a small hill in your view, directly ahead. She glanced up, looking for the hill. The dust had finally started to settle and sure enough she spotted a small hill. All around it a bronzed desert stretched to the horizon, speckled by prickly shrubs. The breeze that remained brought a different fragrance than what she was used to. It smelled faintly tangy and rich with nature.

Annabelle swallowed hard and jumped the trench before she could talk herself out of it. A thrill jolted through her as she headed toward the hill. She was outside the Colony and aside from her own trepidation, nothing had tried to stop her—it had been so easy. With each step she took, curiosity began to stir within her, chasing some of her fears away. She would get away with this, and it would be exciting to see something new.

In less than five minutes, she arrived at the hill. She wanted to climb up to the top, to stand there and gaze into the wilderness. Instead, she listened to common sense and walked around to the other side. *Go to the far side of the hill. At the halfway point of the hill, dig under the sand until you find planks that cover the entrance. Go down and through the tunnel and enter the room. Once inside, look behind the mirror.*

She headed to the middle of the hill. Upon inspection, she found only regular ground. She couldn't see any evidence of a hatch, so she stomped her feet around in the sand. Her stomach twisted with worry that it might not be there anymore. On her sixth stomp something lifted the ground a fraction and she smiled with triumph. *Gran's entrance still existed!* She dropped to her knees and started brushing the sand away until she hit wooden planks a few inches below. She shoved aside the rest of the sand and flipped the planks over, revealing a shaft. Darkness filled the hole and she couldn't see how deep it was. Uneasiness started to chase away her momentary victory. She bit her lip, kneeling down to take a look into the hole. Still unable to see anything she retrieved a flashlight from her backpack. She took a deep breath and flicked it on, then pointed the beam down the hole. *Gran, I won't let you down, not now.*

The beam of light illuminated a metal bar embedded in the side of the shaft. *Must be a ladder.* Holding the flashlight with one hand, she lowered down until a foot landed on the metal bar. She didn't know how old the ladder was and worried it would break under her weight. She held her breath while continuing down and focused on each step instead of letting panic enter her thoughts.

Cold air slithered up her legs and tickled her nose with a stale, earthy aroma. She felt like she was descending into the mouth of an unknown creature and had to fight the urge to go back up. She would not turn back now, not after coming this far. Finally, her feet hit solid ground and she lurched back from the ladder, panting. She shone the flashlight around, catching large particles of dust in the beam. There was only one direction to go, so she crouched down to enter a shallow tunnel. The narrow walls and darkness smothered her, choking out her previous sense of freedom.

Annabelle crept forward, and a minute later arrived at the end of the short tunnel. A hole in the wall lay before her, blocked with debris. She turned the flashlight on it and reached out to investigate. She encountered the smoothness of wooden furniture—the back of a bookcase or dresser.

She put the flashlight in her mouth and rested both palms on the surface of the wood. She took a breath and tried to push it to the side. It wouldn't budge. She would have to kick it over.

Annabelle set her backpack down and rested the flashlight on the top so it illuminated her target. She lined herself parallel to the door and squatted. She clenched her fists and bobbed down once and kicked at the obstruction. The piece of furniture rocked back and forth but settled back in its previous position. Annabelle clenched her fists harder, she needed more force.

She took a few steps back and then, crouching down, ran full speed with her shoulder first. She made contact and sharp pain shot down her arm as she collapsed forward with the piece of furniture. The force of the abrupt crash reverberated through the room and sent dust flying.

She rested where she fell, catching her breath. Once the pain in her arm subsided, she retrieved the flashlight and backpack and crept back over the now toppled obstacle.

She found herself in an empty concrete room with stale air and a low ceiling. Craters dotted the crumbling gray walls, and piles of rubble covered the floor. After a few seconds Annabelle wanted to get out of the dank prison. No wonder her grandfather had built the tunnel as an escape. How had he been able to keep it a secret all these years? And more importantly, where was the key that held another secret?

Chapter Two
Annabelle

Annabelle took two deep breaths and set to work looking for the key. The walls were bare apart from a rusty metal door to her right, and a mirrored medicine cabinet to her left. *Bingo.*

She approached the mirror. The orange light from her flashlight cast ominous shadows, making her reflection appear sunken and skeletal. She ripped the door open to avoid her image and found three empty shelves. She winced and her heart sank, the key wasn't there. Either someone had stolen it, or it had fallen out somehow. Gran had feared it getting into the wrong hands. Annabelle hoped that wasn't the case.

Annabelle spun around, she needed to find it. She reached inside the wall crevices, sifted through the piles of rubble but found nothing. While she studied every inch of the floor, the darkness closed in around her, the small flashlight unable to keep it at bay. She felt dizzy and found it hard to breathe. She wanted to leave but forced herself to keep looking.

She paused for a moment to examine the metal door. It rose almost to the ceiling with a lever lifted up from its latch, seemingly in an unlocked position. She stared at the door and tapped her lip with a finger. Her dizziness subsided while she considered what might be on the other side. She had no idea how big the bunker was or what it looked like because her grandparents hated talking about this part of their lives. She had the opportunity to find out if she went through that door.

Annabelle forced the flashlight away from the door and turned around, finding herself staring at the medicine cabinet again. From this angle, she noticed it hung on the wall with a slight tilt. Gran's directions popped into her head and she wanted to slap herself out of frustration. They said *behind* the mirror—Gran must have meant behind the medicine cabinet, not inside it.

She propped the flashlight up with her backpack, shining light onto the cabinet. She grabbed the sides of the medicine cabinet and braced her muscles to pull with all her might. She yanked and the cabinet released into her hands, causing her to stumble back a step. The flashlight now illuminated a deep square hole in the wall.

She set the cabinet down and hurried to the hole. Reaching inside her fingers grasped around a metal tin. "Gotcha," she said and pulled it out.

The lid wouldn't budge when she pulled on it, so she started shimmying it back and forth until it popped off with a little cloud of red rust. Annabelle tossed the lid on the ground and peered inside the tin. She saw the outline of a key and turned the tin over to drop it into her hand. The shiny, silver key hit her skin like ice and felt heavy in her palm. It stretched across her palm and uneven teeth adorned the bottom. Someone had looped a long chain through the key's clover shaped top.

She felt unsteady while gazing at the key and slumped to the ground. She grasped the key tight in her fist and closed her eyes. "I did it Gran. You can rest in peace now." Tears fell from her closed eyes and streamed down her cheeks.

She let the relief pulse through her for a few more moments before opening her eyes and gathering the flashlight and backpack. She took a deep breath and, with a satisfied smile, put the chain over her head and tucked the key under her shirt. The hardest part was behind her.

She turned toward the opening to the tunnel but hesitated. She glanced back at the door and chewed on her lip. She could never risk coming to the bunker again but questions tugged at her body, urging her to go forward. She wanted to know what was behind that door. This was her only chance to see this part of Gran's life.

She returned to the door and grabbed the lever. With one pull, the door clicked open, falling ajar. She pulled it all the way open, shivers running through her body.

She stepped over the threshold and into a cavernous hallway. White tile flooring covered the ground and identical metal doors lined the hall, all closed. She turned left and started down the hall, her footsteps echoing around her. She wanted to discover where they ate, see where they relaxed, find out how they grew food. She roamed through a piece of history, a place she had minimal information about and she wanted to fill in all the blanks. Her skin tingled while she tried opening the doors, anticipating the clues from the past that she might soon find.

Annabelle passed ten locked doors and came to a T. She looked down each hallway and they both extended out of her view. She went left again, making a mental note so she'd remember her way back. Double doors with thick black hinges and engraved white numbers lined this hallway.

She passed four more locked doors and came to one that had the word *Library* etched into it. She held her breath and approached the door. *Please let it be unlocked.* Libraries held high importance within the Colony—everyone wanted to make sure they rebuilt the world without repeating past mistakes. She'd love to get her hands on some new books.

She grasped the lever and pulled up. It didn't budge.

She sighed and shone the flashlight further down the hall. She wanted to get in at least one room but wasn't sure how much further she should go. She could easily get lost in here, but hadn't discovered anything interesting yet. She tapped her leg while staring down the dark hallway, debating with herself.

An echoing screech interrupted her thoughts. *What was that?* She widened her eyes and her heartbeat pounded in her ears. No crashing sound followed the screech, it must have come from something living rather than from the bunker caving in or settling. She shut off her flashlight. With all animals extinct, the only living thing down here would be another person or a horde of insects. She stood frozen in place, trying to calm her breathing.

Laughter travelled down the hall and jolted her back into action. She rattled the library lever again. It still didn't give. She slipped her shoes off, then running her hand along the wall crept to the next door. That lever wouldn't budge either. She didn't want to run down the dark hallway, but didn't dare turn on her flashlight either. She should never have ventured in here. She'd be out of the bunker by now if she hadn't gotten curious.

"Clyde, stop it!" echoed down the hall.

Annabelle yanked on the lever again. *Come on, open!*

"Why? Are you scared of the dark?"

The voices sounded familiar and Annabelle relaxed her grip on the handle. A teenage boy named Clyde lived two houses down from her. She cocked her head to listen.

"Hurry up, will ya? Your mom could go faster than that."

She bit her lip. They were coming her way and blocked her exit. If they saw her and told the accountability council she could possibly lose her job, maybe get an act of defiance placed in her parenthood file. It could ruin her whole future. She slid to the next door—needing to find a place to hide.

She pulled on the lever. Locked. She heard their laughter again and realized they'd be in big trouble if caught down here as well. A couple of teens certainly wouldn't have permission to enter the bunkers. She slipped her shoes back on and started walking toward their voices.

Just as she got to the fork in the hallway she heard them again.

"What the hell? An open door!"

That's Gran's door! She couldn't let them discover Gran's secret passage. "Stop!" she hollered and clicked on her flashlight.

Both boys let out a scream and turned to run.

"Clyde and Jackson, I already know it's you, running will make it worse." She walked toward them with shoulders back. They stopped and turned around. "What do you think you're doing in here?" She pointed the light on their faces.

"Nothing!" Clyde said.

"You aren't permitted down here," Annabelle said, stopping in front of them.

"What are *you* doing down here, Miss Annabelle?" Jackson asked.

Annabelle was grateful they couldn't hear the racing of her heart. "I've been sent down here to catch trespassers. Looks like I found some."

"It was all Jackson's idea," Clyde said.

"Whatever! You dared me!"

Annabelle thought for a moment. She needed them to keep quiet about seeing her down here. "Okay, listen. Since I know you, I'll cut you a break. No one needs to know about this, but I can't completely let you off the hook."

"Okay, thank you!" Clyde said.

"I'll have to make a report in your parenthood file, but I'll say I overheard you talking about coming down here, not that I actually found you down here. Sound good?"

"Yes ma'am," Clyde said.

"Now get out of here before I change my mind."

They turned and scurried down the hall and out of her view. She should've asked them how they got into the bunker. *Is this a new thing teens are doing these days?*

Annabelle thought about the fake report she'd have to write and her heart felt heavy. A defiant act on file could significantly hurt their ability to obtain permission for parenthood in the future. If they couldn't get parenthood, it almost guaranteed failure within the Colony. They would never be able to move up in status, never enjoy comforts allowed only to those who had children. It would bring shame on their family. They might never be free from this infraction. She didn't want to face the same consequences if she got caught down here.

Annabelle stepped back into Gran's room and secured the door. She took two deep breaths to calm her heart rate, then headed out the opening and down the hall to the ladder. The light from above seemed much brighter now that her eyes had adjusted to the darkness. She clicked her flashlight off and stashed it back in her pack. She grasped the first metal bar and ascended.

At the top, she pulled the planks back over the opening then covered them with sand once again. She sat for a moment with her back against the hill. Her hand went to her chest where she felt Gran's key under her shirt. Did she want to laugh or cry? What had she been thinking? This was the riskiest, yet most thrilling thing she'd ever done. She shook her head and pushed those dangerous thoughts out. She couldn't do something like this again. She tapped Gran's key, considering what she should do about it. It might take longer, but she'd have to take only safe opportunities to discover the key's secret.

***

Annabelle managed to make it back to her dad's house undetected and forced herself into a relaxed posture while blocking the bunker excursion from her mind. Inside, she found her coworker and bestfriend, Margaret. Annabelle embraced her. Her face met black curls and she breathed in Margaret's familiar scent of curry powder. She pulled back and glanced at her friend's clear, hazel eyes. The neutral colors Margaret tended to wear always highlighted her eyes, as did the cream color dress she wore today. Margaret saved up her own fabric ration until she had enough of the same to make a single color garment. Trading with Margaret benefitted Annabelle because she preferred bright colors herself.

"How are you holding up?" Margaret asked, studying Annabelle's face.

"I'm alright." Annabelle forced her voice to remain steady. Margaret knew her better than anyone and might be able to detect her guilt. "It's good to see you," she added.

"I wanted to check on you, and I brought you guys some lab steaks to grill up." Margaret turned to the kitchen counter and slapped her hand on a cooler.

"What? Seriously?" Annabelle opened the cooler and found it filled to the top. "This is more than a whole month's ration! Margaret, this is too generous."

Margaret closed the cooler and waved a hand. "It's nothing. Fredrick didn't do so well trading this week." Annabelle knew this was a lie. Margaret's husband, Fredrick, worked in the meat lab and people waited for hours in the barter market to trade for the extra steaks he made.

"If you really want to repay me, you can do a sketch of the kids for me," Margaret said.

"Of course." Annabelle shifted her weight from one leg to the other. Images of the bunker swirled in her head. She squeezed her lips shut and forced a breath out of her nose, trying to focus on the conversation.

"Annabelle, there you are." Annabelle turned to find her father entering from the living room. "I'm glad you're here. I've been waiting to give this to you." He reached into his pocket and pulled out a small black bag. He handed it to Annabelle.

Annabelle opened the bag and peered inside. "Gran's wedding ring," she said under her breath.

"Aside from the fact that you're the last to need a wedding ring, I know Gran would've wanted you to have it." He patted Annabelle on the shoulder.

Annabelle took the ring out and held it close to her face, studying it. The gold band had a single diamond the size and shape of a small apple seed. "It's lovely," she said, keeping her eyes on the ring so she didn't have to see her dad's face. He loomed over her, and she felt him staring at her. She knew he wanted to say something, wanted to fight.

Finally she met his eyes and discovered sadness there, not anger. She lowered her eyebrows—he rarely showed sadness. Her dad blinked and the sadness left. He didn't say anything though, pursing his lips instead.

"Go ahead, spit it out," Annabelle said.

He shook his head. "I just know Gran would've loved to see you married before she died."

Annabelle narrowed her eyes. She didn't want to have this conversation right now.

"Annabelle, you're 22 years old. I just don't understand what you're waiting for."

"Dad, I'm *only* 22!" She couldn't keep it in—she'd been through too much that morning.

"Your brothers were all married by 20."

Annabelle closed her eyes and sighed. This conversation went the same every time. She didn't respond, which seemed to soften her dad. He rested his hand on her shoulder. "Time goes so fast. I just don't want you to waste it and miss your chance."

"Dad, I'm learning so much at work. Once I actually find someone I want to marry, I'll get parenthood approval easily. It buys me more time to have kids." She had lots of time. "I still have eight years before the cutoff," she added.

That didn't appease her dad. "No you don't, you only have until you're 25 as a first time mom." He glanced over at Margaret, looking for backup. "Maybe you're not learning much at that job of yours."

27

Heat rushed to Annabelle's face, and she didn't dare look at Margaret. Her dad played dirty now. Margaret was her friend, but she also was her work mentor, and Annabelle didn't want to look like she didn't know her job. Margaret also enjoyed pressuring her to get married. Annabelle stared at the ground—she couldn't win this argument. No matter where she worked, he wouldn't let up until she got married.

"I just want you to be successful, that's all," her dad said when she didn't respond.

His words bound her, trapping her retorts inside. They lived in the last city on Earth, after all, and she couldn't argue with it being their duty to repopulate. She didn't want to bring shame on her family, but she wished her dad would trust her. She crossed her arms and her body tensed.

"Maybe I don't want to have kids," she lied. She did want them, but on her own timeline, with the correct man. Someone she loved. Someone she wanted to spend forever with. Not just someone to help her raise children.

Her dad clenched his jaw and stepped back. "Think how crushed Gran would be to hear you say that. And your mother. They both spent their lives giving back to the Colony. Think of how much they sacrificed! For the first time, I'm grateful your mother isn't here to hear what you just said." He shook his head and left the kitchen.

"Dad..." She took a step after him but he didn't turn back. She turned to Margaret. "I didn't mean it," she said.

"I know." Margaret rubbed Annabelle's arm. "You guys are going through a hard time, so everyone's on edge. Your dad will come around."

"I hope you're right." Annabelle rested her chin in her hand. She needed to process all these emotions along with the events of the day.

"Are you sure you're ready to come back to work on Monday? We have a Life and Death Tour to lead, but I'm sure I can find someone to cover," Margaret said.

Annabelle had forgotten all about the Life and Death tour. She knew she could take more time off if she needed it. However, at the moment her pressing need wasn't to grieve, but to satiate her curiosity. Gran had mentioned pain and loss. What better place to see if she could find a clue to the key than on the Life and Death Tour?

"Yes, I'm sure. It'll be nice to get back into the swing of things."

Chapter Three
Harold

Ernie lit the fuse. "Come on," he said, turning around and sauntering toward the hotel's exit. Harold followed at his heels. He told himself that Ernie was the best damn explosives expert he knew, so if he didn't run, Harold shouldn't either. Dashing through the ancient hotel would be dangerous anyway, Harold noted, as he jumped over a hole in the floorboards. Exposed beams held up the hotel and peeling, crispy wallpaper clung to the sections of wall that still remained. He hated coming into dried out skeletons like this—he preferred places that had already fallen down completely. At least it didn't smell moldy.

The sizzling sound of the burning fuse made Harold's body tense. It seemed to be moving towards the vault faster than they were exiting the building. They emerged outside a few seconds later, however, and had time to walk to the space that once was a parking lot. Large grasses and bushes now occupied the area.

Ernie stopped and turned back to look at the building, a large toothy smile on his face. Ernie's face rarely lacked a smile.

He didn't seem self-conscious at all about the gap between his two front teeth or his long, gangly limbs.

They made it out with time to spare, but the anticipation started to get to Harold. He counted down in his head. *Five, four, three, two, one...one...one...one...*

"Do you think—" Ernie held his hand up, cutting Harold off.

"Now." Ernie raised his eyebrows.

Harold squinted at the building, then heard a small boom. "That was it?"

Ernie's smile grew bigger. "You didn't want to blow up the whole building, right?" He patted Harold on the shoulder. "That old vault just needed a little push."

"Okay, let's go check it out then." Harold started for the building but Ernie pulled him back.

"Whoa, it may have been small, but we should wait to make sure the building stays standing. You never know with these old places."

"Right."

Harold glanced back to the wooden building. From the outside, the six story hotel looked sturdy despite its age and was the only building still standing on this block. He squinted at the staircase leading up to the entrance, expecting to see dust roll down as the air from the explosion settled. Nothing happened.

"What are you hoping is in there anyway?" Ernie asked.

"I don't know. I've always wondered what was in that vault. And since we've gutted this town, it seemed like it was time to finally blow it open. I doubt it has anything valuable for the Colony though."

"Maybe we saved the best for last."

"I hope so." They stared at the building in silence for a moment. Harold wasn't superstitious, but his wife was. If he found something worthwhile today, Clara would likely see it as a sign of good things to come.

"How many years before we suck Spokane dry too?" Ernie said.

This question always lurked in Harold's mind. His supervisors mentioned it on a weekly basis as resources became more and more scarce.

"Oh, many more years, I'm sure." Better to be vague, he decided. *No reason to stress out the ground men.* "And by the time it's picked dry, we'll have routes to new ruins established." He gave Ernie a strong pat on the back. "Makes the Seattle mission all the more exciting." *And crucial.*

Ernie grinned back. When Harold had delivered the news to Ernie that he'd be joining Harold's team to Seattle, Ernie had shown more enthusiasm than anyone. "I can't wait." Ernie rubbed his hands together. "But first let's go find out what Richland's final offering is."

As they approached the building, Harold thought again about the real reason he'd wanted to open the vault: he hoped to find something for Clara. She'd been a wreck anticipating the Life and Death tour. He wanted to cheer her up before they started the parenthood approval process. He didn't know how anything he found would calm her nerves, but his gut told him this vault contained something special.

Upon entering the hotel, a slight gunpowder scent greeted them. They headed to the far end of the room and around rubble that once was a front desk. Near the back wall, a large hole gaped where the vault door used to be.

Harold quickened his pace. Once they reached the vault, he stepped over the door and entered the exposed room, pulling a small flashlight from his pocket and clicking it on.

Metal drawers lined the walls and Harold yanked on one closest to him. It creaked open. When he shone his flashlight into it, he found nothing. He opened the next one. Empty again. He heard the clang of Ernie opening and closing drawers as well. Harold found drawers filled with useless paperwork.

"I found some coins. Keepable?" Ernie asked.

"Sure, why not?"

Ernie carried several small boxes to the entrance. Harold now stood at a bank of larger drawers. He pulled one open and found a three foot long plastic box. Inside, his flashlight illuminated a white gown that felt silky as he pulled it from the box. *A wedding dress?*

The next drawer contained a red dress. As he found dress after dress, a smile spread across his face. *Perfect*. Clara would be thrilled about the dresses, especially the bright colors. His superiors would see it as a good find as well, since fabric was valuable to the Colony. This was just the kind of good omen he'd been hoping for.

"I've got some dresses here." He started carrying the plastic containers to the entrance and stacked them next to Ernie's boxes.

"Huh. Who would've thought?" Ernie said.

"I know, something actually useful. Now I wish I had decided to blow this place open a while ago." Ernie helped him carry the remaining boxes. In total they had fifteen gowns, but Harold believed the seamstresses could repurpose them to make three times as many dresses.

"Hey, take a look at this," Ernie said, holding up a piece of thick paper that had slipped off one of the boxes. The yellowing paper had golden lettering which read: *You are cordially invited to celebrate the wedding of Elizabeth Mimi Lampson and Luke Caden Teal on Tuesday afternoon, June the 2nd, at four o'clock.*

Harold glanced at the dresses and shook his head, frowning. "I guess it was a wedding that never happened." *Had this wedding been scheduled right before The End?* He folded the invitation and put it in his pocket. Clara would love to know the history behind the dresses, despite the tragic ending.

"Go ahead and finish checking the rest of the drawers, I'll start loading up." Harold wanted to take the dresses out of the boxes and carry them all at once, but he'd never hear the end of it if they ended up damaged. Better to keep them safe. The boxes weren't heavy, but he could only manage to stack and carry four at a time.

As he headed down the hotel steps, he hoped he would be able to pull some strings in order to keep a bit of fabric. Those with first status would get to choose from the spoils before everyone else, but Harold had been able to work out deals before.

It took him a few minutes to reach the wagon. The overgrown field made it difficult to pull into the parking lot so they had parked close to the road. He shuffled some items around, making space for the gowns. When he turned back to the hotel, his eyes widened at the sight of smoke billowing out a back window. A window right next to the vault.

"What the—!" As he ran across the parking lot, the smoke thickened with each step he took. His stomach tightened. He had ordered the vault blown open, and even though Ernie insisted it could be done safely, Harold should have known better. The dilapidated hotel was clearly dry as kindling, why did he think it could handle an explosion? He would never forgive himself if something happened to Ernie.

When he finally reached the steps, he sprinted up two stairs at a time and into the building. He froze, staring as the raging fire consumed half the lobby. Yellow flames crawled up the walls, while fuzzy smoke scurried across the ceiling. The heat possessed its own force, seeming to want to chase him out.

"Ernie!" As soon as the shout left his mouth the roar around him swallowed it up. The smoke made it difficult to see, but he could make out Ernie's limp body lying near the vault entrance. Harold ducked and ran to him. The room grew darker every second as the smoke won the fight for space.

"Harold? Help!"

Harold could see why Ernie was motionless, he was stuck in the floor!

"What happened?" He leaned down to Ernie and tried to pull him out.

"I was trying to get to the fire to put it out, and next thing I knew I was dangling here. Hurry!"

"Wrap your arms around me." Harold tried pulling but Ernie wouldn't budge.

Above them, the fire crackled and debris rained down on them. Another large snap and a whole wooden beam fell, blocking their path to the door. A second later, flames covered the beam. Fire encircled them.

Harold knew they had to get out, and fast. "Hold on!" he shouted over the fire. He went behind Ernie and kicked at the floorboards. Ernie started coughing. Harold stomped as hard as he could, again and again, until a coughing fit forced him to stop. He tried to suck in a deep breath and brought his foot down with all his strength. Finally the boards gave way.

"Harold!" Ernie slipped down through the expanded hole until only his fingers clung to the floorboards.

"I've got ya!" Harold jumped over the hole and grabbed Ernie's wrists. Harold got his torso above the floorboards and then dragged him out. "Come on." He tried to pull Ernie up but he struggled to stand, and his ripped pants were covered with blood.

"Give me your arm." He ducked his shoulder under Ernie's weight and straightened up. They had to move fast, and he couldn't worry about being gentle. He stepped forward and Ernie limped as best he could. Harold knew they should be crawling. Standing put them closer to the dangerous smoke and soon it would overtake them. They had to get out now.

Harold found breathing a struggle, and his mind grew foggy. He knew they needed to move, but he felt disoriented and didn't know where to go. The smoke gave the fire form and bulk and Harold felt like a breathing animal had surrounded them. He gaped at the smoke, unable to move. How could they possibly escape it?

"There!" Ernie pointed toward a window at the right side of the room. It was surrounded by flames but was their only exit. Harold snapped back into action and dragged Ernie to it.

"Ready?" He asked Ernie. They were on the first floor, but the window wasn't at ground level. He would have to throw Ernie out and hope for the best.

"Yeah!"

Harold threw Ernie over the flames and out the window as if he weighed nothing more than a doll. Then he dove head first after him, fearing the fire much more than a small fall.

Luckily, he didn't flatten Ernie, who had managed to roll over to the side. Harold somersaulted as he landed, an aikido move he'd taught himself, and then stood. He took a deep breath and pulled Ernie up while coughing out smoke. Together they coughed and stumbled as fast as possible away from the building.

A few minutes later they collapsed in a nearby building's ruins. They lay on the ground, staring at the sky.

"That was close," Ernie said.

"Yeah." Harold took a deep breath and didn't cough it back out. Then he took another breath. Ernie had stopped coughing as well. "How's your leg?" Fighting dizziness, Harold sat up and turned to Ernie.

Black soot covered Ernie's body and his sandy blonde hair looked black. Aside from his leg, however, he didn't seem to have any injuries.

"Oh, it's not so bad," Ernie said with a pained smile.

"I don't think so." Harold pulled Ernie's torn pants away from the injury to get a look. It still bled and Harold ripped a section from his shirt to cover the wound. The flow slowed and Harold ventured another peek. The cut wasn't deep. Ernie would be fine. Harold let out a sigh of relief.

"I told you it wasn't so bad," Ernie said.

"Maybe not for you, but now I'm gonna have to bike the wagon back by myself, lugging your sorry ass in the back." He grinned at Ernie.

"Just let me rest a while and I'm sure I'll be able to ride." Ernie sounded as if he really believed this possible. "Just lighten the load a little. A crew can come back for it tomorrow."

Harold studied Ernie for a moment then nodded once. "Good idea. But not the dresses. We take those today." He closed his eyes and leaned back on his elbows. "It's a shame we only got four though."

"You never struck me as the type of guy to care so much about a dress."

"Well..." Harold hesitated. He wanted to talk about it with someone, and after what he'd just been through with Ernie, it felt strange to hold back. "I was hoping I could pull some strings and keep some material, so Clara could have a new dress for the

Fertility Festival. When I first saw the dresses, they seemed like a good omen." He glanced at the building, now engulfed in flames. So much for the good omen.

"Did you guys already get approval?"

"No, we just started the process. We attend the Life and Death Tour tomorrow." Saying the words out loud made Harold's stomach tense up.

"Hey congrats man, I'm sure you'll make a great first impression." The two silently watched the building burn. Harold hoped Ernie was right.

"But wait a minute, what about the Seattle mission? Will you have time to get approval before we leave?" Ernie asked.

"Well, we have exactly enough time to get approval, and if all goes as planned she'll be able to get pregnant right before we leave for Seattle." Harold didn't like the idea of being away during the first trimester, but Clara didn't seem to think it mattered. It was like a switch had flipped, and once she decided she wanted to get pregnant, she didn't want to wait a second longer than necessary.

Ernie nodded. "You're lucky man. You're gonna have it all."

"Hey now, you could have it all too."

"Nah. It's not like I have ladies knocking down doors for me." Ernie let out a laugh. "It's okay though, I have the Seattle mission. That's enough for me."

An uncomfortable silence settled over them as they faced the unfortunate reality of Ernie's fatherless future.

Ernie stood. "We'll have to take extra special care of you on the mission, to make sure you get back in one piece to your pregnant wife."

"Look who's talking." Harold stood and forced a smile but inside his gut twisted as he thought about all the things that could go wrong. Did Clara want to get pregnant before he left just in case he didn't come back? He was stuck. He couldn't quit the mission—aside from it being vital for the Colony's future, he really wanted to go. He longed to see Seattle, and to lead the first mission there, but he also couldn't tell Clara to wait. He shook his head. Now wasn't the time to worry about any of this. Besides, as the Seattle mission leader, he couldn't let Ernie see his concerns.

"Come on man, it'll be all good." He patted Ernie on the back.

Chapter Four
Harold

"Are you sure the purple shoes are okay?" Clara asked looking down at her feet while pedaling her bike.

"Yes, you look beautiful," Harold told her again. Was she even listening to him anymore? "I don't think you have worried about your clothes this much since you were five." He smiled at her—maybe a gentle jest would be more effective than a compliment.

"What if standing out is actually a bad thing?" Clara chewed on her lip for a second. "Before, I thought it was a good thing, but now maybe it's better to just be lost in the crowd, just one of the applicants. Not many people have colorful shoes. Mine are sure to be noticed. I guess it's good I didn't wear the dress with sequins…"

Harold sighed. She definitely wasn't listening to him. But at this point it didn't matter, they were almost there. The Colony didn't build houses this close to the boundary and they started passing fields filled with sagebrush and tumbleweeds. Without shade from the city, the sun beat down on his neck, making him sweat. They approached a large concrete building that reached three stories high. The building's bright red door glistened in the sunlight and he couldn't take his eyes off it as they drew near. They'd painted the door red years ago as a warning to people: keep out. That was their destination today.

Clara was silent now. Harold flashed her a reassuring smile, but she didn't pull her gaze away from the applicants who stood around the red door. They parked their bikes and he grabbed her hand before leading her to join the others. They stood at the back, and he glanced around, wondering if he knew anyone. Sure enough, he recognized a few familiar faces and received some nervous smiles. Clara's shoes were definitely the brightest clothing item amongst the group. Yet others wore their festival clothes, dresses and slacks patched together with muted fabrics. Men's shirts were crisp and clean as if they'd been dried in the sun, like Harold's. They fit right in.

Two women faced them at the front of the group. They wore similar outfits, navy patchwork skirts with white blouses. Neither smiled, but their faces were relaxed. The taller woman had long brown hair and clutched a clipboard to her chest. The shorter woman had black curly hair and nodded her head while looking over the applicants, as if she were taking a head count. Seeing them without smiles and with matching outfits made them seem very official to Harold and he felt queasy. This was the real deal and once they went through that door there was no going back. His ability to be a father was in these two ladies' hands. Clara's grip tightened, and he looked down at her. She gave him a half smile and he squeezed her hand twice. At least they were in this together.

"Isn't the taller woman Annabelle, the famous sketch artist?" Clara asked.

Harold studied the woman, and thought she looked like the person who always traded valuable sketches in the barter market. Her sketches were all over the Federal Building as well. "I think so," he said.

"I don't know if that makes me more excited or nervous," Clara said under her breath.

"Welcome, applicants," the shorter woman said after about twenty-five couples had arrived. "Thank you all for joining us on the Life and Death Tour. I'm Margaret, and this is Annabelle, and we'll be leading the tour today. First off, I'd like to congratulate you for taking the first step toward obtaining parenthood. I'm sure you're all feeling apprehensive about what you're going to see today. I assure you, that despite some unpleasant things, the purpose of the tour is to allow you to have a better idea of what your pregnancy will be like, as well as why it must be this way. Once you have this knowledge, I hope it'll better prepare you for the rest of the application process and for your pregnancy, if you are granted parenthood." If her words were meant to reassure Harold, they didn't. Instead his stomach tightened, almost making it hard to breathe. He forced himself to take some deep breaths. All they had to do was listen and witness today, right? This should be easy.

Instead of opening the red door, however, Margaret and Annabelle walked a few feet away from the door and stood over an open hatch. "First we'll be going down into a bunker, for the Life Tour. Please feel free to ask any questions at any time." Margaret motioned for everyone to approach the hatch. "Annabelle will check you in and then you'll enter the bunker." She took a couple steps down and added, "I'll meet you down there." She disappeared down the stairs.

Harold and Clara stood in line holding hands. Quiet descended over the group, and he only heard feet shuffling and names murmured as they approached the hatch. When they were face to face with Annabelle she wore a smile, one that brightened up her eyes.

"Name?" she said softly.

"Clara and Harold Hunt," Clara said.

Annabelle looked down at her clipboard, flipped a page over, made a mark, and looked back at them. "Nice to meet you," she said and pulled two name tags off her form. She gently pinned Clara's name tag and then Harold's. "You're all set to go."

Harold noticed the thick stack of paper she had on her clipboard, way more pages than she needed for just checking applicants in. What else would she be writing down throughout the tour? Harold forced himself to take another deep breath.

"Thanks, Annabelle. Nice to meet you too," Clara said with her voice steady now, as if all the worries about her shoes had vanished from her mind. Her grip on his hand had loosened significantly. Harold wondered how she could already be at ease.

He didn't have much time to think about it because Clara had already entered the stairway and pulled him after her. Harold wasn't thrilled about going down there. He hadn't ever been inside a bunker, and had heard too many stories from his grandfather about how suffocating living inside one was. He had no desire to discover what his grandfather meant.

A light illuminated the steep and narrow stairs but that didn't make his legs feel any less shaky. After descending two flights, they entered a rounded, tunnel-like hallway. Margaret waited next to white French doors with frosted windows.

Margaret gave a proud smile. "Our first stop is a little taste of where you'll be spending your year in the Colony's Womb." She let her eyes travel back and forth making eye contact with a few of the applicants. "Of course, no one wants to live underground. But, since it's a necessity for the survival of future generations, the Colony has done everything possible to make your year as comfortable as possible. This is a replica of one of the apartments. All are identical in layout, but some have different color schemes. Those who already have children will have additional bedrooms to accommodate their families. Obviously the Colony has some experience with living underground, so the ability to make it an enjoyable experience wasn't a difficult feat." She opened the doors and motioned the applicants in.

Clara followed the group, not even holding his hand anymore. Harold let everyone ahead of him and then entered before Annabelle. He avoided making eye contact with her—worried it might look bad that he was separated from his wife.

Annabellee didn't make any notes on her clipboard, so he turned his attention to the room.

His eyes widened as he looked around. It didn't feel like they were underground at all. He certainly didn't feel like he was suffocating. The raised ceiling and exposed wooden beams caused the room to feel larger than it was. The mahogany furnishings were nicer than any he'd ever seen. Where did they come from? He hadn't ever brought such nice pieces back from Spokane. Someone very talented must have pieced them together from recycled materials. The walls and tile flooring had a golden hue. Harold stared at the aqua blue curtains that gave the illusion of being above ground.

Clara materialized at his side and grabbed his shoulder. "Harold, you have to see the bedroom."

He followed her into the bedroom where she stopped by a king sized bed adorned in silky gold linens. "Check out this bed!" Clara rubbed her hand over the top. "It's so soft, and look what you would wake up to each morning." She pointed up. A chandelier hung there with crystals so close together the fixture twinkled like one giant diamond. Harold surveyed the scene with a small smile—there couldn't be a bedroom better suited for Clara.

"Come see the bathroom," Clara said, already cutting across the room. Harold followed reluctantly and considered what it would be like when he returned to a pregnant Clara. He should be looking forward to living in this fantasy world, but his steps felt heavy.

In the bathroom, Margaret stood next to a green-tiled soaker tub which could easily accommodate two people, maybe three. She and some other applicants discussed water birth and Clara gravitated toward the conversation. As a nurse's aid, Clara loved talking about these types of things, but Harold didn't want to hear it. In fact, he didn't want to be inside this apartment anymore. His grandfather was right, it was suffocating.

He headed back to the living room. Conversation surrounded him and he spotted Annabelle standing near the door, clipboard clutched to her chest again, watching everyone. Could she tell he wanted to run out of there? Was it bad that he felt that way? He walked over to a wall to examine a painting, his back to Annabelle. He focused on the picture, which depicted a vast sea, with calm waves and a single sailboat in the middle. He needed to get through this. For Clara, and for their future. They'd been preparing for this for months and he should be ready.

"Everything alright?" Annabelle asked.

He spun around and forced a toothy smile. "Yeah... I was just," he pointed at the painting with his thumb, "looking at the painting."

Annabelle gave a half smile. "It just got real for you, huh?" she said.

Harold looked at his feet. "Yeah." He couldn't think of anything else to say.

She didn't respond, so Harold slowly lifted his head back up—maybe he shouldn't have admitted to it. How could he make this better?

He found her smiling still. "It's going to be alright, you know," she said and studied his face for a second. She nodded once before turning away. Even though she still held onto the clipboard, she didn't write anything down and Harold found it easier to breathe.

Clara emerged from the bedroom again, along with Margaret and the other applicants.

"Let's proceed." Margaret said, and led them out.

Harold and Clara followed the group further down the hallway, surrounded by conversation. "You know, it's so much nicer than I expected. I think I might really enjoy living down here," Clara said. He smiled at her and grabbed her hand again. It was nice seeing her at ease.

"Welcome to the Colony's Womb," Margaret said when they arrived at a long viewing window. Clara found an empty spot at the window, Harold joined her and looked down. About thirty pregnant women gathered below, waving enthusiastically at them. Clara waved back. She nudged Harold, and started waving again. "Look at them, they're beautiful."

Harold gazed at the women. He'd only seen pregnant women once before when he attended a Fertility Festival to honor his pregnant cousin, and he was too young to pay much attention.

Even though the women appeared excited to see the tour group, staring at them from above felt voyeuristic. Harold rubbed the back of his neck while he took in the strange scene. Below, the women wore identical white, silky dresses that flowed down to their feet. The fabric fit snugly around the middle putting their pregnant bellies proudly on display. Their matching gowns and facial expressions made Harold suspect they were putting on a show.

Their dwelling seemed as artificial as their wide smiles. They stood on a purple and gold tile mosaic that surrounded a white, pregnant statue who looked down at her stomach while cradling it with both hands. Splashes of color, arched doorways, greenery and flowers adorned the rest of the space. He blinked his eyes. He'd never seen such an idyllic place before. He put his arm around Clara and pulled her close. Would she change when she became a face in this crowd?

Clara stopped waving and turned toward Harold. "It's so perfect, don't you think?" Her blue eyes sparkled. "It just feels so right, you know?" She turned back toward the window. "All these months we've been talking about applying for parenthood, and I've just been going through the process. But seeing all this makes it so real, and I really do want it. I want it more than anything."

Unable to agree, Harold simply squeezed her to him. While glancing down at the women again a new fear crept into his mind. What if they didn't get approval?

"Not too shabby, huh?" Margaret said, gaining the applicant's attention. "Trust me, these women aren't acting, they really are as happy as they seem. I speak from experience." She gazed through the window for a moment before continuing. "I personally think it's a fabulous way to spend your pregnancy. You don't even realize most of the time that you're underground and are able to live in a stress-free and safe environment. The Colony only needed to create a haven that would protect your baby from radiation, but they went above and beyond to create a resort type setting for you. You will be nourished, mind, body and soul, without even needing to ask. But most importantly, just as your baby is safe in your womb, you are safe in the Colony's Womb." She paused, giving the applicants a moment to take in her words.

Margaret answered a few questions before leading them to another viewing window. Harold didn't know what they were supposed to find at this window, and looking down didn't bring him any clarity. The white room below contained rows of gray freezers. It was clean, sterile and devoid of anything exciting.

"What is it?" he asked Clara.

She shook her head and shrugged, keeping her eyes on the room.

"Ladies, here is where your pregnancy will begin," Margaret said, her voice more serious now. "This is where your eggs have been safely stored since your birth. As you know, in order to protect your eggs from a lifetime of radiation exposure they had to be removed before you left the Colony's Womb as a baby. We discovered, through a lot of unfortunate trial and error, that this was the only way to save the human race," Margaret frowned, "and we'll cover that on the death tour. We just wanted to give you the opportunity to see that your eggs are safe, that they've been safe, and are waiting for you right down there." She smiled and pointed through the window. "Are there any questions?"

Harold nodded to himself. He glanced at Clara and saw she rested her hands on her lower abdomen. He knew underneath those hands were two small scars, identical to ones all women had in the Colony, marking the egg removal surgery. Was she thinking of those scars as well?

While Margaret answered questions, Harold looked back at the room. Where were Clara's eggs? The beginning of their baby was down there, along with all the last remaining human eggs on Earth. Didn't it make human existence too vulnerable to have all their future generations contained in a single room? Harold didn't dare express this fear. There was no other way to protect their species. This was the best they could do. Still, it revealed mankind's fragile state and how, even though the Colony made them feel safe, humans flirted with extinction.

Chapter Five
Annabelle

Annabelle followed the last applicants out of the bunker and closed the hatch. The wind teased through her hair while she walked toward the concrete building where Margaret stood.

"We'll now conclude our presentation with the Death Tour." Margaret stood in front of the red door. The applicants gathered around her, and Annabelle went to stand by her side.

Margaret spoke with a slightly deeper voice, like someone telling ghost stories around a campfire. "Because this is so emotional, you're only required to see it once. It'll instill in you a great gratitude for the journey you're about to embark on, as well as make you eternally grateful for what the Colony has accomplished to save the human race." Like everyone else, Annabelle stared at the red door. It had lost luster over the years, and even though Annabelle now dreaded going through it, the door still enticed her with its scarlet color.

"Let's proceed," Margaret said.

Annabelle tucked the clipboard under her arm and opened the door. She stood aside while Margaret led the group in. As the applicants passed, she flashed them each a solemn smile. *Yes, it is sad, but we can be grateful it isn't like this anymore*, she tried to convey. Once they were all in, she followed, closed the door and locked it.

The applicants milled around inside, expressing astonishment to find the building had no roof. What appeared to be a three story concrete building from the outside was actually a walled off cemetery.

At this point during the tour, Annabelle usually lingered by the door, answering questions. She'd never had a desire to explore with the applicants. But with Gran's sorrow lingering fresh in her thoughts, her eyes saw the graveyard differently for the first time. The impact of the thousand uniform gray tombstones threatened to pierce her heart. She attempted to count the graves to distract herself from giving into the grief but they were so close together—impossible to count. They didn't need much space in between since under each marker lay a tiny infant.

She looked away from the graves and focused on the nursery themed murals covering the inside walls. The chubby little angels playing amongst clouds usually made her smile. Today it only reinforced her grief, reinforced Gran's grief. Another mural depicting hippos, giraffes, elephants and monkeys surrounding a watering hole now felt garish instead of whimsical. She sucked in a breath. Maybe she wasn't ready to come back to work.

"It isn't easy to see, is it?" Margaret said as she walked toward the grave closest to the door. "Page Mathews, was the first to die. She was one of the lucky ones, too. As you can see on her tombstone, she lived a full three months. All the others died within weeks after being born. Most within days." Margaret backed away from the grave.

"Look around you. All these babies, lost over the course of a decade. A decade when our species was at risk of extinction. When the first colonists left the bunkers sixty-five years ago, they didn't realize how much radiation still remained from the nuclear winter until it was too late. Everyone's body was toxic and unfortunately it was too much for the unborn. Thankfully, our lead scientists and doctors were able to step in and save us.

"This black mark on our history is a reminder of how far we have come. The Colony is committed to our survival, and the survival of our offspring." Margaret's voice projected across the graveyard despite her small frame. All eyes were glued to her, entranced.

"Now I'd like to invite you to look around and think about what the first colonists went through to save mankind. Look around and read the names on the tombstones. You may even find an aunt or uncle. If you start to feel uncomfortable, I hope you're able to shift your sorrow to gratitude. We wouldn't be here right now if it wasn't for the drastic measures the Colony had to take. Please take a few minutes to explore and return to the front for the conclusion of our tour." Margaret gestured toward the graves and the group dissipated as people broke off in pairs.

Annabelle's emotions bubbled to the surface and she turned away from the group, avoiding eye contact. To remain professional, she always blocked the graveyard's grief, but today she couldn't help but face it. She hugged the clipboard and took a deep breath. Gran had lost five children who were buried here, and today she would find them. She doubted it would reveal any clues to the key's secret, but forced herself to move anyway. It was time to acknowledge Gran's hardships.

Annabelle knew the area where Gran's plot was located and found the section after cutting halfway across the cemetery. She approached the tombstones, staring at the names. *Francis Mills, Edwin Mills, Lucy Mills, Scarlett Mills, Owen Mills.* Her aunts and uncles. She bent down and traced a finger over the letters on Owen's grave and a pit hardened in her stomach. She blinked a few times and backed up.

Gran had carried these babies for nine months and only held them for a few days before they were taken from her. *How does someone ever fully recover from that?* Annabelle turned away. No wonder Gran had wanted to die in the darkness.

Annabelle kept her eyes down and joined Margaret, who called for the group to return to the front. "We cannot let this happen again. Ever," Margaret said. "We are the last colony. The last fifteen thousand souls on Earth. We can't take our responsibility to our species lightly. It was a close call." She motioned at the graves again. "We will not let all these infants' deaths be in vain." Many applicants nodded, hopeful expressions on their faces.

"As you know, we're in the process of slowly rebuilding the human race and you have the privilege of being a part of that. We must be grateful to the Colony for safeguarding our eggs until we're ready to bring healthy children into this world, as you all hope to do in the coming year. Feel free to spend a few more minutes looking around. Annabelle and I will answer any questions you have." Conversations started around Annabelle and she kept her eyes glued to her clipboard.

The gratitude and hopefulness she was supposed to feel from the tour was not happening. She touched the key, hidden under her shirt, and thought about Gran's life. After losing her first five children, Gran spent her sixth pregnancy inside the bunker and was finally blessed with a child who survived, Annabelle's mother. Yes, the Colony's drastic interventions worked. But Annabelle felt cheated, and Gran probaby did too because Annabelle's mother died thirty years later, along with her baby sister, during childbirth. Where had the Colony's safeguards been then? Annabelle clenched her jaw and tried to slow her breathing. These dangerous thoughts raced through her but she didn't know how to stop them.

She shouldn't have come to work today. This had all been a mistake. She was foolish to think she'd find a clue to the key's mystery. Of course there weren't any surprise locks on the tour that she hadn't noticed before. She took a deep breath. The tour was almost over—she just had to get through the last few minutes.

She stood near the exit, hoping Margaret would announce the end of the tour soon. A couple walked by her, hand in hand. "My heart breaks for Nana Mae. I just want to go home and give her a hug," the woman said to her husband. That was usually the kind of statement Annabelle would be waiting to hear, but instead of making a positive mark on her clipboard she fought back tears. Annabelle couldn't give Gran a hug. *Deep breathes, only a few more minutes.*

"Excuse me, Annabelle?" Annabelle looked to her right and found Clara. "Is everything all right?" Clara asked in a soothing tone.

Heat rushed to Annabelle's face and she forced herself to stand up straighter. "Of course, did you have a question?"

Clara looked at her with sympathetic eyes but didn't push the issue. "I was just wondering if you knew when they fenced the graveyard off." Clara gave Annabelle a comforting smile and something about her felt familiar to Annabelle.

Annabelle nodded. "The Colony built the wall about ten years after reproduction was successful again. They made it into a monument in order to proclaim that infant deaths were a problem of the past."

"But didn't the parents want to visit the graves?" Clara asked. Her husband, Harold, joined the women but listened quietly while Clara led the conversation. With them both facing her, Annabelle noticed a difference in their appearance. Harold towered over Clara and put his strong arm protectively around her. Distinct ethnicity no longer existed in the Colony, everyone had mixed ancestry, but sometimes traits stood out. Clara's light brown, almost blonde hair and lightly tan skin were in contrast to his darker skin and eyes.

"Since the whole Colony went through the grieving process together, I think it was viewed as a monument for all, instead of just for individuals," Annabelle said. Clara nodded slowly, but narrowed her eyes as if she didn't completely buy the explanation. Before Clara could ask a follow-up question, however, Margaret announced the tour's end.

As the applicants headed to the exit, Annabelle overheard Clara talking to her husband. "You know, we're always calling ourselves the Last Colony. But I'm not so sure we should be called that. We're the First Colony now, wouldn't you say?"

Annabelle managed a small smile. It appeared someone gained hopefulness from the tour. It was just the type of thing Annabelle needed to hear, yet it was hard to fully embrace the sentiment.

"Do you think we still have time to make it to the barter market?" Margaret asked after the applicants had left.

"Yeah, let's do a quick final sweep."

Margaret nodded and the two headed through the graveyard, making sure no applicants remained huddled near a tombstone. "You feeling okay?" Margaret asked when they reached the back.

Annabelle turned toward her friend but didn't make eye contact. Of course Margaret would notice she was off. But didn't she have a good reason? "You know, just a hard week." She glanced up at Margaret, but kept her head bowed slightly.

"Of course." Margaret didn't say anything for a moment and then added, "I think we're good here, let's just head out."

Annabelle nodded and followed Margaret back to the entrance. She needed to get a grip. For now, Margaret would think she grieved Gran's death, but Annabelle didn't want her to figure out that something else was on her mind. She needed to decide what to do with the necklace, or else her preoccupation with it would eventually give her away and Margaret would ask more prying questions.

"So, did you write down any important first impressions?" Margaret asked while they exited. She turned back toward the door to lock it before continuing, "There was one guy who I think we might have to disqualify already. I think his name was Bruce, I'll have to look at the profile sketches to be sure. Did you hear the questions he was asking? I just…"

Annabelle stopped hearing what Margaret was saying and instead stared at three people who stood near the edge of the wall: Harold, Clara, and a Suit. What was a government official doing here? And why was he talking to Harold and Clara? Seeing a government official outside of an office building either meant accolades or punishment, rarely anything in between. While the Suit spoke, Harold crossed his arms and Clara's gaze was fixed on the ground. Annabelle couldn't hear what the official was saying, but then Harold raised his voice.

"We aren't ready," Harold said. Margaret heard him too and spun around.

"What's a Suit doing here?" she asked under her breath.

"I don't know," Annabelle whispered back. The two stared for a minute, still unnoticed by the others. The Suit spoke again, but Annabelle still couldn't hear what he said. Margaret cleared her throat and the Suit's head turned in their direction.

He appeared to be in his sixties, and was gray, balding, and slightly overweight. "Hello ladies. I apologize for the intrusion," he walked toward them with a wide smile that made his eyes squint. "I presume one of you is Annabelle Vangard?" His friendly voice matched his smile. "Your office said I would find you here."

Annabelle didn't take a step forward or return his smile. With each step he took toward them, her pulse increased. Someone maybe saw her go into the old bunkers, or leave the boundary. Or maybe he was here for the necklace. She swallowed. He stopped in front of them, looking from Annabelle to Margaret. His smile dropped a little.

"Hello. I'm Margaret." Margaret shook his hand and gave Annabelle a piercing look. Annabelle swallowed again and forced her hand into the Suit's.

"I'm Annabelle. What can I do for you?" She shook his hand. His was soft but not sweaty, like warm pie dough.

"I'm Tully Foster. It's a pleasure to meet you," he said to Annabelle. The necklace suddenly felt itchy around her neck. Annabelle desperately wanted to scratch it. Instead, she forced herself to smile.

"Nice to meet you too," she said. She felt like a mannequin.

"Annabelle, is there a place where we could chat? I'd love a moment of your time." He looked from her to Margaret.

Annabelle glanced at Margaret. Margaret smiled and rested her chin in her hand, as if pondering something, but Annabelle saw her thumb moving slightly back and forth under her chin. Margaret had a single chin hair and she was playing with it, which she did when something agitated her. *What's bothering her?* Seeing her friend anxious made Annabelle's heart race faster.

"I guess we could go inside…" Annabelle looked around, not seeing any other place. *Would it be weird to have a meeting in the graveyard? Was it even appropriate?*

"All right then," Mr. Foster said without hesitation. "Harold, come with us please."

Harold took Clara's hand and the two joined them at the red door.

"All right." Annabelle turned back toward the graveyard. She had a hard time keeping her hand steady as she unlocked the door. She took a few slow breaths, opened the door, and followed Mr. Foster, Harold and Clara through the door with a forced smile.

"I'll wait for you out here," Margaret said as if it had been her idea. Annabelle nodded and closed the door.

She turned and glanced around the empty graveyard. An eerie quiet hung in the air. She bit her lip. Why had Mr. Foster come to meet her here? What was so urgent that he had to seek her out? She glanced at Harold and Clara, unable to understand how they fit into this. She took a deep breath. Perhaps the meeting was unrelated to Annabelle retrieving the key.

"Shall we go for a stroll?" Mr. Foster asked.

"Yes, a stroll would be lovely," Annabelle said. *Lovely? A stroll in the graveyard?* She shook her head—she needed to get a hold of herself.

Mr. Foster turned toward Harold. "If you don't mind, I'd like to speak with Annabelle for a moment. I'd like you to wait here, so we can finish our conversation afterward."

"Of course," Harold said. He looked at Annabelle then, his eyebrows furrowed and his lips pursed. Maybe he was as confused about this as Annabelle was.

Mr. Foster set a slow pace, as if they were enjoying the afternoon in a park and the tombstones were roses instead of grave markers.

"First off, I want to let you know that I am a great admirer of your artwork," Mr. Foster said.

"Thank you. That really means a lot." Annabelle tried to make her tone match their casual stroll.

"You have a profound ability to capture reality," he said, looking straight ahead. Annabelle kept a small smile on her face. Where was this going? He said nothing for a moment while they walked, but Annabelle waited for him to go on. "I believe you are the best in the Colony," he finally said.

"Thank you." Was he buttering her up?

"Can you draw anything as long as you have a reference? Or is your talent only driven by inspiration?" He sounded serious now, no longer like a grandfather but like a government official.

"Well," she paused to reflect. No one had ever asked this question before. How could she explain her drawing process? Her drive had always been to draw the one picture she couldn't master, despite being able to perfectly illustrate everything else she saw. "I guess a little bit of both. It's easiest to draw something I'm looking at but I have a good memory, so if I see something I feel inspired to illustrate it will stick with me until I draw it."

"But if I asked you to draw something would you be able to do it, even if inspiration didn't hit?"

Annabelle stopped walking and turned to face Mr. Foster. "I'm sorry, but I'm not sure what you're getting at."

He must have seen the apprehension on her face because he smiled again, making his forehead a wrinkled mess. "This must seem unusual to you. It's the first time we've sought out an illustrator, so I can understand that. Let me explain." He started walking again. "You know people are starting to get curious about the outside world. I'm sure even you've wondered what it's like outside." Annabelle's mind flashed to jumping the trench, making her stomach flutter. She could feel the thrill all over again and smell the desert breeze. She held her breath, trying to suppress the memory.

"I know I have," he continued. He looked at her and winked. Annabelle kept her face emotionless, she didn't dare give anything away. "We've been sending teams as far as Spokane these past few years in order to collect supplies. People are grateful for the goods, but they also want to *see* what it's like." Annabelle thought about the boys she'd encountered in the bunker. Maybe their rebelliousness hadn't been unique. How long had the Suits been aware of this?

They reached the back wall, turned right and continued alongside the perimeter. "This is where your expertise comes in." Mr. Foster stopped abruptly as if his explanation had been enough and he wanted to measure her response.

"Oh," Annabelle said, putting her hand to her chest. They wanted her to sketch in Spokane. This really had nothing to do with the necklace. She leaned against the wall and let out a breath. Images started dashing through her mind. Snapshots of what she imagined Spokane must look like. She could feel the pencil's solidness squeezed between fingertips, her mind poised and ready to spit the images out on paper. "Yes, I could draw Spokane," she said, feeling the sketches inside her come alive with eagerness. They wanted their story to be told.

"Not Spokane." Mr. Foster raised his eyebrows slowly. "We've done preliminary testing and all results show that it's now safe to cross the Cascades. We'd like to send a team in to assess the areas west of the Cascades, with a final destination of Seattle."

His final word hung in the air. Seattle.

Annabelle straightened up. "Seattle?" She didn't know what to say. Anywhere that far outside the Colony seemed hazardous and impossibly distant. Seattle felt as accessible to her as ancient Rome. She'd promised herself to never do something so risky again after retrieving the key. However, she knew people who came back from Spokane unharmed. No radiation poisoning, no side effects, no illness—even months later. But Spokane had already been established as safe, Seattle hadn't.

Mr. Foster chuckled. "I guess I sprung that on you kind of abruptly. Don't worry, you're free to ask any questions. And of course, this mission would be completely voluntary." He sounded genuine but Annabelle repressed her questions—they might make her look disloyal.

"Of course, I'd be incredibly honored. I'd take any opportunity that would benefit the Colony. It's just," she paused, "I wasn't expecting this." She didn't want to sound ungrateful and knew if the Colony needed her she shouldn't refuse. It would be like turning her back on mankind, an attitude which surely would stigmatize her, and might be noted in her parenthood file as well.

"I know it would bring us great joy to be able to see another piece of the world. That's a gift you could give us," Mr. Foster said and they started moving again.

"I'm humbled by this opportunity, and I certainly would enjoy the challenge of drawing new things—things that I've never seen or even dreamed of seeing." She gazed up at the sky for a moment, then made eye contact with Mr. Foster—worrying that further hesitation might look defiant. "So…when do we leave?" she said and smiled.

Mr. Foster laughed. "I think you'll be an excellent addition to the team. I'll let you think this over tonight. You don't have to make a decision right now although I do appreciate your enthusiasm. Time is, however, of the essence. You see, there is a reason I sought you out here." He paused for a moment and for the first time avoided making eye contact with her. Before speaking, he started walking again. "The mission has been moved up actually. It was originally set for next spring, but I'm afraid it's of the utmost importance to the Colony that this mission happens sooner."

How soon? Hugging her elbows, she waited for him to answer.

"The President actually sent me here today to report the change in plans. And imagine my surprise when I learned that the two people I needed to contact would be in the same place." So Harold and Clara had something to do with the mission as well, Annabelle realized. He stopped before they met up with the others, however. Mr. Foster turned to Annabelle and lightly touched her elbow. "It clearly is fate that you're meant to come along on the mission, and the Colony would be honored to have you as a member on the team." His eyes looked desperate, almost pleading. "The team leaves on Friday. Think about it tonight and meet me tomorrow at my office to let me know your answer. Now, let's not keep the team leader waiting any longer."

Annabelle followed to where Harold and Clara stood, staring at them. Her legs felt like they were going to buckle under her. *Friday? They would leave Friday?*

"So Harold, we were talking about the fact that your team's incomplete." Mr. Foster looked from Harold to Annabelle, his cheeks popping out over his smile. "Allow me to present to you the newest member." He patted Annabelle's shoulder once. "Our new illustrator!" he announced.

"An illustrator?" Harold's eyes widened, his mouth hung open slightly. "With all due respect, Tully, we need a medic, not an illustrator." He peeked at Annabelle and added, "No offense to you, of course."

Annabelle felt a strange power shift between her and Harold. Moments before he'd been panicked and jumpy around her. But now he had no problem standing up to a Suit.

Mr. Foster swatted his hand through the air. "We can find a medic, no problem. Everyone on your team is experienced. I wouldn't be requesting the change if I didn't think the mission would be successful." He reached into his jacket pocket and pulled out a bundle wrapped in a white dish cloth. "I'm counting on you to gather your team together and get them prepped. Leave the medic to me." He unwrapped the dish cloth and pulled something out. "Cookie?" he offered.

"No thanks," Annabelle said, not wanting to eat a snack in the graveyard.

Harold shook his head and looked at Clara, who was frowning. Her shoulders drooped and she didn't seem to be paying attention to anything anyone said. It was quite a contrast to the Clara Annabelle had witnessed during the tour. The one who had offered optimistic antidotes and who'd practically skipped down the hall during the Life Tour. Annabelle had the urge to comfort her, although she didn't know how.

Harold sighed. "You're right, our team is ready. With a medic, we could leave tomorrow. That's a fact." Clara's head snapped up at this remark, and she glared at Harold, but he was looking at Mr. Foster now. "It's just that we… we were just starting…" He glanced at Clara, whose expression softened. The two gazed at each other for a moment. Mr. Foster munched on his cookie, waiting. "Actually, you know what, I think I have the perfect solution." Harold stood up taller and smiled. "Clara can be our medic!"

Mr. Foster stopped eating and a few crumbs fell off his cookie. "Clara?"

"Yes, she is a very talented nurse's aid and is skilled with herbal medicinals. Actually, with such short notice, I wouldn't feel comfortable with someone I didn't know." He nodded his head while talking. "Clara, what do you think?" He smiled down at her.

Clara wore a stern expression. "Of course." Her voice came out monotoned. "I'd be honored to take part in any opportunity that might bring glory to the Colony." Harold's smile dropped, but Mr. Foster's returned.

"Great, I'll work this out on my end. I don't think it'll be a problem. It does make perfect sense actually. Now, if you'll excuse me." He wrapped his cookies back up and returned them to his pocket, then brushed his hand on his pants. "Annabelle," he extended his hand, "it was very nice meeting you, and I look forward to seeing you tomorrow."

Annabelle shook his hand. "It was nice meeting you as well, Mr. Foster. Thank you for this opportunity."

"Thank you for considering it. And please, call me Tully." With that, he opened the red door and left.

Chapter Six
Annabelle

"Hey Margaret, how'd your Meet and Greet go?" Annabelle sat down at their office conference table to eat lunch with Margaret.

"Another one bites the dust." Margaret wore a smirk.

"Really?" Annabelle said. "What happened?"

"I think it could work out, they just aren't ready yet. The husband was a ball of nerves and it annoyed the wife who kept snapping at him." Margaret took a bite of her sandwich. "They met all the criteria in their answers, but I could tell they were canned answers, and not completely genuine. They're going to have to do more to prove their loyalty to the Colony before I can approve them. But enough about that. Have you decided what you're going to tell Mr. Foster?"

Margaret had pestered Annabelle about the mission all morning, making it impossible for Annabelle to avoid thinking about it. Annabelle preferred blocking hard decisions from her mind. Every time she thought about the mission, conflict flooded her. Warning bells rang in her head, fear gripped her chest, but there was something else there too, something underneath it all trying to push the other emotions out. A stirring, a curiosity, a thirst for adventure. She kept remembering the few moments she'd spent outside the Colony and secretly wanted more.

She didn't like housing the conflicting emotions so she pushed them out by imagining what she might discover in Tully's office. She envisioned rows of file cabinets behind his desk. A small lock at the top of each drawer. It hadn't occurred to her before but the key would be the perfect size to fit into a file cabinet lock. She craved an opportunity to try it. Focusing on that gave her relief from worrying about the mission. She glanced up at Margaret, who watched her while she munched on an apple. Sometimes she wondered if Margaret enjoyed torturing her.

"Honestly, I don't know what I'll tell Tully," Annabelle said.

Margaret took another bite of her apple. "What does your family think?"

Annabelle sighed. "I stopped by to tell them yesterday, and of course they *said* I couldn't turn it down. That I couldn't give up an opportunity to honor the Colony. But I saw the worry in my dad's eyes. I don't know, things have been weird with him since Gran died. He can't deny the mission would bring me status though. I think he's conflicted." She rested her chin in her hands. "That makes two of us I guess."

"You'll go," Margaret said. "And you're probably excited about it."

"I don't think I really have a choice."

"That may be true. But you *want* to go."

"How can you say that?" Annabelle shifted in her chair. Sometimes it seemed like Margaret could read her mind.

Margaret set her apple core down. "Annabelle, I've gotten to know you pretty well over the last couple years. There's more to you than the sweet, quiet vibe you have going on. You have an adventurous side. It used to shock me, but I expect it now. Like when you had us kidnap Julie for her birthday and you had decked out the Life Tour bunker for a surprise party."

Annabelle grinned. "That was fun," she said.

"Yeah, and totally risky."

"It wasn't breaking any rules!"

Margaret smiled back. "Maybe not breaking any rules, but definitely bending them."

"Okay, so you have one example. That doesn't prove I want to risk my life going to Seattle." Annabelle chewed the inside of her cheek, thinking of the other big risk she'd taken that Margaret *didn't* know about.

Margaret shook her head. "I see the way you look beyond the Colony boundary all the time. You daydream about it, I know. And there's the fact that you've never settled down with anyone."

"Now you sound like my dad."

"No, hear me out. I think you haven't found anyone because they don't excite you enough. Deep down you're looking for adventure."

Annabelle couldn't help but smile. Margaret did understand her—maybe even better than she understood herself. The stirring curiosity grew inside her, fluttering up, chasing away the fears. "Maybe you're right," she said.

Margaret shrugged. "Of course I am." She stood and carried her dishes to the sink and started washing them. "By the way, Tully had a message sent over for you."

"What message?"

"I put it in your mail file."

Annabelle abandoned her lunch and rushed to retrieve the letter. In long loopy letters the message said:

"Annabelle, my dear, it appears tonight will be a lovely evening. Please meet me at the plaza instead of my office at 5:00. I'll provide you with dinner. Tully."

No file cabinets at the plaza. Annabelle sighed and let the letter droop down. "He wants to meet at the plaza."

"I know."

"You read it?"

"Well it's not like the letter was sealed." Margaret shut the water off and turned to face Annabelle. "Is there a problem with meeting at the plaza?"

Annabelle knew she couldn't tell Margaret about why she preferred to meet in the office. "Ah no. I just don't go there very often is all," she stammered.

"I'm sure it'll be fine," Margaret said, patting her on the shoulder then heading for her office.

***

As Annabelle rode her bike through neighborhoods, the last rays of evening sun glistened off the solar paneled rooftops. The first warm evening of spring always brought people outdoors, and she felt a buzz in the air. She passed by a barter market, filled with people and the noise of spirited negotiations. The smell of spicy food wafting from food carts enticed her but she pushed on.

She had to slow down to avoid a group of kids playing soccer in the street. She maneuvered around them and approached the plaza. The Colony permitted grass to be grown at the plaza, making the park feel like an oasis in the dusty city. Annabelle smiled, why *didn't* she come here more often? She parked her bike in the lot next to hundreds of others.

To her right, kids screeched and splashed in the community pool, but she turned left—drawn by folk music coming from the gazebo at the courtyard's center. She pushed through dancing couples who spun around to the upbeat tune. The warmth in the air and the dancing couples' cheerful laughter made the evening feel like a spring festival, and Annabelle found herself swaying to the music with a wide smile on her face.

On the stage, she saw five child musicians. One sang while the others played banjos and fiddles. Annabelle became oblivious to everyone around her and couldn't take her eyes off the young talent, soaking in their vibrant rhythm. How could young kids have such captivating power? Before she could come up with an answer, she felt a tap on her shoulder. She turned to find Tully's warm smile.

"Enjoying the music, I see," he said.

"Yes, I am. They're phenomenal."

"I know," Tully said. "They're my grandchildren." He looked up at the stage, his face beaming with pride. Just then the song ended and the crowd burst into applause.

"Come along. I'd love for us to stay here and listen up close but we have business to attend to. We'll still be able to hear them from the back." Tully guided Annabelle back through the crowd. Tully's grandchildren started playing a softer song, and couples embraced each other for a slow dance. Tully led them to the grassy perimeter on the courtyard's outskirts, where a blanket sat in the shade of a tree.

"Please sit. I had my wife pack a special picnic dinner for us. A special picnic for a special occasion." Tully pulled food packets from a basket. He set out flatbread, roasted red peppers, curried beef, and chickpeas with cucumbers along with a colorful fruit salad. To drink, he presented a dark tea. Instead of sitting, Annabelle stared at the food. Her picnics usually consisted of tea and strawberries, never her weekly meat ration. How strange to eat an extravagant meal in a casual setting. It felt all wrong, like wearing fancy clothes to shovel snow. This must be standard fare for government officials, she finally concluded and sat down. Tully filled two plates with a little of everything and handed one to her.

"Thank you," she said, taking the plate and setting it on her lap. "Your grandchildren are very talented. Is that the reason you wanted us to meet here—so you could see them perform?" She took a bite of flatbread, detecting rosemary.

"Oh no. I've seen them play many times. I hate to boast, but I've been integral in their training. Music is my passion, as drawing is yours, and I've been lucky to be blessed with five very talented grandchildren who share the same enthusiasm." Tully took a sip of tea. "I do have ulterior motives for bringing you here, but first I must ask if you have come to a decision." Tully turned to Annabelle and met her gaze, his face serious now.

Annabelle's stomach dropped at the mention of the meeting's true purpose. Tully stared at her without taking another bite of his dinner or another sip of tea. Conflict still swam in her mind. Margaret was right. She did want to go but that didn't completely erase her fears of danger. Planning a surprise party was one thing, going out to the ruins of a radioactive city was quite another. What would happen if she said no? Sure, he would smile and laugh and make some comment about the weather, but what would he go back and report? Would this be seen as an act of disloyalty?

"Yes. Of course it's yes." She forced a smile.

"Oh, brilliant!" Tully clapped his hands together once. "I'll confess that I wanted to see my grandchildren perform, but this is also the perfect venue for something else I have in mind. Please finish your dinner and then we'll talk business."

Relieved that they weren't going to talk about the mission yet, Annabelle dug into her dinner. Tully started talking about his grandchildren while shoveling more food onto her plate. The evening's serenity hugged Annabelle once again while Tully sucked her into his storytelling. The dedication and love he had for his grandchildren touched Annabelle. Her full stomach and Tully's good humor filled her with a warmth she hadn't felt in a long time.

When the sun started to set and the band took an intermission, Tully began packing up the picnic. "Before we call it a night, I was hoping you could do me a favor." He handed her a sketchpad and a pencil. "Do you think you could draw a sketch of my grandchildren for me?" He grinned at her.

"Is this a test?"

"I won't lie, it would be nice to show off an original to my supervisors—one I witnessed you complete myself. But in all honesty, it isn't a test. I'd just really like to have the drawing."

"Challenge accepted," Annabelle said. "Do I have a time limit?" She started the gazebo's outline on the paper.

Tully grinned. "I think they only have three songs left to play."

Annabelle knew she could do the drawing easily, but couldn't shake the feeling that it was a test. After completing the rough outline, she paused. Now was her chance to botch the drawing—disqualifying her from the mission. It would be so easy. She could explain that she didn't have enough time, or blame the distractions. Tully had only seen finished products and didn't really know what her process entailed... But what if he knew she lied? Perhaps it would be worse if she messed up on purpose.

She glanced up at Tully. He waited with his hands folded in his lap. He really seemed to just want this drawing of his grandchildren, whom he loved so much. Besides, what would be the motivation for lying about it not being a test?

She pressed her lips together and immersed herself in drawing. While she produced the picture of the children, their music filled her head. The melody influenced every stroke and the pencil became a dancer in her hand, swirling and frolicking across the page. At the end of the third song she made the final mark and the illustration was complete.

She looked up from the paper as if coming out of a trance, becoming suddenly aware of life around her—people clapping, laughing, and packing things up. She shook her head to clear it. She turned to Tully and presented the drawing to him. Instead of taking the drawing, he continued to look directly at Annabelle, a serious expression on his face.

"My dear, watching you work is remarkable," he said. He took the drawing from her and the grandfatherly smile returned to his face when he saw it. "Remarkable indeed!"

Annabelle blushed. "Thank you. I guess this means I passed the test then?" she joked.

"Absolutely!" Tully let out a chuckle. "Your talent is going to be invaluable to our team. I knew you could do it. I guess I just didn't realize how exceptional you really are. Now come, I want you to meet my grandchildren before I send you on your way."

Annabelle's momentary thrill at pleasing Tully vanished when she realized that her talent had just sealed her fate. He'd confirmed that it was a test, and that she had passed. At first, she felt tricked but then realized she didn't care. Maybe messing up the drawing had been her ticket out—but she didn't want it. As she followed Tully, a small smile grew on her face and she felt lightheaded thinking about what was to come.

Chapter Seven
Annabelle

On Friday, Annabelle strode silently with Margaret to the mission meeting point. Annabelle hadn't anticipated it taking so long to get to the western gate. She wasn't used to walking long distances since they biked everywhere. The sun beat down on them and her back felt wet with sweat under her heavy backpack.

Annabelle rarely came to the industrial district, and the buildings they passed fascinated her. She stared at the large warehouse buildings, which housed items brought in from scavenging. The concrete buildings had no windows, and she wondered what valuables might be inside. Then she remembered she'd be helping to bring back new treasures from Seattle…if they made it. Her stomach fluttered with anticipation.

They rounded the recycling factory which spewed smoke into the air from some of its many towers. In the distance, she saw four large wagons lined up near the western gate, which stood wide open. A gravel road led up to the gate with what looked like a wide hiking trail stretching out into the desert. Annabelle stopped. Could she do this? Her hand went unconsciously to her chest where she felt Gran's necklace.

The wagons looked strange, unlike anything she'd ever seen in person. The word *automobile* came to her mind. The wagon frames were black and had large wheels with thick tires. A bench seat sat above one set of wheels and a steering wheel extended over the left side. Arched white fabric covered the wagons and solar panels lined the roof.

"I didn't realize you guys were going on the Oregon Trail," Margaret joked.

Annabelle let out a laugh and it felt good to release some tension.

"I guess they do look like wagons from the Oregon Trail, except no oxen."

"Yeah, what are those things? Did we invent cars again?"

Annabelle shook her head. "I have no idea."

The two started walking again, but it seemed Margaret had slowed their pace. Annabelle turned to look at her and found Margaret staring beyond the gate, her brows furrowed.

"What's wrong?" Annabelle asked, stopping again.

Margaret pulled her eyes away from the distance and stared at Annabelle. She compressed her lips. "Don't go," she finally said.

"Margaret, it's too late for that," Annabelle said. She didn't like seeing anxiety on Margaret's face. "Don't worry," she added.

"How can I not worry? How can *you* not be worried?"

Annabelle took a deep breath. "I am worried, trust me. I'm not sure what's keeping me going, to be honest."

"Yes you do. It's the adventure, just like I predicted," Margaret said, raising her eyebrows.

Annabelle swallowed. "I'm trying to focus on that, but trust me, I'm nervous too."

Margaret nodded slowly.

"Besides, maybe I'll meet a man on the mission," Annabelle said, knowing this comment would please Margaret.

Margaret laughed. "One can only hope," she said. "Seriously though, Annabelle, I'm gonna miss you. And before I send you on your way, I have something for you." Margaret fished through her backpack and pulled out a bundle. "Here." She handed it to Annabelle.

Annabelle unwrapped the towel. "Beef jerky!"

"I didn't think you'd be getting much meat out there, so naturally I had to take matters into my own hands."

"This means a lot, Margaret, thank you," Annabelle said. "Hey, this might be the thing that lands me a man," she joked and rewrapped the bundle before tucking it into her own backpack.

"If you don't mind, I'll send you off from here," Margaret said.

"Are you sure? Don't you want to find out how the wagons work?"

"You can tell me all about it when you get back," Margaret said and began flicking her single chin hair. Annabelle wondered if Margaret couldn't bear to watch her leave.

"Of course I will," Annabelle said, giving a small smile. Margaret smiled back, then threw her arms around her.

"Take care of yourself," Margaret said.

"You too. I'll see you in a couple of months."

Margaret pulled away and nodded. Then she turned around, and started walking the way they'd come.

Annabelle watched Margaret for a moment then turned back toward the wagons. This was it. Ready or not, she had to put one foot in front of the other. Her wobbly legs made her feel like she floated the rest of the way, as if in a dream. She kept her eyes on the land beyond the Colony until she arrived.

"Annabelle, it's so good to see you again," Clara said, bringing the world back into focus.

"Clara, hi." Annabelle blinked a few times. "I'm here," she added.

Clara chuckled. "I see that. Come with me. We're still waiting on a couple of people but plan on heading out in the next hour. Let me get you settled in your wagon. We'll wait for introductions once everyone is here."

Annabelle followed Clara and watched the bustle of activity around her. People with clipboards stood around the wagons, jotting notes, while others lay on the ground under the wagons with tools, tightening bolts. While walking, she and Clara stepped over someone's legs, and Annabelle wanted to ask if the wagons were secure. Surely they were just doing last minute checks, right? Other people loaded the wagons with boxes, and someone else carried a mattress pad through a doorway. If the wagons weren't ready to go, how in the world could she be ready? Fear threatened to overwhelm her previous sense of adventure.

Ignoring the growing pressure in her stomach, she forced herself to follow Clara through the activity. If Clara hadn't come to guide her, she would have gaped motionless at the scene.

"Harold, Annabelle is here. You want her in the second wagon with Thomas, right?" Clara said.

Harold stood next to a wagon, studying a book of maps with another young man. "Yes, that's right. Hello, Annabelle," he said. His tone was friendly, but he didn't look up from the book. "Thomas, can you help get Annabelle settled into the wagon? I've got to find Tully." He closed the book and hurried off.

"Your husband seems a bit distracted and forgot to introduce me to my wagon mate," the young man said to Clara. "Hello, I'm Thomas, second in command." He gave Annabelle a cocky smile and picked up a large crate that sat at the entrance to the wagon.

Annabelle reached out her hand to shake his and then let it drop awkwardly when she realized his hands were full. "I'm Annabelle, nice to meet you," she said, feeling like it wasn't complete without a handshake. Thomas wasn't much taller than her, but had a wider build. His dark hair was slicked over to the side, and it looked hard and shiny, as if it were plastic. Despite his large nose, his face was handsome, and he had thick eyebrows and a strong chin. He didn't seem dressed for a mission, wearing a crisp white shirt tucked neatly into his black pants. Annabelle felt frumpy next to him. Her brown shirt and cargo pants suddenly seemed too baggy.

"I'll let you two get settled," Clara said and followed the direction Harold had gone.

"Okay, come on up. I'll give you the grand tour," Thomas said and set the crate down just inside the wagon entrance.

Annabelle could easily climb up the three stairs on her own, but Thomas offered his hand to help and she humored him. His clammy hand left sweat on hers, and she wanted to wipe it off on her pants but forced her arm to stay slack at her side.

The wagon was roomier inside than she would've imagined. The curved white walls brightened the space and a plastic window at the opposite end allowed more light to come in. Stacked crates lined the sides, leaving a small hallway down the center of the wagon to the beds at the other end. The raised beds sat atop three long teal blue drawers.

"Welcome to the Blue Wagon," Thomas picked up the crate again and stacked it on another. "We're all stocked up with the finest freeze-dried food the Colony could offer. Just add water and we'll be eating gourmet."

Thomas strutted down between the beds and stopped at the end of the wagon. "Which bed do you want?" he asked.

Annabelle shrugged her shoulders. The foam mattresses were about an inch thick. Folded brown quilts sat at the foot of each bed. "What's in the drawers under them?"

"The bottom drawers are actually cabinets and hold batteries and engine parts." He lifted up the bottom panel, revealing a collection of black machinery and blinking lights. "The other drawers are empty for now but hopefully we'll fill them with loot from Seattle." He lowered the panel back down and snapped it into place.

"So these really are automobiles?" Annabelle leaned back against the bed, feeling dizzy.

"Yeah, pretty cool, huh? And don't worry, I've been test driving them for weeks, so you can just kick back and file your pretty little nails." He looked at her with an arrogant smile. "So which bed would you like? Ladies choice." Annabelle looked from one bed to the other but couldn't focus on his simple question. *I'm inside a vehicle!* She was about to ask a question when Thomas started talking again.

"There's an alternative, of course." Thomas bobbed his eyebrows at her. "We can always share one bed—you know, to keep us warm on cold nights."

Annabelle stood up straight, forgetting all about her vehicle questions. "Excuse me?" she said, crossing her arms. The three feet between the beds suddenly didn't seem like enough.

Thomas started laughing. "You should see your face right now! Don't worry, I'm only teasing."

"Oh." Annabelle chuckled once and relaxed her arms at her sides again.

"And don't worry, it gets better." He reached up and pulled on a string which released a blue patchwork curtain from the ceiling—creating privacy between the beds. Annabelle relaxed her shoulders. Having her own little space felt right and made everything seem possible. Having a safe place to escape and draw, and especially a place away from Thomas, would make bunking with him bearable. Could they just keep the curtain down permanently between the beds though?

Thomas started rolling the curtain back up. "Don't look so relieved, honey. You'll still be able to hear me fart."

Annabelle curled her lip and took a step back. She was used to being around boys, but her brothers hadn't acted like this since their preteens. Was he being rude or trying to be funny?

"Thomas, are you being a creep again?" asked a woman climbing the stairs into their wagon. "Hi, I'm Francine," she said when she entered the wagon. She took a few steps and offered her hand to Annabelle.

Annabelle turned away from Thomas, grateful for the interruption. "Nice to meet you, I'm Annabelle." She shook Francine's hand and gave her a polite smile.

"The famous artist," Francine said. "I've been waiting to meet you."

"Thanks, that's nice to hear."

"And sorry you're stuck with my smart-aleck nephew here. I would've bunked with you but I promised Ernie I'd teach him how to drive. And we have to bunk in the wagon we drive, just in case we get separated."

"That's okay. He's your nephew?" Annabelle looked from Francine to Thomas. Francine had salt and pepper shoulder length hair, but her dark eyes and eyebrows matched Thomas's. Annabelle could tell they were related. However, Francine's shaggy hair and untucked shirt gave her a more relaxed look than Thomas.

"Yes, unfortunately, every family has a bad apple." Francine grinned and punched Thomas in the arm.

"Hey now, don't start throwing me under the wagon just to impress the prettiest lady on the trip," Thomas said with puppy-dog eyes and raised brows. He couldn't hold the expression for long, though, and started cracking up. Francine started laughing and Annabelle joined in—the joke was just too stupid not to laugh. She realized she'd have to make an effort, as hard as it would be, to prevent Thomas's comments from offending her.

"Anyway, everyone is here, and Tully is ready to see us off," Francine said. "Are you guys all settled in?"

Annabelle walked to the beds and placed her backpack in the top drawer under the bed on the left. "As settled in as I could be. Let's go."

Outside, she met the remaining three men: two brothers, Calvin and Curtis, and Ernie who shared a wagon with Francine. Everyone stood in a circle around Tully. Silence spread over the group and Annabelle realized all the activity she had seen before entering her wagon had ceased. The only people still at the site were those going on the mission, and Tully. It was good seeing Tully. He could make everything okay, and if he said things would be fine, she would believe him. He didn't let the silence last for long though, and took his opportunity to address the group.

"It brings great joy to the Colony that this day has arrived," Tully began. His words were authoritative but filled with the warmth that emanated from him. "I am proud of each and every one of you and am confident that this mission will be successful and bring great glory to the Colony. Everyone knows the sacrifices you are making and the risks involved in this undertaking, so for that I thank you.

"I'm leaving you in good hands. Harold's the best leader we have, and Francine happens to be the inventor of the solar-powered wagons and knows them inside and out."

Thomas let out a cheer.

"Don't get too excited, they can't go above twenty miles per hour," Francine said.

"We look forward to hearing how they handle the trip. If all goes as planned, we'll likely build more," Tully said. "We also decided to fill the wagons with an extra month's worth of food so you can feel comfortable taking your time. And there's still plenty of space for you to bring goods back from Seattle.

"As you head west and cross the Cascade Mountains, you'll be rising in elevation and the vegetation will be different than you've ever seen. We're expecting lush forests and pristine lakes. I'll admit I'm jealous I don't get to see it myself. But that's why we've asked Annabelle to come along. She'll illustrate your trip, so we can all get a taste when you return. I can't tell you how excited I am to send you on your way. Does anyone have any final questions?"

Annabelle looked around at the others. Had they discussed the risks involved amongst themselves? Nobody, other than her imagination, had given her that information. Annabelle took a deep breath to steady herself. Tully waited in front of them with a calm smile. She had a million questions but couldn't put any into words.

"I'd love it if you could do a final inspection of the inventory with me, Tully," Harold finally said.

"Of course. It'll put me at ease knowing I sent you off with everything you need. Is that all?" Tully looked back at the others, giving them one more chance to ask questions. *Is he asking us for final words? Giving us the opportunity to back out?* She looked at the others. They all had serious looks on their faces, even Thomas. No one seemed at all on the verge of backing out.

"Very well, let's do the inventory. I'll be around until you depart, so you'll still have an opportunity to ask something if you think of it." Tully and Harold headed off to the first wagon and the rest of the group came together.

"What do you think he was fishing for?" Thomas asked with an irritated tone. Annabelle glanced over at Harold and Tully, making sure they were out of earshot. She couldn't believe that anyone would speak of Tully in such a tone. "Here's a question," Thomas went on, "If we're bringing the Colony such great honor, then why don't we get a grand send off with a band and a feast?"

"Thomas," Clara said, "knock it off." Thomas relaxed his face and flashed a smile.

"You know I'm only kidding, boss," he said. Clara didn't respond, but she didn't look angry. Annabelle liked how Clara put him in his place.

Yet, Thomas had a point. Why was Tully the only one sending them off on the mission? Maybe the party was being saved for when they came back? If they came back...

"Hey Annabelle, did you hear that Calvin and Curtis are quite the musicians?" Clara asked, rescuing Annabelle from her thoughts.

"No, I didn't. What do you play?" she asked, looking at the brothers. It was easy to tell the two were related. They were both tall and had the same medium build. Both had freckled faces and dark hair but Curtis had red highlights in his brown hair.

"I play the guitar and Curtis sings," Calvin answered, "but we only mess around most of the time."

"Oh, don't be modest," Clara said. "They're fantastic. You brought your guitar didn't you?"

"Of course."

"Oh good! Then we'll have to get you to play for us tonight," Clara said. With the mood slightly lightened, the group began to talk about how excited they were to drive the wagons. Annabelle watched Harold and Tully as they did their inspection. If they found something, perhaps the mission would be cancelled or postponed. *Do I hope they'll find something wrong or am I worried that they will?* She tried to control her breath and focus on what Clara was saying, but all she heard was her heartbeat pounding in her ears.

Before she knew it, however, Tully and Harold returned to the group. "Everything looks good," Harold said. "When we head out, keep a good distance between the wagons. These things kick up a good amount of dirt. Everybody ready?"

"Hell yeah!" Calvin said.

Francine clapped her hands together and the others shouted agreement while Annabelle only nodded.

"Alright, let's go!" Harold turned toward his wagon, a wide smile on his face.

Annabelle had no choice but to follow Thomas to their wagon. Her legs felt wobbly and she hoped sitting on the bench would make her feel more centered.

"Annabelle, wait," Tully said, coming over to her. "I nearly forgot to give this to you." He handed her a sketchbook that had an old Space Needle photograph on the front cover. It was a faded picture, but beautiful nonetheless. She rarely encountered photographs in good condition. She hugged the book to her chest. "It's beautiful," she said. "Thank you, Tully." She treasured holding such an artifact. Hopefully, she could fill it with illustrations on the inside that would match the cover's beauty.

"I can't wait to see what you fill it with. Take care of yourself. And make sure Thomas here stays out of trouble."

"See you soon, Mr. Foster," Thomas said, extending his hand to Tully.

"Yes, good luck, Thomas," Tully said, shaking his hand. He shook Annabelle's hand next and turned to say his final goodbyes to the others.

"Let me put this in the wagon real quick before we go," Annabelle said over her shoulder to Thomas as she walked to the wagon's entrance. Holding the sketchbook reminded her of her true purpose on the mission. Soon, she would get to draw things she'd never seen before.

She entered the wagon and headed to the drawers under her

bed and stashed the sketchbook inside her backpack. She started to leave, but then stopped and pulled the curtain down between the beds. She took a deep breath in her own private space and a satisfied smile spread across her lips.

This was it. Within minutes, they'd be outside the Colony. She touched the necklace hiding under her shirt and wondered if she'd ever have the opportunity to discover what Gran's key opened. A world existed out there and she was going to discover it before anyone else. She would get to illustrate it. A sense of awe rushed through her and washed away all the tension. After seeing Seattle, she would come back and discover her grandfather's secret. Step one, step two. It really was rather simple. Her smile grew and she left the wagon.

"Okay, let's go," she said and sat on the wagon bench next to Thomas.

"Buckle your seat belt," Thomas said and motioned at a strap around his lap and pointed to a latch on his right.

"Seat belt?" Annabelle looked to her right and found a flat metal piece. She pulled on it and a strap extended which she pulled across and latched on the other side of her body.

"Safety first," Thomas said and pushed a button under the steering wheel. A quiet hum came from behind them and the wagon lurched forward. Annabelle grabbed onto the bar lining the front of the wagon. Thomas let out a laugh. "Don't worry, sweetheart, I've got this," he said and adjusted a mirror that hung to the left of the steering wheel.

Annabelle forced herself back in the seat while Thomas turned the wagon and followed Harold through the western gate.

Chapter Eight
Harold

Harold couldn't have asked for a better morning to start the mission. The warm sun welcomed him and the clear sky stretched as far as he could see over the dusty landscape. The Columbia River sparkled in the distance and its dark water looked beautiful, despite its toxicity. He drove at a steady pace, grateful to be out on the road. He gripped the steering wheel, loving the feel of it in his hands. He'd been itching to take one of these wagons out on a mission ever since they started test driving them. They got to be the first ones to go to Seattle, and the first ones to drive.

He started whistling a tune and glanced at Clara, thrilled to have her along. The wind blew her hair back, and she looked straight ahead. "Driving is pretty awesome, don't you think?" he said.

"I guess," Clara said simply.

"And what a beautiful day. Not too hot and not too cold."

"Uh-huh," Clara replied.

She was unusually quiet. "Is something wrong?" he asked.

"No."

He knew that had to be a lie. "Come on, Clara, what's going on?"

"Don't act like you don't know."

Harold gritted his teeth. He did know. How could she still be mad about going on the mission now that they'd started? How could she not be excited? They were *driving* to *Seattle*! Together! How did she not get how amazing that was?

"This again?"

"What do you mean, 'this again?' You're the one who brought it up!" Clara said.

Harold wanted to shake her. They'd been over this a million times this week. "I just don't understand what you want. How can you not see that this is what's best for us?"

"Best for you, you mean."

"No, I mean best for us! This way I'll get to be there for your whole pregnancy. We'll get to be together for the whole mission, we'll get to experience Seattle together. How exactly is this a bad thing?"

"Harold." Clara pressed her lips together and blew a few breaths from her nose. "I don't care about Seattle. I don't want to go to Seattle! Okay?"

"You don't want to go?" Harold felt like she'd kicked him down. During all of their previous arguments, she'd never said she didn't want to go. It had always been about wanting a baby. Why did she wait until now to tell him?

Clara sighed. "No, I don't. But it's obviously too late."

Harold didn't know what to say. Why wouldn't she want to go? It was the opportunity of a lifetime. They would return as heroes to the Colony. They would share in the glory. And didn't she want to be with him? Share this experience with him?

"Harold, just think how you would've felt if the mission had to be cancelled. Let's say you had to sacrifice the mission for our pregnancy for some reason."

"But you aren't sacrificing the pregnancy! We'll continue the process as soon as we get back." He clenched his jaw. How could she bring up sacrifice? It was his last mission, after all. He was giving up the job he loved so he could be home after the baby was born. Couldn't she see what he was sacrificing for them? For their family?

"I don't understand why you have such a hard time seeing this from my perspective. Look, I'm going. A little empathy wouldn't be too much to ask, would it?"

"What about empathy for me? This is my last mission. I'm giving up my career for your baby." He regretted the words as soon as they left his mouth.

"*My* baby?"

"You know that's not what I meant."

"It's what you said. I can't believe you, Harold! Your true colors are really showing."

He knew he'd screwed up, but she'd be hung up on semantics now. There was no way to win this. Harold trapped his words in, let them stew. Why did she always have to be right? She always expected him to apologize. He was hurt that she didn't want to go on the mission with him. He didn't want to deal with this conflict. He had a mission to run. Why couldn't she support him? He didn't want to fight about it anymore but wasn't ready to give in either. This wasn't how he'd wanted to start the mission.

It was the hottest part of the day and they had a significant lead on the others. He must've been driving faster than he'd intended, fueled by anger. He hit the steering wheel, frustrated that he'd let the fight interfere with his leadership.

"We have to deal with this later. Let's break for lunch and let the others catch up," he said.

They stopped and waited. He needed to put the argument aside for now and make the mission a priority. He would take Clara along to scout ahead while the others rested so they could put this behind them once and for all.

He paced while waiting for the others. He could see Thomas and Annabelle's wagon a hundred yards back and the next another hundred yards. At first he couldn't see Ernie and Francine's wagon but just as Thomas and Annabelle's approached, it appeared in the distance. Harold stopped pacing, relieved everyone was right on track.

He needed to keep the mission focused and start out on a positive note. He hoped Clara would see the importance of it all. He watched the wagons arrive smoothly. What a privilege it was to lead such a fine team. He wouldn't let them down. He wouldn't let the Colony down.

"Lunch break?" Thomas asked, approaching Harold.

"That's right. I was hoping you could organize the lunch while Clara and I take the scouting bikes up ahead to make sure we're on the right course. We probably don't need to check for radiation levels yet, but I'll take the readers with us just to be safe."

"Sounds good, boss."

Harold retrieved the scouting bikes. They probably didn't need to scout ahead yet because this area was already charted, but he wanted to set a routine.

"We should be back in around forty-five minutes, save some lunch for us," Harold told Thomas.

"Sure thing," Thomas said.

Harold and Clara set off. The ground was still flat and dusty, and biking felt like flying. They rode a while in silence as Harold tried to figure out how to fix this.

"Listen, I don't want to fight with you, Clara."

"Me either." She didn't sound mad anymore, just defeated.

He sighed. The break in the argument had alleviated his frustration and he was ready to let it go. But Clara spoke first.

"I can see the benefit of the mission, truly I can. I'm sure I'll be thanking you someday. This was just such a sudden change, and you were so wrapped up in it that you didn't see how hard it was for me."

"I know. I see that now." Ahead, he spotted some rock formations and turned toward them, thinking it would be a good spot for a heart to heart. "Let's stop here."

They got off their bikes and found a shady place next to a rock wall. Harold faced her. "Listen, I want a baby just as bad as you, really, I do. I didn't choose to make the mission earlier, you know that. If it was up to me, we wouldn't have left yet, you know?"

Clara nodded but didn't say anything. She blinked her eyes a few times as if trying to keep tears in.

"I'm sorry this happened so fast," Harold continued. "But you have no idea how glad I am that you're with me. I'll try my hardest to make it up to you, I promise."

Clara sighed. "I know." She looked down at her hands. "It's okay, it'll be okay." She smiled at him now. Her hair looked golden in the sunlight and a film of dust covered her skin. Her cheeks were flushed red from the sun. It was the face of someone who'd been riding all day on their first expedition, and she'd never looked more beautiful. She hadn't wanted to come but she did.

"Come here." He scooped her into his lap, needing her to be closer to him. Her smile grew and his heart fluttered. "And before you know it, we'll be back and you'll be fat and pregnant." He tucked a piece of hair behind her ear and then she kissed him.

It felt so good to have her in his arms. For them to be a team again. He'd make it up to her, and he vowed to show her what an amazing time they'd have on the mission.

On the ride back to the others, he started to worry that maybe Clara was right though. Had it been a mistake bringing her along? Had he been so blinded by the excitement of having her with him that he couldn't see how difficult it might be? It was only the first day, and they'd had one of their biggest fights ever. What if something happened and he had to put the mission first, before his marriage? Did he really want to put himself in that situation? It was too late now.

***

Annabelle

"Hey Annabelle, before we head to the fire can I talk to you for a minute?" Thomas asked that evening.

They'd been in the sun all day, sitting on the hard bench, and Annabelle wanted nothing more than to curl up next to the fire and eat a bowl of sweet potato stew. What was Thomas up to? He wore a serious expression so she decided to humor him. "Sure," she said, and followed him into their wagon.

She stood by the doorway, the fire's crackle calling to her from outside. "So," Thomas brushed his hand over his still stiff hair, "I want to apologize for how I acted when we first met." Annabelle watched him, not sure if he was really serious. He finally met her gaze. "Oh hell, I guess I get a little nervous when I first meet a pretty girl and don't handle myself in the best way." He gave her a genuine smile. "Friends?" He held his hand out to her.

Annabelle smiled, and felt heat rush to her face. She shook his hand. "Yes, friends." It was a sincere apology, and she appreciated it.

"Well, since we're friends now, let me share something with you." She wanted to show him that she accepted his apology. She retrieved her backpack and pulled out the beef jerky. "Jerky?"

"For real?" Thomas accepted a piece and bit into it. "Thanks, roomie."

"No problem. Let's go join the others."

They'd parked the wagons in a circle, providing a sense of shelter in the center where everyone sat on folding chairs around a blazing fire. She'd only known this team for one day, but sharing a fire made her feel close to them. They all gazed at the dancing flames, soaking in the warmth and anticipating the dinner they would soon eat. Laughter and chatter erupted once they had bowlfuls of stew in their laps.

Clara sat in Harold's lap and he whispered something in Clara's ear, making her laugh. Then she looked up at him and gave him a quick kiss. Annabelle smiled. They seemed so in love. What was their secret?

"How did you two meet?" she asked, moving her chair closer to them.

"I don't remember, do you Harold?" Clara said.

"Um, no," he said. Clara laughed. Obviously sharing an inside joke.

"Let me explain," Clara started. "Our mothers were neighbors so we've known each other since before we can remember."

"And Clara got all my hand-me-downs!" Harold added with a chuckle.

"Yes, unfortunately that's true," Clara said, shaking her head, "so you can't get upset at me when I wear your shirts as pajamas. I've been programmed to wear your clothes since birth."

Harold laughed. "You can wear my shirts anytime, just stay away from my underwear."

"Gross! And besides, you wouldn't be in underwear if it wasn't for me."

"Oh yeah, that's right." Harold said, putting his face in his hand.

"You see, even though I was younger than Harold, I was potty trained before him, and in fact, according to our mothers, it was me who ultimately potty trained him," Clara said.

Now Annabelle laughed. "Is that so?"

"What can I say?" Harold said, "She's always had a big influence on me." He brought her hand to his lips and kissed it, "And I'm eternally grateful for everything she's taught me in life."

"When did you start dating?" Annabelle asked, still trying to flush out their secret.

"You know, for years we were just friends. It probably wasn't until I was sixteen that we noticed there was something more there," Clara said.

"Speak for yourself!" Harold objected. "I knew something was there long before that. I was just sitting around, waiting for you to realize it too."

"Well you should've made a move then."

"I did. I followed you around everywhere and chased away every guy that looked at you."

"Now that's true." Clara said, shaking her head and smiling.

"So that's the secret then, friends first?" Annabelle said, tired of beating around the bush.

Before Clara could answer, laughter from the others interrupted them.

"What did we miss?" Harold asked.

"We just found out that Calvin and Ernie have essentially slept together!" Thomas roared.

"No," Ernie said, "We just figured out we were dating the same girl a while back, that's all."

"Yikes," Clara said, "Who ended up winning her?"

Calvin and Ernie looked at each other. "She broke up with me," Ernie said.

"Same," Calvin said, "So I guess we both lost."

"At least you guys still have each other," Thomas said and howled with laughter again.

Annabelle rolled her eyes. Thomas wasn't funny at all, but as she surveyed the group she couldn't help but smile. They jived together so well, and it excited her to be a part of it. There was something freeing about being outside of the Colony with a group of strangers. They didn't expect anything from her, didn't really know who she was. She could be anyone she wanted to be, and they wouldn't know the difference.

"Hey Calvin, I thought you guys were going to play for us tonight," Clara said, changing the subject.

"Oh yeah, sing us your love ballad for the one that got away," Thomas joked.

Calvin ignored him and said, "Of course, you in Curt?"

"I'll go get the guitar."

"Okay, good. I've got something planned for us as well," Clara said, and stood. "Something I've always wanted to try and will be good for relaxation after our long ride today. Any takers?"

"Sounds good to me," Annabelle said, rubbing her back.

"Alright. Harold, will you help me? And Annabelle, can you fetch some jugs of water?""

"Sure," Harold said, following Clara into the cold night. The others stayed around the dying fire, listening to the brothers' music.

When Annabelle returned with the water, Clara and Harold were still gone. Only coals remained in the fire and she sat, wanting more than ever to just go to bed. Finally, Clara and Harold reappeared, carrying sagebrush branches, a blanket, and a cooking pot.

"What in the world?" Thomas asked.

"Don't look at me, she won't tell me a thing," Harold said.

"Okay," Clara began, "I've read sagebrush is good for treating all kinds of ailments, but I've never had a chance to use it. The fragrance released in the smoke is very medicinal." She looked around at everyone. "Who's up for it?"

"I'll try it," Thomas said, rubbing his bottom.

"Yeah, me too," said Ernie. "But what are we going to do? Smoke it?"

Clara laughed. "No, you're going to take a smoke bath. Not only will it make you feel better, but it'll make you smell better too." She nudged Harold.

"Oh, that's your true intention?" Harold said with a laugh.

Clara placed coals in a cooking pot and poured water over the sagebrush leaves. She put the wet leaves over the coals then placed the pot underneath one of the folding chairs. "Who's first?"

"I'll go," Thomas said.

Clara wrapped a blanket around him, covering his whole body and head. She led Thomas to the prepared chair and draped the bottom of the blanket over the chair so it touched the ground.

Clara worked with precision, yet Annabelle still felt hesitant. *What if the blanket catches on fire? Would it be hard to breath?*

Minutes passed and Thomas didn't show any signs of wanting to come out. Clara added more leaves. Calvin and Curtis started playing again.

Finally Thomas pulled the blanket off his head and took a deep breath.

"How was it?" Clara asked.

"Good," Thomas said. "Thank you." Then he wandered off toward his wagon without smiling or making any jokes.

"Well, okay then," Clara said. "Who's next?"

After Francine and Ernie tried the smoke bath and sauntered off to their wagon, Annabelle decided she wanted to try. Clearly, it had been incredibly relaxing.

The blanket was already warm when Clara wrapped it around Annabelle. Clara guided her to the chair and moments later she felt heat coming from underneath. The smoke swirled around her ankles and made its way up her body. Soon the blanket filled with the sagebrush aroma. It smelled of sweet summer nights in the desert and Annabelle took deep, slow breaths, wanting to fill herself up with its serenity. With each breath, the smoke wrapped her in its arms and she felt safe and protected. Something about the embrace made her feel as if everyone shared in it. She visualized the mission group swimming in a lake together, all enveloped by the same water. They were all together, safe and warm and protected by an all-encompassing oneness. Annabelle understood why Thomas hadn't been in a big hurry to leave the smoke bath. She didn't want it to end either.

But before long, Clara pulled the blanket back. "Sorry to cut you short, Annabelle, but we're out of coals."

"Oh." Annabelle blinked a few times. "That's okay."

"Should we start another fire? I know you wanted to try it, Clara, and we likely won't find sagebrush again," Harold said.

"It's all right," Clara said. "I'll do it on the trip back."

Chapter Nine
Annabelle

Annabelle already felt like a different person when they headed out on the second day. The further from the Colony they went the more free she felt. Maybe it had been the smoke bath, maybe it was doing something new, maybe it was being out on her own. The reason didn't matter, Annabelle was just grateful for being on the mission. The fear of radiation still hovered in the back of her mind, however. Harold had said that they'd be entering uncharted territory by the end of the day and everyone strapped radiation monitors to their wagons. Harold and Clara had scouted ahead that morning to test for radiation and all readings came back negative.

The lack of radiation allowed Annabelle to totally relax, at least for a while. When they stopped for the afternoon she joined an impromptu game of football with the team. They'd stopped at a grassy plain near a tree lined river. Harold had instructed them to have lunch, refill their water stores, sent Curtis and Francine ahead to scout, and then dozed off under a tree. With their leader snoozing, the others couldn't resist having a little fun.

Ernie hiked the ball to Thomas, who headed toward the end zone and Annabelle closed in on him.

"Thomas, come here!" Harold shouted. His abrupt command distracted Thomas and Annabelle tackled him to the ground. Everyone laughed and Annabelle jumped up, triumphant.

"I was distracted," Thomas said and kicked the ball down toward the river.

"You've gotta keep your head in the game!" Annabelle teased.

"Yeah, yeah." Thomas said and headed over to Harold, "What's up, boss?"

Annabelle chased the ball, and Ernie followed her. They wove their way through the curtain of tree branches, Ernie hunched over because of his height.

"Where did you learn to tackle like that?" Ernie asked, sounding impressed.

"I've got three older brothers," she answered, enjoying the compliment. They reached the river bank but didn't see the ball.

"Where do you think the ball got to?" she asked, looking around. The cool air around the river refreshed her. The water enticed her to jump in. They hadn't had a chance to bathe, aside from the smoke bath, and dust and sweat caked her whole body.

"What's that?" Ernie said, pointing up the river. Annabelle saw a thick cable tied to a tree on their side of the riverbank that extended across the river and was tied to a tree on the other side.

"What the heck?" she whispered, and followed Ernie up the bank toward the rope. When they reached the tree, Ernie pointed up. "It's a zip line."

Someone had constructed a log platform half way up the evergreen tree and a set of handlebars attached to a pulley hung from the cable above the platform.

"How'd it get out here?" Annabelle asked, looking at him. They were pretty far from the Colony, but someone had constructed the zip line, and it couldn't have been too long ago.

Ernie shrugged. "Maybe someone on a Spokane expedition built it?"

"But isn't this a different course?"

"Yeah, but not by much."

Annabelle glanced back up at the pulley. A Spokane expedition could be the only logical explanation for why it was here, she told herself. It looked sturdy and well made. She'd never been on anything like it and wanted to try. "Should we try it?" she said, bouncing on her feet.

"I'm game!" Ernie said, matching her mood.

"You go first," she said.

Thin logs lined the trunk, making a ladder, and Ernie climbed up them and eased onto the platform. He tapped the logs with a foot while holding the tree trunk and then gave a thumbs up to Annabelle. Once at the platform's edge, he grabbed the handlebars but then glanced down, hesitating.

"Go for it!" Annabelle said. He gave another thumbs up and lifted his feet. He propelled across the river with his long legs hanging awkwardly beneath him. Seconds later, he reached the lower platform on the other side and Annabelle itched to try it herself.

"How was it?" she shouted.

"That was awesome! And look!" He started unwinding a rope from around the bar that connected the handlebars to the pulley. "I think this is for pulling the rope back to the otherside." He let the rope fall to the ground and stared at the river.

He would need to swim across the river to bring it back. The only river Annabelle had ever seen was the toxic Columbia River which skirted the Colony's boundary. "Let me check the water real quick!" Annabelle shouted. She already had the water monitor in her pocket since she had intended to fill their water stores that day. She dipped the cylinder in the water and waited for the double beep. She held her breath. *What if it's toxic and Ernie is stuck on the other side?* The double beep sounded and she let out her breath.

"All clear!"

Ernie jumped off the platform onto the ground. "I guess I'll have to get my clothes wet. We really didn't think this through."

Annabelle laughed and watched Ernie wade into the water while holding the rope. "It's cold!" Ernie said in a higher pitched voice and Annabelle snickered again. He took a few quick breaths then dove the rest of his body in. While he swam across the river, Annabelle scrambled up the ladder, filled with giddiness.

She gazed around the river, enjoying the vantage point. She'd never seen so many trees together. The trees grew sparsely amongst desert shrubs everywhere except near the river. It wasn't a forest yet, but was more lush than home. She took a mental picture so she could draw the scene later. Tully would appreciate it.

Ernie approached the bank and she reached out and grabbed the rope and pulled the handlebars to the tree. She looked down at Ernie while he stepped up on shore, dripping wet. "Are you going to go again?" she asked him.

Ernie flashed her a big toothy grin. "It was actually super refreshing. But I'll need to ditch some wet clothes before going again."

He started peeling off his wet pants and Annablle studied the water. She'd get wet swimming back so should lose some extra clothes as well. She grabbed her shirt and began pulling it off, then remembered Gran's necklace and yanked the shirt back down. She'd been so caught up in the moment that it had completely consumed her, even causing her to forget Gran's key. She stood frozen, head down. *We probably should go retrieve the water jugs instead of goofing around.*

Ernie joined her on the platform wearing his boxers. "Having second thoughts?" His wet hair stuck out at crazy angles, making Annabelle laugh again and she shook her head. She realized Gran would want her to have some fun, plus a swim would be wonderful. She slipped her pants off, but left her shirt on—it felt more modest and also concealed the key.

She grabbed the handlebars and walked to the edge. "How deep was it?"

"Pretty deep, I could only walk a few feet before I couldn't touch."

She glanced back at Ernie, a mischievous smile on her face. "Good," she said and jumped off. Everything in her peripheral vision blurred as she flew through the air. She relished the speed and the cool wind on her face but forced herself to let go of the handlebars half way across.

She plunged into the water below. The icy water made all her muscles tense at the same time and she kicked until her head broke the surface.

"Are you okay?" Ernie shouted.

"Yeah! I did it on purpose!" She treaded water and the current rushed around her skin, cleaning all the grime off her. "You've got to try it!" She grabbed the rope and started swimming to shore. Her body adjusted to the water temperature and she relished the refreshing river.

"That was amazing," she said, and waded in the shallow water toward shore.

"Yeah," Ernie said, reaching for the zip line rope from the platform. "Almost as good as the smoke bath last night."

Annabelle shot him a glance. "What was it like for you?" Had he experienced the same thing as her?

Ernie held the handlebars but didn't jump, he looked down at her. "I felt this strange sense of… togetherness? Or…"

"Oneness?" Annabelle offered.

"Yes! That's it. It was like—"

"What are you doing?" Harold interrupted. Ernie dropped the handle bars, and took a step back—holding his hands in the air. Annabelle came onto shore. She couldn't look Harold in the eyes. She hadn't intended to disrespect the mission.

"I, we, you see we found this, uh, this zip line," she stammered. Harold kept a stern look on his face. Annabelle stood in front of him now, hugging herself.

Harold studied the zip line for a moment with a pensive expression on his face. "I'm sure a swim feels good," he finally said, "I'll go get the others so they can freshen up as well. While they're doing that, would you two mind filling up the water reserves?"

"No problem," Ernie responded, climbing down the ladder. He tossed Annabelle her pants without looking at her.

They walked silently to the wagons, but Ernie had a smile plastered on his face making Annabelle smile too. She really enjoyed his company. When they got back to work, the origin of the zip line started nagging at the back of her mind, though. Who had built it? A banished person couldn't have built it because they lacked the materials needed for its construction. No other group of people could be around because they wouldn't have survived past infancy. That was a fact. *But what if there are others out there?* Annabelle shook her head, trying to clear it. Of course there weren't others, that was impossible. Ernie was right, the zip line had been built by someone on an expedition. It was the only logical explanation.

***

The next morning Annabelle woke feeling refreshed and energetic. Embracing the energy, she got out her drawing supplies. She glanced over at Thomas, still sleeping soundly. He actually looked vulnerable. She wanted to draw him, but her job was to chronicle new things they found. She watched him sleep a few seconds to store the memory for later.

She quietly left the wagon and stepped into the cool air. Morning sunlight illuminated their campsite—just enough light to get started on illustrations. Francine was the only one up and hunched over several pieces of paper.

"What are you working on?" Annabelle asked her.

"Maps," she answered without looking up.

She didn't want to disturb Francine so she didn't question her further. Instead, she sat down and opened her sketchbook. What should she draw first? Annabelle smiled to herself, remembering the previous afternoon. She could still feel the rush of the wind, the coolness of the water. Yes, she would draw the zip line. She did a few sketches of it from different angles, and then a final one with Ernie swimming across the river. She looked around and started to sketch a wagon, then added the others, parked in a circle with the campfire in the center. By the time she finished this drawing, Harold and Clara had joined them and started getting breakfast ready. Annabelle was on a roll and didn't want to stop.

She hesitated on the next page. She knew what she wanted to draw, but wasn't sure how. She wanted to draw the smoke bath. However, when she tried to conjure up an image of what it looked like, it was too abstract for her to put down on paper. In the end, she settled for a basic drawing of the sagebrush plant itself. By the time she finished, Harold had woken everyone up and sent Calvin and Curtis to scout ahead. Satisfied with the work she'd done for the day, she got up to help with breakfast.

She found Thomas in the wagon when she went to stash her sketchbook. "Hey Roomie," he said with his mouth full. It took her a second to realize what he was eating.

"Are you eating my jerky?" Heat flushed through her. She took a step forward, clenching her fists. Not only had he gone through her stuff, but he'd stolen from her.

"Yeah, I thought we were friends now?" He grinned.

"How dare you." She ripped the jerky from his hand and returned it to her backpack. "Stay out of my stuff," she said and stormed from the wagon. Thomas's tender moments were rare, she realized. She just needed to get away from him for now or else she couldn't stand to ride with him all day.

She'd calmed down by the time they were on the road but sat as far away as possible from Thomas. She rested her chin on her fist and faced away from him. They rode in silence for a while, and Annabelle eyed the radiation detector. It remained completely silent. She turned her gaze back to the scenery and hoped Thomas wouldn't say anything.

"How ya holding up?" Thomas asked after a while. He actually sounded sincere. Was he going to try and make peace with her again?

"Good, how about you?" she replied, guarded.

"Good. Except, God, I stink. I could really go for another smoke bath. That was sure something, wasn't it?"

Annabelle didn't expect Thomas to bring up the smoke bath, but was glad he did. It swirled in the back of her thoughts and she wanted to talk about it with someone. She and Ernie hadn't gotten a chance to finish their conversation about it before. "Yeah. It did more than I expected. I kinda feel like it, uh," Annabelle paused, it had been easy to talk about it with Ernie but now she felt self-conscious about sharing with Thomas.

"Yeah, I know what you mean, it's hard to explain," he said.

"You felt it too?"

"I think so."

They rode along for a while in silence. Annabelle reflected on the smoke bath and tried conjuring the emotions it had elicited in her. The morning sun's warmth embraced her, and the rhythmic rocking from the wagon lulled her into a trance like state. Once again, she felt the strong presence of comfort encompassing everything. And she realized it brought her something else that she rarely felt in her life: clarity. She was meant to go on the mission. She wanted to be here. Nothing had ever felt so right.

"What a beautiful sight," Thomas said, interrupting Annabelle's reverie.

Annabelle looked around but didn't see anything especially beautiful. The terrain had changed a bit over the last day, small trees and thick bushes replaced the desert shrubbery completely. The vegetation grew sparsely across the landscape, still not quite a forest but more abundant than before. She smiled, maybe Thomas's experience during the smoke bath had made him appreciate the outdoors more. Then she heard him snicker behind her.

"How can such a fine specimen like you be single?"

"I beg your pardon?" She glared at him, struggling to hold onto her peaceful state.

"You heard me," Thomas said and snickered again. "Seriously, why are you single? Aren't you getting to be an old maid?"

Annabelle clenched her jaw. She shouldn't take the bait. He wanted to upset her. It gave him a weird power trip to make her uncomfortable. However, he'd struck a nerve. She'd heard this criticism over and over and couldn't stop herself from sputtering defensive retorts.

"I love my job, and I haven't met the right guy yet. I'm not going to just settle down with any old jerk. Sure I want to have kids, but I know I still have plenty of time for that. Not that any of this is your business anyway!"

"Wow, touchy subject."

"Shut up! Why are you such a jerk? And why does everyone let you get away with it?"

"Whoa, whoa, whoa. I was only toying with you. I didn't expect you to erupt like that."

Annabelle crossed her arms. "Well, look who's talking. No one will ever marry you. You're the one who needs to worry, not me."

Thomas stared straight ahead, clenching the steering wheel, and said nothing. She turned back to the scenery, a small smile on her face. She had actually shut him up. She took a breath to calm herself and wished she could recapture the peaceful feeling that Thomas had squashed. This would be a good exercise—trying to stay tranquil despite being in Thomas's presence. However, she kept mulling over her outburst. She hated that Thomas could so easily play with her emotions.When they stopped for lunch, she'd made up her mind: she needed a break from Thomas.

Chapter Ten
Harold

Happy with their morning progress, Harold decided they would take a longer lunch break. This would not only allow everyone a good rest but also give him more time to scout ahead. Since they were in uncharted territory, he wanted extra time to make sure things were safe.

"Thomas you're going to scout ahead with me, finish up lunch and let's head out in ten minutes."

Thomas glanced up with a big smile. "All right, no problem." He stood and shoved the last bite of mashed potato in his mouth.

Harold watched with a satisfied smile. Thomas sure was easy to please, all you had to do was make him feel important. He hadn't intended to stroke Thomas's ego; however, he really wanted the second in command with him. Despite Thomas's flaws, Harold had learned to depend on him after they went on multiple Spokane expeditions together. Thomas was hardworking, reliable and always followed protocol. Finding the zip line yesterday disturbed

Harold. He'd never heard of it, so it was unlikely that someone on an expedition team built it. He needed someone he could trust with him, unsure about what else they might encounter.

"Francine, we should be back in ninety minutes. Can you make sure everyone's ready to depart?" He knew Francine would keep them on track. He grabbed his pack and found Thomas already on a scouting bike, waiting for him.

They set off and made excellent time. The team had been climbing in elevation all morning. By tomorrow they would reach Snoqualmie Pass. Francine was confident they had found the old freeway, which would take them over the pass. Although overgrown, hopefully it still forged a path through the forested terrain they would soon encounter.

They stopped every fifteen minutes to check for radiation levels and to mark trees with the easiest pathway for the wagons. With each stop, they'd found nothing alarming and Harold's earlier trepidations started to fade.

Harold biked at a more relaxed speed and marveled at the greenery that surrounded them. Evergreen trees towered above with fuzzy moss crawling up their trunks. Fluorescent ferns that reached as high as the bike huddled along the forest floor. He took a deep breath and filled his lungs with the delightful, fresh aroma.

At the fourth stop the two rested for a while before heading back. He and Thomas settled under a small cluster of trees and he gratefully rested his back against a rock.

"Do you really think they'll start doing expeditions to Seattle after our mission?" Thomas asked. He set his water bottle on the ground next to him and wiped a drop from his mouth.

"That's the ultimate goal. I hope whatever we find will be useful for the Colony. And since we haven't found a trace of radiation, I think there's a good chance that Seattle will be accessible for long-term salvaging."

"Do you think they'll start sending missions to other cities too? Like Portland?"

Harold hadn't considered this. After all, the initial discussion about exploring Seattle had surprised him. The Colony remained closed off as a means for survival. It was hard to imagine they would ever start to expand beyond Spokane. He certainly didn't think it would happen in his lifetime. Yet, they hadn't found any evidence of radiation, or any danger for that matter, so why not Portland?

"You might be onto something, Thomas. I guess we can take pride in the fact that we proved it's safe to start exploring."

Since this was his last mission, what would he be missing out on? After Portland, where would they go? San Francisco? LA? And would they start sending out boats to explore regions further away? Maybe even start setting up permanent settlements in new towns? The opportunities seemed endless, and Harold couldn't stop these exploration images from haunting his thoughts. He stared at his feet, grimacing. He couldn't bear to miss out on seeing those places.

"I can't wait," Thomas said, interrupting his thoughts.

"You'll probably be leading many of the missions."

"This mission better be a success then."

Harold took a last drink and stood up. "It will be," he said. "Let's head back. Everything looks good."

"Let me mark one last tree." Thomas pulled the large wax marker from his pack. He went to the nearest tree and drew a giant red X.

"What the hell?" he said.

"What?"

Thomas held a rope that hung from a branch above. It reached the ground and continued along the forest floor. The brown rope contained fibers braided together and could only be a couple years old. Harold's stomach tightened as he and Thomas followed the rope. A few feet down, they discovered a dingy blue shirt wrapped around the rope. Next they found a brown pair of pants.

"A clothesline," Harold said. His heart pounded.

He and Thomas looked silently at each other. What did this mean? No expedition came out this far. How would a clothesline get here? Thomas continued down the rope and found another shirt attached and then the rope's end, lying in the dirt.

He held his breath and scanned the area for more evidence. The wind rustled through the trees and goosebumps covered his arms. His gaze landed on something red and fuzzy about twenty feet away and half buried in the dirt. He walked to it and Thomas followed. He picked it up. "A teddy bear?" He stared at it.

"Boss." Thomas grabbed his arm. "Look."

Harold looked up and saw that the ground sloped away. At the bottom of the hill, four tiny cabins surrounded a fire pit. Dishes and a kettle lay in a pile next to one of the cabins. No noise or movement came from the area. Harold hugged the teddy bear and headed toward the cabins.

"You know what this means, don't you?" Thomas said.

Harold did know what it meant, but blocked the implications from entering his thoughts. "I've got a bad feeling about this," he said.

***

Annabelle

Francine upheld her order and kept everyone on task. Annabelle carried a pot of hot water to Clara for washing dishes. Calvin and Curtis brought water from a nearby stream and Ernie purified the water over a fire. With everyone busy, Francine did maintenance on the solar engines.

Clara poured water over her hands and washed them. "Washing dishes never sounded so appealing. It'll be nice to at least have clean hands."

"No kidding," Annabelle said, and reached to scrub her hands. "A shower sure would be nice though."

"Maybe tonight we'll be able to boil some water for a sponge bath. It's either that or we'll have to wait until tomorrow and hope we find a river or lake."

Annabelle let out a laugh. "There's no way I'll take a sponge bath in my wagon, not with Thomas around."

"I don't blame you there. Sorry you're stuck with him. Has he been giving you a hard time?"

"Yeah, you could say that. I'm glad to have a little break from him this afternoon. I don't know how I'm going to be able to handle the rest of the evening with him, much less the rest of the trip."

"Sounds like you need some space from him," Clara said while handing a dish to Annabelle to rinse.

"Yeah, if I want to stop myself from punching that fat nose of his."

Clara laughed and Annabelle joined in the laughter. It felt good to have a friend along to talk to.

"I'll tell you what," Clara said. "When Harold comes back, I'll see if I can swap wagons with Thomas for a night or two. I'll say it's because we need some girl time. He should go for it. I usually have a girl's night out at least once a week at home, so it won't seem too strange to him."

Annabelle's eyes lit up. "That would be perfect." Hopefully a night away from Thomas would allow her to recapture her patience.

Everyone was ready to go long before Harold and Thomas returned. When they were thirty minutes late, Clara started pacing and murmuring. Annabelle rested a steady hand on Clara's shoulder to comfort her. "I'm sure they'll be back soon," she said.

Clara looked startled at first, then smiled anxiously. "Is it that obvious that I'm a little worried?" she said, shaking her head. "You're probably right. But what are we going to do with ourselves while we wait? We were too efficient getting everything set to go.

What a difference from yesterday. Annabelle, where could they be? Do you think something happ—"

"Here they come," Annabelle said, turning Clara around so she could see. Harold and Thomas sped toward the group.

Clara rushed over to greet them but before she had a chance to say anything, Harold addressed the group while he dismounted from his bike. "Oh good, you're all ready to go. We'll leave shortly. Thomas, stash our bikes and packs while I talk to Francine." He walked away from the others with Francine without giving Clara a glance.

"Harold, is everything okay?" Clara asked his back.

Harold turned and flashed her an exaggerated smile. "Of course, we just have to make a slight modification to our route," he said, and continued walking away before Clara had a chance to ask another question.

Clara stood in silence with her arms crossed. Annabelle suspected she didn't like being out of the loop. Something was definitely up, but what? Had they finally found radiation? Annabelle hoped she'd still get to share a wagon with Clara. If something had gone wrong being with Thomas would make her more anxious. She stood next to Clara trying to think of something to say, staring at Harold and Francine in silence until they returned.

When Harold walked back to them, he put an arm around Clara. "Hey Babe, how was your afternoon?" He kissed the top of her head.

"Fine—"

"We're all ready to go boss," Thomas interrupted.

"Good, let's head out," Harold said and started toward the wagons.

Annabelle gave Clara a desperate look.

"Harold, before we go I need to talk to you," Clara said.

"We can talk while we drive. Let's go, we still have a lot of ground to cover before we stop for the night." His tone was sharp.

"No. Now," Clara said.

Annabelle didn't want to cause tension between Harold and Clara. "It's all right, Clara, no worries, let's just get moving."

"No, it's not all right. Harold, come here."

Harold marched over to them and rested his fists on his hips. "Clara, what in the world is this about? We really need to get going."

"What's going on with you?" Clara lowered her eyebrows. "Did you detect radiation?"

"No, of course not. I wouldn't be pushing forward if we did. You think I would lead you into danger?" He turned to leave.

"No, actually," she said grabbing his arm. "I, uh, was wondering if Thomas and I could switch wagons. Uh, you see, Annabelle and I need some girl time."

Harold relaxed his shoulders. "Is that all?" he cracked a smile, "Of course, no problem," he said nodding his head.

"Oh, okay." Clara glanced at Annabelle, eyebrows raised. Annabelle was impressed at how quickly Clara got Harold to agree.

"Thomas, you and Clara are switching places. Everyone, let's go!"

Annabelle and Clara climbed into her wagon, and Clara got behind the wheel.

"Wait, you know how to drive?" Annabelle said when Clara pushed the start button.

"I sure do. Harold's been teaching me. I drove all day yesterday. It's fun."

Annabelle laughed. It would be great to be with Clara instead of Thomas. "Thanks for doing this, Clara."

"Don't thank me," Clara said. "Something's up."

Chapter Eleven
Annabelle

They drove hard and stopped well after dark. Harold let everyone know that they were to eat individual dinners that evening and should get to bed early. No one protested, it would be difficult to set up a fire and dinner in the dark anyway. Still, to Annabelle it felt like the day didn't have a proper close without the communal fire.

In the light of a lantern, Annabelle placed a blanket down in the front of the wagon. She set up a picnic of assorted dried fruits, nuts, and food bars while she waited for Clara to return from a quick visit to Harold. She heard the wagon door swing open and much to her dismay, in walked Thomas. Her disgust must have shown on her face because he immediately grinned.

"Don't worry, I'm not here to crash your little slumber party. I just need some clothes."

"Oh, of course," Annabelle said, "No problem." She went back to getting the dinner ready while Thomas rifled through his stuff.

"See you tomorrow," he finally said and left without making another remark. Annabelle knew Clara was right: something was up. Thomas had made only one rude comment and didn't crack any jokes.

A few minutes later Clara returned.

"So did you find anything out?" Annabelle asked.

"No," Clara settled down on the blanket next to Annabelle and grabbed a handful of dried apricots, "I got the distinct impression that Harold doesn't want me to know, so I didn't push him on it. I know he'll tell me in due time. And as much as it drives me crazy that he's keeping it from me, I have to remember that he's the leader and I have to respect him as such."

"What do you think it is?"

"I have no idea, but Harold's acting strange. He's very hot and cold. And he only calls me Babe when he's hiding something." She sat back and smiled. "It's kind of cute to see him like that; actually, it's a different side of him that I don't usually see. The leadership side, I mean."

"He's a good leader," Annabelle said, munching on a dried mango.

"Yes, he is. It makes me proud of him, actually." Clara took a drink of water and held the cup in her hands while she gazed into it. "Still, I wonder what they could've possibly found today. The most logical thing would be radiation."

"But would they be so secretive about that?" Annabelle said.

"I don't think so but maybe he's trying to keep us all calm."

"You don't think we're the only ones out of the loop?"

"It seems that only Thomas and Francine are *in* the loop," Clara said. "It sure makes me want to eavesdrop on their conversation."

"How serious do you think it is?"

"Serious enough that Harold was relieved when I suggested switching bunks with Thomas. He loved the idea of having some space from me, probably because he didn't want me to pry the truth out of him." Clara sighed. "Did Thomas give any clues when he came by?"

Annabelle shook her head. "He just grabbed some clothes and left."

"Did he grab his hair products too?" Clara asked and laughed.

Annabelle snickered. "Yeah, how does he get his hair so stiff?"

"I was hoping you had the answer! It really is a marvel. Who's he trying to impress anyway?"

"I have no idea," Annabelle said.

Clara gave her a mischievous grin. "I bet it's you."

"Never in a million years would that happen." Annabelle wrinkled her nose and Clara started laughing.

"I'm only kidding!"

Annabelle joined in her laughter and the two joked while finishing dinner.

"Hey, do you mind if I see your illustrations?" Clara asked while cleaning up the picnic.

"Not at all." Annabelle retrieved her sketchbook and passed it to Clara.

Clara leaned against the crates and slowly flipped through the pages, studying each image. "These are really good. I bet you can draw anything."

"Thanks," Annabelle said.

"Do you mind me asking how you got so good?"

Annabelle sat down across from Clara. Usually, she lied and told people she was born with the talent. She didn't want to lie to Clara, it didn't feel right. "I..." she began, looking at Clara. Clara gave her a patient smile, comforting Annabelle. "I actually started drawing a lot as a little girl. When I was around five years old, I couldn't remember what my mother looked like anymore. She died when I was three." She dropped her eyes from Clara's. "We didn't have a drawing of her, and it drove me crazy. I felt guilty that I couldn't remember what she looked like. I started torturing myself about it. I was too afraid to ask my brothers or dad what she looked like, out of shame that I didn't remember. I missed her so much, so why couldn't I remember her face?" Tears were threatening to well up in Annabelle's eyes, but she continued. "So I decided I would try to draw her face. Thinking once I saw it, I would recognize her and never forget again." Annabelle stopped, feeling a thickness in her throat.

"The problem was, I never could get it right," she whispered. "I tried and tried, but every time I looked at the finished product, I could tell it wasn't her. I probably drew hundreds of different faces and none were right. Finally, I gave up and started drawing other things because it was the only way I knew to pass the time. To this day, I still haven't been able to reproduce her face. You say I can draw anything, but that isn't true. I can't draw the one thing that I want to draw more than anything." Annabelle sat hunched forward with her eyes down. She put her face in her hand.

Clara sat next to her and put her arm around Annabelle's shoulders. "I'm sorry you went through that," she said. "I can't imagine how hard that must've been. That's a lot for a little girl to carry."

Annabelle leaned into Clara, needing the comfort. Clara's quiet understanding had made her the right person to tell. Annabelle took a deep, slow breath and her chest didn't feel tight anymore—telling her story to Clara allowed her to forgive herself.

"I'm sorry," she said, blinking back tears. "I haven't ever told anyone that before. I guess it hit me kind of hard."

"No need to apologize. Your feelings are very valid," Clara responded, her voice soft with concern.

"Thank you though, for listening. I do feel better, if you can believe it," she said with shining eyes. She took Clara's hand and squeezed it—she hoped they'd be lifelong friends.

Once the lantern was out and they settled into bed, the quiet darkness brought back the mystery of the afternoon. Annabelle lay in her bed, wide awake, wondering what Harold and Thomas had found. She couldn't quiet her mind, and her stomach felt rock hard as she entertained the possibilities. She rolled over and gripped the blankets.

"Annabelle, you still awake?" Clara whispered.

"Yeah."

"I thought of something."

Annabelle sat up in her bed. "What?"

"Did Thomas leave his scouting pack in here? Maybe there's something in it that will—"

"Let's check," Annabelle said, and switched on a flashlight she had next to her bed. Thomas had it coming to him after he'd gone through her pack to steal jerky.

They found Thomas's scouting pack in the compartment under his bed. The two women sat cross-legged on the floor with the pack in between them.

"Okay, here goes," Clara said, and unzipped the pack. Annabelle shined the flashlight over the contents as Clara pulled out a hat, the red wax marker, and some dried fruit. "What is making this pack so heavy?" she asked, reaching in again. Out came a dirty shirt followed by the radiation detector. She set it on the ground and looked up at Annabelle. "That wasn't the heavy thing." She clunked the bag on the ground to demonstrate its weight. "See."

"So what is it then?" Annabelle asked, scooting around next to Clara and shining the flashlight directly into the pack.

The light illuminated something black and metallic. Clara took it from the pack and set it between them. Annabelle had only seen something like it in books but still recognized it instantly. A gun.

***

Thunder woke Annabelle up. Darkness covered the wagon, making her unsure if morning had dawned. She felt rested though and decided to get up. Clara had her back turned to her but when Annabelle's feet touched the ground, she rolled over.

"Hey," Clara said. Her hair looked as if she'd been rolling down a hill all night, but her eyes were wide open.

"Didn't sleep well?" Annabelle asked her. Clara pursed her lips and shook her head. "Do you think anyone else is up?"

Clara sat up and swung her feet onto the ground. "I've been listening for a while but haven't heard anything." She stood and shoved her arms into a jacket. "I think it's morning. It seems brighter than it did a while ago. I'm going to go see." Clara marched to the door.

"Wait, Clara."

"Yeah?" Clara stopped with her hand on the door handle.

"Are we going to ask about, well the…you know?"

"I'm not sure yet, but we have to find out what's going on." Clara opened the door and stepped outside.

Annabelle took a minute to slip on her jacket and followed. Outside, black rain clouds darkened the quiet morning. Clara tramped back from Harold's wagon, her arms rigid at her sides.

"I think everyone is gone!" she said when she saw Annabelle.

"What?" Annabelle looked at the wagons, as if they would give her an answer.

"What the hell is going on here? I can't believe Harold would sneak off like this!" Clara starting pacing back and forth, "I can't believe this. And what about the gun? What else could he be hiding from me? I just can't—"

"What gun?" Ernie said from behind them.

Clara spun around. "Where's Harold?"

"Whoa, calm down, okay?" Ernie said, holding his hands up in the air. "I'm sure everything's going to be all right. Let's have some breakfast, and I'll tell you what I know."

"No, tell us now," Clara said and poked his chest. Ernie took a step back, recoiling.

"Clara, it's okay," Annabelle said, trying to calm Clara down. The sticky air smelled like compost, and the dark clouds loomed above them. "How about we go inside? I think it's going to rain soon." She gently put her hand on Clara's shoulder.

Clara turned toward her. "Okay," she said. Her stormy eyes filled with tears as her anger shifted to worry. "Sorry Ernie, I don't usually freak out like that. I was just so shocked to find everyone gone."

"It's all good," Ernie said and followed them to Annabelle's wagon.

As soon as they entered the wagon, Annabelle went to get some breakfast from the food crates. "So where is everyone?" she asked casually, hoping it would foster tranquility.

Ernie sighed and sat on the ground near the door. "I don't know everything that's going on. I, like you," he looked from Clara to Annabelle, "am not privy to all the information." He started scratching his elbow. "I don't know what Harold and Thomas found yesterday, but I do know that Francine and Thomas took shifts last night patrolling. Thomas took the first half of the night, and well, Francine took the second, but…" He looked up at Clara, hesitating.

"Yeah?" Annabelle prompted, handing a plate of dried fruit and nuts to Ernie.

"Well, Francine never came back."

"What do you mean?" Clara asked. Annabelle handed her a plate and they sat down across from Ernie.

"I mean, she never came back. I woke up this morning, and she was still gone. When I told Harold and Thomas, they looked shocked. They woke up Calvin and Curtis, and split up. Thomas and Calvin went ahead scouting, and Curtis and Harold went to search for Francine."

"And you obviously did all this very quietly because I didn't hear a thing," Clara accused.

"Well, yeah, Harold said that, uh," Ernie grabbed a handful of nuts, "that he didn't want to wake you two up."

"I knew it!" Clara said and crossed her arms. "He's really going out of his way to hide this from me."

"And what was all that business about a gun?" Ernie asked with raised eyebrows.

Annabelle and Clara looked at each other, silently locking eyes.

"Uh, about that…" Annabelle started.

"You really don't know?" Clara said, squinting at Ernie.

"No! Hey come on, I feel as lost as you guys, and now you say there's a gun. Can we help each other out? We're all on the same team here."

"Obviously we're not, because *you* guys have been sneaking around all morning," Clara said, the edge back in her voice.

Thunder rolled outside.

"Ernie is telling us what he knows, right?" Annabelle said. "We should share what we know, okay Clara?" She hoped she sounded diplomatic.

Clara didn't say anything but grabbed a dried cherry. Annabelle interpreted that as confirmation. "Well, we sort of, found a gun in Thomas's scouting pack."

"A real gun? What for?"

"We obviously don't know," Clara said and tilted her head to the side. "The only thing I can think of is to keep us in line."

"I don't know what to say," Ernie said, and for a moment they were all quiet.

The rain interrupted their thoughts as it began pounding on the wagon.

"Okay, so what we all know is that something was found yesterday that we needed to be guarded against," Annabelle began, "Francine is out there missing and for some reason Thomas has a gun."

"That about sums it up," Ernie said.

"So you don't have a gun?" Clara asked.

"No!"

"And what about Francine and the others?"

"Honestly, I really don't know." The two were practically shouting. Were they angry or yelling because the rain was so loud? Annabelle stood up and opened the door to see what they were up against.

"It's really coming down out there," Annabelle said. A cascade of water fell from the sky, making it look like the wagon stood underneath a waterfall. The sight of the downpour shocked them into silence. "I hope they all come back soon." Annabelle closed the door and sat back down. "How long have they been gone?"

"I don't know, maybe like an hour?"

"Did they say when they'd be back?" Clara asked, frowning.

"Thomas and Calvin were just going on the morning scout, which should only take about an hour, right? But with this weather, I don't know…"

"And Harold?" Clara chewed on her knuckle.

"He didn't say. They all left in such a rush."

"They're going to be soaked to the bone," Annabelle said.

Chapter Twelve
Harold

Harold and Curtis trudged through the forest to the area Francine had patrolled. "Francine!" Harold knew he had to keep it together. If he wavered, the whole group would fall apart. He glanced at the ominous clouds. They needed to find Francine soon.

Francine had the best compass skills in the group and shouldn't have wandered astray. Harold wouldn't allow any other possibility to enter his mind—somehow she *was* lost.

Thankfully, Curtis behaved like a true soldier. He couldn't imagine all the questions everyone had at this point, and Curtis didn't ask any of them. It made it much easier for Harold to behave like a leader when the others behaved like followers. Now Clara, she was a different story. He'd avoided her questions so far, but how long could he keep it up?

He gritted his teeth and pushed his way into a clearing filled with waist high, leafy shrubs. He wasn't really hiding anything from Clara. Nothing had happened. They'd only found some cabins… Yet, no matter how much he tried to minimize the evidence, it kept filling his mind. Nothing had happened, but he had to face the truth about other people existing. He didn't know how the others would react to this revelation. Some might panic, others might want to seek out the mystery people. He brushed his hand through his hair. To maintain control, he had to keep a lid on the secret. Only he, Thomas, and Francine knew, and that's how it had to stay, even though Clara wouldn't like it. But where was Francine?

Lightning flashed, bringing Harold and Curtis to a stop. He stopped and listened for a few seconds as thunder rumbled around them.

Harold set his pack down. "It looks like it's gonna rain soon." He wanted to add: *we gotta find Francine soon*, but worried it would sound panicked. "Let's put our rain ponchos on," he said instead.

Trying to keep his hands steady, he fished his poncho out and put it on. While zipping the pack back up, something caught his eye on a bush a few feet away. A dark red smudge covered a leaf. He walked to the bush and wiped a finger across the smudge. Chills ran through his body as he stared at his finger. It was blood.

"Curtis," he said quietly. Curtis joined him and looked at his hand. They locked eyes. Curtis swallowed, then took a step past the bush and gasped. Harold followed his gaze and his stomach dropped. A bright red puddle of blood covered smashed branches and a trail of blood coated the bushes through the clearing.

They stood frozen, looking at the trail. Harold knew he needed to go first, needed to lead, but the blood made his limbs heavy, holding him in place. *What if a group of people are watching us right now, waiting to attack?* Harold wanted to close his eyes, make this all go away.

"Do you think Francine is hurt?" Curtis asked.

Hurt? Of course! Francine was probably just hurt. He jumped into action. "We'd better check," he said, grabbing his pack and following the trail. Large rain drops began pelting them.

"Francine!" he shouted.

The rain quickly increased to a downpour, muffling their shouts. Rain began pooling on the blood trail, washing it away into the ground. The two men began frantically following the trail of blood.

"Francine!" Curtis shouted.

Harold tripped and landed with his face in a bush. His cheek felt scratched and the fall dazed him for a moment.

"Oh, no." Curtis said.

Harold rolled over and got up. Curtis was looking down at the place where Harold had tripped. Harold squinted through the rain and spotted Francine's boot hidden under a branch.

"Francine?" Harold jumped over the bush that was concealing Francine's leg. His momentary burst of energy stopped as soon as he saw her body.

She lay on her stomach with one arm reaching out, blood covering her whole body. One of her legs bent up at an impossible angle and the side of her face looked distorted. Her eye was next to her nose. Harold scrambled around to her head, trying to make sense of the mangled, bloody mess. "Oh, god," he said and covered his mouth. Her blood seeped from gaping punctures covering her bashed in head. Deep lacerations stripped her neck and shoulders. "Oh, god," he said again and stumbled backward.

Curtis stared at Francine with bulging eyes. "What the hell happened?"

"I don't. . ." Harold looked around for answers. Something had bashed her head in, brutally slit her throat and dragged her here. But how? He'd never seen an injury like this on an expedition. And there was nothing in the vicinity that could cause this kind of trauma. *It's the people, it must be, we need to get out of here.* Trembling, his heart thumped with fear.

"Let's get moving." Harold's voice shook and he fought the urge to flee. "Help me carry her back." His poncho stuck to his body and water dripped down his face but he didn't notice it. *We need to go. We need to go.*

Curtis nodded and reluctantly approached the body. Harold pulled his poncho off and wrapped it around Francine's head and shoulders. He couldn't stomach looking at the injuries. "Let's turn her over, I'll carry her torso, you carry her legs."

They rolled her onto her back and Harold crouched behind her head. He looked away and gasped for breath while putting his arms under Francine's armpits and lifting her until her covered head rested against his chest. Curtis squatted down between her legs, facing away from Harold and grabbed her ankles.

Harold squeezed his eyes shut. "Lift on three. One. Two. Three." He and Curtis stood. He held Francine tight to his body, the rain and blood making everything slippery. Curtis began walking toward camp and the body wobbled awkwardly until Harold matched Curtis' pace. Harold glanced behind them. Were they being watched? Would they lead the others back to camp? *Go faster, dammit! We need to get out of here!*

They entered the forest, which provided some shelter from the rain. They'd be back at camp soon and Harold needed to figure out what to say. It had to be something that wouldn't panic the group. But, he also needed to get everyone evacuated as quickly as possibly without telling them why. He swallowed hard.

As they neared the wagons, Harold thought he heard a sob come from Curtis. His shoulders were shuddering.

The reality hit Harold. Francine, who he'd known for years and worked with on several expeditions, was dead. Francine, with her strong presence and calm demeanor. Francine, his friend, was dead. Possibly murdered. And Harold was responsible for her death. His feelings threatened to overwhelm him. He sucked in a slow breath through his nose. *I'm sorry, Francine, I'll give you some time later. For now, I have to stay strong for everyone.*

He saw the wagons and forced a calm expression on his face. Clara ran to them, with Annabelle and Ernie directly behind.

"Oh my God, what happened?" Clara said, and covered her mouth with her hands.

Harold stopped and lowered Francine to the ground as Curtis gently placed her legs down.

"Is she. . ." Clara said when she reached them.

"I'm afraid so," Harold said and hugged Clara to him. She needed to trust him, but he didn't know how to make her. She pulled away quickly. He couldn't tell if tears or rain streamed down her face, but her eyes were wide with shock and her lip quivered. She turned to look at the body.

"What happened?" she demanded again as she hovered over the body.

Ernie stared at Francine, frozen in place. Annabelle clutched Ernie's arm. "Francine," she sobbed.

Harold knew that any hesitation would bring more questions and said the first thing that came into his mind. "She fell out of a tree." Curtis glanced at him briefly, but didn't say anything.

"Why was she in a tree?" Clara asked incredulously. Instead of looking at Harold, she pulled the poncho off Francine's head.

"Oh god!" Annabelle cried and lurched back.

"She was patrolling last night, and I guess she climbed up a tree to get a better look. We found her on a large boulder. She must have landed on her head." Harold said. He knew he had to tell some truth, plus he figured Ernie had probably told them that Francine had been keeping watch.

"Why was she patrolling?" Clara stepped away from Francine and looked at Harold. Her eyes were filled with tears. He wouldn't give her that answer.

"Yesterday we found a giant mudslide that looked like it happened recently," Harold addressed the whole group. "We knew this storm was coming and put us at risk for another mudslide, so we needed to have scouts out all night in order to assess the danger," he turned and looked Clara right in the eye, "in case we needed to move on quickly." When had he become such a good liar? He couldn't believe the confidence he'd said it with. Clara didn't say anything but narrowed her eyes. He held her gaze and kept his expression neutral, so she wouldn't think he challenged her.

"Was she like this when you found her?" Annabelle asked, voice trembling.

"I'm sorry, there wasn't anything we could do for her," Harold said and lowered his head.

"Hey man, it wasn't your fault," Ernie said and gave Harold a hug. *Yes it is. I sent her out there.* Harold trapped a sob in his throat. *Stay strong, stay strong.*

Clara covered Francine's face again, then put her arm around Annabelle. Curtis stayed away from the group and stared at the ground, hunched over.

"I know how heartbreaking this is for everyone, but we need to bury Francine." He looked up at the sky. The rain had slowed and patches of blue peeked from behind the clouds but another storm churned in the distance. "Then we need to get moving again."

"I can get the shovel," Curtis murmured, still staring at the ground. "Where should we, uh…dig?"

Harold looked around, hesitant to make this decision. It felt too significant to be taken lightly. He'd never chosen someone's final resting place and wanted to give Francine the respect she deserved. He wanted to make up for sending her to her death, but picking the perfect gravesite wouldn't absolve him. No spot could give Francine the dignity she warranted. No spot could bring forgiveness to Harold. Hell, no spot could bring Francine back, which is what Harold was truly searching for.

"I," Harold sucked in a breath to keep a sob from escaping, "I, uh..."

"How about over here?" Clara said and led the group to a clearing on the other side of the wagons. Evergreens encircled the area where tiny white flowers sprouted from moss covered ground. Baby ferns grew on top of a large stump that sat in the back of the glade. "We can carve her name into the stump," Clara added.

Harold nodded.

Curtis and Ernie headed silently to the wagons for the shovel. Harold held his breath, trying to prevent emotion from taking over.

"It's okay, you're allowed to feel this too," Clara said softly, and wrapped an arm around his waist. Her face was somber, her voice controlled. Harold envied her composure. He needed to be the sympathetic leader who maintained control, not her. He should be grateful that she took charge right when he almost lost it, but he didn't like her undermining him. He didn't say anything and didn't put his arm around her either. She didn't seem to notice and studied his eyes instead. What was she looking for? He broke her gaze.

"Listen. . ." she said, "I know there's a lot going on right now," she put her hand on his cheek and guided him to face her again, "but I really need to talk to you." Her eyes were pleading, almost urgent. *Oh god, here it comes.* She wanted to know what was going on, every last detail.

"You just need to trust me," he snapped, and pushed her hand from his face. She stepped back, her mouth wide open. Harold grimaced, he'd been too harsh. "Clara, listen, I—"

"Auntie Fran!" Thomas shouted. He and Calvin had returned, and he ran to Francine's body. "What the f—"

"Francine!" Calvin called out.

Thomas knelt down and lifted the poncho from her body. He gasped and the blood drained from his face in shock. He saw Harold approach and glared at him. "What the hell happened?" he screamed and took a menacing step toward Harold.

"Thomas, she—"

"Why are you covered in her blood? What did you do?" Thomas stomped to Harold and punched him in the face. Harold spun sideways from the blow and the world blurred for a second. Everyone ran to intervene.

"I didn't do anything!" Harold put his hand to his injured jaw. Calvin stepped between him and Thomas, holding his arms out.

Thomas came at Harold again with his chest thrust out. "What the hell happened?"

"Thomas, calm down," Clara said firmly. Thomas looked at her, waiting for an explanation. "She fell out of a tree," she said.

"A tree?" Thomas looked at Harold.

"Let's talk." Harold put an arm around Thomas and they walked away from the wagons. "I'm so sorry, Thomas," Harold said. Thomas nodded but didn't reply.

As they walked, Harold glanced back. Clara was directing Ernie and Curtis where to dig. He turned away. *She needs to let me lead, but clearly doesn't think I'm capable.*

"Okay, so what really happened?" Thomas asked when they were out of earshot. His face was white and his jaw was clenched. He struggled to blink back tears.

"Honestly, I don't know," Harold said. "We just found her like that." He shook his head and recounted the morning's events.

"Whoever did this will pay," Thomas said.

Chapter Thirteen
Annabelle

Annabelle carved Francine's name into the stump while the others covered her grave. There was a reprieve from the rain but mud caked everyone's wet clothes. She added a carving of a solar wagon under Francine's name, along with a row of flowers.

"Let's say a few words," Harold said when the work was done. Everyone gathered around but Thomas stood apart from the group. Annabelle hugged herself, shivering, while Harold spoke.

"Francine was one of the most extraordinary people I've ever had the pleasure of knowing. This marks a tragic day for all of us and especially for the Colony. Her drive benefited humanity in so many ways. I think we can all agree that the Colony will suffer without her." He took a deep breath and looked to the sky. "She was also a loving mother. It breaks my heart to have to bring this news back to her family. They'll feel the loss more than anyone else. And Thomas, we're all so sorry for your loss. Do you want to say a few words?"

Thomas clenched his fists at his sides and blew a sharp breath from his nose. "Not here," he said.

Harold nodded. "I wish there was more we could do to honor Francine, but she would've wanted us to continue on. We need to head out, and soon. Everybody get some dry clothes on and bundle up. We have a lot of ground to cover."

The others headed for the wagons but Annabelle lingered at the grave. She couldn't pull her eyes away. This was Francine now, just a lonely mound of mud. It wasn't fair. It didn't make any sense.

Her shivering increased and she forced herself to go to her wagon. Harold seemed in a hurry to get away. Annabelle didn't understand. Why couldn't they stay the night? Why were they even continuing on? She couldn't think straight, all the mission's excitement had been washed away with the rain. Only questions remained.

Annabelle slipped into dry clothes. Doing something helped alleviate the numbness she felt. She wondered if Clara would be bunking with her again tonight. And what about the gun? She quickly opened the drawer under Thomas's bed. The pack was gone.

She closed the drawer, and the vision of Francine's mangled body flashed through her mind. She sat on the bed and held her head in her hands. Francine hadn't looked like she'd fallen from a tree, and Annabelle didn't believe the mudslide explanation either. She closed her eyes. Too many unanswered questions. She wanted to curl up under the blankets and not come out. It would be easier to not look for answers and to ignore the questions.

"Ready to head out?"

Annabelle opened her eyes to find Clara standing in the doorway.

"Yeah, just let me get my poncho." Annabelle stood and started rifling through her clothes. "Are you driving with me again?"

Clara sighed, and crossed her arms. "It appears so." She shook her head. "I can't get a word out of Harold, and Thomas won't leave his side, like he's his bodyguard or something. It's so frustrating. I know he's lying, and that hurts more than anything."

"Do you think she fell out of a tree?"

Clara didn't answer right away and studied the ground for a moment. "I looked at the injuries closely, and," she pursed her lips and took a few breaths, "there were puncture wounds, lacerations and her skull was crushed. This is going to sound crazy, but the only thing that seems likely to cause those injuries would be some kind of animal attack." She looked up at Annabelle.

"Impossible." Clara had to be wrong. Animals had been extinct ever since the nuclear winter, hadn't they? She put her head in her hands again. This was too much, and she didn't want to think about what it implied. Yet the question slipped through her mental block anyway: was the Colony wrong?

"I know it's impossible, but, who really knows?" Clara looked at the floor again, her voice shaking. "With all this lying, and sneaking around, I don't know what to believe, or even who to believe." Annabelle closed the space between them and put an arm around her friend, needing the comfort as much as Clara.

"I'm sure we'll get answers soon," she said.

"Answers to what?" Thomas stood in the doorway, his hair wet and disheveled, mud and blood streaking his cheeks.

"Thomas, I can't imagine how hard this must be for you," Clara said. "We really are so sorry for your loss." She approached him, and rested a hand on his shoulder. "We just want to know what's going on. Can you blame us?"

Thomas stepped away from her touch. "I always knew it was a mistake bringing girls along on a mission like this. If it wasn't for your irrationality we wouldn't need any secrecy, we could trust that all members of our team could handle possible dangers."

"So you admit there are things that are being hidden," Clara accused.

"And we're the only ones who don't know?" Annabelle added.

"You two are just proving my point. You aren't in a position to know." Thomas crossed his arms. "There are bigger things going on here than your precious little egos. You don't understand the implications of them, or the importance of this mission. Our success is more important than your pride."

"Now that people are dying, we have a right to know!" Clara said.

Thomas glared at her. "Tell me this, Clara, why did you even come along on this mission, huh?" he took a step toward her. "Was it just to play vacation with hubby before you get all fat and pregnant? Because some of us actually care about the mission and are dedicated to it for the sake of the Colony."

"Are you questioning my loyalty?"

"You're the one asking questions, doesn't that speak for itself?"

"So you think we should just blindly go along with whatever you say, no matter who ends up dead in the morning?" Clara shouted. The two stood face to face. Annabelle's breath quickened.

"Damn it Clara, don't you trust your own husband? Your lack of faith could compromise this whole mission. The only thing that *I* question about Harold's judgment is bringing you along." Thomas raised his eyebrows, challenging her. "On second thought, I take that back, you have one thing that you're good for." Thomas motioned his hand up and down her body.

"You're an ass," Clara said.

Before Thomas could reply, Harold stepped into the wagon. "What's the hold up? We need to leave."

"Harold, did you hear what Thomas just said?" Clara spat, and walked to her husband's side. She looped her arm around his and glared at Thomas.

Harold looked from Thomas to Clara. He hesitated a second, then stepped away from Clara's grasp. "All I heard was you calling Thomas an ass. Look, we don't have time for squabbles. We need to leave. Now."

"That's what I came in here to tell them, boss," Thomas said.

Clara stared at Harold, speechless. The space between them seemed to harden.

"So, let's roll then," Harold said, turning to leave the wagon.

"Fine, let's *roll*," Clara mocked.

Harold ignored her comment. "We're leaving a wagon behind since we're one man down. Thomas and Ernie will ride with me in front. You two will ride together again today."

Annabelle and Clara followed Harold and Thomas out of the wagon without further comment, and climbed on to their wagon bench.

As they rode away, Annabelle wanted to comfort Clara, but she didn't know what to say. Besides, she wanted to avoid the swirl of questions and speculations, which she feared would surface if they talked.

Instead, the image of Francine's body continued to haunt her. She tried to process what had happened—tried to accept Clara's theory about Francine's death. Accepting it would mean accepting a world that was different than she thought. A world where animals did exist and where the Colony was wrong. Gran's key felt warm under her shirt. If the Colony had lied about animals, what else had they lied about? She grabbed her shirt and the key underneath, clutching them in her fist. *Gran, I think the Colony lies. And I think this key uncovers more lies. I hope I still have the chance to solve its mystery.*

The rain started again and as they headed into thick fog, one question consumed her, breaking through her sorrow. It felt like an ice cold droplet running down her spine. *Who's next?* it whispered.

***

Harold

Harold knew he was setting an impossible pace but the harder he pushed, the less he thought about the day. They had a lot of ground to make up to stay on schedule. And…he wanted to get far away from whatever had gotten Francine. Since they had found the old highway from before The End, they at least had smoother terrain to drive on. Grass and a few small shrubs covered the road now, but the cement underneath had prevented the forest from taking over.

"Harold, I can't see any of the other wagons," Ernie said.

Harold glanced in his side mirror and saw only fog. Should they stop and wait for the others? He clenched his jaw, why couldn't they keep up? He slowed but didn't stop. He eyed the radiation monitor which was still silent. At least one thing was going their way. If it went off, would he continue onward anyway? He pushed the thought aside and kept going.

As they climbed higher in elevation, the misty rain changed to a rain and snow mix, making driving and visibility even worse. He checked the mirror again, still no sign of the other wagons.

"Let's wait for a bit," he finally said, "and we may as well get a bite to eat while we wait." They stopped and Ernie headed inside the wagon, hunched over and hugging himself. Thomas followed him. Harold stood outside with arms crossed, waiting for the other wagons to appear.

"Come on, where are you?" he said under his breath and started pacing. What a mess this all was. Death, lies, pushing everyone to impossible limits...others being out there. And what would he do if the rest of the group was now lost? He tapped his lip and thought about Clara. Quite frankly, he missed her. He missed being a team with her. He'd never shut her out before. Begrudgingly, he accepted that she would know what to do if he asked her for help.

Finally in the distance, he saw a wagon. He let out a sigh of relief and headed inside his wagon.

Ernie sat on the bed wrapped in several blankets and Thomas handed him a drinking glass.

"Ernie isn't doing so well," Thomas said.

Harold rushed to the bed. "What's wrong?"

"Oh nothing, just a cold." Ernie tried to smile, but his eyelids were drooping.

"No, it's not nothing," Thomas said. "You're burning up." Thomas didn't look so good himself. His puffy eyes were as red as his nose. Harold pressed his hand to Ernie's forehead and felt the heat radiating from him. How serious was this? Should they stop and make camp so Clara could have a look at him, and he could rest? No, Ernie could rest while they rode. He didn't have to sit in the front. Harold pulled his hand away from Ernie's forehead.

"Thomas's right. You need to rest. Do you think you'll be okay back here when we continue?"

"Sure thing," Ernie said, still trying to smile.

"Okay, we're just taking a short break, letting everyone catch up and then we'll be on our way. I'd better go see if the others are here."

When he headed back outside, he saw both wagons approaching and breathed a sigh of relief. He knew they needed to keep going; they had already lost so much of the day. But he wanted to see how everyone was, especially Clara.

Slowly Calvin and Curtis arrived. They didn't look well. Their waterlogged hair stuck to their heads, their faces were flushed red, their eyes sullen. Harold's stomach tightened with panic. *Are they sick too?*

"How are you guys holding up?"

"Not bad," Calvin said. "A break would be nice though." Curtis simply nodded.

Calvin sounded fine, should he check their foreheads? "We'll rest for about fifteen minutes. Head inside and grab a bite and warm up, and let me know if you need anything."

The brothers nodded and went inside just as Clara and Annabelle pulled up. They looked just as bad as Calvin and Curtis. The difficult drive added strain to an already emotional day.

Clara parked and walked toward him with Annabelle. Clara wouldn't make eye contact with him but he took a step toward her, his arms out, wanting to hold her close, tell her everything was all right, and explain it all. Why couldn't he? Would it really make the others respect him less if he did? Would it betray the Colony? Betray Tully?

The night before they'd left for Seattle flashed in his mind.

He sat in Tully's office drinking tea and studying maps. A cool spring breeze came from the window on that beautiful evening. At first the conversation was lighthearted, and relaxed.

Tully folded up his map and put his hand on top, suddenly quiet.

"Harold," he said finally, staring down at his hand. "Listen, you may see things that you never could've imagined."

"Of course." That always was the case on every expedition.

"No, this may be different," Tully looked at him now. "You need to stay strong for the group, no matter what you find, you need to keep everyone focused and calm. Whatever it takes, you must do this in order to succeed. It only takes one false step to make everyone panic. If there's panic, your mission will fail. People will want to return to the Colony, and not only will this hinder our progress, it will bring great shame to the Colony."

Harold didn't respond, Tully had never said anything like this before an expedition. What did he think was out there?

"Remember your training, all of it. There are things you may need to do on this mission that you didn't have to do before."

Suspecting what Tully referred to made it hard to swallow as dread blocked his airway. He shouldn't ask, but before he could stop them, the words escaped. "The guns?"

Tully closed his eyes for a moment before nodding. Then he stood and closed the window. This struck Harold as unusual. Who would be listening outside?

"Same protocol as always with the guns. If you see another person, they're to be considered dangerous because they've been banished from the Colony."

"Absolutely."

"Only you and Thomas have guns, and have received the proper," Tully paused for a moment searching for the right word, *"education,"* he finally said. *"There's no reason to alarm the others, they might not understand. And it's your job to keep everyone on task."*

Rain and snow pelted Harold as he stared at evergreens poking through the fog. The Colony and Tully felt very far away. Clara was right here, right now, and she looked miserable. She'd been his best friend his entire life and she needed him. And quite frankly, he needed her just as much. He felt a strong pull toward her, the kind of pull he always felt after they'd had a fight and tempers had calmed.

"Clara," he said as she approached him. Saying nothing, she looked past him. Harold glanced back and saw Thomas walking toward them.

"Ernie's sick Clara, can you check on him?" Thomas said.

"Of course I will." Clara said. She followed Thomas without acknowledging Harold.

He watched her walk away. He'd lost his chance to talk to her.

He turned back to Annabelle. "We'll rest for about fifteen minutes. We still have a lot of ground to make up." Annabelle gave him a sideways glance. He must have spoken too harshly. "And get some food and dry clothes, hopefully that will help a little," he added, trying to sound more sympathetic.

"Okay," Annabelle said. "How sick is Ernie?"

Harold rubbed his hand over his head. "He's running a fever. We're going to have him stay in the wagon for the rest of the ride."

Annabelle nodded and her teeth chattered from shivering.

"You should get inside too and bundle up some more," he said.

She nodded again and retreated to her wagon.

Harold sighed. He didn't talk to Clara and they'd have to push on soon. Once they got far enough away and he had everything back on track, then he could make it right with her.

The fifteen minute break seemed to help a little and without any complaints, Harold had everyone moving again. The fog swallowed them up as they rode deeper into the unknown. He had no idea where it would spit them out, and what or *who* they would find.

Chapter Fourteen
Harold

Overnight, Ernie got worse. As his fever raged, Harold and Thomas took turns cooling him with wet rags and sips of water. By morning, Harold's head pounded from lack of sleep. Through the cobwebs in his mind he did, however, see one thing clearly. He needed Clara. This was too much for him. He needed her and accepted whatever consequences that would bring. His fear from the first day had come true—he was split between the mission and his marriage, and both were at a breaking point. He couldn't lose both. He would take her ahead scouting and tell her everything.

When he and Thomas stepped outside in the morning, the bright morning sunlight worsened his headache. He squinted through the pain, looking for Clara. She and Annabelle rushed toward him. Did that mean Clara was ready to put this behind them as well? He gave her a welcoming smile. Clara wouldn't make eye contact with him. "Clara, I want you to—"

"Have you guys heard that musical noise?" Annabelle said. She looked refreshed and her excited eyes sparkled.

"No, what noise?" Harold furrowed his brow.

"Shhh, listen." Annabelle put a finger to her lips and tilted her head.

The four stood in silence. He stared at Clara, who gazed into the trees, concentrating. He waited.

Dring, dreeen, drrrring.

"What the hell?" Thomas said.

"You heard it?" Annabelle said.

Dring, dreeen, drrrring.

"There it is again, what is it?" Harold asked.

"That's what we're going to find out." Clara shook her head in exasperation.

"Hey boss, I think it, uh," Thomas said, looking at the girls then hesitating for a second, "might be a bird. My cousin has an old antique whistle that makes bird calls, it sounded sort of like that."

"That's what I was wondering too." Clara added, looking at Harold. He felt like she was accusing him of holding this back as well.

"A bird?" Annabelle exclaimed. "How can that be?" Her excitement had been replaced with disbelief. "First a bear and now a bird, what's going on?"

"A bear? What are you talking about?" Thomas squared his shoulders and stared at Annabelle.

"Can we stop with the lies, please?" Clara said. "I examined Francine's body. It was clearly an animal attack."

"Like hell it was!" Thomas yelled.

Harold didn't know what to say. Had an animal killed Francine? He hadn't considered it before. He thought about the injuries and it seemed possible, that is, if animals existed, which they didn't.

"It wasn't a bear, she fell from a tree," he finally said.

Clara finally faced him. "Did you see her fall from the tree?" She put her hands on her hips.

"No, but—"

Dring, dreeen, drrrring.

"Well, I want to know what that is," Clara said and went into the forest with Annabelle following.

Harold and Thomas looked at each other silently.

"A bear?" Thomas finally asked.

"Of course not!" Harold said, trying to convince himself.

Thomas studied the ground, nostrils flaring. "I know it was those bastards with the cabins. If we ever find them, they'll pay for what they did."

"Whoa, Thomas, we don't know that for sure." Harold shook his head. "I mean a bear might be possible, who knows what we can believe anymore? Clara wouldn't just make it up."

Thomas glared at Harold. "Wrong. You know it as well as I do. Come on, a bear? That's as believable as her falling from a tree."

Thomas had every right to be angry, but his anger made him irrational. Harold's headache prevented him from thinking of words to calm Thomas down. Anything he said would be futile anyway. He had no answers to any of these questions.

Harold rubbed his temples, he needed Clara. "Come on, let's go see if they found anything." He slung on his scouting pack and headed in the direction she and Annabelle went.

They walked deeper into the forest, Clara leading in the distance. Harold had stopped hearing the noise, but Clara kept pushing forward. Before he could call her back, she and Annabelle descended down a hill and disappeared from his sight.

He sighed and lumbered forward, feeling disoriented from his lack of sleep. When he reached the hilltop, he saw what had drawn Clara: a lake peeked through the trees at the bottom of the hill.

Clara and Annabelle got to the bottom of the hill, then broke through the trees and out of his view again. Thomas started down the hill and Harold increased his pace.

They passed through the trees at the bottom of the hill and Harold froze, staring at the view with fingers touching his parted lips. A powerful sense of calm wrapped around him. Snow-capped mountains rose from the lake as if they had sat on the shore to put their feet in. The mountains and blue sky reflected across the calm, pristine lake. Everything seemed frozen in time, like he stood within a photograph.

Movement caught his eye and he spotted Clara and Annabelle a ways down the beach. But they weren't alone. There was a third person—a child, with them. Harold blinked and his mouth dropped open. Despite all the evidence they'd seen of other people, he still couldn't believe it. And a child... how could that be?

Thomas wasn't stuck in denial, however, and started sprinting down the beach while reaching into his pack. Harold sprinted after Thomas once he realized what Thomas was retrieving.

"Thomas, wait!" he yelled. Thomas wasn't listening. He stopped within shooting range of the boy. He pulled his gun out and pointed it right at him.

"Thomas, what are you doing?" Clara screamed.

"Shut up, Clara, this doesn't concern you." Thomas cocked the gun. The boy stared at Thomas, seeming unaware of the danger the gun posed.

"Thomas, you put that gun down," Harold commanded.

"We have orders. He's a threat to the Colony," Thomas spat. "This is for Francine."

"No!" Clara grabbed the child and dove to the ground as the shot echoed across the lake.

Harold heard a guttural scream and sprinted toward Clara and the boy. They lay in a heap on the rocky shore, motionless. He ran as fast as he could but everything moved in slow motion except the blood that quickly expanded under them.

"Clara!" Annabelle yelled, reaching her right before Harold. Harold hardly heard her and rolled Clara off the boy. The boy looked up at him with wide, terrified eyes. Blood covered him but he was alive. Annabelle helped the boy up and pulled him away.

Harold held Clara in his lap. Blood covered her body from the chin down and her eyes bulged. She gasped for breath and a gurgling sound came from her mouth. "Oh god, Clara! No!"

Harold cried. "Stay with me! Hold on!" Blood gushed from her neck. Harold pressed the bullet wound with his palm, trying to stop the bleeding from the exit wound. He placed his other hand on the back of her neck, hoping to stop the bleeding there as well. "Please, Clara, please hold on."

Annabelle came to his side. "Use your shirt to stop the bleeding," she said and cradled Clara's head. "Stay with us Clara!" She stroked Clara's forehead with her thumb.

Harold removed his hand from Clara's neck just long enough to pull his shirt off and wrap it around her wounds. "I don't know what else to do," Annabelle said, her voice trembling.

Clara's eyes fluttered closed. "No! Clara! You can't go. You can't go! Stay with me!" Harold gasped frantically.

Clara's skin started to pale. Her arms lay limp at her sides, and she didn't open her eyes. Her breathing became more labored. *You can't die! This can't be happening!* He glared at Thomas, who stood at the edge of the forest, his gun on the ground next to him. Harold's heart pounded with rage, and Thomas swam in the sea of his hatred.

"Burn in hell!" Harold screamed, pulling his own gun from the pack and aiming at Thomas.

"Whoa, wait boss I—"

The shot rang out, and Thomas fell to the ground. Harold threw his gun and turned his attention back to Clara.

Clara's eyes remained closed. Harold cupped her cheeks in his hands. "Clara!" he sobbed desperately. He didn't know what to do. How could he make her open her eyes? She couldn't be gone. "Clara." He hugged her to him. "Come back to me," he pleaded. How could this be happening? Wasn't he supposed to get a moment to say goodbye? To say I love you, and I'm sorry? He clung to her, as if he could keep her spirit inside if he held on to her hard enough. He didn't want to let her go, he could never let her go.

***

Annabelle

The world looked distorted through Annabelle's tears. She turned back to the boy, who stood motionless, eyes wide and mouth gaping. He appeared to be about eight years old, had shaggy brown hair and skin covered in freckles. His deep blue eyes darted between Harold and Thomas. Driven by a need to comfort him, she gained some composure.

"Can I help you get home?" she asked and put her hands on his shoulders.

He didn't say anything, but nodded. He seemed to understand her.

"What's your name?" she asked. Before he had a chance to answer, Calvin and Curtis broke through the trees lining the beach.

"What happened?" Calvin shouted. "We heard screaming."

Annabelle looked at the carnage, then back at Calvin, struggling to find words to describe what had happened. Harold held Clara and rocked back and forth. She doubted he even knew they were there.

"Thomas was going to shoot this boy so Clara," Annabelle started choking up again, "jumped in front of the bullet to save him. Then . . .then—Harold shot Thomas."

Calvin sprinted to Harold's side and Curtis headed toward Thomas's body.

"Mom!" the boy shouted and ran down the beach. A woman opened her arms and hugged him. She had the same brown hair and freckled skin as the boy. Her loose brown skirt and a grey shirt were well worn.

She clung to the child's shoulders and frantically inspected him. "Hogget, are you hurt? Why are you covered in blood?" Her panicked voice had a slight accent. She looked at Annabelle and the others, her eyes growing wide as she took in the scene. "What's going on here?" she demanded, backing away.

"We need help. Can you help us?" Annabelle glanced at Clara, fresh tears springing from her eyes. *It's probably already too late.*

"Hogget, are you okay? Who's blood is this?" she shouted.

"It's not mine, Mom," Hogget said. The woman looked at the scene again then grabbed Hogget's hand and started running.

"Wait! Please don't go!" Annabelle ran after them. "Please," she sobbed. "We really need some help. I promise we won't hurt you. Please help us, she's dying!"

The woman stopped. "Hogget, what happened?"

"I don't know, Mom. He had a magic stick that made her bleed. I think he wanted to hurt me with it." He pointed at Thomas.

"Why?" she asked.

"He thought the boy was a threat to us," Annabelle said.

"My Hogget, a threat? Who are you people?" She took a few more steps back, pulling Hogget with her.

"Wait, please. I know this is all strange, it is for us too. Please help us. This woman, Clara, saved your son's life."

The woman looked at Clara for a moment. Harold still held her in his arms but had stopped rocking. She pointed at Thomas. "What about him?"

"We leave him," Harold said. "He was the one who tried to hurt your son. He got what he deserved."

Harold stood, lifting Clara in his arms. "Please help me. Please, this is my wife. She means everything to me. Please."

The woman stared at him with pursed lips, then gave an understanding nod. "Bring her. Our camp is not far from here. We have an herbalist that might be able to help. Let's hurry." She started running and the others followed. As they left the beach, Thomas's lifeless body lay face down and nobody looked back.

They followed Hogget and his mother back into the forest, away from the lake. Annabelle tried not to think about what was happening. This, on the heels of Francine's death, was too much to deal with. She forced herself to follow Calvin's footsteps. Her shoulders shook with sobs when she saw Clara's blood speckled on the ground.

"Ezra!" the woman shouted. Annabelle looked up and saw a shirtless man chopping wood. He stopped chopping and watched them approach.

"What's going on?" He gripped his ax. "Hogget, are you hurt?"

"Ezra, we need help. Hogget's fine. Get Minnie!"

"Why is he covered in blood?" Ezra took a step toward them.

"It's her blood!" Hogget's mother pointed at Clara then strode past Ezra. The others followed. "Minnie!"

Ezra glowered at them while they walked by. Annabelle glanced up, hesitating to meet his gaze. The man shared a resemblance with Hogget, and Annabelle assumed he was his father. He had short, dark hair and thick eyebrows which stood out on his handsome face. She made eye contact with him and instantly looked away, heat springing to her cheeks.

She turned her attention forward and found they had arrived at a small camp. Five single room cabins were situated around a large fire pit.

As they approached the cabins, a woman with long, graying blonde hair stepped out from one. She was bony and had a pointy nose like a rat. When she spotted Clara, she rushed over to them.

"Who are you?" She looked around at the group. "What happened?"

"She's bleeding a lot, can you help her?" Hogget's mother said.

"Bring her in," the woman said. Harold carried Clara in and laid her on a cot. Unable to fit inside, Annabelle and the others stood silently around the entrance.

Annabelle leaned against the cabin, hugging herself. She didn't have any tears left.

Chapter Fifteen
Annabelle

Annabelle didn't know how long they waited. She'd lost all sense of time and huddled outside the cabin, in shock and heartbroken. It could have been minutes or hours, but at some point the herbalist came out. She faced everyone but didn't say anything. The silence stretched out, then she simply shook her head and looked down. Someone gasped, but Annabelle didn't know who—maybe it was herself. *Clara was really gone?* New tears streamed down her face as she headed toward the door.

The woman held her hand up, however, and prevented Annabelle from entering. "No," she said, "he asked to be alone with her."

Annabelle stepped back—bumping into Calvin. She turned to him, her lip quivering and Calvin hugged her. Annabelle accepted the comfort and squeezed her eyes shut.

"I'm so sorry. There was nothing I could do," the woman said.

Calvin nodded. "Thank you for trying."

"Let me offer you and your friends some tea," the woman said. "Ezra dear, could you get a fire going?"

"Of course," Ezra said and headed back around the hut.

Hogget's mother motioned to stumps situated around a fire pit. "Please sit," she said.

Annabelle pulled away from Calvin, and they sat on the stumps. None of them said anything. What could they say?

So many fears had plagued her prior to leaving: radiation sickness, injuries, getting lost, running out of food... but she never really, truly believed death would visit them. She thought they'd return to the Colony as heroes with legends of Seattle and new opportunities. Her drawings would be put on display throughout the Colony. Could they even go back to the Colony? What would happen if they said there were other people? Clearly, Thomas had been instructed to shoot others so did that mean the Colony thought people were a threat? Why?

Annabelle buried her head in her hands, wanting to stop the thoughts from firing at her. Ezra had been building the fire, and she heard a crackle and him blowing into the flame. She peeked at him through her fingers, grateful for the distraction from her thoughts.

Soon she smelled smoke and Annabelle sat up as the fire grew. Hogget's mother carried a tea kettle and hooked it on a rustic, metal tripod that hung over the flames. "I think some introductions are in order." She sat down and smoothed out her skirt. Hogget sat next to her.

No one responded and the woman didn't press them. "I'm Minnie, this is Hazel," she gestured toward Hogget's mother,

"Ezra, and this strapping young boy is Hogget." Hogget rolled his eyes at his introduction. Annabelle smiled at that, maybe some things were universal.

"Where did you come from?" Calvin asked, unable to hide the wonder in his voice. Annabelle wanted to know the same thing, but Calvin's question made it sound like their hosts were a group of mythical fairies.

"Seattle, of course." Minnie said, seemingly oblivious to Calvin's astonishment. "And what about you?"

"Seattle?" Calvin said, gaping at the strangers. "But. . .how?"

Minnie let out a chuckle. "What do you mean, how? That's where we live."

"Minnie, they've been through a lot today," Hazel said. She seemed to have forgiven that someone in their group had tried to murder her son. "Where are you from? It's always a treat to meet others," Hazel said tenderly and gave them a smile, which lit up her face.

"We're from the southeast," Calvin said. "I'm Calvin, this here is my brother Curtis, and that's Annabelle." Curtis nodded.

"From the southeast, you say? What brings you up in these parts?" Ezra said. He stood with his arms crossed, no expression on his face. Annabelle couldn't read him. Was he curious, or did he think they were a threat?

"We, um. . ." Calvin said, "were actually headed to Seattle."

"Were you looking for us?" Ezra asked, again sounding neutral.

"Well," Calvin looked at Annabelle as if for permission to say more. Annabelle shrugged her shoulders and he continued. "No. In fact, we didn't know anyone lived in Seattle."

"We get that a lot," Hazel said. "Not many people know there's a settlement there. We can take you there if you'd like."

Just then the tea kettle whistled and Minnie jumped up to pull it away from the fire.

"Hogget, will you be a dear and get three mugs for our friends?" Minnie said. Hogget bounded off his stump as if he'd been looking for an excuse to get up. Minnie reached into a bag and pulled out a few small satchels. "I'll give you all something that'll help calm your nerves. I think you need it."

Hogget returned with the mugs. They silently waited while Minnie prepared and distributed the tea. "Let it steep for a few minutes. I'll tell you when," she said.

Annabelle looked into her tea. Just holding the mug brought her the comfort warm tea always did. Then she smelled lavender and peppermint and her shoulders relaxed. Just like seeing Hogget roll his eyes, the universality of a comforting cup of tea made Annabelle calmer. Out of everything unimaginable that had happened to them, some things would never change, and despite all her questions, she needed these constants to maintain a sense of control.

"So why were you heading to Seattle?" Minnie pressed when everyone had their tea.

Annabelle looked from Curtis to Calvin, waiting for them to respond. Neither said anything. The strangers were too nice, and Annabelle thought about Hansel and Gretel. These people were kind and had offered to help them. Given them tea and a warm fire—but that didn't mean they didn't plan on "eating" them later.

"Well.." Annabelle stared at the fire. "You see we—"

"Oh my God, Ernie!" Calvin interrupted and stood.

"What?" Hazel asked.

"Our friend, Ernie. Oh god, how could we forget about him? We better go check on him," Calvin sputtered.

"There's someone else with you?" Hazel said.

"Yeah, and he's really sick. Come on Curtis, we have to check on him." Calvin set his tea down on the stump and sprinted away.

Curtis stood and set his tea down. "Thank you," he said to Minnie and went after his brother.

Annabelle watched them go. She wanted to go with them, to run away from these new people and their questions but at the same time she wanted to stay and ask her own. She couldn't believe they'd forgotten about Ernie.

"You were saying," Ezra said and picked up Calvin's mug so he could sit down on the vacated stump.

The pressure Annabelle had felt before couldn't compare to what she felt now. Three sets of eyes were on her, including Hogget's who now seemed suddenly very interested in their conversation. Annabelle was torn. Should she tell them everything when she knew nothing about them, and how they might react?

"I'm from a place we call the Colony," she began, her voice hoarse from crying. She looked down at her mug and swirled it around in her hands. At this point, what did she have to lose? "We thought we were the only people left in the world, which clearly is incorrect." She took a deep breath. "Anyway, we decided it was safe enough to venture to Seattle, so we were on a scouting mission there."

"Safe enough from what?" Hazel asked

Annabelle shook her head and felt her face flush. Had there ever been a risk? Clearly not, since there had been people living outside the Colony for a while. The only risk apparently was bears.

"Well. . . from radiation," she said and looked up from her mug to see Hazel's reaction.

"Ah, of course," Hazel said and shot Ezra a look. Ezra had a knowing smile, were they sharing some inside joke?

"What were you hoping to find in Seattle?" Ezra asked, sitting slightly forward. He held his mug between both hands, and it was the first time he sounded gentle, almost the same way Hazel did.

"We've been collecting from Spokane for a while and were hoping to find materials in Seattle as well." Too emotionally drained, she could only tell the truth, simply and to the best of her knowledge.

"Things of use for you?" Ezra asked, the gentleness gone from his voice.

Annabelle was confused about why this would upset him, was he worried that they would take things from his group?

"Yeah, we have limited raw materials, so it's useful for us to bring back things like glass, plastics, rubber...."

"I knew it," Ezra said and stood up. "I'm done here," he handed his mug to Minnie, then turned and marched away from the fire pit.

"Ezra!" Hazel called after him. He didn't turn but held one hand up in the air as he disappeared around a cabin.

"Sorry, don't worry about him, he doesn't really interact well with new people," Hazel explained in a matronly tone.

Annabelle stared in the direction he went. What had she said that upset him so much? "So, do you guys know about the Colony?"

Now Hazel and Minnie clammed up. Annabelle gripped her mug and narrowed her eyes. She had just opened up, and now they wouldn't? "Is this ready?" she demanded. She didn't feel so shy now, her confidence fueled by irritation.

"Oh yes, please drink," Minnie said and sipped from the mug she held.

Annabelle took a drink, but her mind wasn't on the tea. What were they hiding?

"To answer your question, yes, we do know about your Colony," Hazel finally said.

Annabelle looked up at her, unable to believe what she had just heard. *They knew about us, but we didn't know about them.*

"Isn't that where Ovid is from?" Hogget asked. He stood up and retrieved the tea that Calvin had left. "Can I have this?"

"Yes, yes," Minnie said, and waved her hand back and forth as if swatting at a bug.

Annabelle leaned forward. "Who's Ovid?"

"Apparently, he's from your Colony but was banished. He's lived with us for over ten years." Minnie said.

Annabelle started piecing things together. This Ovid person had told them about the Colony, and Ezra must have been upset because Ovid had probably said bad things about the Colony—angry about his banishment.

"Oh," was all Annabelle could think to say. She felt her sense of reality threaten to crumble around her. Had the Colony lied about everything? Maybe the Colony didn't know about others. That was possible wasn't it? She wanted the truth. "How did your people survive the nuclear winter?" she asked.

"All of us have relatives who hid in bunkers for a time," Minnie said.

"But how were they able to survive when they came out?" Annabelle's voice shook. "How were you able to reproduce?" She didn't want to hear this answer, but she knew it was the key to getting to the truth. Everything in the Colony revolved around the fact that radiation killed babies. It was why they needed their eggs taken out and kept safe underground. If this wasn't true…if the Colony had lied about that…

"Well," Hazel said, "after the nuclear winter cleared, those who had survived came out of their bunkers and tried to carry on the best they could."

"But their babies didn't die from radiation poisoning?"

Hazel and Minnie exchanged a look before Hazel answered. "Life was incredibly difficult, for sure, but there wasn't really any radiation on the West Coast. Bombs were only dropped on the East Coast. Your people had a problem with radiation? I think I remember Ovid mentioning that."

Annabelle stared into her tea. She didn't know if she should laugh or cry. "Yeah, we did," she said. Had the radiation

177

been a lie? It certainly was a good way to keep everyone in line. Everyone was too scared to leave. Everyone willingly gave up their eggs for protection. And by taking complete control of reproduction, the Colony had complete control of the people. They couldn't justify that control without radiation.

"It's hard to have a good handle on history," Hazel said. "Every group we meet has a slightly different version of what happened." Annabelle felt like it was Hazel's attempt to make her feel better.

"Could radiation affect the Colony and not Seattle?" Annabelle asked. Maybe there was still hope.

"I'm not sure," Minnie said. "Maybe? None of us are from Seattle. When we got there, the city was empty. Maybe it was radioactive for a while? We really don't know."

"Really?" Annabelle said, she looked at them now, blinking back tears. Maybe the Colony hadn't lied. Maybe it was just ignorance. It had to be. She needed it to be.

However, deep down, a disturbing revelation stirred within Annabelle. Even if radiation posed a threat to reproduction at one point, that didn't mean it continued to. Clearly, there was no radiation risk here. Did the Colony really still need to remove all females' eggs? This news should be cause for celebration in the Colony but something told her it would be met with resistance.

***

Harold

Harold didn't know how long he'd been holding Clara's hand, but it no longer felt like a hand. It was cold and rigid. Startled, he dropped it and looked at Clara's face for the first time since he had carried her into the cabin. Strangely, it didn't look like her anymore, should that make him feel better or worse?

Clara was his life force and losing her eviscerated him. His freshly hollowed insides ached with emptiness, and he had no idea how he would ever heal. She'd been in his life as long as he could remember, living without her was like continuing on without vital organs. He didn't know how to do it. Could he do it?

I never got to tell her how sorry I was. How much I loved her. She died angry with me. I'll never get her forgiveness. I'll never forgive myself. A knife stabbed at his internal injuries.

He wiped tears from his face. He couldn't stay in here forever with her lifeless body. He looked back at Clara's face. It was as pale as paper and her skin had sunken around her cheekbones. Those cheekbones that used to make her look like a goddess now made her look like a skeleton. He found a blanket under the cot and draped it over her body. Before pulling it up over her face, he kissed her one last time on the forehead.

He stood and dizziness struck. He blinked his eyes and waited for them to focus, but they were so puffy it was hard to see. He wiped his face, took a deep breath, and stepped outside.

Annabelle and the others sat around a fire. He stood and watched them, not sure what to say. Finally, Annabelle saw him and stood up.

"Harold?" she said softly, taking a step toward him. Her tone made him think she was asking if she could come over to him.

He nodded and she walked to him and embraced him. He hugged her back, and felt a little comforted. He began crying again, and so did Annabelle.

"I'm so sorry," she sobbed into his shoulder.

Harold pulled away from the embrace. "She would've wanted to be cremated," he said. He focused on the next step in order to keep going on. If he gave into the grief right now, he would lose himself. Annabelle just nodded. "Will you help me?" he asked.

Annabelle took a step back, her eyebrows drawn. "Of course," she said after a moment's hesitation.

"Can we help?" Hogget's mother said, approaching them.

"You have all done enough for us already, and I thank you, but—"

"Harold, it's okay, let them help us," Annabelle said.

Harold didn't want to further burden this group, but he didn't have any fight in him.

He made eye contact with the woman. "Thank you," he said in a weak voice.

She gave him a sad smile and rubbed his back.

Chapter Sixteen
Annabelle

They cremated Clara on a pyre away from the camp. Watching the flames dance around Clara's body made Annabelle's heart ache, and she couldn't bear to watch for long. She left Harold with Ezra and headed back to the camp in a daze.

As Minnie and Hazel prepared food, Annabelle wondered what time it was. She looked at the sky to gauge but clouds and trees blocked the sun. She hugged herself. Not being able to see from horizon to horizon like in the Colony felt claustrophobic.

She offered to help cook and was put to work cutting vegetables. Neither Hazel nor Minnie said much and Annabelle was grateful, she wasn't in the mood for talking. It was nice to get lost in the monotony of meal preparation. Focusing on the simple things kept Annabelle going. She wondered if she should go check on Ernie, but she didn't want to leave Harold alone. She would stay until he was ready to depart—to wherever that might be.

Ezra joined them for dinner, but Harold stayed by Clara's fire. Ezra tried to take him some dinner, but Harold refused to eat. "He's probably going to stay out there all night," Ezra said and took the last few bites of his stew. He'd eaten very quickly, as if he had somewhere he needed to go.

"That's fine, let the man mourn," Hazel said, blowing on a bite and then chewing slowly. Annabelle looked in her bowl. She had gobbled up everything without realizing it. She swallowed her last bite and stared in her empty bowl. How could she be so ravenous? After everything they'd been through, she should've lost her appetite like Harold. She sighed and set her bowl on the ground.

The sky turned gray and a chill filled the air. Where would she sleep since she had decided to stay with Harold? Was she welcome to stay? She didn't know how to ask.

Ezra still hadn't said anything to her since he'd stormed off that afternoon. Hazel and Minnie put Annabelle at ease, but having Ezra near made her self-conscious about everything she did. She didn't want to inadvertently set him off again.

However, his presence captivated her, and she started wondering about him. She had noticed he had identical tattoos on his forearms. They looked like some kind of sea animal, maybe the Orca whale. Did whales still exist, like bears and birds? And why did Ezra have them tattooed on his arms? She wanted to know about him but couldn't bring herself to ask the questions.

"Ezra, you and Annabelle are on dish duty, Hogget and I will fetch more water before it's dark. Minnie, do you mind checking on Harold?" Hazel said when they'd finished dinner.

Annabelle looked at her own feet and shifted on the stump but didn't object.

Once they had a pot of hot water, Ezra placed it on a waist high stump behind the cabins. He handed her a cloth and they started washing dishes in silence.

"Thank you for all your help." She had rehearsed the words in her head over and over before speaking.

He met her gaze. He didn't seem mad anymore, but his expression didn't give anything away. When she gazed into his eyes, she found herself drawn to him. His thick eyelashes invited her to look into his dark brown eyes. They weren't just brown though, they were clear and dynamic, like a polished tree stump, with rings and different shades.

He looked away and handed her a dish to dry. "Is it surprising to you that people would want to help each other out?"

Was he trying to be mean? Was he teasing her? "What do you mean? I was just thanking you, that's all."

"You know what I mean."

Annabelle didn't respond at first. She really didn't know what he meant. "No, I don't," she finally said under her breath. If he heard her, he didn't respond. They finished the dishes in silence, and he retreated into his cabin without saying a word to her.

Annabelle sat down at the fire alone, hoping Hazel or Minnie would return soon. The fire had died down, and she rubbed her arms for warmth. Where was she going to sleep? How was Harold doing?

Ezra exited his cabin, carrying a bundle. "Here. It's getting cold, and I thought you might need this." He handed her a gray wool sweater similar to one he wore. She put it on immediately and hugged her arms. Then he handed her a wool blanket. "Take this out to your friend."

"Thanks," she said, and then remembered that he hadn't liked it when she thanked him before. He didn't chastise her this time though.

"We're only using three of the cabins. You can sleep in either of those." He pointed at two cabins.

This time, instead of saying thanks, she just nodded. She couldn't understand why he was being kind to her now. Or was he? The darkness hid his expression and his voice still gave nothing away.

"See you in the morning," he said, and headed back to his cabin.

Annabelle sat there, more confused than before. She shook her head and set off to see Harold.

***

Annabelle

When Annabelle settled into bed, her mind began spinning like a kaleidoscope. Round and round, the same thoughts shifted and morphed into each other. Despair about Clara, questions about the Seattle people, and what they should do next. Yet, everything centered around one image, the way she'd just left Harold. Instead of looking at her or responding, he stared into the fire, motionless. She'd put a blanket in his lap and thought she saw him nod his head slightly, but she couldn't be sure.

Seeing Harold that way disturbed Annabelle. She worried that he might not recover. Clara had been everything to him, how would he find his way?

Annabelle sighed and tears rolled down her cheeks. Clara had been so full of life. It wasn't fair that she was gone. If she could capture that life on paper it might help Harold. It was a small thing Annabelle could do for him. She wiped her tears and tried conjuring up Clara's face. For some reason she couldn't see it, Clara kept turning her head the other way. Annabelle buried her face in the pillow, frustrated. She squeezed her eyes shut and concentrated, staring at Clara's face with her mind's eye. Finally, Clara turned and she'd never looked more beautiful. Annabelle felt a pull toward her. She looked different, yet familiar. Her hair was shorter for some reason. She started to solidify the face in her mind, memorizing every shadow and curve when she heard breathing near her.

She bolted upright and opened her eyes to darkness. She held her breath, trying to listen. Had she imagined it?

Something wet nudged her hand. She jerked her hand back, her heart pounding in her ears. What was in the room with her? The thing blocked her exit. She froze, unable to do anything else. It jumped onto the foot of the cot, and she saw its outline as moonlight shone through a crack in the wall.

"Wolf!" She darted past it and ran from the cabin toward the fire pit, not caring where she went. Arms suddenly restrained her and she continued to try and run but couldn't.

"What happened?" Ezra said above her ear.

"Wolf!" Annabelle shouted, pulling away from his grasp.

Ezra laughed. "A wolf?"

"Yes! Let me go!"

"You mean this threatening little girl?" Ezra pointed to an animal, which now sat next to him, cocking its head to one side. It looked so harmless that Annabelle stopped trying to get away from Ezra and studied the animal. Her ears weren't erect like a wolf, instead they drooped down. She was scruffy and dark, although Annabelle couldn't tell what color she was exactly. Her tongue hung out, making her look goofy. Ezra released Annabelle, and she stepped back a little.

"Annabelle, I present to you, Hogget's dog, Speeda."

"Oh." Annabelle felt foolish but was still wary of the dog. "She startled me. I was trying to remember..." Clara's face came back into her mind. The image was clear, and she knew she could reproduce it exactly. But it wasn't Clara. . .it was her mother.

She turned to Ezra, urgent now. She needed to draw before she lost the image. But her sketchbook was all the way back at her wagon. "Do you have any paper?"

The grin Ezra wore before changed to a straight line across his face. "Paper?" he asked, confused.

She must have seemed crazy to him, running around screaming about wolves and now demanding paper, but she didn't care. She remembered her mother's face! "Yes, I know this sounds crazy, but I've remembered something important, and I really need to draw it."

Ezra studied her, his eyes searching hers but giving nothing away. For the first time, Annabelle didn't feel intimidated by him. "Please," she insisted. She needed to draw it now. She didn't want to lose it!

"Okay, I'll get you some," he said and turned toward his cabin. Annabelle relaxed and followed him. The dog was right behind them, wagging her tail. Annabelle didn't really want her to come any closer but didn't know how to keep her away.

"So dogs exist too?" she asked. Could anything surprise her anymore?

"What do they teach you at this Colony of yours?" Ezra directed her inside and retrieved a lantern.

"That dogs are extinct."

"Clearly, they aren't." Ezra lit the lantern, bathing the room in warm light.

"Clearly." Why did the Colony bother him so much? She didn't feel like arguing with him right now, she just wanted to draw her mother's face.

The cabin was arranged like the one she'd just left. A beige cot was against one wall and a row of rustic chests lined the other. Ezra dug through a chest and retrieved a journal. He flipped through it to the back and ripped out a page.

"Will this work?" he asked, handing it to her.

"Yes," Annabelle said, grasping the paper. The thick texture surprised her, she noticed flecks of different colors in it and the edges weren't smooth. She usually sketched on uniform hemp paper made in the Colony's factory, but Ezra's homemade paper had a charming quality. It was perfect for her task.

Ezra ripped out a couple more pages and handed them to her along with a carved wooden pen. "Thanks," she said, "I'll only need one piece though." Annabelle had the image so clear in her mind she knew she would get it perfect on the first try.

She kneeled and smoothed the paper out on top of a chest, feeling giddy. So many times she'd tried and so many times she'd failed. This time it would be right. She held her breath and made the first mark.

She started with a rough outline of the head and neck, wanting a close up of her mother's face, and then started on the eyes. In a flash, early memories exploded in her mind, and she could remember now that her mother had a kindness in her eyes that showed through even when she wasn't smiling. She drew her mother's full eyelashes and recalled looking up at her mother while they held hands and walked down the street. Just looking at her mother's eyes had been enough to bring Annabelle security and warmth.

Next she drew two thick eyebrows. Even though they were prominent, they were shaped well with a nice arch. Annabelle remembered the way her mother would arch them even higher, making them almost look clown-like, when Annabelle amused her with something she did.

When she moved to her mother's lips, she stopped for a moment and closed her eyes. She could remember what her mouth looked like but wanted to see if she could conjure her voice. As if her mother had pulled her into a dream, she could hear her singing the chorus of a lullaby. Annabelle opened her eyes and drew a simple closed-mouth smile. It was the smile that her mother would make after kissing her goodnight.

Her mother's nose was longer than wide, curving up. It was the perfect nose for giving little nuzzles, and Annabelle could remember how her mom would scrunch it up when she laughed.

For the finishing touches, she focused on the cheekbones. Her mother's whole face seemed held in place by those cheekbones. They gave her a youthful look, and also made her face appear long and slender. To Annabelle, her mother was the most beautiful woman she'd ever known.

After making the final stroke, she set the pen down and held the drawing up to look at it. Annabelle let out a breath—one that she felt like she'd been holding ever since her first failed attempt to draw her mother. This was her. An exact copy. Annabelle wanted to hug the picture, to twirl around with it. Tears filled her eyes. She felt an enormous sense of satisfaction having finally done it. Now she could look in her mother's eyes again.

"Is that your friend who passed away today?" Ezra asked, breaking Annabelle's trance. She'd completely forgotten him.

"No, it's my mother. Well, was my mother." Annabelle looked at the drawing again and saw why he had asked. She did look a lot like Clara. They had the same cheekbones, the same eyes, the same beauty. Was that why Annabelle had felt so comfortable around Clara the first time she met her?

"Thank you, for the paper and letting me draw. You have no idea how much it means to me."

"You're talented. I've never seen anyone draw like that."

Annabelle narrowed her eyes. Ezra confused her. Why was he being nice to her now?

The dog came in and jumped on the cot. Ezra sat and petted her. Curious, Annabelle hushed the warnings that blinked in her mind and approached the animal.

"How do I...?" she asked, reaching her hand toward Speeda.

"Seriously?" Ezra asked, scrunching his forehead.

"Listen, I know there's a lot I don't know about but just imagine how I feel. This is the first animal I've ever seen." Annabelle wasn't going to let him push her around anymore.

Ezra didn't respond at first, opened his mouth then closed it. Finally, he shook his head. "Fair enough," he said and took her hand. His touch zapped away her momentary irritation with him. His large hand fit perfectly over hers, as if they were made to fit together. He set her hand on Speeda's back and guided it down.

Speeda's warmth and solidness surprised Annabelle. She was used to handling stuffed animals from her childhood, but this was much different. Her coarse fur had the earthy smell of life. After a couple of strokes, Ezra released her hand to let her pet the dog on her own. Annabelle ventured to Speeda's head and petted her between the ears. Speeda turned her head and looked at her, amazing Annabelle with how human her gaze appeared.

"Nice to meet you, Speeda," she said. She decided she liked the dog. Quiet settled around them as the excitement of the evening faded away. Annabelle fought the urge to yawn and her eyes felt heavy. "I should probably get back to bed," she said to Ezra.

"Me too."

She turned to the entrance and waved her drawing at Ezra. Then, without thinking, she flashed her flirtatious smile at him. "Thanks again," she said and stepped out.

Chapter Seventeen
Annabelle

The next morning Annabelle found herself with Hogget. She didn't mind, his carefree attitude gave her an escape from all that had happened the last few days. Speeda followed with an exuberance that matched Hogget's.

"Someday, I'll find a berry that can make you invisible," Hogget said to her while inspecting a leaf he'd just picked. Annabelle had offered to help him collect some herbs for Minnie, although she honestly had no idea what to look for. She ended up just following him around and carrying the basket.

"Oh really, and what would you do once you were invisible?"

"You know, mess with people."

This amused Annabelle. "How so?"

"Move stuff around, sneak up and scare people, you know, stuff like that." Hogget tossed the leaf aside and jumped onto a fallen tree. "I could eavesdrop on people, but that would probably be boring." He walked along the tree trunk. "It would be fun to spy on my sheep too, see what they are like when no humans are around."

"Sheep?" Annabelle had decided the night before that nothing would surprise her anymore, but she couldn't help but feel it anyway.

"Yeah, my sheep. You know, baaaaa." Hogget jumped off the tree and gestured his hands above his head back and forth. Annabelle had no idea what he meant.

"I actually haven't ever seen a sheep before."

"You have to come back with us then! You'll love my flock."

Hogget put Annabelle at ease. He shared his world without questioning her. It made it a lot easier to accept that things were different when introduced to her without judgment.

"I would love to meet them," she said. "What other animals have you seen?"

Hogget crouched down, examining another bush. "Not many. A few birds, and some deers once."

"What about a bear?" Annabelle said.

"No, I've never seen one, but my uncle thinks he saw bear footprints and bear poop."

She nodded. The affirmation that bears existed provided partial closure with Francine's death and gave credence to Clara's theory.

"The best place to spot animals is probably the sea," Hogget said.

This brought Ezra's tattoos to Annabelle's mind and she couldn't resist asking. "You mean like whales?"

"Yeah—whales, fish, octopus, sharks." He inspected the bush again, then started picking leaves while Annabelle held the basket out to him. "We'll have to take you to the beach sometime. You'd love it!"

"That would be nice. Would I get to see a whale?"

"We'd have to canoe a ways for that, but we'd probably see a few." Hogget moved on with Annabelle and Speeda following.

"Is that why your dad has whale tattoos? Because you guys go see them often?"

Hogget stopped. "My dad?" he asked.

"Yeah, Ezra."

Hogget turned around to face her, a smirk on his face, "He's not my dad, he's my *uncle*." He shook his head and started forward again.

"Oh." This new information felt like a gift—Ezra wasn't married. She smiled to herself. She could feel all mixed up about him without some of the mix-up being that he was married.

"Did your dad stay in Seattle?" she asked.

"No, he died when I was four."

"I'm sorry, that's terrible." Why did she have to ask that? She, of all people, should have known better than to ask about a missing parent.

"It was a long time ago," he murmured. Annabelle could barely hear him.

"My mother died when I was three. It was a long time ago too, but that doesn't mean it doesn't still hurt sometimes, and that's okay."

Hogget gave her a small smile and nodded. He then looked past her and his face lit up. "Huckleberries!" He pushed by her

194

and stopped at a leafy shrub, bursting with green berries. "Oh wow, this is a jackpot spot!"

Annabelle joined him by the bush. "They aren't ready though, right?"

Hogget laughed. "Of course not. But we'll come back in the summer. They're my favorite! Do you like them?"

"I've never had one before, but I can't wait to try."

After they filled the basket, they headed toward camp. Annabelle didn't want to go back. It was a nice break from reality exploring through the forest with Hogget.

When the cabins came into view, Annabelle saw one of the wagons parked near the camp. "Oh no, Ernie," she said, and quickened her pace.

"Who?" Hogget sped up as well.

"He was the one the other two went back for yesterday."

"You mean Calvin and Curtis?"

"You have a good memory," Annabelle said, as they approached Calvin who stood outside the wagon.

It'd been less than twenty-four hours since she'd seen Calvin last, but it felt like a lifetime. "How's Ernie?" she asked.

Calvin took a deep breath and looked her in the eyes. "Not good," he said. Annabelle nodded. Her heart felt heavy with worry. Would she lose Ernie as well?

"Last night he was joking around and we thought he was doing better," Calvin continued, "Maybe he was just trying to hide how bad off he really was because this morning his cough was worse. Once his fever started to climb, we decided to see if Minnie could help. She's in there with him now."

"Can I see him?"

"You could peek in and check with Minnie."

Annabelle started up the stairs. "Hey Annabelle, how's Harold doing?" Calvin asked.

She turned back, "You haven't seen him?"

"No, he wasn't around when we got here."

"He isn't doing so well." She didn't really know what else to say.

"Of course." Calvin stared at his feet with a pained look on his face. "This is all insane. Can you believe that others exist?" He looked at Annabelle now. "I keep hoping I'm going to wake up from this nightmare."

Annabelle took a slow, shaky breath. "I honestly think the Colony didn't know," she said.

Calvin's face relaxed. "You really think so?"

Annabelle nodded, realizing he felt the same conflict she did. She turned to enter the wagon, not wanting to engage in the discussion at this time.

Inside, Ernie was sitting up in bed and covered with a heap of blankets. Minnie and Curtis stood by his bedside, and the wagon smelled like sweat and rotting tomatoes.

"How is he?" Annabelle whispered even though Ernie was awake.

"He's hanging in there." Curtis held a glass of water to Ernie's lips. "Right Ernie?"

"Annabelle?" When he made eye contact with Annabelle, he attempted a smile. "I'm fine, everyone's just making a big. . ." he hunched forward, coughing.

"There, there," Minnie said, patting the blankets. "You take it easy."

Annabelle approached the bed. "You just rest so you can get better and we can go find another zip line, okay Ernie?" she said when his coughing had subsided.

Ernie opened his mouth to say something, but another coughing fit escaped instead.

"You'll feel better in no time, I'm sure." She gave his hand a squeeze. He nodded but his face was strained and ashen. He didn't seem to have any fight left in him and that worried Annabelle more than the coughing.

"Tea's ready," Hazel announced, entering the wagon. She marched to the sickbed and brushed hair off Ernie's forehead. "Hi, I'm Hazel." Her voice was warm and comforting. "Do you think you can drink this for me?"

Ernie looked at Hazel and he attempted to smile. "I'll try."

Hazel held the mug to his lips and he started drinking, but then took the mug from her. "Thank you," he said, "although I'm afraid I can't thank you for the taste of this."

Hazel laughed. "Yeah, sorry about that. And, you have to drink it every six hours, I'm afraid. Right Minnie?"

Minnie nodded, "That's right. It'll help with the inflammation in your lungs. We have broth cooking, which you'll eat after it's simmered a few more hours. It's very important that you stay hydrated."

"And that you rest," Hazel added, "Do you feel sleepy?" She took back the mug.

"I feel a little better. Maybe that tea did the trick. I think I can sleep now." Ernie slid under the blankets.

"Good." Hazel fluffed up his pillow with her free hand. "Let's get some air in here too, it'll help you sleep better." At the window, she tinkered with the latch a moment before pushing it open. "Everyone out," Hazel commanded. "Ernie, we'll check on you later. I expect to hear you snoring loudly." She patted his shoulder.

Ernie nodded. His face looked like it had some color back. As they said brief goodbyes, Ernie's eyes remained fixed on Hazel.

Annabelle smiled as she left the wagon. Ernie was smitten with Hazel. How could he not be though?

When Hazel emerged from the wagon, Annabelle approached her. "You're a natural," she said.

"I've had a lot of practice." Hazel looked down at the half-empty mug. Based on her conversation with Hogget earlier, Annabelle guessed she referred to her late husband, and decided not to press her for details.

"I think your presence alone made him feel better." Annabelle looked at the wagon. "It sure seemed like that anyway."

As if on cue, they heard coughing erupt from the wagon. Minnie sighed and headed to the fire.

"Do you think he'll be okay?" Curtis asked Hazel.

Hazel studied the wagon. "I do," she said after a few seconds, and then smiled. Everyone let out a collective sigh of relief. Those simple words seemed to lighten the burden of emotions they'd been carrying.

Throughout the day, Annabelle carried wood to the fire for cooking the broth, and fetched water. Minnie showed her how to prepare Holy Basil tea for Ernie, and she prepped several tea bags. She also took turns checking in on Ernie, who slept the day away just as Hazel had instructed. Tending to Ernie was a great distraction from everything that had happened. Annabelle focused on helping Ernie get better—she couldn't lose him too.

Calvin spent the day asking Minnie and Hazel the same questions Annabelle had asked the evening before. He couldn't accept that they'd been born above ground. Annabelle didn't participate in the conversion and instead concentrated on her tasks—wanting to avoid contemplating the implications of their answers.

She found herself looking up anytime she heard a rustle in the bushes, hoping it was Ezra. He'd disappeared, and she wondered where he was. This man who *wasn't* married. She wanted to see him again.

***

Harold

Harold's mouth was dry. He looked in the water canteen. Empty. How long had it been since someone had brought him water? His thirst woke him up and his surroundings came alive for the first time. Where could he get water?

He heard a laugh in the distance, and the sound stung his ears. He didn't want to hear laughter in a world where Clara didn't exist. How could laughter even exist? He barely recognized it, like it had come from some other species than his own.

Without Clara, everything seemed wrong. The wind blowing through the trees sounded like a thousand zaps of electricity, shocking his ears. The lush green forest looked moldy and dark, the fresh air smelled of death. He covered his ears and closed his eyes. *No, I don't want to experience this world without Clara, I can't, I don't know how, it hurts too much.* He lay down and covered himself with the blanket that Annabelle had brought him. He needed to block it all out. He had to make it all go away.

He stayed there for a few minutes, gratefully embracing the numbness which enveloped him. Before long, thirst inflamed his mouth again, forcing him to pay attention to it instead.

"Damn it!" He yelled and stood up. He staggered around the encampment and kicked every rock he came to. Then his eyes fell upon Clara's funeral pyre. The fire had died out a while ago and now only ashes remained. He stared at the light gray mound and thought about how soft it looked. He didn't want to think about what those ashes really were. He didn't want to acknowledge that this was all that was left of her. But it was. Falling to his knees, his chest heaved with anguished sobs.

Once again thirst roused him. His tongue throbbed and felt like it stuck to the roof of his mouth. He gulped air, which stabbed his tongue instead of bringing relief. He needed water and he needed it now.

He looked around for a nearby water source. He didn't see anything obvious but noticed a pathway through the brush and followed it.

He found everyone around the fire, busy with tasks. The smell of barbecue beans assaulted him. His stomach clenched against his wishes. How could he be hungry? How dare he want to feed his body? Nourishing it would take him further away from Clara.

Everyone stared at him, but his eyes fell on a water jug and he couldn't resist water at this moment. "Water?" he whispered, barely able to force the word out. Annabelle and Hazel jumped up. He limped toward the fire; his legs ached.

Hazel handed him a cup, and Annabelle put her arm around him to steady him. "Come sit down and let us know if you need anything else," she said. Instead of sitting, he guzzled the water. A cold rush surged through his body with each swallow. He emptied the cup and needed more. He held the cup out, and Hazel refilled it. He drank too quickly, however, and had to stop to cough. He bent over coughing, heaving and was afraid he would vomit. He straightened up, and Annabelle patted him on the back. She bit her lip and nodded at him with eyebrows furrowed.

Hazel refilled his mug, and Annabelle guided him to a stump. He sipped on the water, and Annabelle pulled some leaves from his hair.

As if on cue, everyone picked up where they'd left off when he'd staggered into camp. Minnie went on stirring a pot over the fire, Hogget carried fire wood. Hazel, Calvin, Curtis and

Annabelle ate flatbread wraps. All their tasks seemed impossible to him. Pointless. How would he ever do anything again? No one offered him food, and he was grateful for it. He wanted to just waste away.

A tea kettle screamed and Hazel removed it from the fire. "I'll go check on Ernie. Minnie, do you think he should try to eat something other than broth?" She poured the hot water into a mug.

"If he feels up for it then I'd say yes. See if he has an appetite," Minnie instructed.

Hazel turned toward Ernie's wagon and a rush of awareness assaulted Harold the same way the thirst had earlier. Ernie! Was he okay?

"How's Ernie doing?" Harold asked. His voice sounded hoarse and quiet. Everyone stopped what they were doing again and stared at him.

"He's getting better. He slept most of today, and this afternoon his fever finally broke. He still has the cough, but I think he'll be fine." Hazel took a step back toward the fire.

"Can I see him?"

"Of course." Hazel smiled and Harold followed her into the wagon.

"Harold?" Ernie said, his eyes wide. He looked paler and thinner than the last time Harold had seen him, but his voice sounded strong.

Harold nodded and sat on a stump next to the bed. Hazel gave Ernie his tea. "How are you feeling Ernie?" Harold asked.

"You should eat something," he added. He needed Ernie to be okay, to get better.

"You both need to eat something," Hazel said, placing her hand on his shoulder. Harold winced. He didn't want to eat anything.

"She's right, Harold," Ernie said. "Look, I'll make you a deal. I'll eat if you will?"

Harold looked at Ernie. Food would bring back Ernie's strength, and if his appetite grew he'd be on the mend. Harold needed Ernie to recover. "Okay," he mumbled.

Hazel smiled. "I'll be right back with two dinners," she said and marched off.

Harold decided he would stay with Ernie until he got better. He desperately wanted to join Clara but knew that she would've wanted him to tend to Ernie first. As soon as Ernie recovered, he would find a way to be with Clara again.

Chapter Eighteen
Annabelle

"Hey Annabelle, want to go swimming with me?" Hogget asked the following morning after breakfast.

A layer of filth covered Annabelle's whole body, making the prospect of swimming very appealing. "That sounds great," she said. Besides, she felt useless again. Harold had parked himself by Ernie's side, and Hazel brought them food and drink so escaping to Hogget's carefree world would be perfect.

"How about you take her to the falls?" Hazel suggested.

"Okay!"

"Let me get you something to swim in," Hazel said with a smile.

She returned later with a simple white undergarment, which looked like a white shirt sewn to a pair of men's underwear. "It has a zipper in the back," Hazel explained, handing her the garment.

"Thank you," Annabelle said and turned to Hogget, "Well, looks like I'm ready to go."

"Come on!" He started off with Speeda at his heels, without looking back. She smiled and followed him, feeling a bit like an eight-year-old herself.

They hiked for about twenty minutes and Annabelle admired Hogget's sense of direction. Without a clear trail through the evergreen forest, he seemed to lead based on landmarks which Annabelle couldn't detect herself. Everywhere they turned looked the same to her. She speed walked to keep up with him, knowing she would get lost by herself.

Eventually, they followed a large creek downstream. Speeda frolicked in the shallow water and attacked small rapids created by rocks. Annabelle put her hand in the icy water, probably chilled from snow melt. Hopefully, the brisk hike would warm her enough to make her want to swim in the cold water.

Life thrived around the creek with spring in full bloom. She wanted to draw the red, purple, and white wildflowers, which freckled the lush green landscape. She hoped she could properly capture it in black and white.

The creek grew in size until it dropped off over a cliff. They had made it to the falls. Hogget jogged toward the edge, stripped off his shirt and pants and hurled himself over.

Annabelle jogged as well. She stopped at the top just in time to see him land in the pool below. Before she had a chance to worry, his head emerged and he grinned. Speeda barked and paced back and forth and then bounded down a path at the cliff's side. The waterfall probably dropped no more than fifteen feet, yet it gave her vertigo.

"Come on, jump!" Hogget challenged, and climbed on shore.

"I need to change first!" she shouted back, grateful to have an excuse to not jump yet. She found a place with good tree coverage to change. She slipped the swimsuit on and couldn't zip it all the way up, no matter how she stretched her arms. She decided it stayed on well enough and headed back to the waterfall. Just as she arrived, Hogget jumped again.

She watched him emerge from the water, knowing that if she hesitated any longer she wouldn't jump. She swung her arms forward and let her legs follow off the ledge. The wind crawled up her legs and body as she plummeted. In an instant, the icy water seized her and she fought to get back to the surface. She pushed her head above the water and took a deep breath.

"Bombs away!" shouted a deep voice from above. She looked up and recognized Ezra plunging through the air.

Annabelle swam to the shore, and the cold water pulled at her swimming suit as she climbed out. She realized with horror that it had come off her shoulders, and she quickly pulled it back up, tugging on the zipper again.

"Here, let me help you," Ezra said, suddenly on the shore next to her. He zipped her up, and Annabelle turned around to face him. He wore only white boxers, similar to her swimsuit's bottom. His hair clung to the side of his head, dripping wet and looking black. He gave her the same smile Hogget often did, the same smile as his *nephew*, Annabelle reminded herself and smiled. She hadn't seen him since drawing her mother and even though she'd been anxiously wanting to see him, she now found herself tongue-tied.

"Ezra, where did you come from?" Hogget joined them on the shore.

"I've been following you two for a while. I spotted you on my way back to the camp."

Annabelle wondered if he'd seen her undress and felt heat rush to her face.

"Don't worry, I turned away," he said, as if he could read her mind.

Could she believe him? She hugged her body, and avoided eye contact with him. "I—"

"Come on you guys, what are you waiting for? Let's jump again!" Hogget ran up the trail.

"Hey, what's with you and the kid?" Ezra asked her. His eyebrows and mouth both made straight lines across his face now.

Was he challenging her right to hang out with Hogget? Questioning her motives? Why did he care? "What do you mean?"

"I mean, every time I've seen you lately you're at his tail." Ezra crossed his arms.

"And what's wrong with that?" She liked Hogget and didn't think she should have to justify being with him. "Does it bother you?" she challenged, taking a step toward him.

He narrowed his eyes and hesitated. "No, I just don't see why you would need to spend all your time with a kid."

She didn't want to tell him the real reason, that Hogget was a good distraction at the moment, or quite simply, that she enjoyed his companionship. "We both have parents who have died," she said instead, thinking it was a more credible reason.

He shook his head and scowled. "We've all lost parents. Trust me, that doesn't make you special." He turned and walked up the path.

"Hey, what's your problem?" She followed him up the path, gritting her teeth.

"Woohoo!" Hogget shouted while falling through the air next to them.

"Why do you hate me so much? What did I ever do to you?" Annabelle snapped at Ezra's back.

When they reached the top, he faced her. He studied her for a moment. "I don't hate you," he finally said.

She couldn't break his gaze, not sure who should speak next. She rubbed her finger and thumb together, waiting.

"You really don't get it, do you?" he said. "Maybe that's what drives me crazy, your complete naivete."

It was true, she didn't have any idea what he was talking about, but she didn't want to give him the satisfaction of being right. "But you've treated me like this from the moment you laid eyes on me, before I ever even said anything. I know it's because you hate the Colony. Why?"

"Seriously?" Ezra shook his head. "How can you be so blind?"

"Please, enlighten me." Annabelle crossed her arms and shifted her weight to one hip.

"I don't even know where to start."

"How about telling me what the Colony did to make you so angry."

Ezra snorted and shook his head. "Nothing. They did *nothing*." Then he turned and jumped over the waterfall. Annabelle watched until his head popped above water. She hugged her elbows and clenched her jaw. He confused her and she wanted to go after him and demand answers. But at the same time, she didn't want to waste any more breath on him. He clearly wouldn't open up no matter how hard she pressed.

Below, Hogget laughed as he and Ezra wrestled in the shallow water. Speeda barked and pranced near the shore. Annabelle suddenly felt very unwelcome. Ezra always seemed like he wanted nothing to do with her. For the first time since meeting him, she didn't want to be around him anymore either. She turned to retrieve her clothes. If she followed the stream she could find her way back, right?

She struggled out of the wet swimsuit then paused before getting dressed. She felt cleaner from the brief swim and putting on dirty clothes seemed equivalent to rolling in garbage.

"Annabelle?" She heard Ezra shout a second before he came into view. She gasped and quickly held her clothes up to cover herself. "Oh! Sorry!" he said and turned around. "You're not going to run off are you? There's no way you'll get back all by yourself."

His tone and words were condescending. Especially since he'd used the term "run off" like she was irrational and moody. "I don't need your help, thank you."

"So you think you can find your way back?"

"Yes, I have a very good sense of direction," she lied. Why did he make her feel so defensive?

He snorted again and this made her want to throw something at the back of his head. "Are you dressed yet? Can I turn around?" he said.

Annabelle looked down at the clothes she held against her body. She wrinkled her nose at the thought of putting them on.

"Well, no actually. I don't want to put them back on because they're so dirty."

"I can help you with that." Ezra walked into the woods and returned a moment later with a pack. He approached her with his eyes on the ground. His chivalry contradicted the way he'd been treating her.

He tossed the bag at her feet and turned back around. "I have a change of clothes in there. You're welcome to wear them until yours are clean."

His kindness again confused her. Maybe he was conflicted. He seemed to be at war with himself, unable to stop helping her despite his disdain toward her. "Thanks," she said.

"Bring your clothes down when you're dressed, we can wash them and there should still be enough daylight for them to dry." Before she could respond, he ran toward the waterfall and jumped off.

Annabelle dropped her clothes and rummaged through the pack. Inside, she found tan shorts and a short sleeve wool shirt with buttons down the center. Both would be too large for her, but she put them on anyway. They were clean but she could detect a musky, slightly sweet scent on them, which she hated to admit attracted her.

She tightened Ezra's shorts around her waist with one hand and in the other carried the dirty clothes to the cliff's edge. "Bombs away." She tossed the clothes over the edge. They fluttered and spun before splatting on the water. Hogget laughed.

She held the shorts up while she went down the path, wishing that she had a belt. By the time she reached the bottom, Hogget had her clothes on the shore.

She squatted near the edge of the water and scrubbed her pants. "Here, let me help," Ezra said and started washing her shirt.

Annabelle shook her head. "You, my friend, are a contradiction," she said with a steady voice, happy she finally sounded like herself again.

"Oh really? How do you mean?"

Annabelle liked putting him on the spot. "You can't stand to be around me, yet you can't stop yourself from helping me every chance you get."

"Hmmmm, I guess I could see why you'd think that." He stopped washing the shirt for a moment and looked at her with soft eyes.

He seemed much kinder when she was direct with him. She should call him out more often, she decided.

Hogget's teeth chattered. "I'm starting to get cold, do you guys want to head back?"

"You go ahead, Hogget. I'm going to take Annabelle on a little field trip."

"Okay, see ya guys later." Hogget headed up the path and Speeda followed.

"A field trip?" Annabelle asked.

"Yes, I want to show you something."

Annabelle was intrigued, but what if he turned back into her adversary? "What makes you think I'd want to go with you?" She put her hands on her hips.

"Because I'll answer your questions."

Chapter Nineteen
Annabelle

They left her clothes drying on a sunny rock and headed into the forest. Ezra forged through the trees like it was his natural habitat. It seemed as if the same branches that whipped Annabelle in the face miraculously parted for him. It didn't help that she had to hold the back of her shorts to keep them up. Finally, he looked back and saw that she was struggling. He shook his head and laughed.

"You don't have much experience hiking, do you?" He'd stopped and let her catch up.

"The first time I ever saw a forest like this was just a few days ago, so yeah, no experience." Was he mocking her or toying with her?

Ezra started inspecting the foliage around them. Was he going to collect plants for Minnie? Finally, he broke a branch from a sapling and stripped the leaves off it.

"Where are we going?" Annabelle asked.

Ezra waved the branch back and forth at her. "It's a surprise," he said. "Now turn around, let me help you with this."

She turned around and he looped the branch through the back belt loops and then she felt the pants tighten as he made a knot. "Better?" he asked.

She gave him a half smile. "Yeah, thanks." Why hadn't she thought of that? She wasn't usually so helpless.

With both hands free, she kept up with him as they headed deeper into the forest. As they hiked, Annabelle realized how dependent she made herself by following him. The forest became darker and darker the further in they went. Each turn they made looked the same as the last. She would never find her way back. Ezra said he'd give her answers, but what if she upset him again somehow? She wanted to know so much. But maybe it would be smartest to hold back.

As they hiked, Annabelle began to wonder if she should have come at all. Where was he taking her? How much further would it be? She had to push herself to keep going, but she started to lag behind a bit. Ezra turned back and waited patiently while she caught up.

"We're almost there." He put his hand on her back and guided her forward. Was the gesture to hurry her along, or something more? She felt like all the blood rushed to the place where he touched her. Her back tingled from his hand's warmth.

Suddenly they broke into a clearing which seemed out of place. Fifty feet straight ahead, the deep woods began again, yet to her left and right the clearing continued on as far as she could see. It looked like a long grass canal carved into the middle of the forest.

Ezra dropped his hand from her back and they headed down the clearing. The sun beat down on Annabelle's neck, and she realized she was thirsty. Hungry as well, when did she last eat? It had to be mid-afternoon by now.

Soon the clearing curved and started descending down a hill. Annabelle could see for miles, and at the bottom of the hill, she spotted their destination and instantly forgot her hunger. A long, snake-like machine stretched into the distance. The clearing suddenly made perfect sense—they were following an old train track, and now approached the remains of a train.

They hurried down the hill. Ezra glanced back at her, his smile still wide and Annabelle returned the smile. Foliage and rust covered the train, adding to its intrigue. This was the first ruin she'd ever seen, and she couldn't get to the train fast enough.

Finally, they arrived at the first car which slanted forward like a snake's head. The train car towered over her and standing next to it made her feel small.

Ezra placed his hand on it. "Isn't it impressive?" He brushed away some foliage, revealing a smooth white surface.

"Yeah, it is." Annabelle wanted to see more. Would it be possible to see the inside? Would it be safe?

"It's a maglev train." Ezra started walking next to the cars. The train took up most of the clearing so they didn't have much room to walk beside it. "What do you think?"

Annabelle didn't know what to say, being next to the massive machinery left her with a sense of wonderment. "How fast could it go?" she finally asked.

"Probably around three hundred miles an hour, so it would take about an hour to get from Seattle to your Colony if it was up and running. This was a passenger train. Want to go inside?"

"Can we?"

"Yeah, where do you think I was last night?"

"You slept in there?" Annabelle asked.

"Sure did, come on." Ezra stopped at a car missing a door. Inside, nature had taken over the train with sprouting trees and bushes. Ezra grabbed the edge of the doorway and pulled himself up. He offered his hand to Annabelle and helped her up.

"Where did you sleep?" she asked, looking around. Plants crowded every inch of space.

"Come on," Ezra said and took her hand again. He led her through the overgrowth to the back wall where he pushed his way through moss and found a handle. He pulled on it and a door opened. They crossed through to the next car and Ezra closed the door.

Being closed off from the outside world had kept the second car preserved and Annabelle could imagine what it must have once looked like. They walked down the center aisle, three seat rows lining each side. The teal seats still looked comfortable, with cushioned backs and side head rests. Each row had a window, bringing in light but also making the car hot and stuffy. Despite rust dusting the walls, the space still seemed clean. Annabelle felt like they'd stepped into a time capsule. She even spotted an old magazine peeking up from a seat's back pocket.

Ezra stopped at the front where the last two rows of seats faced each other, making a six chair cluster. "Hungry?" Ezra sat in a window seat and opened his pack. He handed her water, which she accepted gratefully and guzzled half the bottle before sitting down across from him.

"This is incredible," she said looking up at the perfectly intact plastic ceiling. "Did you just stumble upon it?"

"No." He handed her a flatbread and took a bite of one himself. "I was looking for it."

"How did you know it was here?" Annabelle took a bite. It was dry but it felt good to get something in her belly.

Ezra's smile brightened his face. His features were softer than she'd ever seen before. He wasn't trying to hide anything from her right now, she realized. Instead, he seemed thrilled that she'd showed interest in his discovery.

He pulled a journal from his pack. "I've been charting all the train routes that I come across." He flipped through the journal and held up a page for her to see. It was a map, although Annabelle couldn't understand it. She just nodded. Ezra turned the book and admired his work. She wanted to ask him why. But, she didn't want him to start on his, "you really don't know anything" rant. She got the sense that he wanted to talk and would if she waited.

"This is the most intact train I've found. I've gotten into several of the cars, except the front car which is what I really want to see." Ezra gazed out the window. "I just can't help but wonder if…now I know this is going to sound crazy, but I want to see if I could get it to run again."

Crazy or not, Annabelle didn't want to break his reverie. She wanted to know how far his aspirations went. "How could you get it to run again?"

"It used to run by magnets, if we cleared enough of the track and were able to get it started, maybe it would work."

Annabelle knew it would take months and lots of manpower to clear the track. And nature had trapped the rusted train, how could it ever run? But, she didn't want to voice her concerns. "Maybe," she said instead and gave him a half smile.

"I know, I know, it's crazy. But think of the implications if we could get trains going again! We could take supplies across long distances. Bring people together. It would be the first step in rebuilding civilization." Annabelle could see the appeal. However, it seemed as likely as him showing her a rocket ship and claiming they could fly to the moon. "Infrastructure has always been key in building civilizations," he added, gazing over her head.

"Do you think civilization will ever get back to what it once was?" she asked.

Ezra looked at her and smiled. "I think we can make it better. First step is infrastructure." He held his water bottle up like he was making a toast then took a drink. Annabelle loved seeing this idealistic side of him. "In a way, you guys are doing the same thing, right? Expanding out of the Colony, exploring new places, establishing new routes."

"Yeah, that's true." It wasn't really the main reason for the mission, but she could see how he had come to that conclusion.

"Tell me, Annabelle, I can see why Harold and the other guys were selected for the mission, but why were you asked to go along?"

"What, you didn't notice my hard-core, outdoorsy skills?" Annabelle flashed a grin. "Yeah, I can see how I might seem a little out of place. Well, you witnessed my contribution to the mission a couple nights ago." She ate some flatbread to give him a second to ponder her words.

He narrowed his eyes for a moment and asked: "Your drawing?"

"Bingo," she said and raised her water bottle. "I'm supposed to illustrate what we find. No one's been this far west before. They wanted documentation of what everything looks like, and my drawings will be a way for everyone to see what we saw."

Ezra nodded. "You're really talented. That drawing of your mother was the best I've ever seen." Even though many people had told her this, getting the compliment from Ezra felt like a gift, and she treasured it. She gave him a nod but didn't say anything, feeling heat rise to her cheeks. "If you don't mind me asking," he continued, "how did your mother die?"

"Oh, she died when I was little. In childbirth actually." Annabelle didn't mind him asking.

"Childbirth? But I thought that the Colony had that all figured out?" He looked genuinely surprised.

"You sure know a lot about the Colony," Annabelle said. "Yes, it's actually really rare to die during childbirth. My mother, in fact, is the only case that I've ever heard of." She shifted and tucked her legs up under her. "Your mother died as well?"

"Yeah, she died from an infection."

"I'm sorry to hear that." Ezra wasn't looking at her. Maybe he didn't like talking about his mother's death?

"It devastated my father," he said and then looked back at her. "He killed himself after she died."

Annabelle covered her mouth. She hadn't expected that. Although her father had checked out when her mother died, she couldn't imagine how devastating it would've been if he had killed himself.

Annabelle shook her head. "I'm so sorry." She sensed it was an uncomfortable subject for Ezra, and even though they had both lost a mother, it didn't feel like a commonality. It was like they stared down into the same deep canyon but stood on opposite sides.

"We see a lot of death," Ezra said. They were both quiet for a minute. Annabelle didn't know what to say. She felt as if the canyon expanded between them. She'd taken health and life for granted inside the Colony.

Ezra sighed and set his water bottle on the windowsill. He held his arms out, motioning at the train around them. "You see, that's why infrastructure is so important. If we can bring people together and share knowledge, we'll advance. Maybe we can stop preventable deaths."

Annabelle saw it now, the train's significance to him. She saw his vision, and what it meant to him personally. She felt like a bridge expanded over the canyon now, bringing them together. His willingness to share his dream flattered her.

"So how many people are there?" she asked. He seemed open to talk and she was ready to claim the promised answers.

"Not many. A few small groups spread across vast distances." Talking about his world seemed to ease the tension and Ezra relaxed back in his seat. "Most are very wary of strangers and a few refuse to interact with each other. We've tried to establish trade routes with other groups and after years of trying we have a few established."

"What goods do you trade?" Annabelle leaned forward, fascinated.

"You'll see that in Seattle our specialty is wool. We have a flock of sheep, which is really rare. The flock belongs to our leader, but we all work together to take care of the animals and procure the wool." Ezra tugged on the wool shirt Annabelle wore. "As you can see, it's what we all wear, and it's pretty valuable to other groups as well."

Annabelle smiled at him. It was the first time he'd mentioned that she'd be going to Seattle.

"So I'm going to Seattle, am I?" She tilted her head to one side.

"Where else would you go?" He raised his eyebrows.

Annabelle felt her pulse quicken, he wanted her around. She had the impulse to switch to the seat next to him. If they were standing, she would've closed the gap between them. Instead she leaned further forward, resting her head in hand. "Yesterday you didn't want to be anywhere near me, and now you want to take me home. I gotta say I'm a little confused." Their knees were almost touching.

Ezra studied her for a moment then looked away. "Hmmmm," he said. He nudged her knee with his and glanced into her eyes for another second. He seemed to be quietly mulling over what he wanted to say, and Annabelle couldn't look away. His calm glance sent rushes of energy through her body. His stoicism captivated her. Even though he didn't speak, she guessed thoughts flashed rapidly through his mind. Finally, he broke her glance. "Well, why would you want to go back to the Colony?" Annabelle felt let down. He was holding back, pulling back. Maybe she didn't like his stoicism after all. What was he hiding?

Annabelle leaned back into her seat and glanced out the window. "What do you mean? It's my home." He didn't answer and she looked back at him. *Oh no,* she thought when she saw his eyes narrow.

"I don't understand why anyone would want to go *there.*"

Why was he picking a fight? Why did he insist on insulting her home? She gritted her teeth. "My whole life is there, my family, everyone I love. Why is it so hard for you to understand me wanting to be with them?" As soon as she said the words, she realized she didn't believe them completely. A small part of her didn't want to go back. She had so much to learn, and the more she learned, the less credibility the Colony had. Could she really go back when it was all possibly built on lies? At the moment, however, she didn't want to give Ezra the satisfaction of being right.

"I guess I was wrong about you." Ezra crossed his arms.

"What does that mean? What did you think you knew about me?"This confirmed that he had been mulling something over in his mind before. "Do you only see things in black and white?"

Ezra opened his pack and shoved in the contents of their picnic. "Come on, we need to head back if we're going to make it before dark," he said and stood.

"Ezra, I asked you a question." Annabelle stood and took the pack from his hands.

He looked at her without expression again, hiding behind his walls. "Why did you even bring me here," she pressed when he didn't answer.

"Like I said, I thought you were different." He turned and headed toward the door.

She followed him. "What does that mean? You promised me answers, and you're as cryptic as ever." They were in the overgrown train car now. Ezra expertly jumped over the opening and landed on the ground, still refusing to answer.

"Ezra!" Annabelle demanded. She stood in the train opening and looked down at him.

"I don't know what you want me to say." He sounded a little defeated, his voice wasn't as hard as it had been before.

"Just tell me the truth."

"The truth?" he shook his head. "The truth is, we're from different worlds, Annabelle. Nothing can change that."

"That doesn't have to be a bad thing," she said and tossed him the backpack. "We can learn from each other."

Ezra sighed and held his arms up like he intended to help her down, "We'll see. Now come on, we really do need to head back."

Annabelle sat and scooted off the edge into his arms. He let her drop an instant after he caught her. He turned and started walking up the hill. She followed him silently, but vowed to prove him wrong. As different as they might be, they could see eye to eye someday.

Chapter Twenty
Curtis

During the afternoon break, Curtis paced alongside the last wagon, out of view of the others. He didn't want to go to Seattle. He needed to think of a way to stop them from going. It was their duty to return to the Colony and report everything they'd seen and experienced. The Colony had a right to know there were others—he felt like a traitor continuing on to Seattle. Why didn't anyone else seem to feel that way? Feeling outnumbered, Curtis couldn't bring himself to speak up, and needed to stall the group until he figured something out.

This was his last chance to do something—they'd be in Seattle by night fall. He'd chickened out all week while they'd waited for Ernie to recover. He hadn't said anything while everyone was getting driving lessons. Curtis needed to act now. What could he do to slow them down? He ran his hand through his hair, wincing at how long it had gotten. Curtis examined his hair in the wagon's side mirror. It was starting to curl and he hated that, the longer it got the more noticeable the red was. He hadn't tended to it since before leaving the Colony and now the curly tendrils made his head look extra round.

He got his reddish hair from his mother, and it seemed to be the only thing about him that she liked. She had a strange relationship with his hair. She always wanted him to grow it out, and she loved to ring her fingers through the curls. He flinched at the memory of her putting pigtails in his hair when he was a small child. Would she like his hair now? Would she put bows in it and make him use a special conditioner?

He gritted his teeth and headed into his wagon to retrieve a pair of scissors. He couldn't stand it this long for another second. He dug through his belongings in the drawer under his bed. He couldn't find scissors so he turned his attention to his half-full backpack and reached carefully in. He glanced back at the wagon door, and listened for a second, making sure no one was coming. He opened the pack as wide as he could and stared in. His eyes went immediately to Thomas's gun. He'd collected it from the beach when no one was looking. He'd wanted to check on Thomas as well, but Harold had ordered them not too. His stomach tightened while he thought about them walking away from Thomas. Curtis understood why Thomas had done what he did. But he had killed Clara and understood why Harold reacted the way he did as well. Still, remembering that day on the beach haunted him, and made him wonder: could Harold really be trusted?

He covered the gun with a shirt and dug around until he found his scissors. Clutching them in his hand, he returned to the side mirror furthest from the others. He began cutting and little red curls fell to the ground like sparks from a flame. He cut faster— once he got started he couldn't get rid of it fast enough. He hated it. It marked him as his mother's doll, a plaything that she tossed aside when she grew bored. He hadn't let it grow this long in years and seeing it now ran the risk of uncovering buried emotions. The faster he got rid of the hair the faster he could find peace again.

When the curl was gone, he finally lowered the scissors. He rubbed his hand over his head and exhaled. There, that was better. It was a little rough around the edges, but he liked it. He brushed stray hairs from his shoulders and took a deep breath. He felt better, calmer. Now he could focus on delaying the trip to Seattle.

The front wagon tire caught his eye. He looked at the scissors in his hand. This was the wagon Ezra had been driving. He didn't want to hurt anyone, but a flat tire would definitely stop the wagon. He approached the tire, holding the scissors at his hip. Standing tall, he stabbed the scissors into the tire while still looking up. The thick rubber resisted his force and when he pulled the scissors away nothing happened. He pursed his lips. Of course—he couldn't do anything right.

"Curtis, you ready?" Calvin shouted, making Curtis jump away from the tire.

"Be right there!" He slunk back inside his wagon and returned the scissors, then joined the others.

Ernie was up and walking around, and color had returned to his face. "Good to see you feeling better," Calvin said to him.

"Feels good to be up." Ernie flashed his toothy grin. "I think I'd like to ride up—" He bent over, coughing.

Calvin shook his head. "I think you should stay in bed, sorry man. Everyone ready?"

Hogget bolted up to Annabelle. "Annabelle, can we trade spots? I really want to ride in the front wagon!"

Annabelle nodded and looked at Hazel. "If it's all right with your mother?"

"Of course, if Harold doesn't mind," Hazel said.

Harold shrugged and Hogget raced to the first wagon, with Hazel following.

Annabelle wore a small smile as she passed the other wagons. She climbed into the driver's seat of the one Curtis had just stabbed. Ezra got in the passenger seat next to her.

"Let's go!" Calvin commanded before Curtis had a chance to do anything.

As they drove away, Curtis gripped the side of the bench and focused on the route ahead of them, resisting the urge to glance behind every second. Mountain peaks surrounded them, and patches of snow dotted the landscape. They drove over flat terrain now and thin, crisp air surrounded them. All the wagons crossed the grass-covered highway with no trouble, and Seattle was just beyond these mountains. He clenched his jaw. He'd failed at stopping them. It had been a lame attempt anyway. Why did he always have to be such a screw up?

The grassy road slowly descended down the mountain. Waterfalls and streams replaced the snow patches. They began to speed up as gravity propelled them forward. The terrain also became rockier, and Curtis grasped the front bar while they bounded over bumps. As the road became increasingly steep, Curtis wished they would slow down. Off to the left side, a large bank dropped off to a ravine below. He glanced at Calvin, who casually held the steering wheel with one hand. Curtis looked away and narrowed his eyes. Calvin the fearless, always making him look like Curtis the weak.

A loud pop and rumble echoed behind them.

"What the hell?" Calvin said, glancing in his mirror. "They're swerving!"

Curtis held his breath. He didn't need to look to know what had happened. But, he did anyway, and found Annabelle's wagon swerving back and forth, then heading straight for the bank of the ravine.

"Annabelle!" Calvin screamed and hit the breaks. Gravity grabbed Annabelle's wagon and pulled it over the edge.

"No!" Curtis shouted and covered his mouth with his hands. What had he done? The wagon barreled down the bank, gaining speed.

Calvin parked the wagon behind Harold's and they all jumped out and ran to the side of the ravine. Annabelle's wagon had reached the bottom, and lumbered forward. He couldn't see Annabelle or Ezra, only the back of the wagon. Finally, the terrain flattened out and the wagon began to slow, but it was approaching a forested area. Curtis' heart pounded while he watched helplessly. The wagon continued to slow until it crashed into a tree.

"Ezra!" Hazel screamed. She turned to the others. "It wasn't going very fast when it hit that tree, right? Do you think they're okay?"

"I don't know. I hope so," Calvin said.

Curtis thought he should run down after them, but the cliff was steep. It didn't drop straight down, but would be impossible to climb back up. Besides he didn't see any way someone could catch their footing. Going down would be like sitting on a rocky slide.

He squinted at the wagon below. Annabelle and Ezra hadn't emerged yet. "I'll go after them," Calvin said. Why could Calvin always muster the words before him?

"Wait, look!" Hazel pointed while Ezra and Annabelle exited the wagon. Annabelle had her hand on her head and Ezra steadied her with an arm. He waved at them with his free arm.

"They're okay!" Hazel clapped her hands together.

Curtis let out a sigh of relief. Then looked at the others to measure their response. Harold stood apart from the others, staring below. Ernie had come out to see what had happened and stood next to Hazel, Minnie and Hogget.

"What do we do now?" Calvin asked.

Hazel examined the slope. "There's no way they can get back up here." She cupped her hands around her mouth. "What can we do?" she shouted.

Ezra stared at them and tapped his ear. "I don't think he can hear us," Hazel said.

Ezra stepped away from Annabelle and started doing hand movements. He pointed forward then motioned both arms and then pointed to himself.

Hogget laughed and started motioning with his arms.

"What's he trying to say?" Ernie asked.

"I think he's saying he'll lead Annabelle back from there?" Minnie rubbed her chin while studying his movements. "At least I hope so. We don't really have any other option." She pointed at Ezra and Annabelle, then made a big gesture with both hands—pointing the way Ezra had pointed.

Ezra gave a thumbs up.

"Will he know the way?" Calvin asked.

Hazel let out a laugh. "Of course."

Minnie gasped, and Curtis looked below just in time to see Annabelle stagger backward and collapse.

***

Annabelle

"Annabelle?" The voice swirled in the distance. "Annabelle?" It seemed closer and beckoned her to open her eyes. She blinked a few times, the world and her stomach spun. She closed her eyes tight. "Annabelle," he insisted. *Ezra.* She cracked her eyes open and his face floated above her.

"Ezra?"

His concerned smile came into focus and there wasn't anything else she'd rather see. "Are you okay?" he asked.

The crash came back to her all at once. Pain shot through her head. "My head," she said.

"You hit it on the steering wheel. I think you'll have a bump for a while." He took a deep breath. "That was terrifying. But, you handled the wagon so well."

Ezra placed his hand on the side of her cheek and held her head in his hands and examined the bump on her forehead. "I bet it hurts but doesn't look too bad." His hands felt soft, nurturing. They eased the pain a little.

Ezra stood and turned around. Annabelle saw the others at the top of the hill in the distance. They made hand movements at each other, but Annabelle's eyes felt heavy and they fluttered closed.

***

Later she opened her eyes to a star filled sky. Blankets cocooned her and a fire crackled nearby. The pain in her head had eased, and she sat up.

"Hey," Ezra said, coming from behind her. "How are you feeling?"

She blinked a few times and pulled the blanket back over her shoulders. "Better, I think."

"Are you hungry?"

Annabelle smelled food and her stomach growled. "Yeah." He handed her a plateful of food.

"My mother's favorite springtime recipe," he said. "A lentil-curry-lettuce wrap. I found some wild greens and improvised with what was in the wagon, but it tastes damn good."

Annabelle took a bite. She sighed with satisfaction while the flavors filled her mouth with warmth and spice. "Where are the others?" she asked after a few more bites.

"I encouraged them to continue on. We'll meet them in Seattle."

Annabelle nodded, glad she didn't hold anyone up. Then it occurred to her that she and Ezra were alone. And they'd be alone until they got to Seattle. Her stomach tingled at the thought. He was stuck with her, and she didn't think he would abandon her. While Ernie had been recovering, she hadn't gotten any time alone with Ezra, but she couldn't get him off her mind. She didn't just want answers from him; she wanted to be around him—to hear him get all idealistic about the future again and to prove to him that they could see eye to eye. "How long will it take us to get there?"

"It's less than a day's hike away. If we start out early tomorrow, we could be home in time for dinner."

She had him for a whole day. They ate quietly for a minute. Annabelle tried to think of what to ask. She had so many questions. Would he actually answer some now?

"So what'll it be like when we get to Seattle?" she asked. She hoped she'd be accepted by the people there, but didn't want Ezra to see her insecurities.

"I think you'll like it." Ezra set his plate down and leaned back on his elbows, gazing at the sky.

"What's it like?" Annabelle prompted when he didn't add anything.

"When our founder, Raymond, first settled in Seattle he didn't want to live in old abandoned homes, and who can blame him? But he didn't have the manpower to build from the ground up, so they decided to move into a well-preserved compound." Ezra stood up and placed a log on the fire, then poked at it. "By the time I joined them, their population had grown to about one hundred and they had really fixed the place up."

"What kind of a compound?"

Ezra sat down. "I'll let it be a surprise because I have a feeling you'll be as awed as I was the first time I saw it."

Annabelle breathed in the smoky air and wondered what he meant. She liked the idea of a surprise. "How long have you lived there?"

"Hazel, Hogget and I settled there around four years ago. We came with another couple from San Francisco."

"Why did you guys leave San Francisco?"

"Do you want the official reason or the unofficial reason?"

"Both." Annabelle rubbed her arms under the blanket. It was starting to get cold, but she didn't dare leave their conversation to fetch a sweater. She couldn't believe Ezra was answering her questions uninhibited. Instead she inched her way a little closer to the fire, and also a little closer to Ezra.

"Officially, it was to establish new trading routes. We didn't really know what we were going to find. We didn't even know if there were people this far north, but it was time for someone to go find out." Ezra got up again and silently poked the fire.

"And unofficially?"

"Well," Ezra sat back down, next to Annabelle this time. "Really the timing was just perfect. Hazel wasn't doing too good; her husband had just died, and I thought getting away from all that pain would be best for her." He stared at the fire for a second, then at Annabelle. "I've never told anyone that. Hazel doesn't even know."

Annabelle held his gaze. "Did it work?"

"I think so. Seattle was good for all of us, it gave us purpose, kept us busy. It was really good for Hogget."

How many places existed that she'd never known about? Again, her feelings oscillated between wondering if the Colony was ignorant or intentionally misleading. Her stomach tightened as she faced the conflict full on. But, she wanted to know more.

"Where all have you traveled?" she asked.

"All up and down the coast," Ezra said. "I've crossed the mountains into your territory, but we keep a good distance from the Colony. I'd like to venture east though, all the way to the Atlantic Ocean."

"Why is that?"

"There are so many reasons to explore. Now that you've seen what you have, don't you want to know what else is out there?"

"No, I mean why do you always keep a good distance from the Colony?" she asked.

Ezra turned to face her. "Seriously?" He studied her, and she let him. The firelight danced across his skin, only illuminating parts of his face. This was how he revealed himself to her, she realized, sometimes open, but always keeping something hidden. She finally broke his stare. What could she say?

"Well tell me this. What do you think would happen if an outsider marched into the Colony?" he pressed.

"I think it would be a call for celebration." She hoped so anyway.

"Do you really? Think about it for a second."

She did think about it. And the same questions emerged. If someone else existed would that threaten the Colony's entire way of life?

"But if they thought outsiders were a threat, why send us on a mission? Wouldn't they worry we'd find others?" She was trying to convince herself just as much as Ezra.

"One of you tried to kill an outsider as soon as they saw one! And a child no less. Clearly they did know about us, and thought we were a threat. Can you blame us for steering clear?"

Annabelle rested her head between her hands. She didn't want to look at him, but she knew he was right. Evidence crept into her mind. Like the night Tully had her draw his grandchildren. She had felt like it had been a test, was he testing how well she could draw *people*? Was that what they'd intended her to draw all along? But why? What would they need a record of people for?

She didn't want to share these thoughts with Ezra though, no need to add to his disdain for the Colony. He wasn't being mean, just stating facts, but the truth hurt. "So why help us then?" She saw his side now. They didn't deserve any kindness.

Ezra laughed. Startled, Annabelle looked at him. Shaking his head, he said, "I've been wondering the same thing." He gave her a half smile. "Hazel's too damn nice to turn anyone away. And trust me, I wanted to stay away. But something kept me coming back."

Annabelle's heart pounded. She wanted to press him further. What? What kept him coming back? She wanted confirmation that he felt the electricity between them too. His smile grew, was he challenging her to ask? The question almost escaped but then he stood.

"We should probably get to bed if we're going to get an early start. The wagon's a little beat up, but I think it would be safe for you to sleep in there." He stirred the fire. "Do you think you'll be ready to go tomorrow? How does your head feel?"

Annabelle had completely forgotten about her head. Although now that he mentioned it, she did feel tired. She didn't want to go to bed, she wanted him to finish his thought. "I think I'll be ready tomorrow," she said instead. The moment had passed. Maybe she'd get another moment in the morning.

Chapter Twenty-One
Curtis

Curtis hated being such a screw up. Here they were, about to get to Seattle, and he'd yet to think of a way to stop them from proceeding. They'd abandoned their wagons and now rowed across a lake in two four-person canoes. Hazel informed them *home* was right across the water. They rowed toward a structure that looked like a backward C jutting up toward the sky, which Hazel said was the ruins of a football stadium.

He couldn't believe his previous stunt had almost killed Annabelle. Luckily, no one suspected him. They assumed a sharp rock, or something else in the road, caused it instead. He needed a better thought out plan. No more knee-jerk reactions. At this point, he acknowledged the fact that they were going to meet the Seattle people, and he couldn't change that. He needed to figure out how to convince his group to go back to the Colony. Of course, he could just leave by himself. But, as much as seeing Calvin assume the new leadership role tortured him, he didn't want to leave without his brother. His mother would never forgive him. If it came down to it, though, he'd return alone and report everything.

The stadium seemed to remain tiny in the distance, as if they hadn't gotten any closer. As much as he dreaded arriving, his shoulders had begun to burn and he wanted to be done with rowing. He should just stop—that would slow them down and give him a break. He studied Calvin, who sat in the front of the boat. Calvin set a quick pace and showed no signs of slowing. Curtis bared his teeth and pushed on.

With each stroke of the oar, he let his mind descend to a darker place, a colder place. He reveled in his own personal cave of emotion and let the feelings swirl around him like thick, black fog.

Curtis would keep some distance between himself and the Seattle people. He didn't trust them, and his loyalty still remained with the Colony. Thomas's instincts were correct: outsiders were a threat. Especially since they harbored people who had been banished from the Colony.

He needed time to figure out his plan, so keeping a low profile with the Seattle people would be key. He'd always been terrible at meeting new people, so matching and mirroring would be vital when he met them. He'd learned about matching and mirroring from an old book he'd found in the self-help section of the library. It argued that if you smiled at people the way they smiled at you, and positioned your arms and legs the same way they did, they would like you better and feel more comfortable around you. It was a trick Curtis had mastered. People always seemed amiable toward him and never saw him as a threat. Being sociable had never come naturally to Curtis, the way it did for Calvin, so matching and mirroring was the only way to keep up with him.

He glanced at Calvin again and smiled smugly when he noticed Calvin's right arm shake each time he pulled the oar. When he looked beyond Calvin he was surprised to see they were almost at the stadium. *Thank God. Get me off this damn boat.*

When they docked, Speeda leapt off the boat, and barked at the others. Next, Hogget disembarked and ran toward the stadium with Speeda at his side. "I'll let the others know you're coming!" he hollered. Would the arrival announcement be good news to the Seattle people, or would they take it as a warning?

Curtis watched Hogget disappear around the stadium ruins and then turned to help carry the boat inside a shed.

"How's everyone feeling?" Hazel asked looking around at the group. "Let's drink some water and then head on up. Ernie, you doing okay?"

"Yeah, I feel fine. Water sounds good though." Hazel retrieved water canteens from the back of the shed and distributed them. Curtis didn't want to drink water given to him by Hazel, but he forced himself to match her kind expression and took a drink.

Minnie paced near the shed entrance. "All right, everyone ready to head out?" she asked in a nagging tone. Curtis didn't like her and felt tempted to stall.

"Let's do it," Calvin said and walked toward Minnie. Everyone filed in behind him like ants following their leader. Seeing Calvin embrace the leadership role caused a twinge of loathing to throb through him. He sighed and followed the others.

They walked around the stadium's rubble and up a hill where they passed some more ruined buildings and entered a trail through a wooded area. Curtis guessed it had once been an open field based on the size of the trees growing. He'd seen these types of forests all over Spokane, in old children's parks, backyards, parking lots and driveways. New forests filled up every empty space it could, even growing through an orange plastic slide, or through an old car's windshield. Nature didn't let the obstacles of a fallen civilization stop it from reclaiming the land.

Curtis saw buildings through the trees and figured they must be almost to the Seattle people's home. What were they going to find at the end of this trail? Curtis had gone on many similar hikes through Spokane but never one that ended with meeting another clan of people. Each trip had always been about collecting supplies, finding things that were useful, and each mission had zero tension. But this hike was different. On the other side of these woods, *people* waited for them. How could they be sure they'd be welcomed? What if this was an elaborate trap? He touched his backpack for comfort. Hopefully he could access it's contents quickly if need be.

Sure enough, as they approached the end of the trail, Curtis heard voices. Did Hogget rally the whole village? *I'll just stay in the back like always*.

However, when the forest finally spit them out, Curtis momentarily forgot about all plans and fears. Ivy covered brick buildings with towers and spires surrounded them. He gaped at the gothic buildings, feeling like they'd been transported back to a different land, somewhere far away and haunted. The buildings surrounded a courtyard, which contained a large round pond in the center.

Ten people with fake smiles stood next to the pond. They wore knit clothing and leaned forward with exaggerated laughs while greeting Hazel and Minnie. A skinny man with soulless, black eyes gave Curtis a wide smile, making the hair on the back of Curtis' neck stand up. *These people are fakes. This is a trap!* Curtis matched the skinny man's wide smile and shuffled behind Calvin to meet him.

"Thank you for welcoming us. This place is remarkable." Calvin said to the skinny man.

"The pleasure is all ours, we love having visitors. It's a rare treat for us." The skinny man kept one hand on his hip and extended the other to shake Calvin's hand. "I'm Raymond," he added. He had salt and pepper hair, and Curtis guessed he was in his late forties.

"I'm Calvin, and this is my brother Curtis."

Raymond reached out to shake Curtis' hand, and Curtis matched the tension in the grip. "Nice to meet you, Curtis," Raymond said.

"Nice to meet you too, Raymond." Curtis pulled his hand away and gripped his backpack strap. He could pull it off, and access its contents in seconds, if need be.

"What is this place? I've never seen anything like it," Calvin said. Raymond beamed, while Hazel joined them with Ernie, Harold, and a blonde woman in tow.

"It used to be a university. We've worked very hard at restoring it and making it livable." He put his arm around the blond woman, "My daughter can vouch for that."

Raymond's daughter rolled her eyes but she smiled. "Hi, I'm Poppy." She shook Calvin's hand. Raymond turned to greet Ernie and Harold, and Curtis stuck by Calvin's side, unable to take his eyes off Poppy.

Of course Curtis noticed when a girl was attractive, but he couldn't remember a time when he couldn't stop himself from staring at a girl. She wore a tight white shirt and an aqua knit short skirt. Her golden hair cascaded down her shoulders and rested next to her cleavage.

"I'm Calvin." Calvin motioned to Curtis. "And this is my brother Curtis."

Curtis took her soft hand tentatively.

"Curtis," she said. Her voice was high and sweet.

"Poppy," he said. She nodded and smiled at him but raised her eyebrows ever so slightly, as if they shared an inside joke. Her golden brown eyes were lively and mischievous and she seemed different from the others. Genuine. But could she see straight through him? Did she know that *he* was a phony from one glance? Before he could ponder her expression any longer, she turned away to meet the others. Curtis stared at the back of her head feeling dumbfounded.

Calvin patted him on the back. "Looks like we stumbled into paradise, huh?" Dismay grabbed Curtis. Was his brother referring to the campus or to Poppy?

Chapter Twenty-Two
Annabelle

Annabelle crammed her pack full of food. She wanted to get out of the wagon as quickly as possible. Being near the wagon brought the terrifying accident back to her mind, making her head throb. She would be happy to never see a vehicle again. She just needed to pack and they'd leave the wagon in the dust.

Ezra said they'd only need enough food to get through the day. She went through her belongings and found she only had one piece of jerky left. She tucked it in her pack, even though she doubted she could eat it. It was all she had left of Margaret. Would she ever see her again? Would going to Seattle mean they would never return?

There was just enough room in the pack for her sketchbook. She studied the Space Needle picture adorning the front cover. Tonight she would be in Seattle and would get to see the Space Needle in real life. It felt impossible, and she'd never wanted anything more in her life. Even if she were to go back to the

Colony, she had to see Seattle first. It was the only thing she knew for sure.

Ezra peeked into the wagon. "Ready?"

Annabelle nodded and smiled. "Hey look at this." She held up the sketchbook so he could see the Space Needle picture.

Ezra approached her, eyes glued to the sketchbook. "That's a really good photo." He took the book in his hands and gazed at it.

"Is it still standing?" Annabelle feared that it wasn't, but couldn't resist asking.

Ezra smiled at her. "Yes it is. I'll take you there." His warm smile was inviting and pulled her in. Not only did he want to take her home, he wanted to show her around, that had to mean something, right?

"So another field trip then?"

His smile faded and he didn't answer. She realized she'd already gotten used to this from him. Letting his eyes silently scrutinize her while he mulled over what to say. She wished she could hear his thoughts. What was he holding back? How could she release the floodgate? The silent seconds felt like an eternity—the tension made her lightheaded. Yet the suspense was thrilling. She didn't want it to end.

"You're trouble," he finally said, shaking his head. "Now come on, let's get moving."

She followed him from the wagon, smiling to herself. She knew he was cracking.

While they hiked, Ezra chatted about Seattle, San Francisco, and his life. Annabelle soaked it up. She kept quiet about the

Colony, not wanting to ruin his openness by reminding him where she was from.

They began to descend in altitude and the day grew warmer. They followed a riverbank, making the hike easy to navigate, and they made good time. Annabelle wished they could go slower, not wanting the day to end. Around lunchtime, Ezra stopped abruptly.

"Wait here," he said and headed toward a nearby clearing. Moments later he returned with a wide grin on his face. "Hungry?"

Annabelle set her pack down. "Yes," she said and followed him. In the clearing she immediately saw what had drawn him in. "Strawberries!" She couldn't believe her eyes.

"You've had them before?"

Annabelle laughed. "Yeah, you could say that."

"Huh, I thought you guys were more limited on what you ate. Well, come on, troublemaker, dig in!"

Annabelle wanted to dive into the strawberry field. The familiarity of a strawberry brought her comfort and nostalgia, and she wanted to cover herself in them. Instead she crouched down and plucked a berry hidden under thick leaves. Dirt speckled the bright red berry. Even though it was significantly smaller in size than her berries, it smelled sweeter than a whole crateful of hers.

"So does the Colony have a lot of farms?" Ezra asked with a full mouth. It was the first time he'd asked about the Colony and seemed genuinely interested. Maybe he really wanted to get to know her and was putting aside whatever made him so angry with the Colony.

"Oh no, not farms: biodomes. They are controlled environments, so we can grow just about anything. Everyone is in charge of a crop that they grow for their neighborhood."

"Sounds interesting." Ezra said, shoving another handful in his mouth. Annabelle froze. Did he just call the Colony interesting? "Well, what are you waiting for? Try it!"

Annabelle brushed the dirt off and ate the berry. Sweet juice filled her mouth and she grabbed another.

"Well?" Ezra asked impatiently.

Annabelle realized she had closed her eyes in order to keep her full concentration on the flavor in her mouth. She opened them and smiled. "Impossible! How can a berry have that much depth? I can only get this flavor in jam with mine." She reached for another and shoved it in her mouth.

The two gorged on strawberries for a while. Annabelle crept on the ground for closer access to the berries. Dirt soon caked her knees and hands, but she didn't care. She looked up and saw Ezra doing the same. Annabelle sat back, and took a deep, satisfied breath. Mountains surrounded their secret strawberry field, the sun warmed her back and a gentle breeze surrounded them with sweet berry fragrance.

"Done already?" Ezra asked.

Annabelle glanced over at him and started laughing. The lower part of his face was stained red. "You, uh, have a little something on your face," she choked out in between laughs.

"Oh is that so?" Ezra gave her a flirtatious smile and inched his way toward her. "You mean like this?" He squished a berry on her chin.

"Big mistake!" Annabelle scooped up a handful of strawberries. Ezra stood and took a few steps back. With her hands loaded, she charged at him. She intended to squish them on the top of his head but he dodged to the side and she made contact on his neck instead. He laughed and threw a berry at her while she bent down to reload. He ran from her this time, and she chased him, throwing berries with each step. He stopped suddenly and let her catch up. She aimed for his face, but he grabbed her and threw her over his shoulder.

"Hey!" she laughed. Ezra squished a handful of berries on her back before putting her back on the ground. He didn't release her, however, and Annabelle loved having his arms around her. He grinned at her and she felt heat rush to her cheeks.

"I've had a really good day with you today," she said.

His grin faded and his eyes searched hers. Had she said too much?

He continued to stare, and she stared back. Usually locking eyes with someone made her uncomfortable, but not with Ezra. Staring into his brown eyes connected her to him. Her heart pounded as he silently scrutinized her.

"God, you're beautiful," he said and put his hand around her waist. He pulled her closer, lifted her chin, and kissed her.

All sensation went to her lips, and it didn't seem to matter at all if she closed her eyes and broke their gaze. He tasted like strawberries and dirt and everything mischievous they had shared that afternoon. He kissed her fiercely, and she reciprocated, feeling like they shared more in the kiss than they could in a million glances. He had invited her in, he wanted her, and she wanted him back.

The kiss slowed and became tender and soft before he pulled away his lips and embraced her. She rested her head on his chest and swooned when she heard his heart thumping loudly. Even though he tried to hide his emotions all the time, his heart gave away his true feelings. Her own raced just as fast, yet she felt calm, safe, and protected in his arms.

"I hate to say it, but we probably need to head out soon if we want to make it back tonight," Ezra said softly. He stroked her arm, making Annabelle shiver with pleasure. She didn't want to leave, couldn't they just stay like this forever? "But first, how about a swim?" he added.

"Yeah, that sounds good." She pulled back, just enough to make eye contact with him.

Neither made any indication of wanting to move. Annabelle took the initiative and reached up to kiss him. This time the kiss started slow and stayed that way. Annabelle laced her fingers through his hair. He pulled her tighter into his body. She felt like one with Ezra, like water from a river flowing together, flowing through each other.

When the kiss finally ended, Annabelle became aware of her own distinct body, and yearned to mix her soul with his again. Ezra looked up at the sky and sighed. "We do need to get going," he said and then planted a kiss on her forehead. It was a kiss that marked the end of something. It seemed so awkward after the kiss they'd just shared that it actually made Annabelle laugh.

"You are pretty dirty. We should take that swim," she teased pulling away from him.

"Look who's talking," he grabbed her hand and led them toward the river.

At the riverbank, Ezra stripped down to his boxers and waded into the water. Annabelle followed suit, shedding her shirt and pants before stepping into the river. She clenched her teeth at the cold. Ezra pushed forward until he was waist-deep, seemingly unaffected by the cold. After a few seconds, he dunked himself underwater. He emerged and pushed his dark hair out of his eyes and Annabelle stared at him. Water dripped down his defined muscles and she wanted to run her hands along them. He kept secrets from her, but she didn't care. She wanted him, even more than before.

"Don't make me throw you in!" he shouted when he saw her only ankle deep. He charged toward her, making big waves with each step. Annabelle screeched when he splashed her.

"All right! I'm coming in." She laughed and waded in deeper. After a second, she plunged into the water down to her shoulders.

Once her face was near the water's surface, she noticed how dirty the river was. It was murky and thick with grime. She stood to get some distance from it's strong swampy smell.

"Is this river going to make us cleaner or dirtier?" she asked and pooled muddy water in her hand.

"You haven't ever heard of a mud bath? Very good for your skin."

"Ha, ha." Annabelle walked toward Ezra, who was waist deep again, trying not to think about why the ground felt like mashed potatoes squishing between her toes.

"What's this?" Ezra cupped her necklace in his palm.

Annabelle widened her eyes at the key. How had she forgotten? Instinctively, she pulled it away from him and concealed it in her hand. Then she realized that it would mean nothing to Ezra. If anyone could see it, it would be him.

"It was my Grandmother's," she said, letting go of the key. "She gave it to me just before she died."

"What does it unlock?"

She glanced at him. "I actually don't know." Ezra held the key again in his hand. Annabelle had the urge to tell him everything. She knew he would love knowing that it revealed a deep, dark secret about the Colony, one that was potentially damaging. He seemed to actually be warming a little to the Colony, and she didn't want to ruin that. At least not right now. "It was important to my Grandmother. It's all I have left of her, so that's why I wear it." Thinking about Gran brought a painful tightness to her throat and she splashed water at Ezra to distract herself. "I know that probably sounds crazy."

"Not crazy at all." He splashed her back. She dodged the water but then he scooped her up into his arms and plunged them both under.

She laughed when they emerged. "Hey!" she sputtered and splashed him again.

"You hadn't gone all the way under yet. I was just helping you out," Ezra said, pulling her to him. She wrapped her arms around his shoulders and kissed him.

"I don't know why I ever tried to resist you," Ezra said when they pulled away. His gaze was intense but he held her cheek tenderly.

"So why did you?"

"Annabelle, seriously?" He started floating on his back. "We're from two different worlds."

"So? That didn't stop me." She went after him.

"I'm glad it didn't," Ezra said, standing again. He held his hands out to her. She swatted one away playfully before he grabbed her for another kiss.

His words prevented the kiss from completely overwhelming her this time, however. *We're from two different worlds*, bounced around in her mind. His resistance to her had been very strong initially, and a part of it still lingered. Now that they were heading back to *his world*, would things change?

Chapter Twenty-Three
Curtis

Curtis didn't sleep well his first night in Seattle. How could he? He didn't trust these people. Luckily, no one noticed how groggy he was since they only saw him follow his brother around all morning. Calvin, on the other hand, seemed to be having a great time meeting everyone. Everyone assumed he was the leader, and no one from the Colony corrected the assumption. After all, it would take too much explanation. Maybe Hazel had filled everyone in, but Curtis had his doubts. She didn't seem like someone who would want to create tension.

He'd yet to come up with a plan, increasing his frustration, and making it more difficult to hide his irritation. However, a small part of him wanted to linger: the part of him that was curious about Poppy. He fought to set that aside though, it could hinder his loyalty to the Colony.

When they left their guest quarters to head to the cafeteria for lunch, Curtis spotted Poppy across the courtyard.

Her hair was in a loose braid that hung down her back. She wore a navy oversized sweater which fell off one shoulder and white knit shorts. Curtis glanced at his own clothes—the same beat up cargo pants and black patchwork shirt he'd worn for days. Thankfully, he'd been able to wash them the night before.

Calvin spotted her too. "Poppy! Good morning!" he shouted. Poppy stopped and waited for them to catch up.

"Good morning boys, how'd you sleep?" Poppy's eyes were lively and her face bright.

"Quite well, thanks," Calvin said. Curtis just nodded. He wouldn't let anyone know his complaints. Especially not Poppy, who was the only genuine one in the group.

"Hey, I've been wondering all morning how your father got this place running so well. Wasn't it in ruins when you found it?" Calvin asked. Curtis doubted Calvin really cared. He just wanted an excuse to talk to Poppy.

"Some of it was." Poppy started walking again, and they followed. "But the bones were well preserved. And the luckiest thing of all, and the main reason Daddy wanted this site, was that it had previously functioned off the grid, so he knew we'd be able to get power and water running relatively easily."

"It's remarkable," Calvin said. Curtis didn't like Calvin's wide eyes and the way he looked at Poppy with them.

"I'm so glad you like it here." They stopped at the end of the courtyard. "I've got to run but maybe I'll see you later in the cafeteria?"

"Oh, okay," Calvin said. Curtis nodded, and they watched her walk away.

They made their way to the cafeteria where they joined Ernie and Hazel's table. "I've had plates made up for you guys. I hope you're hungry," she said.

"Thanks Hazel, this looks great," Curtis said, forcing his words to come out in a friendly tone.

"It's true. You're taking such good care of us, and I don't know how we'll ever repay you," Ernie said.

"Oh stop, it's my pleasure. This is kind of like a mini vacation for me. Since I get to help you guys get settled, I get a break from the sheep."

Curtis clenched a fist under the table. What exactly did she mean by *settled*? No one seemed to question her. Was he the only one who planned to return to the Colony?

"You're not hungry?" Hazel asked him. "Or maybe it doesn't taste good? I can see if they have some salt for you?"

"I had a big breakfast." Curtis looked at his plate. Steamed greens and chickpeas sat next to a side of bread. A meal which would also be eaten at the Colony, however it didn't seem so appetizing to Curtis today. He didn't want Hazel to suspect him though, and resolved to try and eat it. "Thank you," he said to Hazel, hoping to throw her off his tail.

"Well, it's all right if you have a small lunch," Hazel said. "They're planning a feast for tonight, after Ezra and Annabelle return."

"A feast? How thoughtful," Calvin chimed in. Curtis returned to pushing his food around his plate. How could Calvin be falling for this? These people couldn't be trusted. He wanted to smack Calvin for his treachery.

While they talked, Curtis kept an eye on the door, hoping Poppy would come in. If she did, Calvin would probably monopolize her time, forcing Curtis to be like a ventriloquist's dummy—with a painted smile on his face and nothing to say. He needed to get away so he picked up his fork and forced himself to eat.

When Curtis finished, he grabbed his backpack and left the cafeteria alone. He wanted fresh air and to get away from these people.

He walked past the ancient buildings until he found a large red-bricked square surrounded by more gothic structures. If he kept walking straight, stairs would lead him to the pond near the trail entrance they came in through the day before.

Behind the pond, in the distance, he saw a mountain that he hadn't noticed before. The snow covered mountain had a stereotypical triangle shape with a rounded top, and appeared painted in the sky above the campus. Curtis felt dizzy looking at it. What was this place? Everything about it felt like an illusion or a dream and he didn't like it.

Several people gathered in the middle of the square. One person played an annoying harmonica while the others chatted. Curtis didn't want to be spotted and kept his head down while he walked toward the mountain. The Seattle Clan's welcoming attitude made Curtis want to avoid them even more. He knew he needed to keep them at a distance. He needed a clear head until he figured out his plan.

Besides, something seemed off about this place, but what? For the most part, it seemed like a mini version of the Colony, so shouldn't he feel at home? Maybe the intimacy created by a one-hundred-person group made him uncomfortable. Everyone knew everyone, and they all seemed to get along so well. It had to be an act. And, Calvin was falling for it. Well, not Curtis. He wouldn't abandon the Colony so quickly. Didn't they still have a mission to do? Had Calvin forgotten all about that?

The longer he stayed here, the more traitorous he felt. He didn't trust these people, he wondered what their true intentions were. What if the Seattle Clan ultimately were using them to somehow infiltrate the Colony? *They want us to feel comfortable, to feel welcome, that's how they'll trick us.* He gripped his backpack straps for comfort. If anyone tried to mess with him, he'd show them why they should stay away.

Lucky for them, he made it through the square and down the steps without being stopped. At the pond he decided to go back into the woods at the entrance. He smiled, for the first time he was more loyal than Calvin. Wasn't this the moment he had been waiting for his whole life? A chance to upstage his brother? How could Calvin be so enamored that he would turn his back on their home? Well, Curtis wouldn't fall for it.

He followed the path for a ways and came to a fork. He could either go straight, taking him back to the lake, or left. He went left, and after a few minutes entered a clearing.

Well-manicured trees surrounded freshly mowed grass and four large, white pillars lined the far end. Curtis wondered if this was a ceremonial site. An elderly man stood in front of the pillars, washing the side of one. He stopped cleaning when he saw Curtis. Curtis wanted to turn around and leave. He had no interest getting entrapped by this man. But it was too late—the man approached him. Curtis would have to stay on guard during this interaction.

"Hello," the man said. It didn't come out overly friendly like everyone else and also sounded familiar.

"Hello." Curtis met him in the middle of the clearing. He forced his arms to relax at his sides, but his muscles felt tense— ready to fight.

"So, you must be from the Colony," the man said, and it hit Curtis why he sounded familiar. He didn't have the Seattle accent. Curtis' heart pounded. This man was from the Colony. He'd been banished, and was a bigger threat than anyone else here.

"I'm Ovid," the man said, and held his hand out.

"I'm Curtis." He shook the traitor's hand. What lies had he told the Seattle people about the Colony? Curtis clenched his teeth and tried to keep his hand steady.

When Ovid released his hand, Curtis grabbed the strap on his backpack. His purpose was clear to him now. They were isolated from everyone else, and no one would know what happened. *I could rid the world of this filth. This is how I prove my loyalty.*

"Are you feeling all right?" Ovid asked.

"Yes, fine." Curtis stood up straighter. How dare this man question how he felt? Of course, he would be off-kilter, he was standing next to someone who had been banished. Ovid didn't deserve to be alive. Curtis didn't even need to know what he'd done—only the most treasonous got banished. Curtis could see Ovid's agenda clearly now. He'd been with the Seattle group all these years, plotting his revenge. Poisoning the Seattle people with lies about the Colony. The members of the mission were being entranced by everyone's kindness, but no one here could be trusted. And, as the ringleader, Ovid had to be taken out.

"Would you mind helping an old man out? I've got an extra rag, and two more pillars to scrub clean. Besides, I'm sure we have lots to talk about," Ovid said and walked toward the pillars as if he assumed Curtis would follow.

This is my chance. Curtis stared at Ovid's back, frustrated that his looks didn't match his threat level. Ovid's thick, white hair glistened like a little bed of snow atop his head. His slender frame and baggy clothes made him appear like a young boy stuck in an old man's body. *Don't get fooled by his innocent act!*

He swung his backpack around and unzipped it. Ovid was almost at the pillars again. He hadn't even looked back. What a stupid man for not sensing danger. Curtis reached into his backpack and gripped the cold metal with his fingertips.

"Curtis, what are you doing here?"

Minnie's voice startled Curtis and he dropped the backpack. It landed with a thud but all its contents stayed inside.

"Minnie, what a pleasant surprise," Ovid said, making his way back toward Curtis.

"I was, uh, just…" Curtis struggled to keep his body from shaking as adrenaline pulsed through him. He couldn't look

Minnie in the eye, and stared at her shoulder. *Think fast, what would Calvin say?* He picked up his backpack slowly. "Exploring and stumbled into this amazing place. What's it used for?" He zipped his backpack shut and threw it on his back.

Minnie crossed her arms and narrowed her eyes. Did she see right through him? He forced his lips into a smile and hoped he didn't look like a clown. Luckily, Ovid joined them and when she looked at him, her face lit up.

"I didn't see you in the cafeteria for lunch, so I thought I'd bring you a picnic," she said. She lifted up a picnic basket as if she needed to show the evidence.

"Oh, how lovely," Ovid said.

"I figured you must be hungry. You've been out here all day." Minnie shuffled her feet back and forth. "I haven't really gotten to see you since we got back. I thought it'd be nice to have a picnic and catch up."

"Well, Minnie, that's so kind of you."

Curtis saw his opportunity to escape. "I'll just leave you to your picnic then," he mumbled and scurried off.

Idiot! He'd hesitated too long. He stumbled forward on the trail while the world started spinning. He stopped and rested his hands on his knees, gulping for breath. If Minnie had come in a second later she would have witnessed the murder. Was it better that he'd hesitated because that prevented him from getting caught? Or did he fail by hesitating and missing his chance? Either way, he screwed it up, just like he screwed everything up. Would he get another chance?

He closed his eyes and took deep breaths.

After a few minutes, his mind had calmed enough to allow him to walk again. It would be so easy to head to the lake and travel home. But what would he say when he got back to the Colony? He stood at the fork now, hesitating again. If he left now, he would have nothing to show for his time away. No proof of his loyalty. He would return as a coward.

He turned right, back toward the campus. He would get another chance. He knew it. Ovid seemed interested in talking, so he would befriend Ovid, gain his trust, and collect proof of his threat against the Colony. Then when the time came, he would make his move and return home a hero.

Yes, a hero. He liked that idea. He envisioned a parade, a speech, an immediate promotion to level one despite being single and childless. He would have the glory. He would prove who the better brother was.

A small detail conflicted with his fantasy, however. He indulged it anyway—his resolve making him arrogant. While walking through the parade, waving at all his admirers, a girl with golden hair walked alongside him, her arm linked in his.

Chapter Twenty-Four
Annabelle

They were quiet most of the hike back. Annabelle tried to imagine how she'd be received by the Seattle people. Would they like her? Would they accept her? If they were like Hazel and Ezra, she didn't have anything to worry about, but…what if they weren't?

Ezra set a quick pace, and rarely stopped, seeming anxious to get back home. Annabelle would have been perfectly happy to have him for one more night. She stalled him as much as possible, stopping him with kisses he couldn't resist. He'd hold her hand afterward, and she suspected he intended to make her go faster, but she didn't mind.

With her hand in his, she felt calmer. She thought about the sense of oneness that came from the smoke bath, and tried to conjure it again. *Oneness: if we are all one, I am already a part of the Seattle people and they are a part of me, there can be no discord.* She easily embraced this sentiment because the trip with Ezra filled her with warmth.

Clara was with her as well. It was the first time she thought about her friend without pain in her heart. If the oneness could connect her to the people in Seattle, couldn't it connect her to Clara also? And what about to her mother? This thought felt like honey in her veins, delivering sweetness and comfort throughout her body. Yes, her mother was there too.

As they approached Seattle, she saw ruins everywhere: old homes, business buildings, shopping centers. Some barely stood, others were in surprisingly good shape. Vines covered many, as if Mother Nature was eating them. Annabelle became increasingly curious about the past and what life was like before The End. Being here, and with Ezra, she'd have access to so much information. It had been easy to be complacent about mankind's demise when living in the Colony because they were isolated from it. Now the ruined buildings beckoned her with their mysteries, and she was tempted to go inside.

She also felt more connected to the past. These people were her ancestors, her history. She felt part of her had lived during this time among them. Time didn't restrict oneness. She had a claim to this legacy, and she wanted to know more about it. She especially wanted to see the Space Needle and downtown.

They passed many tall buildings, which had floor after floor uniformity. These weren't skyscrapers by any means but still seemed large to Annabelle. It occurred to her that they hadn't seen any skyscrapers yet.

"Will we be going through downtown?" she asked.

Ezra let out a laugh. "Downtown? No. It's flooded, and out of the way."

"Oh." Annabelle's high spirits deflated a little. She wanted to see downtown.

"We'll see it soon, I promise," Ezra said. "Ready for a boat ride?"

"Boat ride?"

Ezra smiled as they suddenly made a turn and approached a large lake. He pointed across it. "There's home."

They rowed across the lake and Ezra led her past more ruins on the other side. She knew they must be getting close when the buildings started to look more intact. They were extraordinary brick buildings, unlike ones Annabelle had ever seen.

"Here we are," Ezra said at the bottom of a staircase. Annabelle followed him up two flights where they emerged onto a large, red brick plaza. Annabelle stopped at the top of the stairs and gasped in astonishment.

"Ezra's back," a woman shouted, and people approached them. Annabelle gazed at the buildings instead of the people, however. The main building that caught her eye was across the square and looked like, well, a castle. Columns held up the building in grandiosity, pinnacles topped each column and gargoyles crouched above stained glass, arched windows. The antiquity of the buildings made her feel like she'd been transported to medieval times.

Ezra hugged several people who now looked at her expectantly. She forced her eyes away from the buildings to greet them.

"This is Annabelle," Ezra said simply. Annabelle smiled shyly, but her meditation from the hike made the others seem familiar.

"Hello," was all she could think of to say. Suddenly, everyone barraged Ezra with questions. He seemed to be a very popular person here.

"Hi, I'm Poppy," a young woman said to Annabelle. Her eyes were shining and she gave Annabelle a gentle smile.

"Nice to meet you," Annabelle said, shaking her hand. Poppy had a stronger grip than she expected, but the squeeze she gave Annabelle had a steady, even pressure. It seemed to say *welcome friend*, and Annabelle nodded at her trying to convey *thank you*. She felt a connection to Poppy already.

"I see you brought Ezra back in one piece to us," Poppy said.

"Hey Annabelle," Ernie interrupted. "It's good to see you're all right. We were pretty worried. Of course, we knew Ezra would be able to get you back though." Hazel stood by his side, their shoulders almost touching. Annabelle looked for Hogget, but couldn't see him.

"It's wonderful to see you guys too."

"Just wait 'til you get the grand tour, you're never going to believe this place," Ernie exclaimed. He sounded back to normal, one hundred percent healthy again. How much of that had to do with Hazel?

"I can't wait," she replied. She looked around and took a deep breath. The air here was moist and earthy, not like the dry air back at the Colony. This air had depth, and it had a story to tell. She filled her lungs trying to extract its secrets. A small thought tickled inside her mind, and she feared facing it straight on, but she let it whisper while she exhaled: *this is home.*

"I'll let these two show you around. I've got to go find Raymond," Ezra said.

"Okay, I'll see you later then," Annabelle said. Ezra nodded and headed up the stairs into the castle building. Annabelle was sad to see him go, but she turned to Ernie and Hazel with a smile, still excited to see the campus.

As they walked through the square, Hazel started the tour, pointing out buildings and sharing facts about them. "This square was the easiest to clean up when the campus was resettled because there's a parking lot underneath, which inhibited growth," she added. She and Ernie held hands and looked like a couple on vacation. Something must have solidified their relationship in the last twenty-four hours, much like herself and Ezra. She wished she was hand in hand with him now, strolling through his world, learning about it from his perspective.

They passed the castle building, which Hazel explained used to be a library and now was the home of Raymond's family. She hadn't met the leader yet but learned that Poppy was his daughter.

"So, she's a princess," Annabelle joked.

"Oh yes, most definitely so," Hazel answered with a laugh.

They went up another staircase into a courtyard surrounded by more castle-like buildings. "This is The Quad," Ernie said, "where most people live, and also where we get to stay."

A brick walkway led down the middle of the courtyard with paths splitting off to the entrances of the buildings. Trees lined the walkway, with vibrant green leaves and trunks with low branches. One tree had three kids sitting on a branch, laughing. Annabelle wanted to sit down in the middle of The Quad and sketch them.

"Wait until you see this place next spring. These are cherry blossom trees, and when they bloom, The Quad transforms into the most enchanting place in the world," Hazel said. Annabelle couldn't imagine it being more captivating than it already was. And Hazel had just implied that they would be there the following spring. Had this already been decided in one day? An anxious excitement sprouted in her chest, and she worried that if she let it grow, the prospect might not come true.

"Heads up Ernie!" someone hollered, and Annabelle turned just in time to see a frisbee hurling toward them. She ducked and Ernie caught it, grinned, tossed it back and then ran to join in the game.

"Well, Ernie sure feels at home here," Annabelle said.

"I know," Hazel said, watching him. Then she turned to face Annabelle, "Isn't it great?"

"I'm happy for you two."

"He's so different than anyone I've ever met."

"Yeah, I know what you mean," Annabelle said, thinking of Ezra.

"Do you have someone special in your life?" Hazel asked. Annabelle raised her eyebrows. How had Hazel not noticed that she and Ezra had been bonding? Of course, they hadn't been affectionate with each other publicly, but she thought it must have been obvious to everyone, especially his own sister.

"Well—"

"Hazel, catch!" Ernie threw the frisbee. Hazel sprinted to catch it but missed by a couple of feet.

"Nice try," he said, retrieving the frisbee and tossing it back to the others. "Should we show Annabelle the inside now?"

"Yes. Come on, Annabelle, we fixed you up a really nice room. I think you're going to love it," Hazel said, while grabbing Ernie's hand and starting down the path again. Annabelle followed the two, feeling a little deflated. She wondered if she'd lost her chance to talk to Hazel about Ezra.

Hazel was right—she loved the room they'd set up for her. The guest quarters were at the north end of The Quad, and her room had two windows which overlooked the courtyard. A twin bed had cherry blossom bedding and the walls were adorned in cherry blossom artwork. A small desk sat along the far wall with an upholstered blue chair next to it. A perfect place for her to sketch. As much as she loved it, she couldn't help feeling a little disappointed that it was meant just for her. How far away did Ezra live?

"Where's everyone else staying?" she asked.

"We're all in the same hall. Calvin and Curtis have a room, and Harold and I share another," Ernie explained.

"Oh, okay," Annabelle said. "How's Harold doing?" she asked, feeling guilty that she hadn't asked sooner. Come to think of it, she hadn't seen him at all since they returned.

Ernie and Hazel looked at each other instead of answering.

"Not so good," Ernie finally said. "I haven't heard him say a complete sentence since we got here. He keeps to himself and mostly just wanders around alone." They were all quiet for a moment. Imagining Harold walking around listlessly made Annabelle frown. "I had hoped this place would be good for him, but I just don't know."

"He just needs time," Hazel said, with sympathetic eyes. Annabelle knew that she spoke from experience. Clearly time had helped Hazel, she'd begun to find happiness again with Ernie. Hopefully, someday, that could be the reality for Harold as well.

"Do you think it would help him if he talked to you?" Annabelle asked her.

Hazel thought for a moment and then said, "I don't think so. He'll find his way. I agree with Ernie though. A new place should help him."

***

Harold

Harold needed to shave. Clara had hated it when he had facial hair. It used to be a joke between the two of them when he came back from Spokane with a beard. She would refuse to kiss him until he had a smooth face. "I like seeing the boy I fell in love with," she would tell him. He, however, liked the look of a little facial hair. Since Clara was never on the missions that was his only chance to grow it out.

But now she was gone forever and he wished he could take back every moment they had spent apart. His facial hair disgusted him. His body betrayed him, forcing him to go on living. If he let it grow, did it mean that he was letting her go? He couldn't face that. He needed it gone, she would want it gone. He needed his face smooth so she'd be happy.

He wandered around the campus, the only thing he'd done since getting there, and kept finding things that reminded him of her. He came across a rose garden where she would've insisted on smelling every single rose. Every time he met someone new, he could imagine the witty things she would've said to win them over. He saw her at dusk when the sunset matched her hair color, and he saw her in the moonlight where every shadow looked like her form.

He needed to end the torture. But first, he needed to shave. Somehow, he'd lost his razor and wondered who he could ask to loan him one.

He rounded the corner and saw movement near a building. Nighttime approached, making it difficult to see, but the movements caught Harold's eye because the rhythm was familiar. He identified a man holding a four-foot-long stick. At first glance he appeared to dance with the stick, but before long Harold identified the precision of the moves. Each step was too rigid, too precise and deliberate to be a dance. *The technique is so familiar, could it be fencing?* Harold strained to see the steps and his feet itched to match the beat, and his body instinctively wanted to follow along. He watched the man practice his moves alongside the building while heading toward him. If he saw Harold, he made no indication of it, instead staying focused on his practice. He would pivot, step back and then sweep the stick around him, going in controlled circles alongside the building.

Clara had always teased Harold about his fencing hobby. She'd said he was too old to play with swords. Yet, when he did get together with a few other guys to practice, she always watched and cheered him on. She'd kiss him on the cheek after they were done, a big smile on her face, and he'd know that she had secretly liked it.

Harold continued to stare at the man, perplexed that he'd stumbled upon this scenario. Was Clara watching from above? Did she want to see him fence?

When the man was about ten feet away, Harold could see that he was Asian. He had black spiked hair, thick dark eyebrows, and a muscular build.

The man stopped near Harold. "Hello, I'm Wataru," he said, extending his free hand.

Harold shook his hand. "Is that fencing?"

"Yeah, are you familiar with it?"

"Well, I'm self-taught from a book." Harold shifted his weight from one foot to the other. "But, I'm not sure if I do it right."

"Wanna try a few moves?" Wataru gave him a challenging smile and passed him a long staff that had a thick handle.

Harold stepped forward with his right foot and bent at the knees with his feet facing opposite directions. His heart rate increased as he focused on Wataru. It had been a long time since he'd practiced, and it felt cathartic.

Wataru came at him and Harold's body took over. He retreated, while parrying all Wataru's blows with swift moves that came to him without thought.

Wataru stepped back, his smile grew. "You're pretty good. Again?"

Harold nodded and Wataru advanced, quicker this time.

As he dodged the blows, he felt like he'd entered a dance with Wataru. His body began to wake up. He had pins and needles all over, chasing the numbness away that had settled in his muscles ever since Clara had died. He felt alive. He lunged at Wataru, who deflected his advances while retreating. Harold gritted his teeth and pushed forward again.

Energy surged through his veins. He struck Wataru in the side causing him to stumble back, interrupting their dance. The pause jolted Harold out of the moment and reality crashed down on him. His arms dropped and he stared at his legs. Again his body had betrayed him. How dare it allow him to feel anything with Clara gone? How dare it allow him to feel alive?

Numbness returned, chasing the adrenaline away. He didn't notice Wataru advancing at him again, until he took a hard blow to the chest. Harold gasped for breath and fell backward to the ground.

"You okay?" Wataru asked, standing over him. "You were doing so good before."

"I must be a little rusty." He grabbed Wataru's hand, and stood.

"Thanks man, I really enjoyed that," Wataru said. "It's been years since I've had someone to practice with."

Harold nodded, looking at the ground. He didn't know what to say.

"You sure you're okay?" Wataru asked. When Harold didn't answer, he added, "There's supposed to be a feast tonight."

The only thing Harold wanted to do was get back to his solitary walk. If he went to a feast how else would his body betray him? He rubbed his face.

"Do you have a razor I can borrow?"

Wataru laughed. "Sure, but let's eat first."

Chapter Twenty-Five
Harold

Harold followed Wataru reluctantly. People already filled the dining hall, and he got in line behind Wataru. He didn't want to be rude so he filled his plate with zucchini noodles covered in marinara, squash, beans, grilled potatoes, salad with berries, and two rolls. Then, he followed Wataru toward the tables, trying to not look at the food.

He saw the others from the Colony sitting at a table together but kept following Wataru. He didn't want to sit with them. When Wataru set his plate at a table, Harold sat at an empty chair next to him, relieved.

"This is my wife, Lily and my daughter Hanako," Wataru said, motioning to the woman and child next to him.

Hanako stared at him with wide eyes. She was a beautiful child, and a perfect mix of her parents. She had dark eyes like her father, but her wavy hair was light brown like her mother's. She continued to stare at Harold and clung to her mother's arm.

Harold wanted to make her feel at ease, because that's what Clara would've done.

He smiled. "I'm Harold, nice to meet you." Hanako narrowed her eyes before looking back at her plate.

"How old is she?" Harold asked.

"Two and a half," Lily answered, smoothing one of Hanako's curls down, a proud smile on her face.

They ate in silence for a minute, but the room was filled with noise. It seemed everyone in the Seattle Clan had crammed into this room. The laughter and chatter burned his ears.

"So what do you think of our campus?" Lily asked him.

Harold looked at her. She smiled at him with warmth in her green eyes. He knew he couldn't be honest with her. What good would it do to tell her how miserable he was? "It's incredible," he said.

Lily's smile grew. "Thanks. It's come a long way, but we think it's pretty great too."

"How long have you lived here?"

"I came with Raymond around ten years ago when he settled the area. Wataru joined us a couple years later."

"It was pretty incredible then too, it's always had an alluring quality to it." Wataru said in between bites. "Did you know that Seattle was called the Emerald City?"

"No, I didn't." Harold had always imagined Seattle to be captivating and unique and decided the name fit.

"Have you seen downtown yet?" Wataru asked.

"You mean the Space Needle? No, not yet."

"The Space Needle isn't technically downtown, but it's the best way to see downtown because so many of the buildings are falling down these days." Wataru chewed for a minute, seeming to think something over. "I'll tell you what, how about I take you to the Space Needle tomorrow, and we can climb to the top? That way you'll get to see the Emerald City in all its glory."

"Can we still get to the top?"

Wataru laughed. "Well it's a little dangerous but was very well constructed. I've climbed it dozens of times. It's a long climb but worth it."

Everything suddenly snapped into focus. The noise around him vanished, and he could see clearly what he was meant to do. It all made sense now, meeting Wataru, coming to the feast, learning about the Space Needle. Clara had been guiding him. Guiding him back to her. He imagined himself climbing the stairs, each step bringing him closer to Clara. He imagined getting to the top and looking out over the Emerald City, twinkling at him in all its glory and ruin. He envisioned feeling the wind and breathing the thin air, being the closest to heaven he'd ever been.

"Yes, I would like that," he said.

***

Annabelle

"This strawberry pie is so good," Annabelle said, closing her eyes, savoring the bite. "Is this a nut crust? I'll have to get the recipe."

Hazel took a bite. "Mmmm, it is good. I haven't had a strawberry since last summer." Annabelle sat next to Hazel at the end of their table. She'd enjoyed the feast and felt content, despite not seeing Ezra since they returned. She scanned the room again looking for him but he was nowhere in sight. She wanted to ask Hazel where he might be but didn't want to sound clingy.

Just as she took the last bite of pie, Ezra finally walked into the dining hall, with Raymond, a pregnant woman, and Poppy. Annabelle stared at the woman. Her body was slender, but her belly protruded in a perfect oval outwards, and she waddled a little when she walked. Even though she knew pregnant women weren't at risk from radiation here, it still shocked Annabelle to see a pregnant woman walking around above ground. It felt so unnatural, so dangerous, so irresponsible. She had to look away.

"Who is that woman with Ezra and Poppy?" she asked Hazel, nodding her head toward them. Raymond's group started through the buffet line.

"Oh, that's Rose, Raymond's wife," Hazel said. "I'm surprised she's here. She's been on bed rest for the last couple weeks."

Annabelle studied the woman. She looked like she was probably in her forties. Women in the Colony weren't even allowed to have children in their forties. Annabelle had to stop herself from shaking her head in disbelief.

"So Poppy is going to be a sister?" Annabelle asked.

"Yes, much to the excitement of Raymond. He's wanted a second child ever since Poppy was born," Hazel said, "so what is that? Twenty years or so? I've never seen him happier."

Raymond's group finished getting their food and walked toward Annabelle's table. Ezra looked right at her, causing her pulse to quicken. The world around him blurred and all she could see was his smiling face approaching hers.

"How are you doing?" Raymond said when they reached the table. "Rose wanted to come out and meet you all."

"I'm Annabelle, nice to meet you." Annabelle shook Rose's hand. Rose attempted a smile, but it didn't reach her eyes. Rose must have looked a lot like her daughter when younger. She still had blonde hair but wrinkles surrounded her eyes and she had a face bony from age or pregnancy.

Rose introduced herself to the rest of the group.

"And this is my son," Raymond said, rubbing her belly.

"Raymond, we don't know that for sure." Rose pushed his hand off.

"Believe me, it is a boy," Raymond said, beaming. "I hope you all enjoy your evening." He turned to leave, and Rose followed. There weren't any empty chairs at their table. Did that mean Ezra wouldn't sit with them? Couldn't he pull up a chair? Poppy smiled before following her parents and then found an empty chair a few tables away, next to Curtis.

Ezra looked at Hazel and then turned to leave himself. He knocked on the table in front of Annabelle before following Raymond and Rose from the dining hall. What was that supposed to mean? Annabelle stared at his back until it disappeared from sight. It baffled her that he didn't even say "hello." It was as if someone had thrown her a frisbee, but at the last minute it turned out to be a boomerang and went the other way. She was confused and didn't know what to think.

"Annabelle, you all right?" Hazel asked.

"I just. . ." Ezra hadn't said that she had to keep it a secret, but now, because of his aloofness, she wondered if she should say anything. "Well," she turned to face Hazel finally, "I sort of…" How would she define the relationship? They hadn't made any commitments to each other. She knew how she felt about Ezra but wasn't sure how he felt about her. "Kissed your brother," she blurted out, it was the only way to describe what had happened. She bit her lower lip, worried what Hazel would say.

Hazel said nothing, her face frozen in shock. Was she mad? Annabelle covered her mouth, regretting that she'd said anything. But she couldn't take it back now.

"Sorry?" Annabelle said, not sure exactly what she apologized for, she just didn't like seeing Hazel all frozen.

Hazel blinked finally. "You're serious?" she said.

"Yeah." Annabelle shifted in her seat. "Is it that hard to believe?"

"Oh no, dear, I don't mean it like that." She placed a hand on Annabelle's shoulder. "I mean, it's just, well…unprecedented, that's all."

"What do you mean? He hasn't ever had a girlfriend?" Annabelle leaned in closer to Hazel. Hazel gazed around the room before talking.

"Not since we were teenagers," she whispered. "Not that I ever knew of anyway." Her eyes darted around. Annabelle turned to see where she was looking. At Poppy?

"Why not?" There had to be a good reason, Ezra was irresistible.

Hazel sighed. "It's a long story, but I think it has a lot to do with our parents." Hazel tapped on her lip for a second before going on. "Did he tell you about our parents?"

"He did." Annabelle looked at her empty plate. It made sense. Ezra had seen a lot of heartbreak in his lifetime. His parents, and also Hazel's late husband. "So he's scared of love?"

"I guess you could say that. Afraid of love, or the pain of loss. You can't be hurt if you never fall in love."

"Right," Annabelle said. Maybe the reason he initially resisted her was that he feared developing romantic feelings, and not because he disliked the Colony. As strange as this revelation was, it actually flattered her. He'd distanced himself because he desired her. She looked at Hazel, unable to hide her smile. Hazel looked over Annabelle's head, seeming to be in a far off place herself. Hadn't Hazel witnessed the same heartache that Ezra did? Yet she was open to loving again. "How were you able to cope with it all?" Annabelle asked.

"Well, I guess I'm not as stubborn as Ezra. And I think maybe I try to heal my wounds with love instead of walls. I don't know. . . we're just different." Hazel shook her head. "Anyway, this is great news. Maybe he's finally ready to let it all go."

Annabelle thought about his abrupt departure. "I don't know. He didn't even say hi to me just now."

"Oh, well," Hazel glanced at Poppy again, "I think it was because Poppy was nearby." she whispered.

"What do you mean? Is there something going on between them? I thought you said he hadn't had any girlfriends."

"No no, it isn't like that," Hazel said, her eyes still darting around the room.

"What is it like then?" Annabelle pressed.

"It's complicated."

Before Annabelle could ask more, Hogget approached her. "Mom, can I have another piece of pie?" he asked. A couple other people at their table stood, along with many others around the room. The feast was coming to an end.

"Yes dear, but after you help me clear some dishes to the kitchen," Hazel said, and stood. "We'll talk later," she said and squeezed Annabelle on the shoulder. Annabelle nodded, but wondered if she really meant it.

***

Curtis

Ovid sang to himself while he ate. He would take a bite, hum while he chewed then sing aloud when stabbing another bite, all while bobbing his head back and forth. The off key singing annoyed Curtis, but he found himself watching Ovid, slightly intrigued. Did music play in Ovid's head all the time?

When not making music of one kind or another, he laughed or chatted with the others at the table. Ovid made everyone laugh easily. It seemed hard to imagine anyone having a bad time with him. This made Curtis more and more uncomfortable about his plan. He needed to stay strong but being around Ovid made it difficult.

"Minnie, don't stress so much about it. You'll find it. It's already out there. You're probably looking too hard and missing it," Ovid said. Minnie had been complaining about some plant that she hadn't been able to find. She and Ovid couldn't be more different. The more jolly Ovid became, the more Minnie crossed her arms and scowled. Yet she never seemed to bring Ovid down, as if he lived in the clouds where nothing could reach him, but he could easily rain down some of his happiness. "Didn't I ever tell you the story about the crab?"

"Yes, of course you have." Minnie rolled her eyes. "The elusive crab just crawled right under your leg when you lay down to take a nap."

"Exactly." Ovid clapped his hands together. "So you see, you have nothing to worry about."

"Yes, but herbs don't crawl," Minnie said. Curtis couldn't believe Ovid had so much patience for Minnie. Ovid just smiled and went on talking about his crab.

Curtis wondered what Ovid had done in the Colony to get himself banished. He had to be putting on an act to seem harmless. The Seattle Clan wouldn't understand the implications of banishment, making them easy to fool. The Colony took banishment very seriously, and it didn't happen often. What had Ovid done to deserve banishment?

Furthermore, how in the world had Ovid survived after banishment? Waiting for food to crawl onto your plate wasn't a very good survival technique, and how could someone so laid back have what it took to cross the mountains by himself?

"I'm ready for some pie, anyone else want me to bring them a slice?" Ovid stood and looked around. Everyone at the table agreed at once.

"I'll help," Minnie said, and the two headed to the dessert table. Curtis laced his fingers together and forced a pleasant smile on his face. He needed to figure out how to make Ovid talk without showing that he was onto Ovid's act. How should he bring it up? He went over different scenarios but hadn't decided by the time they returned.

"Take a look at that, my boy, have you ever seen a sweeter sight?" Ovid placed the pie in front of Curtis and patted him on the back before sitting back down. Curtis looked at his pie.

It did look sweet, and Curtis didn't like desserts very much. Everyone else at the table quietly enjoyed the pie. Curtis took his chance to question Ovid.

"So Ovid," he started, interrupting Ovid's humming, "what exactly did you do to get banished?" His question came out sounding abrupt. Curtis didn't want to sound accusatory, he'd wanted to sound curious, but doubted he had pulled it off.

Ovid just laughed. "You really don't beat around the bush do you?" He stabbed another bite of pie with his fork, his face serious. After chewing and swallowing, silently this time, he turned to Curtis. "You know, I hadn't thought about that in a long time, not until your group showed up that is. " He took another bite. Curtis waited.

"It really is a long story." Ovid finally said. "The short version is that I was curious about the details surrounding the death of my baby sister. And for some reason, the Colony thought that was a threat."

"And what's the long version?" There had to be more. Curiosity wasn't a banish-able offense.

"I'm not entirely sure you want to hear the full story," Ovid said. What was that supposed to mean? Curtis struggled to keep his breathing even. What gave Ovid the right to dictate what Curtis wanted?

"No, I do," he said. "I want to know what happened," he added when Ovid didn't say anything.

Ovid cocked his head to the side. "I should get us some extra tea then," he said. "I was right earlier when I told you we had a lot to talk about, wasn't I?"

"Hey guys, have you tried the pie yet?" Poppy said and sat in the empty chair next to Curtis. Curtis jumped when he heard her. He'd been so distracted by Ovid's story that he'd stopped looking for her. And here she was. He shook his head, realizing she showed up when he stopped looking, just like Ovid's crab.

"Uh, no, actually," Curtis admitted.

"Well, what are you waiting for?" she asked and took a bite of her own pie. She had a dinner plate and a dessert plate and wanted dessert first it seemed. "Oh, that's good," she said. She chewed slowly, and tilted her head back slightly. Her eyes narrowed with pleasure. Curtis watched her, transfixed and unable to come up with any words to say.

"I made it myself, you know." She took another bite.

"It's delicious, Poppy," Ovid said. Hearing Ovid speak allowed Curtis to regain his composure and he decided to eat the pie. However, he barely tasted it. Instead he mulled over what to do. On the one hand he needed to find out more about Ovid's banishment, but on the other hand, Poppy sat next to him. Her arm rested a couple inches away from his. His body wanted everyone else to disappear and to have Poppy all to himself.

"So Curtis," Poppy said, her voice high pitched and excited, "it looks like Hazel and what's-his-name have really hit it off." She arched an eyebrow and leaned in.

"Ernie," he said.

"Yeah, that's right. So, they're an item?"

"I don't know, maybe?"

"And tell me about Ezra and the girl he came in with." She flipped her hair behind a shoulder.

"Annabelle," he supplied.

"Yes, Annabelle. So they're together too?"

"I really don't know. Why do you ask?"

"Oh, my dad just likes to know about all these things," she said.

Curtis wanted to ask so many questions: *Is it really any of his business? Do people need his approval to date? Are you his spy?* But he couldn't muster up the words. He didn't want to throw anything at her that might make her leave. She had chosen to sit by him and he wouldn't take that for granted.

"You'll be the first to know if I hear anything," he promised.

"Thank you." Her face lit up with a dazzling smile. "I knew I could trust you."

Curtis smiled back, he felt dizzy. He saw Calvin at the next table over. Their eyes met and then Calvin looked away. He had obviously been watching Curtis and Poppy talk. He had seen the way Curtis made Poppy light up just now. Was his brother jealous? Of him?

Maybe there was more than one way to beat his brother. Could he have it all? Glory back at the Colony after proving his loyalty and winning the girl that his brother wanted? It all seemed too good to be true.

He turned back toward Ovid hoping to get the rest of his story, but he was gone. Maybe that was good, he didn't want to be fooled by Ovid's charms. He needed to get his plan together, and soon. For now, however, he would indulge in Poppy's presence.

Chapter Twenty-Six
Annabelle

After dinner, Annabelle sat on a bench outside in The Quad. She'd tried sketching with the limited light coming from the quest quarters but couldn't focus on drawing. Instead, she watched every person who walked by, hoping to see Ezra. Wasn't he going to at least come say goodnight to her? Her conversation with Hazel replayed in her mind. What should she say to Ezra? Accusing him of keeping things from her would only make him more defensive. Maybe he really wasn't into her at all, and it had nothing to do with hiding things from her. Or maybe he was just busy? He'd been at the leader's side all day—perhaps he was doing something important.

While she watched people retreat into the buildings surrounding The Quad, she grappled again with the Colony's lies. *No, it's ignorance*, she tried to convince herself. What did she really believe? She still didn't know. Would she ever know? It made her uncomfortable not knowing the truth.

Was everyone in the Colony being lied to intentionally? She clenched her jaw.

Speeda barked, interrupting her thoughts, and galloped toward her.

"Hey, Speeda." Annabelle grinned and patted her head.

"Hi Annabelle," Hogget said, arriving a few seconds after Speeda. "Look! I got two pieces of pie for a midnight snack." He held up a basket.

"Are you going to stay up until midnight?" she asked. She was happy to see him, if she couldn't see Ezra she may as well spend some time with his carefree nephew. She set her sketchbook down.

"Ha, I guess probably not. Maybe a 10:30 snack," Hogget said.

Annabelle laughed. "Well, I know where I'll be at 10:30 then."

"I don't think so. You know how many dishes I had to do to earn this?"

"Fair enough," she said, smiling. "Hey, where do you live anyway? I got a tour of the guest quarters, but Hazel didn't mention where you guys live. I promise I won't stop by to steal pie, I'm just curious."

"Right here." He pointed at the building behind her. "I bet you knew already and were waiting for me to bring you pie."

"What?" Annabelle turned around to look at the building behind them as if it wasn't there before. She laughed again. "Honestly I had no idea!" Did this mean she had been sitting in front of Ezra's home the whole time too? How long would she have to wait? "Does Ezra live here too?" she asked.

"Ezra? No, he lives in the library with Raymond's family."

"Oh." That seemed odd to Annabelle. Was it to be close to Poppy? Did they all share one big room? "Why is that?"

"He likes to do research and stuff. He used to live with us but started spending so much time at the library that we just moved his stuff there, kind of as a joke, and he never came back." Hogget started rubbing his nose back and forth like he wanted to stop a sneeze. "But I think he's happier there, and he's closer to Raymond if he ever needs him," he added.

Annabelle loved Hogget's openness. "Can you do me a favor?" She tucked her sketchbook into her bag and stood. "Could you take me to his place? I need to ask him something."

"Yeah sure, no problem. Just let me drop off my pie real quick." Hogget raced up the stairs, Speeda right at his heels.

They were back in under one minute and weren't even winded. Annabelle missed those days of carefree childhood when she ran everywhere. She wished they could run now to Ezra's, but Hogget led in a nice adult walking pace.

Outdoor lights had come on, bathing the campus in long, ominous shadows. In the twilight, the campus no longer enchanted Annabelle, instead it looked like a place where vampires would hide in the doorways waiting for her to get too close. Annabelle hugged her arms.

They only had to walk through The Quad and down a couple flights of stairs and into Red Square. Speeda must have picked up an interesting scent and took off. Instead of calling her back Hogget continued to the library.

290

"Do you still want to meet my sheep?" he asked.

"That'd be great. When can I?"

"Anytime," Hogget said and started up the steps to the library. Annabelle tried to follow Hogget's carefree gait, but she felt queasy on the inside. She hadn't decided what to say to Ezra. How would he greet her when she marched into his home?

Hogget pulled open the large, windowed door, and flicked on a lightswitch. Annabelle followed him inside. Behind them the door closed and silence surrounded them. Their footsteps echoed while they walked through a marbled entryway and approached two winding staircases on opposite sides of the room. Sconces mounted between stained glass windows bathed the stone steps in golden light. Annabelle rested her hand on one of the thick, marble banisters, awestruck by the staircases. *They must lead to something magnificent.* She wanted to go upstairs but Hogget walked past them, into an area where the light didn't reach. He hummed while he walked, unfazed by the darkness. Annabelle followed, wanting to see Ezra more than the upstairs. Hogget flipped a switch and a light came on. They were in a hallway now.

"What's up the stairs?" Annabelle's voice amplified down the hallway, starling her, and she wished she hadn't spoken.

"That's where Raymond lives. I like to call it the castle room." Hogget didn't hush his voice, so they clearly weren't disturbing anyone. Hogget stopped at the end of the hallway and knocked on a door. He turned and smiled at her and rocked back and forth on his feet while they waited.

Finally, the door opened. "Hey, Hogget," Ezra said kindly. "And Annabelle." When he looked at her his smile became more flirtatious, just a slight rise of the lips and an intense look with his eyes. Annabelle blushed. At the same time, she relaxed; he was happy to see her. "Please come in," he added and opened the door wide.

"I gotta go, I was just dropping her off. I have pie waiting for me at home!" Hogget said gleefully and ran back down the hallway.

Ezra shook his head, laughing at Hogget, and motioned for Annabelle to enter. "It's good to see you," he said and closed the door behind them.

"It's good to see you too." She put her arms around him. They kissed, and Annabelle felt all was right with the world. She had just kissed him this morning but it felt like weeks, making this kiss new and exciting, like lovers reunited.

"So this is your place," she said, turning around to take a look, happy he didn't have a chance to tidy up which gave her a chance to see him in the raw. The long and narrow room had a small bed at the far end, covered with a jumble of blankets and pillows. She liked that he didn't make his bed, for truthfully, she didn't make hers either.

The wall on the left contained floor-to-ceiling bookshelves filled with books. Had he read all these books? It wasn't possible. Annabelle walked along the bookshelves, marveling at them.

Thick burgundy curtains lined the other wall, did that mean they concealed a whole wall of windows? In front of the curtains were piles of unidentifiable lumps and plastic parts. Silver hunks of metal covered the surface of a workbench. Old electronics, she guessed. Papers covered a desk next to the workbench. The stone floor had three large, area rugs which gave the room some warmth. As disorganized as the room looked, everything seemed to be grouped with similar products, making her think Ezra had some order to it.

"So what brings you here?" Ezra asked.

Now it was Annabelle's turn to give him a flirtatious look. "To see you, of course," she said. He raised his eyebrows and pulled her back to him. They kissed again and she savored the closeness.

"What's all this stuff?" Annabelle asked when they pulled away. Seeing his room helped her to get to know him a little better and she enjoyed piecing together the Ezra puzzle. She walked over to the metal things.

"Old computer parts," he said. "My latest project."

"What are you doing with them?" She reached out to touch one, then pulled her hand away, not sure if she should.

"I'm trying to make a computer." He sat next to the workbench and shuffled through the parts.

"Will you be able to?" Annabelle sat next to him.

"I sure hope so. I've been able to collect lots of different parts. So many pieces are rusted or broken, but I'm hoping that I can combine the good pieces together."

Annabelle picked up a piece. It was small, oval, smooth, and fit perfectly in her hand. She turned it over, studying it, fascinated. "What are you hoping to find?" she asked.

"A piece of history," Ezra said. "Just think how groundbreaking it would be if I could access an old hard drive. Who knows what might be on it?"

Annabelle didn't know what a hard drive was. Yet, his musings sucked her in. "Let me know when you get it to work. I'd love to see it," she said.

"Nah, it's probably a fool's errand. I'll keep trying, but who knows?" He stood and brushed rust off his pants.

"So is this what you've been working on all evening?" Annabelle asked.

"Oh, no, I've been catching up with Raymond mostly, going over stuff." He walked to the desk and opened a small cooler. "Do you want something to drink?" He grabbed a water bottle.

"No thank you." Annabelle stood up and pulled one of the curtains back to peek outside. She couldn't see anything in the darkness. She turned back to Ezra. "What's the weather like here?"

"Lots of rain."

Annabelle nodded. "We don't get much rain in the Colony."

Ezra took a drink of water and didn't say anything. Annabelle didn't want to talk about the weather, she really wanted to ask about Poppy.

"What's your job here?" she asked instead. Why did their conversation suddenly feel formal? As if they were strangers meeting for the first time. How could she get them back to the comfort and excitement of when she first arrived?

"I don't know, advisor? Right-hand man?" Ezra shrugged his shoulders. "Second-in-command?" He took another drink and Annabelle couldn't tell if he was kidding or not.

"So does that mean you are next in line for leadership?" Annabelle didn't really want to say *when Raymond dies.*

"Raymond would never admit that someone else would take over someday." Ezra sat at the foot of the bed and rested his arms on his knees, his water bottle dangling between his legs. "Sometimes it feels like I am running this place though." He rubbed his face and yawned.

Annabelle also yawned and sat in the chair at the desk. That one yawn made her realize her exhaustion. It'd been a long day.

"So Poppy wouldn't take over?" Annabelle studied Ezra carefully at the mention of Poppy's name.

"I don't think so," he said, pressing his lips together for a second before going on, "he hasn't ever said she wouldn't, but we all kind of just know. That's probably why he's hoping for a son so bad, so he'll have a male heir." Ezra shook his head. "Poor Poppy," he said.

As much as she wanted to suppress jealousy, she couldn't help it. She agreed with the sentiment of what he said. But she didn't like hearing him say something sympathetic about a girl that things were "complicated" with.

"Is there something going on between you two?" She winced, hating how insecure she sounded, like a possessive girlfriend.

Ezra raised one eyebrow. "Poppy and me?" He let out a laugh. "God no, she was like twelve when I met her. She'll always seem like a little sister to me."

"Oh." Now Annabelle felt even more foolish. So what was Hazel talking about when she said that it was complicated? She looked at Ezra for clues, but he just yawned again. She stood. He clearly needed to get some sleep, and honestly she did too. She wasn't thinking clearly. This conversation probably would be better in the morning.

"I think we both need to get some sleep. Do you mind helping me find my way out of here?" she asked.

"Oh yeah, of course." Ezra stood and walked to the door. "How about I walk you home?" he said with a half grin. She felt a little disappointed that he didn't try to make her stay, but his joking tone made her feel better. He would walk her home like they were teenagers—it was a cute sentiment.

When they reached outside, Annabelle looked up at the stars. She couldn't help but remember that just last night she'd been alone with Ezra, under those same stars, the only two people in the universe. Now he walked alongside her, saying nothing, not even holding her hand.

"So when are you going to take me downtown?" she asked when they entered The Quad.

"Soon, I promise."

"Do you think we could go tomorrow?" She hated being so close to downtown and having to wait to see it. That's what she'd been waiting to see, the Space Needle, tall buildings, all of it. She *needed* to see it and sketch it. Also, if she got him alone she could tear those walls down some more.

"I can't tomorrow," he said. When she didn't answer he added: "I promise soon, but with Rose about to have her baby Raymond's a mess right now. And he's upset with me that I came back a day later than everyone else."

They arrived at Annabelle's building and she turned to face him. "Okay, soon then," she said. She hoped they would part with a kiss and waited for him to make a move.

"Soon," he said and lifted her hand and kissed it. "I promise."

Annabelle didn't want to leave him but when he released her hand she turned and climbed the steps.

By the time she got to her room, she wasn't satisfied with *soon*. She thought about her first meeting with Tully, which seemed like a lifetime ago, in the graveyard. When he'd said the word Seattle, it had stuck in the back of her mind like a bee. The closer to the city she got, the louder the bee buzzed, and it wouldn't stop until she saw the city and let it free. She hadn't come this far just to sit around and wait. Before falling into bed, she resolved that she would go tomorrow, with or without Ezra.

Chapter Twenty-Seven
Harold

They pulled their canoes onto the shore. "You guys are really going to climb to the top?" Annabelle asked, while they stared up at the Space Needle. It was far higher than Harold had anticipated, which was a good thing, he reminded himself. Still, the sight of it made his heart pound and his stomach churn. He was glad Annabelle didn't want to climb with them though. When she'd first approached them that morning saying she wanted to tag along, he feared he couldn't go through with it if she were there.

"Yeah, it'll be the best way to see the city," he said, trying to sound adventurous. He didn't want Annabelle to figure out his true intentions. "Besides I think it will be therapeutic for me, I've really needed to do something like this to get my mind off things, you know?" he added.

Annabelle furrowed her eyebrows and looked down. "Of course," she said. Harold swallowed. That was easy, no more obstacles to stop him now.

"Well, I'll leave you boys to it then. I should just stay away from the streets closest to the Sound, right?" Annabelle said.

"Yes, that's where the buildings are the most unstable," Wataru answered. "Stay further east," he pointed to his left, "on the roadways that are overgrown and you should be fine. And if you hear any loud creaking, it's probably time to head back. Sometimes, the buildings give us a little warning that they're going to fall."

"What does it sound like?" she asked.

"Trust me, you'll know."

"Okay," Annabelle said, "I'll meet you guys back here in a few hours then." She returned to her canoe and waved before rowing toward downtown.

"Shall we?" Wataru asked. "It's still a bit of a walk to the base from here."

"Yeah, let's go." As they walked, the pain of emptiness spread through his body and only the idea of being with Clara again brought him comfort. He ached for her. His life was nothing without her. How could he possibly go on? This was the right thing to do.

Once they reached the Space Needle it looked even higher. Rubble surrounded the base, making the tower appear to grow straight from rock instead of the bare ground. The top looked like a saucer resting on three outer legs that descended in an hourglass shape with one straight leg down the center.

"You've really climbed it?" Harold asked, it didn't look as sturdy as Wataru had made it sound before.

299

"Yes, many times," Wataru replied. "It'll give you the thrill of your life." He smiled and brushed his hand through his hair while glancing up at the top. "And once we get to the staircase, you'll see how stable it feels. When it was functioning, people used to take elevators up. The stairs were only for emergency use."

Harold followed Wataru, scrambling up the rubble surrounding the base of the Space Needle. At the top, they walked into the middle of the structure where the center leg rose up. Harold now saw the stairs which zigzagged around the center leg. Only concrete beams making an X-pattern along the stairwell separated the stairs from the outside world. When they entered the stairway, a set of stairs also went down into the rubble.

"You ready?" Wataru asked. Harold looked up the stairs. He had never seen so many in his lifetime. Clara would have considered the sharp angles artistic and beautiful. She probably wouldn't have wanted to climb the stairs but would've been fascinated by them. Once again the sadness enveloped him. He felt a deep, throbbing pain. He needed relief and there was only one way to get it.

"Yes, let's do it," he said flatly then flashed a forced smile at Wataru, hoping to shield his true intentions.

Wataru leapt forward onto the first step. "Yeah! Okay, follow me."

Harold followed, grateful he couldn't see Wataru's smiling face. He couldn't bear being around someone so full of life, when his was so empty.

Your ticket back to Clara is up there, he reminded himself. He took a breath and entered the stairwell. The concrete stairs still had a handrail near the inside wall, and he grabbed on tight. The stairs did feel stable but what if the whole tower fell down? He took slow, careful steps. So what if it fell, what did that matter? Then he realized it did matter, he had to make it to the top to ensure the job was done.

Wataru waited for him a few flights up. "Trust me, I wouldn't go if it wasn't safe," he shouted down to Harold.

Harold thought about Wataru's family. He thought about the looks of affection he saw between him and his wife. He saw the awe in his eyes as he watched his daughter play. He remembered Wataru placing a loving arm around his wife's shoulder and pulling her to him for a kiss. Again, Wataru's happiness stabbed at Harold's heart. But he knew it was true—Wataru would never do anything that could take him from his family. Strange that his insisting their lives weren't in danger motivated Harold to go forward.

Without saying anything, he climbed the stairs. After a couple of flights, he found a rhythm and the world was silent except for the thump of shoes on stairs. The monotony of the climb provided a break from his pain by focusing on the automatic movement of going up.

Every step up was one step closer to Clara. As they climbed higher, he started to see her face. Her eyes were bright and she smiled at him. She reached her hand down to him. Each time he took another step up, he felt her hand, pulling him up to her. "I'm coming, Clara," he whispered, and started to feel a burden lift off his shoulders.

"You okay, man?" Wataru asked. Harold hadn't realized he'd caught up to Wataru already, who glanced at him with concern. Harold quickly wiped tears from his face and focused on Wataru instead of on his fantasy.

"Yeah, I guess the wind is irritating my eyes, or something," he said. Wataru narrowed his eyes and studied Harold for a moment before turning and ascending again.

"Okay, but seriously, let me know if you want to turn back," Wataru said.

Harold followed but couldn't conjure Clara's face again. He wanted to scream her name, make her come back. He looked around for her but of course, she couldn't be found. The metal beams lining the stairwell let a lot of light in as well as a view of how far up they were already. The vertigo made his stomach and lungs feel light and full of air. He let a breath out, trying to shake the feeling, but it only made the sensation worse.

"Harold, don't look down! Not until we're at the top," Wataru shouted. Harold looked up and saw they were almost there. He also realized he had stopped. He focused carefully on taking a step without looking down. His legs felt wobbly and he gripped the handrail harder. He had to make it to the top, where he would have his opportunity to join Clara.

Harold climbed a couple more flights and Wataru reached a hand down to help pull him into a circular room. "We made it," Wataru said. "Now for the reward, come check out the view." He walked across the room.

They must have been on the first level of the saucer because the stairs continued up. He didn't need to go to the top—he was ready for this to be over. The concrete room was empty, whatever

302

had been here in the Space Needle's previous life must have all blown out long ago. Strong winds whipped around them, like they were inside a large fan, and Harold walked with extra force to push his way through. It didn't seem to bother Wataru who had already reached the outside. Harold followed him through a door frame. A mostly intact fence surrounded the perimeter, cluttered with remnants of old furniture and other unidentifiable things. A quick glance around and Harold saw many holes in the fence, a perfect opening for someone to slip right through. Wataru stood behind the fence marveling at the view and instead of joining him Harold turned toward an opening that beckoned him. He walked, feeling weightless, preparing himself to jump. His heart felt light in his chest. He was only seconds away from Clara and nothing had ever felt so right in his life.

***

Annabelle

Annabelle felt like she was on a different planet. She floated down swampy streets and the salty air clung to her skin like an extra layer of clothing. She had imagined that the ruins of an old city would be dark and dreary, rusty and crumbling, but not Seattle. Seattle teemed with life. Vines climbed up the skyscrapers, covering them in blankets of leaves, giving the buildings a beautiful second life. Now the buildings soared, as if their sole purpose was to nurture the new wildlife.

Reeds grew from the murky water and lily pads floated on top. Ahead in the water she thought she saw movement and stopped rowing. She stared at the spot for a few seconds, waiting for it to settle. Finally, she saw a school of fish swimming down the canal and was awestruck. She trained her eyes to look for movement and saw a frog leap from one log to another. Annabelle gasped with delight. A swimming turtle pulled itself from the water and onto a building's ledge. A flock of birds swooped down the city street, squawking while they made their flight overhead.

Tears of joy and astonishment fell down Annabelle's cheeks. Animals—wildlife, existed! The animals' graceful movements looked like a choreographed ballet. She'd never witnessed a more beautiful scene. Hogget had said wildlife thrived in the oceans, so the increase in fish must have helped support animals who lived in a close proximity to the water.

Annabelle closed her eyes, she wanted to hear what a living habitat sounded like. The hum of life rewarded her. Interrupting the hum every second or so she heard the croak of a frog, a fish jumping or a bird singing. Annabelle wished she could sketch sound.

She rowed slowly, soaking it in. She had to fight the urge to pull out her sketchbook and draw every animal right that second. First she needed to find solid ground, and do some more exploring.

She rowed further east until the canals turned to muddy wetlands. Seattle stretched on for miles—down each street there were skyscrapers as far as she could see. Some tall and sleek buildings rose up with sharp angles while others had columns and arched doorways adorning them. What were they all used for? Again she felt overwhelmed with the desire to illustrate it all. She found a solid place to park her canoe and walked a few blocks up to where trees grew in the streets.

She looked around for a good place to draw. In the woods she couldn't see her surroundings, and she knew that she shouldn't go back to the flooded streets. She hated to admit it, but the vantage point from the Space Needle would have been ideal.

She stopped and studied the building in front of her. It had an older architecture style than the others, and was only about ten stories high, making it more stable than a skyscraper. Like most of the buildings, the windows were gone and nature crawled its way in. It seemed like a perfect building to go inside and explore. Also, if she could make her way up to one of the higher floors, it would be a great place to look out a window and sketch.

Columns reaching three stories high flanked the grand entrance. She climbed the stone steps and entered a lobby that stretched to the back of the building. The ceiling was high: at least three stories up. Decorative columns lined the walls and the second story overlooked the first. She walked around rotting furniture on a mushy floor covered in moss. She headed toward two grand staircases leading to the second floor. However, as she approached the stairs the smell of the place overwhelmed her. It was moldy and dank. Such a contrast to the vibrancy she'd seen outside. Here things died and decayed, while nature slowly ate the building. Should she go back? But where else would she draw? She pressed onward.

She started up the moss-covered steps and held tight to the handrail to avoid slipping. What was this place used for? It didn't seem like an office building, maybe a hotel? That would make sense because of the large lobby area. Perhaps the answer would be on the second floor.

Anxious to get to the top, she quickened her step. Halfway up she lost her footing and slipped back a step. She landed hard, causing the stair to cave under her foot. She screeched while clutching to the handrail to avoid getting stuck. She hopped to the next step and scrambled forward as quickly as she could.

Three steps from the top her foot burst through the stair again, throwing her forward and making her lose her grip on the handrail. Her leg sunk while the whole stair vanished from under her. She grabbed the soggy step above her and held on. *What do I do now?* Worms of panic squirmed inside her, trying to take over her thinking. *No, I must stay calm.* She took a deep breath and pulled herself up. Her arms burned from the effort until she was able to get her knees up on the stair. Then she skipped up the last two steps and stood at the top, breathing hard.

Disbelief replaced her momentary sense of triumph. What had she been thinking? She should have turned around the first time the stairs gave out. Now she was at the top and would have to go back down.

She certainly didn't want to go down yet though, so she may as well look around. Closed doors lined the hallway. She walked further down where more light from the lobby windows brightened the area.

As she went down the hallway, she noticed some of the doors were darker than the others. Was it a different type of wood? Once there was enough light, she approached the first dark door to investigate. It was red. It looked like it had been painted in a hurry, the borders and the bottom half weren't red. Maybe some of the paint had faded over the years? She walked down two more doors, they were both a light oak color and then she came to another red door.

It was dusty red, the color of rust. Even though it was a duller color, it made her think about the red door to the graveyard back at the Colony. Hadn't it been painted as a warning to keep people out? Had that been the same purpose for these doors? Just like the red door from her home these had the same effect on her; she wanted to open it and see inside.

She turned the doorknob and pushed the door open, surprised that it wasn't locked. The plant growth sprouting from the carpet forced her to inch the door open. Before she took a step in, she saw movement and heard a flapping noise. She jumped back, startled. Her eyes hadn't adjusted to the brightness in the room from the open windows, so she didn't see clearly what had made the noise. She stood in the hallway, her heart pounding. Was she scared or excited? She took a deep breath, and stepped back in the room once it was quiet again.

Yep, hotel. Lumpy blankets and pillows covered two beds. Along the opposite wall was a table with a TV on top. The shell of a decaying couch, covered in blanket remnants, sat under the window.

She took a step toward the window and stopped when she heard the flapping noise again. She listened. Yes, there was something in here with her. She tried to stay as quiet as possible in order to identify it, but the quieter she tried to be the louder her heart pounded.

Then she heard a soft chirping noise and her eyes immediately traveled toward the sound.

"Aw," she gushed, noticing a bird's nest in the lamp near the window. In the nest were three baby birds, calling for their mother. She felt her insides melt with affection. "Sweet baby birds," she said and walked over to the lamp. She must have startled the mother when she first came in. As much as she wanted to reach up and hold one of the babies, she resisted the urge and sat on the bed instead. Would it be cruel to sketch them real quick if it made the mother stay away?

The bed, however, was uncomfortable. She had sat on something hard. She stood and tried to push away whatever the blanket concealed, but it didn't move easily. She stared at the bed. What was under the blanket that made it so bumpy? *Don't check*, a small, logical part of her whispered, probably the voice of Margaret. But Margaret wasn't here. She pulled back the blankets.

She screamed and stumbled backward out of the room. Three skulls stared at her, grinning from ear to ear. She couldn't stop her eyes from making one last assessment of the room before she slammed the door shut. It was so obvious now, all the blankets covered skeletons. How many were in there? Seven? Eight?

She ran further down the hallway. She wanted nothing more than to get out of this hotel and as fast as possible. Luckily there was a simple flight of stairs at this end. She jumped down them two at a time. Then she ran to the entrance and out the door and continued to run a few more blocks before stopping.

She turned around and faced the building, hands on her knees. While trying to calm her breath, a thought struck her. Were there skeletons in the rooms with the doors that weren't painted red? She doubted it. People must have painted the doors red because of the skeletons. But why? Were people put in there before they died, or after?

If these people had died during the nuclear winter, why were the hotel rooms used for quarantine? How would death by nuclear winter look? Acid rain, radiation poisoning, starvation, hypothermia, desperation. How did quarantine fit into that?

Had anything they taught her in the Colony been true at all? What was their purpose for lying about all this? Why couldn't they teach that animals existed, that radiation poisoning wasn't a threat and that there were other *people* alive? She ground her teeth, frustrated with the supposed lies again. It couldn't all be ignorance! How much did they really know?

She turned around and headed back to her canoe. She felt defeated. She'd come to the city to learn some secrets, and she'd sure found some. They just weren't the kind that she'd hoped for. She wished she hadn't gone inside the building, now everywhere she looked all she could see were the eye sockets of those skulls, staring at her. She imagined each building full of them, every room, every floor, crammed full with skull after skull. A city rotting with death and decay. Even the greenery around her looked more sinister, like a parasite thriving off the dead's remains.

She wanted nothing more than to get back to the safety of the campus. Back to the safety of Ezra's arms. She didn't know where the two of them stood, but was sure that he was interested in her. Maybe that was enough for now. Maybe he just needed to take things slow. That was okay with her. She would wait for him. He was worth it. She just hoped that she could curl up in his lap and listen to him talk about his computers or trains or anything to take her mind off what she'd just seen. Maybe she would even have the guts to find out some more truth.

By the time she got into her canoe, she felt a little better. She felt kind of silly, actually. How could she expect a city to die without anyone still in it? Of course there had to be people somewhere in the end. Not expecting to see death was foolish. She knew better now, next time she wouldn't go into any buildings, at least not without being prepared mentally.

As she rowed, she continued to regain her composure. The city didn't allure her the way it had before, but she started enjoying herself a little again. She spotted a group of turtles and stopped to watch them.

A loud boom interrupted the peaceful scene. The turtles dove underwater while the thunderous sound echoed down a city street. It was the warning. One of the buildings was about to collapse.

She paddled fast. The sound seemed to come from far away, but was hard to localize. She swallowed and willed the boat to go faster. How far was it to Lake Union? How far into the city had she come? An eerie silence now blanketed the city—interrupted only by the sound of her frantic paddling. All the animals had taken cover, and she was far away from safety. She panted and pushed forward, ignoring the pain in her arms.

She rounded a corner and saw the Space Needle in the distance. It looked small, she had a long way to go.

Chapter Twenty-Eight
Harold

Harold glided toward the opening, feeling weightless. Wouldn't that make the jump even easier? He would just skate right out—it could even be graceful. He got to the edge and the wind clawed at his face, made his eyes water. He blinked, clearing his vision and looked down. He blinked again, trying to comprehend the scene before him. He'd never seen anything like it in his whole life.

The world spread out before him. Vine-covered skyscrapers rose proudly from the water, refusing to be washed out to sea. The Puget Sound glistened sapphire blue under the warm spring sky. Despite all the wind around Harold, the world below seemed incredibly silent and peaceful, like a city preserved in a snow globe. Mother Nature made the city green and the water made it sparkle. Seattle truly was the Emerald City; strong, beautiful, and timeless.

Outside the city, snow-capped mountains surrounded wilderness, and beyond the mountains lay the rest of the world.

What lived past those mountains? How far did the world go? How many people lived there?

The ruins dredged up images of an empire of the past. How had those people lived in their skyscraper jungle? They surely saw the same beauty when they stood at this vantage point. Now they were all gone, steel was the only evidence of their existence. Mankind has always been destined to do amazing things, he realized. *We will rise again.*

He couldn't pull his eyes away; it was like seeing a sunset for the first time. He couldn't leave the world, not when he was only beginning to discover it. Not when the Colony forced his people to live a lie. He sat on the ledge and dangled his feet over the side.

He fixed his eyes on the largest mountain in the distance. Its snowcapped top had a golden glow from the sunlight, the same color as Clara's hair. He stared and saw Clara's face, etched in the mountainside. She smiled and held her arm out, but instead of reaching out to take his, she waved.

"Goodbye Clara," Harold whispered while silent tears fell down his cheeks. He closed his eyes and tipped his head back, embracing a moment of clarity—he knew what he had to do. Not for himself but for Clara. She would have wanted him to discover the world, to uncover all the truths the Colony had hidden from them. He couldn't give up now, not when it was at his fingertips, no matter how much he ached for Clara's loving touch. She had been leading him here all along, but it wasn't so he would jump—it was so he would live.

"The climb sure is worth it, huh?" Wataru asked and sat next to him. "And you're really going for it; this is gutsy, man. I've never sat on the edge like this." He swung his legs back and forth. "But I'll admit it does make it more intense."

Harold turned to Wataru. So much had changed for Harold that he felt like a different person. "Thank you, I really needed this," he said. Should he tell him that it saved his life?

"No problem, I always love finding an excuse to come up here," Wataru said.

"I can see why." He turned back toward the view, overwhelmed with gratitude. Wataru had just saved his life. How could he ever repay him? He took a deep breath, trying to keep his composure. "Where are you from?" he asked, motioning at the view.

"You can't see it from here, unfortunately," Wataru said. "I was born and raised in Hawaii, and then lived my teen years in San Francisco."

"Hawaii?" People lived as far away as Hawaii? He felt foolish that he didn't know this, and he had the Colony to thank for that.

"Yep. True paradise." Wataru leaned back. "I hope someday I can return, with Lily and Hanako of course."

Harold now hoped he could go there someday too. "Why did you leave?"

"When my grandfather needed more medical support we moved to San Fran. I left there to explore north. I guess I inherited the exploring gene from my parents who were brave enough to come over from Japan."

"From Japan to Hawaii and then San Francisco? How did they do it?"

Wataru laughed. "My parents restored an old sail boat and took a crew with them from Japan. I had the pleasure of riding on it to San Fran, although to be honest, it's not something I'd recommend."

"How did your parents know there would be people in Hawaii?"

"They didn't," Wataru said. "They were island hopping and discovered a small clan of settlers living there who had also come by boat."

"Incredible," Harold said. "I didn't realize there were so many people left."

"I imagine it must be hard to believe. You guys didn't even know anyone existed outside of your colony, right?" Harold looked down, embarrassed. "I've never been to Japan," Wataru continued, "but I'd like to. I guess things were pretty bad when my parents left. There's no way to communicate with anyone over there, so we have no idea how things are now. I'd love to be able to find out if things have improved and to see if I could help in any way."

Harold admired Wataru's big plans. No one in the Colony would ever have been able to dream so big. The Colony forced everyone to live in a small, contained world, full of deceit. In fact, wasn't it the Colony's lies that led to Clara's death? The word brainwashing bounced around the back of his mind when he thought about Thomas's willingness to do the Colony's bidding. But Harold had been that loyal as well. Would he have pulled the gun out on Hogget if Thomas hadn't first?

Why hadn't Tully said, "There may be others out there. We don't know if they can be trusted, so be careful, but learn about them, learn from them…"? The Colony must have known there were others. Why would they risk sending a team out that might discover other people? None of it made any sense. He was digging through a pile of mud, looking for answers that would never be clear. The one diamond that he found, however, the one piece of information that he felt so strongly about, and saw so clearly now was that the Colony was responsible for Clara's death.

"I'd like to go with you someday," he said finally. He didn't care if it was Hawaii or Japan or San Francisco. One thing he knew for sure was that he didn't ever want to go back to the Colony.

"Sure thing," Wataru patted him on the shoulder. Harold made his first genuine smile since Clara had died.

Before Harold could respond a loud rumble filled the space around them. He and Wataru looked at each other, eyes wide. "A building?" Harold asked.

"Yep." Wataru stood. He walked around, studying the city. "I wonder where Annabelle is."

"Could she be in danger?" Harold got up too and scanned the streets for her canoe.

"Absolutely."

They circled the Space Needle looking for her, but it was difficult to see detail from high up. He examined the lake, hoping she'd already left the city, and headed toward the bank where they'd last seen her.

"There," he said pointing at a boat in the lake. But as soon as he said it, he realized it wasn't Annabelle. The boat was going the wrong way, *toward* downtown.

Wataru joined his vantage point to see. "What the?"

"Who is it?" Harold asked, squinting his eyes.

"I think it's Ezra. Why's he going so fast?"

Harold watched the boat as it arrived at the edge of downtown.

"I don't know, for Annabelle?" Harold wasn't sure if they were an item, but it wouldn't surprise him.

"Annabelle?" Wataru asked. "Well whatever the reason, I think we'd better stop him."

"Agreed," Harold said and the two men turned to descend.

They ran down the stairs as fast as they could. They scrambled down the rubble at the bottom and jogged to their canoes. A few seconds later, they pushed off into the water.

The two men worked well in unison and rowed swiftly downtown without having to communicate much. Ezra's boat was long gone, however. How were they even going to know where to go?

"Annabelle!" Wataru shouted, when a boat came around the corner. She rowed toward them, smiling and waving. A few minutes later they reached each other.

"I'm okay, see?" she said, holding her arms out.

"Did you see Ezra?" Wataru asked.

"No. What are you talking about?"

"We saw him race through here about fifteen minutes ago," Wataru said.

"Why?"

"We don't know." Wataru raised his eyebrows. "Was he looking for you?"

"I don't know. I don't think so...Well, maybe?"

Another noise boomed in the distance, interrupting their conversation.

"Come on, hurry!" Annabelle started to turn her canoe around.

"Annabelle, get in our canoe, and we'll leave yours on the shore. It'll be faster if we take one," Harold instructed. Wataru nodded, and Annabelle quickly rowed to the nearest bank. After getting out, she stashed her sketchbook in the canoe.

After getting in the canoe, the three rowed as rapidly as they could. Still unable to tell which building had made the noise, they headed south along the street closest to the Puget Sound.

They zoomed down several blocks and didn't see Ezra. Where could he be? How much time did they have?

"Are we certain the building is going to fall?" he asked Wataru.

"Based on the last warning sound, I'd say yes," Wataru answered and they rowed faster.

"Where is he?" Annabelle said after they went another block. "Ezra!" she shouted. The other two joined her.

"Ezra! Ezra!"

Nothing responded aside from some birds who took flight. The street seemed quiet. He only heard the oars hitting the water.

"Ezra!"

But instead of Ezra replying, the ground began to shake. A rumbling noise came from a building in the distance, about ten blocks away. Dust shot out of the top as the building started to collapse.

Instead of tipping over it fell straight down, into itself. They gaped, frozen in place, while it crumbled. Within seconds only clouds of dust remained. The water sizzled for a moment before waves, created from the collapse, raced toward them, carrying large chunks of debris and smoke.

***

Annabelle

They pushed onward, despite the danger they faced. Annabelle leaned forward and rowed with all her might. They needed to get to Ezra, faster now than ever. The waves hammered them, tossing the canoe in the air while they struggled to hold on.

"Row left!" Wataru screamed. A metal chunk the size of a table rushed past. Up ahead a scrap metal wall surged toward them.

"Ezra!" she screamed as a wave crashed next to the boat, soaking them.

Annabelle's wet hair blocked her view and she pushed it to the side just in time to see a metal beam slam into them, cracking the side of the canoe. She lurched right and almost fell overboard. Wataru and Harold shifted their weight to balance the boat. They kept rowing while water gushed through the crack in the canoe.

"Row toward the buildings," Wataru pointed to their right. "It looks like we can pull ourselves into one of those windows." They rowed toward a balcony while more water poured in their boat.

Just before reaching the balcony, something large and rectangular hit them. The boat broke apart, and Annabelle found herself in the water, in the midst of debris. She kicked frantically, dodging everything while looking around for the others. Wataru's head appeared, near the balcony, and behind him Harold emerged. Wataru swam to the balcony first and grabbed the rail, then grabbed Harold's hand. Harold climbed over the rail and Wataru stayed holding the rail, and reached out to Annabelle.

Seeing them gave Annabelle a surge of energy, and she swam harder, making it to the balcony. Wataru grabbed her hand and pulled her to the rail. From the balcony, Harold helped her to stand on the ledge and then she climbed over the rail. Wataru followed.

"Let's see if there's rope or anything useful," Wataru said and the men ran inside. Annabelle stayed outside, watching for Ezra. Her heart raced frantically in her chest. What was he doing down here? Had he really come after her?

"Any sign of him?" Harold shouted from inside. She wasn't sure if they'd found anything useful in there, but she didn't dare take her eyes off the water.

"No," she said, unsure if they heard her. Just then she saw something brown in the distance, standing out next to all the gray debris. She squinted and a second later she could tell it was his boat. "Wait, I see him!"

"Ezra!" she shouted again, relieved he was still in the boat. He wasn't looking at her though, navigating the obstacles around him instead. He surged forward, carried by the waves.

"He's coming fast, what are we going to do?" She waved her arms above her head. "Ezra!" She thought she saw him wave back.

"Ezra?" He waved his oar in the air at her. He had heard her! "Guys, he sees us, he's coming!"

Waving distracted Ezra and he didn't see a pillar floating in the water that quickly approached him from the left.

"Look out!" Annabelle screamed just as it collided with the side of his canoe and capsized him. "Harold, he went under!"

"Where?" Harold asked, by her side now. She pointed to where the boat floated upside down about thirty feet away. Ezra still hadn't come above the surface.

"Where is he?" Annabelle shrieked. What if something happened to him? Annabelle panted with fear as the pressure of needing to save Ezra overwhelmed her. "What are we going to do?" she managed to say between breaths.

Wataru joined them now. "Here, hold this," he said and handed her some fabric. It was the end of a rope made from bedsheets and blankets tied together. Wataru jumped over the balcony with the bedsheet rope tied around his waist. Annabelle tied the other end around her waist, while Harold fed the rope to Wataru.

Ezra's capsized boat sailed past them. How long had Ezra been under? What if he'd hit his head on something? Wataru dove under, and came up with nothing.

"Come on, come on," Annabelle whispered urgently. Her breath had calmed a little, having the purpose of holding the rope made her feel less helpless, however, her stomach dropped each time Wataru came up empty handed.

"Here!" Wataru shouted and went down. A second later he came up, holding Ezra's body, but then sunk back under again.

"Pull the rope!" Harold said, and they pulled. Wataru's head resurfaced, and he held Ezra tight. It seemed to take forever to get them back to the balcony. Was Ezra breathing?

Finally, Wataru grabbed the balcony. Harold and Annabelle took Ezra's arms and pulled him over the rail onto the ground. His face looked waxy, his eyes were closed. She didn't think he was breathing.

Wataru jumped over the rail. She reached down to feel for a pulse, Ezra's hand was cold. "Oh, God," she said. This couldn't be happening.

Harold blew into Ezra's mouth and then started chest compressions. He pushed fast and hard, counting under his breath.

Annabelle squeezed Ezra's hand. *Please live*, she willed. She closed her eyes. *Please live*. She needed to see Ezra open his eyes, she needed to look into them and see the strong, intelligent, determined soul that was Ezra. He had such big plans for this world, plans to make it a better place for all. Out of anyone who should survive, it was him. If she lost him, she would never find his equal—he was the man for her. If he survived, she would follow him to the ends of the Earth and never leave his side. "Please live," she begged.

Ezra coughed and she opened her eyes. He rolled onto his side, coughing up water.

"Ezra?" Wataru patted him on the back gently, "Can you hear me?"

"Where's Annabelle?" Ezra said. His voice was hoarse and weak, but the words were coherent. A rush of relief spread through Annabelle.

"I'm here," she said and kneeled by his side. He gave her a weak smile.

"Let's get him inside," Harold said. Water lapped over the side of the balcony now.

"Do you think you can move?" Annabelle asked Ezra. He nodded and tried to sit up. The three of them helped him hobble inside and lay him on a bed. Annabelle glanced around the room and was relieved there were no skeletons. Vines covered the couch and dresser, weaving around picture frames and jewelry boxes making the room feel like a jungle treehouse.

She sat down on the bed next to Ezra and brushed hair away from his forehead. She wanted to question him, criticize him for coming. But she was too grateful that he was alive. "How are you feeling?" she asked instead.

He blinked a couple of times. "My throat and lungs burn. Do we have any water?" He said.

Annabelle looked at Harold and Wataru, knowing that they probably didn't have any. "Sorry." She kissed him on the forehead. "We will soon, just try to relax."

"What are you guys doing here anyway?" He sat up.

"What are we doing here? Rescuing you, apparently," Wataru said with a laugh.

"We saw you rowing toward downtown so we came after you," Harold added.

"Oh," Ezra said and furrowed his brow.

"What are we going to do now?" Harold asked, looking back outside. "We're stranded."

Wataru walked to the balcony. "The force from the building collapse caused the waves, but it looks like it's settling now." He walked back into the room. "I bet if we wait a little while Harold and I could swim to Annabelle's boat and then go back for help."

"How long do you think it'll take? Is there a risk that another building might collapse?" Harold said. His voice had leadership back in it. In fact, during the whole rescue he'd seemed more like himself again. Warmth flooded through Annabelle and she smiled hopefully. If they got out of here safely, Harold would be okay.

"There's always a risk of that, but I don't think we have any other options," Wataru said.

Chapter Twenty-Nine
Annabelle

A few minutes after Harold and Wataru swam out of sight, Annabelle retrieved the fabric rope. The hot afternoon sun had already started drying the lightweight clothes she wore, but she wanted a dry blanket for Ezra. She slipped her shoes and socks off, to leave in the sun, then dragged the blanket rope inside. Ezra sat up when she sat next to him on the bed.

"What were you thinking coming downtown by yourself?" Ezra asked.

"What was I thinking? What were you thinking? You were the one who almost got us all killed." She tugged on a knot in the rope to get a blanket free.

"Yeah, because you had come down here," he answered. He clearly wasn't going to take responsibility for what had happened. He also seemed to be recovering just fine. "And what about Harold, why in the world did you let him climb the Space Needle? Didn't it occur to you that he might try and jump off?"

"Oh," Annabelle said. She had completely overlooked that possibility, but now it seemed so obvious. Of course she shouldn't have let Harold climb up there. What if he had jumped? She didn't think she would've been able to live with herself. She set the blanket rope in her lap. "God, I should've realized. I feel terrible. If something would've happened..."

"You weren't thinking about anything but yourself," Ezra said.

"And what about you? I was perfectly safe, you were the crazy one who went right toward the falling building, putting us all at risk."

"No, I wasn't putting you at risk."

"What were you doing then?" Annabelle yanked at the blanket rope again. "Why did you come down here?"

He was quiet now, his face tense and lips pursed. Annabelle finally got a blanket free and handed it to Ezra. He pulled his wet shirt off and wrapped the blanket around himself. "I knew you were going to get into some trouble if you went downtown by yourself."

"Oh, you *knew*, did you?" Annabelle crossed her arms. "And I wasn't by myself, I was with Wataru and Harold."

"Then why did you need two boats? I knew your plan. I knew how bad you wanted to see downtown. I bet you even went into some buildings, didn't you?"

Annabelle hated to admit that he was right. It was time for her to play a little offense instead. "You had your chance to 'escort' me downtown to make sure I didn't get into trouble, but you declined. I wasn't going to sit around and wait any longer."

They sat silently for a while. Why were they fighting? Annabelle wanted nothing more than to take him into her arms and kiss him. She had lost him and now he was okay. She didn't understand where all this anger came from.

"Well, I'm glad you're all right," he said finally, his voice a little softer.

Annabelle couldn't help but laugh. "You're glad that *I'm* all right? You almost died. In fact, I think you did die." She shook her head, not wanting those words to sink all the way in. She put her hands on his face. "I'm glad you're all right too." She gazed into his eyes and saw tenderness there. "I was really scared I'd lost you. I don't ever want to lose you again."

He pulled her toward him and kissed her. It had the same ferociousness as their first kiss, and Annabelle relished it. Not only was she in his arms, but she could feel how alive he was and her heart overflowed with gratitude.

Surrounded by mankind's fallen civilization made her feel like they were the last two souls to survive. Everything faded around her, and all she could see was Ezra. He was here. He was breathing and warm. In that moment he was all that mattered, and she wished it could be just the two of them like this forever.

At some point, they dozed off. Annabelle awoke wondering what time it was. She lay on Ezra's bare chest, which lifted slightly with each unconscious breath. She didn't want to wake him, savoring the moment of closeness with him. Besides, he smelled wonderful. When she breathed in his scent, it reached the back of her mind and lingered there. He smelled like peaches and apricots, drying in the summer; warm, sweet, and musky. No one had ever smelled so good.

He stirred then lifted his head and locked eyes with her, smiling tenderly. "Hey, you," he said.

"Hey."

"Any idea what time it is?" He sat up.

"I was wondering the same thing." She sat up as well. "They should be back soon, right?"

"I think so. I'm starving." Ezra got up and looked out the doorway. "It must be late afternoon by now."

"I'm hungry too," Annabelle said. Even though she'd previously wished they could be alone forever, her hunger and thirst made her want the others to hurry.

They went to the balcony to see if anyone approached. The water had receded about three feet below the balcony. The city street seemed peaceful again, the calm after a storm. Closing her eyes, she heard the soft buzz of life again. However, she wasn't as entranced as the first time she'd seen downtown. The memory of the skeletons overshadowed it.

"Ezra?" She wanted to ask him about it all. She was ready to know the truth, even if it meant confirming the Colony's lies.

"Yeah." He faced her and took her hand.

She bit the inside of her lip before answering. "What killed everyone?"

He lowered his eyebrows. "You were taught it was nuclear war, right?"

"Yeah, followed by nuclear winter. Anyone who survived the war died during the 'dark days,' along with all the animals." She looked back out at the city. "That's what they told us anyway. But I know it isn't right. I saw. . ." Should she admit that she went into a building before? He gave her his full attention and squeezed her hand. "Okay, so you were right, I did go into one of the buildings," she gave him a rueful smile.

"I knew it." He shook his head and grinned.

"And, well, I saw something that didn't seem to add up."

"What did you see?" he asked.

"There were these doors painted red, and I wanted to see what was inside—"

"You wanted to see what was behind a red door?"

"Now, I wish I hadn't, but. . ." she wrinkled her nose at the memory, "there were a bunch of skeletons in there, which made me think of—"

"Quarantine," he said.

"Yeah."

He nodded. "Don't get me wrong, there was nuclear war, and I'm sure some areas of the world experienced a nuclear winter. From what I've learned, the end had it all. Over-population, lack of resources, war, famine, to name a few. But the thing that did the human race in, along with most of the land animals, was a killer virus."

"Wow," she said. She looked back at the street. Why did the Colony need to lie about this? For control? To keep everyone scared? Wouldn't a super virus be just as frightening? Was anything she had learned true?

Ezra put his arm around her. "You okay?"

"Yeah, it's just infuriating. To realize that everything you have ever been taught was based on a lie." She pressed her lips together for a second. "I don't understand their motivation." She leaned into him. "But I want to know the truth now, all of it."

He kissed the top of her head. "There's lots of time for that. I'm always learning new things too."

She looked at him and smiled. "So now you'll be my teacher too?"

"Of course." He leaned down and gave her a slow, soft kiss. Ezra: her love, her teacher, her comfort, her guide, her protector. But she wanted him to be more, she wanted to hear him say they had something more. When they got back to the campus would he disappear for days, wrapped up in work? But, she had vowed to take things slow. Maybe for him, what they had was a big commitment.

She gazed into his eyes. "Ezra," she said. "With you, I'm all in."

"All in." He gave her a warm smile. "I like that."

They kissed again and even though he didn't say *he* was all in, Annabelle was okay with that. She had found the man for her, and she didn't care how long she had to wait.

"Ezra!" came a call from the distance.

They ended the kiss and looked down the street. A boat headed toward them about two blocks away. Ezra waved his hands, and a few seconds later the boater waved back.

***

Curtis

"Harold, what happened?" Ernie asked, setting a broom against the wall. Curtis stopped scrubbing the kitchen counter. Harold was wet. His hair had tiny leaves and sticks stuck in it. He stood tall though, a posture Curtis hadn't seen Harold take in a while.

"We went downtown, a building collapsed, we were stranded, and we rescued Ezra. It's a long story. I really just wanted to stop by to let you guys know we need to have a meeting tonight. After Annabelle is back."

"Everyone's okay though?" Calvin asked.

Harold studied the floor for a moment. "Yeah. And Annabelle should be back soon. They sent a boat to pick her and Ezra up."

"Are they alone?" Curtis asked.

"She stayed with him and we went for help. He was in pretty bad shape."

"What happened?" Curtis pressed. Poppy would be interested in these details.

"He came to save Annabelle, I guess. And ended up getting caught up in the waves. He almost drowned." Harold shook his head. "But I think he'll be fine. Listen, it's been a hell of a day. Can we talk later? I really need to change. I just wanted to let you know about the meeting tonight. After dinner, in our guest lounge." He pressed his lips together in a tight line. "And this is a Colony-only meeting, so we can speak openly about everything."

"We'll be there," Ernie said and Calvin nodded.

"Ok, thanks," Harold said and left.

Calvin and Curtis turned back to cleaning the kitchen. "What do you think that was all about?" Calvin said.

"I don't know," Curtis answered. "Is there something going on between Ezra and Annabelle?"

"I think so," Ernie said. "They had that whole night together before arriving here."

"And, it seemed like they were together a lot before that too," Calvin added.

Curtis decided there definitely was something going on between the two of them. Especially if Ezra had gone to save Annabelle. This was the perfect opportunity to tell Poppy what he knew. She would probably be happy to hear the information. He had seen her in the prep kitchen when they came back to clean up.

He rinsed out his rag and grabbed a stack of clean dishes. "I'll put these away," he said and pushed his way through the swinging door that led to the prep room.

Poppy was there. She was hunched over a long counter, rolling out dough. Curtis placed the dishes in a cabinet.

"Poppy?" he said. He stood by the cabinet. Should he walk right up to her?

"Yes?" she answered. She didn't look up from the dough. He approached her so he could speak quieter.

"So, I found out something about Ezra and Annabelle that I thought you might be interested in." He stared at her arms rolling out the dough. Her tank top revealed defined arm muscles. She had always seemed so dainty to him before but now she looked strong, forceful, determined. He liked that.

At the mention of Annabelle's name, she turned toward him. "Do tell." She had a mischievous look in her eyes and a half smile on her lips.

"I guess Ezra went downtown to save her today when a building collapsed."

Poppy narrowed her eyes. "What do you mean 'save her?'"

"I really don't have a lot of details, but that's what I heard," he said. "I guess they've been alone all afternoon."

Poppy took a long, slow breath then turned back to her rolling. "So there is something going on between them, then? He must care about her if he went downtown for her."

"Yeah, I think so," Curtis said, starting to feel weird about the conversation. Why did Poppy want to know about this? Did she scrutinize every relationship? Did her father? Or maybe the more obvious answer was what he didn't want to admit: that she had a thing for Ezra. "Why do you need to know this again?" he asked, staring at her back.

"I told you, my father likes to know these things." She pushed the dough harder, the circle was at least twice as large now.

Not seeing her face gave him courage. "Are you his spy or something?" he asked and then regretted it when she looked at him with glaring eyes.

"Look, all I asked was for you to let me know if you heard anything. And you've done that, so thank you. I'll be sure to ask your brother for information next time." She put her hands on her hips.

Curtis didn't know what to say. Did she already have him figured out? "No you don't have to do that," he fumbled.

"Good," she said and smiled. "You are much more interesting than your brother anyway."

Curtis had never heard those words uttered. Here was a person, a woman, saying he was more interesting than Calvin. He wanted to hug Poppy. Instead, he just stared at her, carving the moment in his memory.

She placed a soft hand on his cheek. "I've got pies to make but keep me posted on anything else you hear, okay?"

"Yeah, of course," he said. She smiled again and turned back to the dough. Curtis left feeling lightheaded. The logical side of him knew she was playing him. But every other ounce in his body didn't care. Her touch sent shivers through him, and her words echoed in his mind, muffling the logical side's arguments. She'd caught him in her web, and he had no interest in escaping.

Chapter Thirty
Curtis

That evening Curtis headed to the meeting and then waited with the others for Annabelle to arrive. The simple room had four mismatched couches situated in a square and a few chairs. Harold paced back and forth, while Curtis, Calvin, and Ernie sat on the couches.

Annabelle hurried in. "Sorry, am I late?" she asked. She looked tired, and her voice sounded scratchy. Ever since she and Ezra had returned, it was pretty obvious they were a couple. They were inseparable all evening and shared intimate glances. Ezra kept his arm protectively around her all through dinner. Curtis wanted to talk to Poppy about it, but she had seen for herself, so what more could he add? Besides, he never saw Poppy alone at dinner, and she went home early. He didn't think he could go there uninvited.

"No problem," Harold said, "I know you've had a long day." He sat on a couch and Annabelle sat next to him.

"Thank you all for coming. This shouldn't take long," Harold started. Harold seemed to be his old self again. He spoke to them tonight as their leader. "I called this meeting for two reasons. First of all, I want to officially declare our mission void and over, which I suppose is probably obvious. And secondly, we need to discuss what we all want to do from here on out. You can do anything, except go back to the Colony. Going back would not only endanger those who have chosen to stay but also endanger all those who live in Seattle. Don't you all agree?"

Curtis couldn't believe what he'd heard. Harold forbade them from going back? And to protect the Seattle people? What about the people in the Colony? He was just going to turn his back on them? And furthermore, if he declared the mission over, that meant Harold wasn't the leader anymore so what gave him the right to dictate what they did?

"Do you think they will send a search party out for us?" Calvin asked.

"I'm not sure, maybe eventually. They aren't expecting us back until fall so they wouldn't be able to send one out until next spring." Harold took a deep breath. "I hate to say it, but it's better that they think we're all dead." Everyone was quiet for a moment. "So what do you all want to do?" Harold finally asked.

"I'd like to stay," Ernie said.

"Me too," Annabelle said.

Calvin didn't say anything at first but then said, "I think I want to stay here too, what about you Harold?"

"I'm not sure. I think I need to see the world. I'll stay here for a while, but I don't think I'll settle here."

"Curtis?" Calvin asked. Why'd they bother asking him his opinion? Didn't they all expect him to follow Calvin?

He couldn't tell them the truth, apparently it wasn't even an option. He was still dead set on going back to the Colony. "What makes you think they're going to just let us settle here?" he said.

"Good point, I guess we can't just assume that we're welcome to stay. Everyone has been very friendly, but we haven't been formally invited," Harold said. "I guess we'll have to make an official request or something."

"I can ask Hazel what the protocol is," Ernie said.

"So we all agree then?" Harold asked. Everyone nodded, including Curtis. He didn't want to give away what he really was thinking. "All right then. Meeting adjourned. Ernie, let me know what Hazel says tomorrow, and we'll go from there. In the meantime, let's all try to be as helpful as possible and start thinking about how you might fit in here."

Everyone retired to their rooms, but Curtis needed fresh air. He wanted to go for a run, the best way to clear his head. He felt dirty from attending a meeting with traitors. He jogged across The Quad and ran full speed through campus, clenching his fists. How could they all turn their backs so quickly on the Colony? How could they forget everything the Colony had done for them? A couple of romances and they were all ready to jump in bed with the enemy? Well, not him, he wasn't giving up on the mission or on the Colony. Everyone here had been duped by these Seattle people. They believed everything they had been told. Couldn't they see that this place maybe wasn't all that they thought it was?

He stopped at the pond to catch his breath. The stars and full moon reflected off the calm surface of the water and the twinkling distracted him for a moment from his frustration.

"Is something bothering you?" someone asked him.

Curtis jumped and whirled to his right, where he found Ovid sitting on a bench.

"Ovid, what are you doing out here?"

Ovid motioned upward, his white hair shimmering in the moonlight. "Star gazing," he said.

Of course he is. Curtis looked at the little man. He saw through the innocent act, and maybe now was his chance to get to the bottom of it.

"What are you doing out here, sprinting around all mad?" Ovid asked.

Curtis grinned. "I'm not angry. You must be mistaken. I was just going for a run." He sat next to Ovid, and leaned all the way back, forcing his body language to look relaxed. He gazed up at the stars. How could he get Ovid to talk?

"When I first came here, I was angry too," Ovid said.

Curtis kept looking up, clenching his jaw. "I bet you were," he said, trying to keep his voice neutral. "I'd still like to hear that story."

The silence of the peaceful night surrounded them for a moment. Curtis watched a shooting star flee across the sky. Was Ovid ever going to speak?

"Curtis, tell me, did you ever go on the Life and Death tour?" he finally said.

"No, I'm not married yet."

"Hmmm. So you've never been in the infant graveyard?"

"Why are you asking me this?" Curtis hated it when people didn't get to the point. At least it seemed like Ovid wanted to talk. He'd flush the truth out of him one way or the other.

Ovid took a long, slow breath. "My baby sister was the first one to be buried there."

He had Curtis's attention now. Why would that lead to his banishment?

"My father believed she was murdered," Ovid added.

Liar. "Why did he think that?" Curtis looked at Ovid now, he wanted to search for proof of his lies, even though it was hard to see his face in the darkness.

Ovid gazed at the moon. "I didn't see the moon until I was 7 years old. Can you imagine that? Or the sun for that matter. I'll never forget the day they opened up the bunkers. The air smelled sweet and light. There was brightness all around, coming from everywhere. It was overwhelming, yet at the same time exhilarating. I ran and ran and ran. So did all the other kids. We just couldn't get enough of the freedom and wide open spaces. Those months were good months. Everyone was happy.

"And we had so much to do! We started building our homes and the biodomes from kits that had been stored in another bunker, waiting all those years to be put together. Everyone was busy, but no one cared. It felt so good to do something different. Something new. And we had big dreams and hopes for the future. The human race had survived!

"My mom was three months pregnant when we went above ground, everyone was excited for the first baby to be born in our new city." Ovid paused. Curtis leaned forward. No one had ever spoken so candidly about this time of the Colony's history to Curtis, and he couldn't help but hang on every word.

"It all changed a few short months later. When my baby sister died. We grieved her, and my mom was a wreck. So was I. But then she became just the first of many." Ovid sighed. "Life went on, but the joy, the sense of hope and freedom was gone. Replaced with fear. You probably don't even notice it because it's been there your whole life. You don't know what it's like to be free from that fear. But I do. I felt it for those few short months. Probably the best months of my life."

Curtis let the story settle around him. Ovid told it well, but he wasn't fooling Curtis. It was full of ingratitude. "I'm sorry about your sister," he said. "I can't imagine how awful that was. But the Colony did what they did to save the human race. If they hadn't intervened, the Colony would've died with your generation. We'd only have something to fear if the Colony wasn't protecting us." Was he explaining this to a five year old? He couldn't believe Ovid's insolence, especially after he had lived through those horrible years of death.

"It's awfully convenient that we needed the Colony's protection."

Curtis ground his teeth. "Are you saying they made the radiation up? We have the radiation detectors, we have our yearly radiation checkups, we know it's real." Curtis had detected radiation many times during missions to Spokane. All this conversation did was further prove Ovid was a liar.

"Maybe. But maybe not," Ovid said.

Curtis couldn't believe what he was hearing. Ovid must be trying to shift the blame of his own banishment onto the Colony. "You still didn't tell me what you did."

"Well, it turned out my father never fully believed the Colony. Before dying, he asked me to look into the circumstances around my sister's death. I broke into the old bunkers, trying to find a secret storage room that my dad said held documents. I returned many times but couldn't find it. Then one day, someone followed me and I was caught. I foolishly thought that if I was honest I would be in less trouble. So I confessed my true intentions. They accused me of conspiracy. Said my ingratitude wasn't welcome, and that if I didn't appreciate what the Colony did for mankind, then I could kindly see myself out. Sounds like their propaganda has stuck with you."

Propaganda! Ovid was the one spewing propaganda. Did he even have any evidence? "But you found nothing." Curtis said.

"No, unfortunately, I was never able to uncover the truth."

Curtis shook his head. This whole story was pointless. The Colony was correct with their assessment of Ovid: he was a conspiracy theorist. Of course they couldn't let him spread his lies through the Colony. It was too dangerous. What if pregnant women started wanting to stay above ground? That wasn't a risk they could take. If anything, Ovid's story just strengthened Curtis's resolve.

Curtis stood. "Thank you for telling me your story, Ovid. I think I'll turn in now," he said.

"It's important to question what you've always been told. It took me years to accept it. But it's hard to deny the evidence when you discover people exist. Clearly, the Colony isn't responsible for saving the human race."

"I'll keep that in mind," Curtis said. "Goodnight." He strolled away, making his arms swing naturally at his sides but inside his heart pounded. Ovid was trying to poison his mind. How many people had Ovid told this conspiracy to? Did everyone in the Seattle Clan think this about the Colony? His muscles tensed while thinking about the misinformation being spread. It wasn't acceptable! Lies were being told and he realized what he had to do. He owed it to the Colony to stamp out this misinformation. It all made sense. He now understood his purpose here. He could still make the Colony proud, and he wouldn't stand for this defamation. He'd find out who believed these rumors. When the time came, he'd take care of it and then report back to the Colony a true hero. A protector of truth.

Curtis would carefully plan his next move. He wouldn't fail this time.

Chapter Thirty-One
Annabelle

As the days faded into weeks, Annabelle grew ever closer to Ezra. They spent every afternoon and evening together. Sometimes they stayed with others, passing time filled with laughter and joy. Sometimes they stayed alone and talked about the world. Ezra's walls of resistance were coming down, and he listened with understanding about her disappointment and anger with the Colony. When they weren't talking, they'd tinker on his projects. Annabelle enjoyed trying to help him build the computer, even though they couldn't ever get it to start.

The moment he had opened his eyes after almost drowning she knew he was the man for her, and every day she spent with him reinforced her resolve. She'd been waiting for him her whole life. Now she rejoiced that she'd never settled in the Colony.

Word spread about her artistic ability and during the day when Ezra was busy helping Raymond, Annabelle found herself drawing for the Seattle Clan. She enjoyed the task, it was a quiet and comfortable way to get to know people, and it allowed her to feel more welcomed into the group.

She continued to grapple with her feelings toward the Colony. Their lies bothered her, and it bothered her that she might never know the full truth about the Colony's intentions or past.

One Saturday morning, Ezra stopped by her room to steal her away for the day. "I have a surprise for you," he said.

Annabelle beamed. She rarely saw him before lunch. "Where are we going? Do I need to bring anything?"

Ezra shook his head and grabbed her hand. "Just bring yourself," he said leading her outside.

He led her through The Quad toward Red Square. A crispness chilled the air that hadn't been there the previous day and the overcast sky blanketed the campus in gray tones. They passed the entrance to his home and went around the side of the building. Ivy covered the whole side of the structure and some of the leaves at the top were starting to change to a vibrant crimson. Ezra dropped her hand and approached the ivy. He then parted the hanging leaves, revealing a door. Annabelle widened her eyes with surprise at the sight of it.

Ezra pushed the door open, then turned back to her. "Come on," he said.

Annabelle took his hand and followed him through the doorway. It took a beat for her eyes to adjust to the darkness, the only light coming from the open door. She could tell instantly this room hadn't been occupied in years. It smelled musty and as things came into view she could only identify heaps of rubble. She slowed down—Ezra wouldn't take her somewhere where there were skeletons, would he? He pulled her forward but looked back at her when he realized she'd slowed.

"It's safe, I promise. Trust me," he said.

Annabelle bit her lip and matched his speed. He led her around piles of broken furniture until they arrived at another door. He opened it and pulled her through.

Ezra left her in the dark doorway and started pulling open curtains, which lined the right wall. Leaf shaped shadows filled the room. Annabelle scanned the row of windows and noticed they were partially blocked by the ivy growing outside. She stepped further into the clean room and gazed up at the left wall where floor to ceiling bookcases towered over her. Ezra approached a long rectangular oak table that sat on top of a green rug. He switched on a light that stood in the middle of the table, bathing the room in warm light.

"Welcome to my library," he said, wearing a satisfied smile.

Annabelle approached the wall of books and let her finger slide across the spines while she walked the length of the room. "I thought your library was in your room," she said.

"It started out that way, but I needed more space, so I started cleaning up this room. This is the collection of all the salvageable books I've found over the years."

Annabelle turned to him now, she could tell how proud he was of the library from his voice, and she loved when he shared his passions with her. "It's marvelous," she said. She looked back at the books, not even sure where she'd start if she wanted to read one. It overwhelmed her.

"You know how you've been saying you want to know where the Colony's lies end and the truth begins?"

Annabelle spun around and faced him. "You found something?" She asked, intrigued. Suddenly, she understood the importance of the trip here, he didn't just want to show off his library; he wanted to help her.

"Maybe." He started pulling books off the shelves and setting them on the table. "I've been scouring the collection for history books, specifically ones that deal with our region. There isn't anything actually detailing the end—no one was around to write that, but I think I found some books that give clues. If we compare our learned history and cross reference it with these books we might have a better idea of the truth."

Pressing fingers to her smiling lips, Annabelle watched while he stacked books on the table. Is this what he'd been so busy doing? She thought he'd been helping Raymond all the time. She felt warmth in her heart when she realized he'd taken the time to get this ready just for her. "This is a lovely surprise," she said.

He stopped pulling books and sat at the table. "Should we get started?"

She sat in the chair next to him, nodding. She loved his determination when he searched for knowledge.

He held up a book called *The Origins of Cascadia*. "I think this will be the most useful book for us."

Annabelle took the book from him and looked at the cover. "We learned about Cascadia in the Colony," she said, feeling good that not everything derived from lies. Still, she hesitated opening the book. Was she ready for confirmation that her reality had been totally built on deception? She felt breathless, frozen on the edge of a great revelation.

"I learned about Cascadia in San Fran also. What did you learn about it—let's compare notes," Ezra said.

Annabelle let out a breath and set the book back on the table, happy to delay the inevitable a little longer. "Well, we learned that after the Second Civil War the United States broke up into five separate countries, and the one in the Pacific Northwest was named Cascadia."

Ezra nodded. "Same. What did you learn happened next?"

Annabelle laughed. "I feel put on the spot all the sudden. I never was very good at history. Let me think though… conflicts intensified around the world, and that eventually led to World War Three, after oil ran out, right?"

"Yeah, that's what I learned as well." Ezra nodded again.

"We were taught that the original leader of the Colony, Cecile Ann Dembowski, set up the bunkers long before World War Three started. All my ancestors were safely thriving underground before the bombs were even dropped. They claim that her early planning saved the human race, which obviously isn't true."

"Interesting," Ezra said.

"But there weren't any bombs dropped on Cascadia, right?" Annabelle asked, glancing at the book again, feeling more ready to open it up.

"I learned that there weren't," Ezra said.

"Well, the Colony had to lie to us about that, I guess. They needed there to be radiation so they could control us with fear."

"So our stories diverge during World War Three; and unfortunately, I don't have any books about it, too close to the end." Ezra started digging through the books. "Let's see what else we can find though."

Annabelle grabbed the *Origins of Cascadia* again, took a deep breath, and opened it to the table of contents. She could still read the text clearly on the browning pages and scanned the chapter titles. Her heart raced thinking about the possibilities of what she might discover. She'd soon learn things no one else knew in the Colony. Now, what information would be the most useful?

She flipped to the chapter titled *Washington*. Would anything about the Colony be mentioned there? She knew it was built on the ruins of three cities that were clustered together, Richland, Kennewick and Pasco. She started reading pages, most of the information was about Western Washington. Interesting, but not what she sought. She flipped forward, scanning for Eastern Washington.

A location started popping up on the pages, one she wasn't familiar with. *Hanford*. The book said Hanford was in Richland, but she'd never heard of it before. The book explained that Hanford was a major driving force of the economy in Richland. She furrowed her eyebrows in confusion and flipped back, trying to figure out what Hanford was. Finally she found the introduction to Hanford and gasped.

Ezra looked up. "What did you find?"

"Listen to this," Annabelle said, reading: "'Established in 1943, Hanford became the site for the Manhattan Project where the first full-scale plutonium production reactor was built.'" She glanced up at Ezra before going on. "It says that the nuclear bomb dropped on Nagasaki in World War Two was made out of plutonium manufactured there. And that later, it expanded to nine nuclear reactors. Ezra, I never learned any of this stuff." She shook her head and turned back to the text, reading again: "'The plutonium production left behind more than fifty million gallons of highly radioactive waste.'" She turned the book to show Ezra a map on the side of the page. She tapped her finger on it. "This is the exact location of the Colony. It was literally built on top of a nuclear waste dump." Coldness trickled down her spine while she processed the new information. "Why would they do that?" she whispered.

Ezra pulled his chair closer to Annabelle to look at the book with her. "Maybe that's why they chose the location?" he offered.

Annabelle's stomach tightened. Would Cecile Ann Dembowski intentionally poison her people? Cecile had always been put up on a pedestal. Everyone called her the savior of the human race. Annabelle suddenly felt sick, not sure if she wanted to learn this after all. Her mind went to the infant's graveyard in the Colony, had all those babies been exposed to radiation on purpose?

"You said the Colony needed radiation in order to control the people," he added. "Looks like this is how she guaranteed there'd be some."

Annabelle sighed. The evidence was pretty damning. She felt another shift take place in her mind. She'd suspected there'd been lies, not just ignorance, and now she had to confront the fact that there could have been nefarious actions. She leaned back in her chair and sighed again.

"What are you thinking?" Ezra said, facing her now.

Annabelle looked at him, her lips pursed. "It's just a lot to take in," she said.

Ezra took the book and set it back on the table. "I'm sorry," he said.

"Oh no, don't be sorry!" Annabelle shook her head. "I'm so grateful you brought me here. I want to know the truth. It's just a little hard to swallow."

"Come here." He pulled her into his lap and wrapped his arms around her. Annabelle instantly felt warmer, and she leaned her head against his chest, savoring the comfort. She could face anything with him by her side. "I'm here for you, let's get through this together," he whispered in her ear.

She shifted so she could face him. "I'd like that," she said. She stared into his eyes, feeling her heart quicken. Who better to help her find the truth than Ezra, who'd spent his life searching for answers? She wanted nothing more than to go through these books with him, making discoveries together. But first she leaned in to kiss him. They'd earned a break.

Ezra let her take the book home that night and she spent most of the night reading it. She hadn't stumbled on anything as revelatory as Hanford, but stayed riveted nonetheless.

The next morning Ezra stopped by again, finding her with her nose still in the book. Annabelle looked up at him, thrilled to see him two mornings in a row. "Another surprise today?" she asked. She'd planned on visiting Hogget's sheep, but wouldn't mind pushing it back another day if Ezra wanted to steal her again.

"I wish," Ezra chuckled. "I just wanted to check in with you, see how you're doing after what we discovered. Find anything else interesting?"

Annabelle dropped the book to her lap. "Nothing like yesterday. But it's all very interesting. It really just makes me think of more questions though. It makes me want to learn more."

Ezra grinned at her. "I know the feeling," he said.

Annabelle laughed. "I guess you're rubbing off on me."

"So you're okay?" he asked.

Annabelle walked over to him and wrapped her arms around his neck. "Yeah, I'm fine. Thanks for checking on me though, that means a lot."

"Be careful today, okay?" Ezra said.

"Don't worry, I'm not going downtown or anything like that," she said.

He laughed. "Please don't do anything like that. But that's not what I meant. A bunch of people are sick this morning, so just keep your distance, wash your hands a lot, stuff like that."

"Is it serious?"

"No, I don't think so." He started toward the door, but turned back toward her. "Want to meet me for dinner tonight?"

"Are you asking me on an official date?"

"Ha, I guess so?"

"I'd love to," she said.

Chapter Thirty-Two
Harold

Harold wanted to help the twenty or so people who'd fallen ill but didn't know how to offer. Or even what he could do. He'd been spending the past few weeks going with the fishing crew, but fishing had been canceled that morning. He loitered around The Quad, trying to figure out how to be useful. Without something to do, he feared where his grief might take him.

He overhead bits of information as people passed by and thought the symptoms implicated a stomach bug: high fevers and trouble keeping fluids down, which brought the larger problem of dehydration.

In the Colony, this kind of illness wouldn't have brought on panic. Twenty out of one hundred was a large part of the population, but he remembered times when half his class would be out from school with a stomach bug. They would stay home and sleep it off. Of course, the medical care in the Colony was better, so if things got serious doctors easily treated them at the hospital. Here there was no hospital and they relied only on herbal treatments.

From one of the homes, he'd heard a mother sobbing all morning. His heart ached for her, thinking she must have lost a child but later he found out that the child had simply fallen ill like the rest. Family members ran back and forth to the kitchen to retrieve various concoctions as if it were a matter of life and death. All operations had shut down and it seemed they were preparing for the worst. Almost like they *expected* the worst to happen.

Finally, he spotted Ernie entering The Quad with Hazel by his side. They both carried trays with mugs and tea kettles. He jogged over, maybe he could finally help with something.

"Can I help with anything?" he asked.

Ernie had his usual big smile, but Hazel's forehead seemed to be frozen in a wrinkled state. "Sure. We're bringing this special tea blend to all the sick. It's supposed to help with their dehydration. Minnie has been working all day putting it together," she said.

"Here, let me carry that for you," he said and took the tray from Hazel.

"How are things looking?" Harold asked as they started up the steps at the first residence.

"Not good," Hazel said, opening the door for him and Ernie. "It seems like our count is up to thirty now."

They walked to the first door on the right, and Hazel knocked lightly. A young teen girl answered the door wearing a face mask.

"Hi, Ava," Hazel said. "How is Francis doing?"

"He's resting now," Ava said.

"Here's a cup of tea for him when he wakes up. Minnie made some for everyone who's sick." She filled a mug and handed it to the girl. Ava nodded and then closed the door.

"If the numbers keep rising, Raymond wants to quarantine them." Hazel said, as they walked down the hall to the next door. "As we speak, he's having a room cleared and set up just in case." She knocked on the next door and they delivered the tea. After the next, Harold suggested they split up so they could cover more ground faster. Hazel agreed.

Harold was happy to be doing something, although the hysteria was starting to affect him. Everyone had worried faces when they answered the door and all the children wore face masks, some even wore gloves and goggles. He started to wonder if he should be wearing protective clothing as well. He caught himself holding his breath when distributing the tea, only taking quick breaths when having to talk.

When they finished distributing the tea, Harold asked if they should go back for more.

"No, other teams were sent to pass out tea too. Everyone should have some by now," Hazel said, "Let's go check in with Raymond and see if he wants to start the quarantine. We'll probably need all the help we can get transporting people."

Harold followed them toward Red Square. "How serious do you think this is, Hazel?"

"I don't know. It's scary though. We've never seen this many ill, all at once. But all of us have lost someone to illness, so it's really hard not to be scared. I think everyone will feel a little better once the sick are quarantined," she said. "Except for the mothers that is, they probably won't like being separated from their kids."

They went inside a building at the north side of Red Square. It was a square, concrete building and seemed out of place next to the other elaborate buildings. Inside, they entered a large room where several men were setting up mats on the floor and clearing out odds and ends.

"Wait here, I'm going to go talk to Raymond," Hazel said and made her way into the crowd.

Ernie set his tray on a table by the door, and Harold followed his lead. It seemed like the campus was taking a sick day. Either everyone stayed home tending to their sick, or they were here getting this room ready for the worst.

"Ernie, what do you make of all this?" he asked.

"It's strange, definitely different than back home, that's for sure." He wasn't smiling now.

"Do you think it's as serious as they all seem to think?"

Ernie turned to him. "You know, I actually don't. That's part of why it seems so strange. Like they're really over reacting."

"Yeah, that's what I was thinking too. But the hysteria is sort of contagious."

"I just hope we're right," Ernie said looking back at the room. Harold nodded, he hoped so too.

Hazel rejoined them a few minutes later. The room had been mostly cleared and looked ready for patients.

"Raymond wants to go ahead with the quarantine. We're to go back to the same wing where we distributed the tea and escort the sick here." She didn't look happy about their new assignment.

They headed back to the first home they had delivered the tea to and knocked again. Once again the girl, Ava, answered the door.

"He's still asleep, he hasn't drank the tea yet," she said when she saw them.

Hazel took a deep breath. "That's fine dear. Can we come in? Raymond wants everyone taken to the hall where they can be kept safe. Can I speak with your mom?" Ava hesitated for a second, but soon opened the door wide.

"Mom, Hazel needs you," she said and disappeared into a room. The three of them entered the home and closed the door. Baskets full of wool cluttered the space, along with dishes and books. A woman emerged from the room Ava had gone into. She had brown hair and eyes, and dark circles under her eyes. She wore an apron stained with yellow streaks over her gray dress.

"How is he doing, Marth?" Hazel asked and walked to her. The two women embraced.

"Oh, I don't know," she said and hugged her elbows. "So Raymond wants to quarantine?"

"Yes, just as a precaution."

Marth gave Harold and Ernie a suspicious glance. "What are they doing here?" she asked.

"Oh, you know Ernie and Harold," Hazel said.

"I know who they are. I asked what they're doing here."

Harold felt uncomfortable. It was strange having someone talk about him as if he wasn't there. He and Ernie just stood there, neither knowing what to say or do.

Hazel looked at them and then back at Marth. "They're here to help," she said.

"We can manage without them," Marth said and flashed them an unkind smile, "Thank you, but your assistance isn't needed here."

"Of course," Harold said and then looked at Ernie. Ernie nodded and the two men walked out.

"What do you think that was all about?" Ernie asked when they were back outside.

"I'm not sure, but I don't think it's good. Hopefully, she just didn't want strangers helping with her children, that would be understandable. But something tells me it was more than that. Like she didn't trust us or something."

"That was the sense I got too," Ernie said, "So what should we do now?"

"I don't know." Harold looked around The Quad, searching for an answer. "Maybe we could help out in the kitchen?"

While they headed toward the cafeteria, the first groups of the sick came from their homes. They walked slowly but seemed stable on their feet. Harold thought that was a good sign. He closed his eyes and took a deep breath, fighting back tears as he wished Clara was there. Not for himself this time but for the sick. Her expertise and calm bedside manner would've been put to good use.

In the cafeteria kitchen, they helped prepare dinner. Hopefully their hard work would help them find acceptance here. Curtis was also in the kitchen helping, and he found out that Annabelle and Calvin had offered to help Hogget tend to the sheep.

As dinnertime approached, Ezra appeared in the kitchen. "Raymond wants the dining hall closed tonight. All healthy individuals should eat in their rooms. Raymond has appointed two teams of five to take shifts tending to the ill. Everyone else should stay home and rest in case your help is needed tomorrow. Help me spread the word as people come for dinner."

Harold approached him before he left. "Can we help take meals over to the sick hall?" Ezra stared at him for a minute, lips pursed.

"You guys should go home and rest," he finally said.

"We're all healthy. We'd like to help," Harold pressed.

"It would be great if you could help clean up here then," Ezra said and then added, "Raymond wants to limit the number of people who are exposed to the sick."

"Okay, no problem," Harold said. Ezra turned to leave.

Harold paced while waiting for people to arrive for dinner. He scanned the buffet and noticed there wasn't any silverware and went to retrieve it.

He placed the silverware at the end of the buffet table and watched people as they went through the line. He tried to give them sympathetic looks and smiles, hoping to convey the sense of calm that Clara would have. No one seemed to notice him. Just as he was about to return to the kitchen he heard a woman gasp.

"Who let him in here?" she said, pointing right at Harold. He recognized her. She was an elderly woman he'd given tea to for her husband. Everyone stopped dishing up their food and stared at him now. "He shouldn't be allowed in the kitchen! My son got sick right after he brought tea to our house."

Harold held his hands up. "I'm sorry," he said. "I'm healthy, I assure you." Those closest to him backed away. Others shouted accusations at him and he retreated to the kitchen.

"What's going on out there?" Poppy asked. Curtis was at her side.

"Um, I think we better go back to our guest quarters," he said to Curtis, "People are pretty stressed out and us being new makes them a little uneasy, I think."

Poppy's face relaxed. "Ah, yes. Good idea. Grab some food from back here and come with me, there's a back door." They called Ernie and made a quick exit out the back.

***

Annabelle

"You need to be calm and gentle with them, and they'll be the same with you," Hogget explained and sat next to Calvin, who had a lamb in his lap. Hogget petted the lamb and she allowed him to move her head and limbs any way he wanted. "Isn't she cute? I think she needs her hooves trimmed, see." He pointed at the lamb's foot. Annabelle had no idea what she was supposed to see, but nodded anyway.

After spending some time with the animals, Annabelle felt confident enough to help Hogget with the trimming. Mainly, she soothed the animal while he did the rest, which she found enjoyable. Being around the sheep forced her to tap into a new state of mind. It was like she had to find an animal part of herself, one that could communicate with energy instead of language. *I am calm, so you should be calm*, she projected.

They were fluffy animals, most of them were white and cream colored. But a few of them were black, or had black spots. Annabelle thought the cutest ones were white with black faces.

All in all, it had been a very relaxing afternoon. As evening approached, Hogget said they should get ready to herd the sheep into the barn. "Speeda will do most of the work," he explained. Annabelle was excited to see Speeda in action. As the dog weaved and darted around the sheep, Ezra appeared in the pasture. He waved at them. Annabelle felt her stomach do summersaults as he approached them.

"How's it going?" he asked, his face tense. Annabelle was perplexed by the expression on his face.

"Great. Hogget's a natural, just like everyone said," she answered.

The pasture was a short walk, about twenty minutes from the campus, but it felt like a world apart. As Ezra surveyed the flock his shoulders relaxed.

"We were just about to put them in for the night," she said.

Hogget let out some whistles, and Speeda answered with a bark. She ran around the sheep and herded them into the barn. Hogget and Calvin went inside after them.

"Listen," Ezra said, turning toward Annabelle. "I want you to stay with me tonight." He faced her but gazed at the barn. Annabelle couldn't suppress a smile, despite the serious look on Ezra's face. His request probably didn't have to do with their relationship, but she wasn't going to argue. "There have been some developments today, and I think it would be best if you're with me." He finally looked her in the eye and laughed when he saw her goofy grin. "It isn't like that," he said.

"Oh sure," she teased. Just then Calvin and Hogget emerged from the barn.

"All set," Hogget announced.

"Let's go," Ezra said. "And Hogget, the dining hall is closed tonight; you'll dine in with your mom at home, all right?"

"Have things gotten worse?" she asked.

Ezra nodded. "The sick have been quarantined and everyone else should stay home tonight. Sort of like a curfew. Calvin, you can go straight back to the guest quarters, I made sure someone took food there for you tonight."

"Sure, no problem. Have more people gotten sick?" Calvin asked.

"A second round hit this afternoon. I believe the count is up to forty or so," Ezra said.

"Jesus, that's almost half," Calvin said.

"Yeah," Ezra said and sighed. "Let's get back."

As she and Ezra walked to his room there weren't many people outside but those that were stopped to stare at Annabelle. They whispered to each other as she passed by. Annabelle felt a shiver crawl up her spine.

"What's going on, Ezra?" she asked.

"I'll let you know as soon as we're inside," he said.

But when they finally got behind closed doors, he didn't divulge the information. "Are you hungry?" he asked instead and walked over to his bed. "I have a picnic for us." She looked around the room, noticing that he had tidied it up a bit.

"That sounds perfect," she said.

He spread a blanket out on the ground and then pulled dishes from a basket. "So, why exactly do you need to keep me safe tonight?" she asked once they started eating.

"Well," Ezra took a bite of flatbread and chewed. "I guess the easiest way to put it is that people are scared, and that's making them suspicious of you."

"They think we're responsible for the illness?" Annabelle was repulsed. She would never infect a group of people. Especially not one that she was hoping to join.

"Word has gotten around that Ernie was sick when he arrived. Many think that he passed on some superbug from the Colony."

"Could that be true?" Annabelle felt a lump in her stomach. What if they were responsible for making everyone sick?

"I don't think so. The symptoms are very different. Ernie's was more of a respiratory illness. This seems to be a stomach bug. Plus it's been so long since Ernie was sick."

"Oh good." Annabelle let out a sigh of relief. "I mean, not good, it's still terrible that people are sick, I just meant that good that, uh—"

"I know what you meant," Ezra said with a smile. "But that doesn't mean you guys are off the hook. Hazel has been trying to explain the difference in symptoms and that has just made people come up with more malicious theories."

"Like what?"

"Like you guys brought a virus to infect them on purpose," he said slowly and clearly. He studied Annabelle, his eyes glued to her face. Was he anticipating a reaction he didn't want to miss?

She leaned forward. "What? You don't agree with them, do you?"

His face relaxed and he shook his head. "No, I know you didn't. But I'm not sure about everyone else."

"What?" Annabelle stood. "Ezra, trust me, no one in my group poisoned your people. Why would we do that?" She was mad now. She knew he had a deep seated distrust of the Colony, and she had hoped they were beyond that. Clearly, it was still there.

He looked at her for a minute quietly and then stood up. "I believe you," he said. "I'm sorry, it's just been a crazy day."

"I bet," she said. He took her hand and they went back to their indoor picnic.

"I have a feeling this will all blow over. Even though there was a second round of illness this afternoon, those who woke up sick were starting to get better. I'll admit I was worried earlier but seeing people recover is a very good sign."

"Thank God," she said. Her flash of anger passed as quickly as it had struck, but she wondered if Ezra still suspected that someone from her group was responsible. Of course they were all innocent, right?

Chapter Thirty-Three
Annabelle

"Ezra!" *Bang bang bang,* "Ezra!"

Annabelle sat up and shook Ezra. She'd been sleeping on his chest. She couldn't believe he hadn't woken up.

"Ezra," she said, "There's someone at the door."

"Huh?" He opened his eyes and squinted.

The loud knock hammered the door again. Ezra jumped out of bed and rubbed his eyes. He walked to the door and opened it but blocked the person's view of his room.

Even though Annabelle knew the person at the door couldn't see her, she still shrunk down into the blankets, trying to be as inconspicuous as possible.

"Ezra, I need you. Now." It was Raymond.

"What's going on? What's happened?" Ezra asked.

"It's those people, this is all their fault!" Raymond's voice was high pitched, he sounded crazed.

"What do you need me to do?" Ezra asked.

"I don't know. I don't know. I don't know."

"What's going on, Raymond?" Ezra asked calmly.

"I just got word two people have died! And Rose is sick! If she dies, if my *son* dies, they'll pay. I need you to take care of this, Ezra. I need you to take care of it now."

"Give me two minutes, I'll be right up."

"You have one minute."

Ezra closed the door and turned to Annabelle.

"You gotta go."

"Trust me, I know," she said getting up.

Ezra opened the door and peeked out.

She joined him at the door and he tenderly held her face in his hand. "Go back to your room and wait for me. I'll smooth this over, I promise." He gave her a slow kiss and brushed her check with his thumb.

"I'll see you soon," he said and opened the door all the way.

Annabelle looked out and ran to the entrance and outside. She looked at the ground as she walked quickly all the way back to the guest quarters.

When she went inside, Harold and Calvin were frantically carrying things to the front of their hall.

"Annabelle, thank God," Harold said. "Get your stuff. We have to leave." She stared at him. Leave? She couldn't leave. "Now, Annabelle, go!"

She turned to her room and stood in the doorway. She didn't really have much stuff. It would take her less than a couple of minutes to gather it. But she wasn't leaving, not without Ezra.

"Annabelle, come on." Harold said. Then Hazel was suddenly by her side.

"Annabelle, listen," she put her hands on her arms. "You really need to go now. Look at me," she said. Annabelle locked eyes with Hazel. She had urgency written all over her face. "People are saying crazy things. I'm not saying we can't ever come back but right now we need to go." So Hazel was going with them? That probably meant that Ezra would go with them too. This snapped Annabelle into action, and she grabbed her bag and shoved things in.

"Let's go," she said seconds later.

Everyone from her group gathered in the hall, ready to go, along with a very unhappy Hogget.

"Why do I have to go?" he asked.

"Hogget, this isn't up for discussion. You can't stay here without me. I'm your mother."

"Why are you going then?"

"Someone has to lead them to safety, Hogget."

"So we're coming back then?" Hogget asked.

"I didn't say that either. We don't have time to discuss this, come on." She started for the door. Everyone followed, except Hogget, who sat down in the middle of the hall, arms crossed.

Hazel walked back to him. "Listen, I'm sure we'll be able to come back. And if we can't, I promise I'll get you a lamb to start your own flock wherever we end up." Hogget looked up now.

"My own flock?" he said. Hazel nodded, smiling. He stood. He didn't look happy about leaving but at least was willing to cooperate.

"I don't want us to go through The Quad and Red Square. There's a back way to the boat launch, hopefully we can get there undetected. Come on," she said and they rushed out. But now Annabelle wanted to protest. She couldn't leave without Ezra. She looked around, and he was nowhere in sight.

"Wait," she said as they rounded behind the buildings. "I have to wait for Ezra."

"There isn't time," Hazel said.

"But I can't just leave him," Annabelle knew she sounded exactly like Hogget had moments before. Was Hazel going to promise the gift of her very own Ezra wherever they ended up?

"Curtis!" Poppy ran toward them, carrying a basket. "I thought you guys might be leaving," she said. "That's probably the best idea. I brought you some muffins, though. It isn't much, but I thought you probably would be hungry." She handed the basket to Curtis.

"Thanks Poppy," Curtis said with a big smile on his face. He stood there awkwardly like he wanted to say or do something else but didn't. Annabelle took the opportunity of the delay to step back, so she could see into The Quad. Where was Ezra? She couldn't leave without him. Hazel thanked Poppy now. *He'd better get here quick.*

Then like a miracle, she saw his head emerge at the top of the stairs at the other end of The Quad. She wanted to shout out his name and wave her arms, but she didn't want to draw attention to them. She would just have to wait. The others were moving on now.

"You better go," Poppy said as she walked past her.

Annabelle just stood with her eyes glued to Ezra. Finally, he arrived at the door to their building, and she called his name. He turned and saw her, then jogged over.

"Ezra," she said, relieved. "Come on, we have to go." She started walking and he followed.

"What do you mean? Where are you going?" They had caught up with Hazel and the others now.

"We'll head north, probably camp at Deception Pass tonight," Hazel said without stopping. "I think they'll be safe in Vancouver, we'll see."

"Annabelle, don't go," Ezra said.

"What? I have to," she said. "Just come with us."

"Come with you?" He scowled. "Annabelle, I can't go." She stopped. They were well out of sight of The Quad now, the buildings around them were all in ruin.

"Why not? You have to."

"I can't just leave."

"Hazel is coming with us," she argued.

"She shouldn't be leaving either. Is this because of Ernie? She can't take Hogget away."

Hazel and the others stopped now. "Annabelle, Ezra, come on!"

"She just expects me to leave too? This is unbelievable," Ezra said.

Annabelle's eyes filled with tears. "Please come." Was this how it was going to end?

"Annabelle, this is going to blow over, just let me talk to Raymond."

Annabelle could remember the hysteria in Raymond's voice all too clearly from his conversation with Ezra earlier. She doubted that he could smooth things over. And if something happened to Rose, heaven forbid, it probably was smart that they be as far away as possible. Before she hadn't wanted to leave, but after seeing everyone else's urgency she knew it was the only option.

"You know I can't stay. Raymond was practically threatening to have us killed already," she said.

Ezra threw his arms up. "I can deal with Raymond," he said. "You can trust me. I thought you were all in?"

Annabelle closed her eyes. She was all in, but she didn't have a choice. "I am," she stepped closer to him. "But you know it isn't safe for me here." She looked him in the eyes, "You have to come with us, aren't you all in too?"

"You just expect me to leave my home, everything that I've worked so hard for?" He crossed his arms.

Annabelle felt hopeless. "Well, I did," she said. It was the truth. She had left her life, her family, everything she had ever known and worked for. She was willing to give it all up for Ezra.

"I can't," he said with no emotion. His suddenly relaxed face showed nothing, and when he looked at her his eyes were distant. It was the same stoic mask he'd worn when they first met.

"So you're saying you aren't all in?"

He looked at the ground. "I guess I'm not," he said.

Annabelle felt more tears coming, and she didn't want him to see them. She turned and ran to catch up with Hazel. She didn't know what else to say. What more could she say? He had made it pretty clear that she wasn't worth much to him. She didn't want to look at him another second because it would hurt too much. She wanted nothing more than to get on the boat and row away as far as possible. Maybe if they went fast enough she could leave the hurt behind too.

***

Harold

After a long day of rowing, they finally stopped at a beach camp, containing small cabins similar to the camp in the mountains. When they sat on stumps around a fire for dinner, they silently ate for the first few minutes. Harold appreciated the comfort of a warm meal, especially with the uncertainty they faced. Perhaps he was the only one excited to leave Seattle. Going north would be the beginning of his world exploration. He wanted to make Clara proud of him. He wanted to show her that he wouldn't waste his freedom from the Colony.

"We can camp here for a couple of days to rest and get our strength back," Hazel said, breaking the silence. "I really doubt anyone will come after us." Harold hoped she was right.

"Hazel, thank you for believing we didn't cause the illness," he said. If she hadn't been on their side, he wasn't sure what they would've done.

"Well, I knew for a fact that the illness was different than Ernie's but no one would listen to me. Once the idea was put in their heads, they wouldn't accept anything else."

"How was the idea put there?" Harold asked.

Hazel shrugged. "I don't know. But people were coming up with all kinds of theories."

"Like what?" Calvin asked.

"Well, stuff like Harold brought them poisoned tea, or they heard Poppy say Curtis had been spending a lot of time in the kitchen or—"

"Poppy said that?" Curtis demanded. Everyone looked at him.

"I guess so. But it was true right?" Hazel said.

"What do you mean? Yes, it was true that I was in the kitchen a lot. But why would Poppy implicate me?" Curtis looked back and forth at them with wide eyes.

"I didn't say Poppy said it, just that others did. Maybe she mentioned you were with her and they made assumptions. Does it matter? I was just saying they were making up ridiculous theories."

Curtis's face suddenly became calm, and he sat back again. "Yeah, ridiculous theories," he said casually.

"What do you think happened?" Calvin asked.

Hazel took a bite. "Honestly, I think it was food poisoning."

"But how could there be secondary infections?" Calvin countered.

"There was probably a contaminated ingredient that was used in a few meals. Plus, everyone's digestive system works a little differently. It maybe just took longer to hit some than others."

Everyone was quiet for a minute.

"Why did everyone overreact?" Harold said, breaking the silence. It had been bugging him ever since the outbreak.

Hazel sighed and looked down. "Disease is no joke for us. It's been ingrained in us since birth that at any moment we could be wiped out like before, and we've all seen illness take its toll in our lifetime. After your loved ones die it's hard not to take it seriously."

"What do you mean 'wiped out like before'?" Harold asked. Had the Seattle people already gone through some terrible loss?

"Well, you know, the super virus that led to the fall of civilization," Hazel said, she wiped sweat from her forehead. "It's hot this evening, isn't it?" Harold glanced at the ground, not sure how to respond. He wanted to know more but felt ashamed by his ignorance.

"It's true," Annabelle said quietly. "I saw the evidence myself. It wasn't the nuclear winter that killed them. It was a virus."

Harold nodded. The Seattle Clan feared disease the same way his people feared radiation. Radiation detection in the Colony would cause hysteria: calls to move back into the bunkers, banishment of anyone responsible. Fear changed the way people behaved, it was universal.

"But you weren't scared," Calvin said to Hazel.

"Oh, yes I was," she said shaking her head. "But I knew in my heart you were innocent so that allowed me to think with a clearer head, I guess."

Harold's eyes drifted toward Curtis. He sat forward now, seeming to hang on every word spoken but remained silent.

"Hogget, why haven't you eaten anything?" Hazel said.

Hogget shifted food around on his plate and looked up. His face was pale, his eyes heavy. "I'm not hungry."

"Hogget, do you feel sick?" Hazel stood and placed her hand on his forehead. She held her breath.

"I gotta…" Hogget jumped up and rushed to the bushes where he began throwing up. Hazel ran after him.

"Oh no," Ernie said.

Harold stared at the bushes, his heart pounding.

A moment later Hogget and Hazel returned. Hogget forced a smile and mumbled an apology.

"Nonsense, you have nothing to be sorry for. Drink some water and I'll get you to bed," Hazel said. She looked a little pale herself.

Everyone turned back to their dinner in silence while Hazel helped Hogget to a cabin.

"I'm sure he'll sleep it off," Hazel said when she returned. She stared at the Puget Sound, wringing her hands together for a moment before sitting back onto her stump and retrieving her dinner.

"What should we do?" Ernie asked.

"What can we do? We'll let him rest and head out in a couple days like before. As long as he stays hydrated, he should be fine. Everyone recovered in Seattle, so we don't need to worry." She poked at her food.

"Hazel, you didn't hear?" Annabelle said.

"Hear what?" Hazel glanced up, her eyes heavier than before.

Annabelle furrowed her eyebrows. "Two people died, Hazel. I overheard Raymond."

"No. I would've heard," Hazel protested, shaking her head.

"That's what Raymond said. I thought that's what caused the hysteria this morning."

"What do I do?" Hazel stood, dropping her plate to the ground. "I have to go back then."

Ernie rushed to her side. "You can't go now, it's too late. We'll leave first thing in the morning."

"Ernie, you can't come! You were patient zero. I can't imagine what they'll do to you if you come back. God, two people died?" Hazel looked at Annabelle. "Who was it?"

"I'm so sorry. I don't know."

"Ernie, I have to go back, you understand, right?" Ernie glanced down at Hazel. Tears rolled down her cheeks.

"Of course." He wiped a tear off Hazel's cheek. "You'll come back, right?"

"Oh God." Hazel held her hand over her mouth for a second then ran to the bushes to empty her stomach. Ernie hurried to assist her.

Calvin stood and paced. "What do we do now?"

Harold didn't know. He rubbed his hand over his head and tried to suppress the panic growing inside him by keeping his breath steady. They needed Hazel to direct them. Would they find their way without her? She and Hogget both needed to get back to Seattle, that much was obvious, but who could take them?

"Maybe we should go back to the Colony," Curtis said.

"What? No," Harold shook his head. "We all agreed that wasn't happening. It isn't safe for anyone."

"Okay." Curtis stared at the ground. Harold watched him for a second. Something seemed off about him, but he couldn't figure out what.

"I'll take Hazel and Hogget back in the morning and then return here. We'll head north like our original plan," Harold said.

"Sounds like our best option," Calvin said. Curtis nodded and smiled.

Chapter Thirty-Four
Annabelle

Annabelle settled into her bed but sleep wouldn't come. In the quiet of her cabin, her heartache kept her up. Twenty-four hours ago everything had seemed so clear. She'd been so happy and felt like she knew what her path was meant to be. Now she was lost again. She didn't want to find her way without Ezra—he was the one she wanted.

A life with him would have been full of adventure and progress. A life she would have been proud to live. Something that made much more sense than trying to advance to level one in the Colony. How did that really help anyone? Ezra had bigger plans and she wanted to be a part of those. He would do it too, go on to do amazing things, she was sure of it. And what would she go on to do?

She clutched Gran's key, still hanging safely under her shirt. She would never uncover it's secret now. She had been willing to let the secret go to be with Ezra, but she didn't have him anymore. She had nothing and was going to let Gran down.

To make it even worse, she loved Ezra. Admitting this fact brought tears again. She closed her eyes trying to make them stop, but they seeped out anyway. She loved him. She'd never been in love before, no one had ever made her feel the way he did. He challenged her, mystified her but also charmed her.

She'd been waiting her whole life to meet someone like Ezra. She'd lacked satisfaction and ambition in the Colony because her life wasn't complete. It all made sense now—she was meant to be with him. It was as if she had found the secret map of her life. But he didn't want her anymore.

This was her own private nuclear winter. She had to navigate a dark world, void of all sunshine. Find her way through a new landscape covered in ash, everything shades of gray. Ash coated her skin, filled her lungs, clouded her thoughts. Maybe she should just give into the numbness, sink into the cold darkness. Maybe her eyes would adjust and she wouldn't need light anymore.

As tempting as it was, she couldn't let go. She still wanted Ezra. How could he do this to her? How could he leave her alone? He said he'd be there for her. But when she needed him most he let her go.

She sat up, needing to draw. She was done crying. With nostrils flaring, she lit a candle and retrieved her sketchbook. She flipped through the last few sketches she'd done. Scenes of the buildings and wildlife downtown. Smiling people from the Seattle Clan. Interspersed among them were sketches of Ezra. His beautiful face, his perfect form. She wanted to run her fingers across his shoulders and down his arms. Would she ever have the chance again? She came to one where he stood on the balcony downtown, his back to her. That was how it was now, his back forever to her. He had turned away from her and left her alone in this nuclear winter. She tore the page out and ripped it up, then flipped to a blank page.

She drew his face, but just the bones. She had seen plenty of skeletons lately to know what it would look like. She gave him eyes though, his beautiful, inquisitive eyes. Then she added exposed muscle and fat, with skin clinging to it in places. He had a surprised look on his face, since the eyes were wide and suspended in the sockets without eyelids. His teeth were exposed as well, and she didn't add lips. His jaw was forever clenched in disbelief.

She sat back and looked at her drawing. The candle bathed it in a warm orange light which was the perfect effect. It was Ezra, after being hit by a nuclear blast.

***

Harold

Harold felt uncomfortably hot under the sun. Sweat dripped down his face and his whole body felt clammy, even his forearms. Why should he feel so uncomfortable? He and Clara were enjoying the afternoon on the beach. Just the two of them sat on a white sandy beach gazing at the endless ocean. It felt like they occupied infinity.

Clara buried her feet under the sand. The sun highlighted her hair from above, making it even lighter, almost golden. "Want to swim?" she asked.

Swim? Why hadn't he thought of that? It would be the perfect way to cool off. "Yes," he said and stood. Clara didn't stand though. She reached her arms up to him.

"Help me up?" she asked. Hearing her voice was like hearing a childhood song that he hadn't heard in years. It made his insides ache.

He grabbed her hands and pulled her up. As she struggled to stand he realized why she needed his help up. She was pregnant. He stared at her belly. This was very confusing although he wasn't sure why. She put her hands on the back of her hips and took a slow deep breath. God, she was so beautiful. More now than ever. Her skin shimmered and she wore a long white dress, making her look like Aphrodite. She put a hand on her stomach and smiled at him.

"Well?" she asked.

His eyes rested on her pregnant belly. It still didn't make sense to him. He felt quite certain that she wasn't pregnant the last time he'd seen her.

"Why are you pregnant?" he finally asked, unable to solve the puzzle.

She laughed and walked to him. She put her hands on his face. "Because this is a dream, silly."

All at once it came back to him. The shock of it hit him so hard he stumbled and fell back onto the ground, although it wasn't the beach anymore. He lifted his hand to inspect what goo he'd landed in, discovering mud. The sun disappeared.

Remembering Clara's death was unbearable, but he still wanted to spend as much time with her as possible, dream or not. He looked up quickly, and she was still there. She kneeled down next to him, mud clinging to her dress. She wasn't smiling anymore.

"Why are you running?" she asked through clenched teeth. She towered over him. She moved closer, her face just inches from his, burning him with her eyes.

"What do you mean?" He leaned back as she inched closer. She grabbed his shirt collar and pulled him up to his feet effortlessly.

"Stop being a coward!" she demanded and let go of his shirt.

Harold realized he was crying. "Clara," he whimpered. He didn't know what to do. He wanted to take her in his arms, and never let her go. But she was so furious and strong. He was actually scared of her.

She slapped him.

"We had to leave Seattle. We weren't welcome there anymore," he explained.

She crossed her arms. "That's not what I meant." He stared at her for a while, trying to find answers in her face. She stared back.

"You mean from the Colony?" he finally asked.

"Yes." Her face softened.

"Clara, I can't go back there." He clenched his teeth, feeling anger now. "It's the Colony's fault I lost you."

Clara nodded. "Yes, I know, and that's why you must go back. Our people need you, Harold. You have a job to do."

"I know," he said. He thought she had already shown him his "job" back when he was on the Space Needle. It was to find answers, to find the truth and to help mankind rebuild again.

"That's only part of it," she said as if she read his mind. "Make them pay." Silent lightning lit the sky above. "Take the truth home."

He pulled her close. "I'll try." He closed his eyes and clung to her, could he stay here forever? She didn't hug him back, though. When he opened his eyes he couldn't see her face, darkness had cloaked them. He squinted, trying to see her. Another round of lightning started and she looked different. Her hair got darker with each blink of light.

"You'll find a way. Do whatever it takes."

The shape of her face started elongating. He hugged her again, not wanting to see it change.

"Promise me," she said into his ear. She hugged him back this time.

"I promise," he said.

"Harold?" she asked. He pulled back to look at her. She looked at him, confused. Her face had changed even more, freckles covered it now. And she looked almost like... Annabelle?

"Harold? Harold?"

He jolted awake and found Curtis looking down at him. "Sorry. You were screaming and thrashing. I think you were having a nightmare."

Harold let out a deep breath. "Just a dream," he said, wishing it wasn't the truth. The traces of the dream started drifting away, evaporating in the face of reality.

He tried to sit up, but his body felt very heavy. Suddenly, all he wanted to do was go back to sleep. Moving and breathing seemed to take too much effort. And it was so hot. He tried to focus on Curtis, why wouldn't he hold still?

"Take it easy," Curtis said and rested a hand on his forehead. "I think you're sick too."

***

Annabelle

Annabelle woke to the sound of footsteps in her cabin. She wanted to turn over and look but she felt too heavy. It was hot in her room as well, maybe she had too many blankets? The heaviness seemed to be all around her too, slowing things down. She rolled over slowly.

Someone struck a match and lit a candle. Annabelle blinked and when she opened her eyes, Ezra stood looking down at her.

"Sorry I woke you," he said and kneeled down next to her bed.

"Ezra?" she said. "What are you doing here?"

His face looked strained. He let out a breath but it didn't seem to give him any relief. He moved closer to her and took her hand, but stayed kneeling at the side of the bed.

"Annabelle, I realized something when you left." She'd never seen him this intense, even when he daydreamed about trains. There was a softer look in his eyes, one she had never seen before. It made him look younger, more vulnerable. "God, I hope I'm not too late. That I didn't mess it up for good." He closed his eyes. She wanted to comfort him, tell him it wasn't too late, but the anger that she had conjured up earlier stopped her.

"What do you want?" she asked instead.

He opened his eyes and searched hers. "It's ridiculous. I've tried from the beginning to keep you at a distance. To push you away."

"I noticed that."

"Well, it wasn't very effective. When I didn't know where you were, or I thought you might be in danger, I couldn't think straight." He gave her a small smile. "It was very irritating."

Annabelle didn't return the smile. Where was he going with this? He'd come all this way to say she was irritating? "Sorry I've been such a burden on your conscience," she said and pulled her hand away from his. "Is that what you came to say?"

"No! That's not what I meant...I...Listen." He took another breath and looked at her again. He still seemed like he was searching. Like he looked over the edge of a cliff, trying to decide if he should jump or not. She would wait for him to jump. She crossed her arms and slowly sat up.

"You weaseled your way into my mind, and I couldn't get rid of you," he sat on the bed next to her. He spoke faster now. "Remember when I was gone that first night in the mountains? Well, I was trying to get you out of my mind, even though I had just met you." He took her hand again and she let him. "At the time, I really thought it was because I couldn't stand you, but I was still so curious about you. I caught myself wondering what you were doing, where you might be. So I tracked you and Hogget at the waterfall. Then after spending the day with you, I knew I was really in trouble." He smiled at her. "Remember you were my little trouble maker in the strawberry patch?"

Annabelle nodded but didn't say anything. She didn't want to interrupt his train of thought; she liked where this was going.

"And we both know how much I panicked when you went downtown. Whenever I tried to put distance between us it only made me more, uh," he stopped for a moment, looking for the right word, "obsessed?" He cringed as if admitting this was embarrassing. "Annabelle, you make me crazy. And honestly, it freaked me out a little bit. I've never felt this way before. I thought that when you left I'd be able to get back to my life the way it was before."

She narrowed her eyes, he hadn't actually said anything nice yet. Was he ever going to get to the point?

"But that didn't happen when you left. I felt empty inside," he shook his head. "And the idea of never seeing you again was unbearable. I realized that you being in my head wasn't just an irritation, and I wasn't just crazy or obsessed. I realized that I didn't need to push you away anymore. That I didn't *want* to push you away. I wanted you to stay. With me. I realized that you were the best thing that ever happened to me."

Annabelle felt relief wash all her anger away. He *wanted* her. She wanted to grab him and smother him in her love, however, looking in his eyes, she saw that he had more to say. She would wait.

"Annabelle, I realized that," he took her other hand. "I realized that I love you, and I never want to lose you again." Annabelle closed her eyes and let the words travel through her body, mind and soul. The words sang as they pulsed through her veins, filling her with warmth. She opened her eyes and saw he looked worried. He had just poured his heart out, and probably feared she wasn't going to. As much as she wanted to toy with him, make him pay, she wanted to kiss him more.

"I love you too," she said. He smiled tenderly and she realized the difference about his eyes: his walls were down. He kissed her sweetly, almost timidly, as if this new plateau they had reached was fragile and they needed to treat it with care. *I love you, and I never want to lose you* pulsed through her again and she felt complete. The man she loved, loved her back. Even as she basked in the magic of knowing his love, old fears crept in. How could she really be sure that he wouldn't try and push her away again? How could she really trust him? Since they were putting everything out on the table, she decided to challenge him. She broke away from their kiss.

"How do I know you won't decide to push me away again tomorrow, or the next day? What's to stop you from packing up and going back to the campus without me someday when I'm asleep? How can I fully trust you?" He gave her a confident smile. She hadn't expected that, she thought maybe he would scramble if she challenged him.

"I hoped you would say that," he said. "I guess I do know you pretty well. I knew I couldn't win you back without a fight." He stood up. "So I was talking about what I realized. I realized that I love you." He kissed her hand and then continued. "I never want to lose you again. That means I want to be with you, always. I want you, Annabelle, forever. I can't live without your charm, your spontaneity, your thirst for life. Every second I'm with you I feel excited, I feel alive. You have woken up a part of me that I never knew existed, and I can't ever let that go. I want to be by your side for the rest of our lives. I don't care where we end up, as long as we're together. I want to start a new life with you. I want to have a family with you. You're the one for me, I'm all in." He smiled and got down on one knee. "Annabelle, my life would be empty without you." He reached into his jacket pocket and pulled out a box. "Will you marry me?" He opened the box, inside a ring twinkled in the candlelight.

Annabelle was speechless. His proposal dazzled her; it floated around like pixie dust, sparkling and lighting up the whole room. He kneeled by her, waiting.

"Yes," she said and he stood and pulled her into his arms. They kissed passionately this time. She felt the pixie dust all through her body. It tickled her and filled her with radiance. Ezra was hers, forever. She had never felt so loved in her whole life. She never wanted this moment to end.

"God, Annabelle," Ezra said, pulling away suddenly. "You're burning up."

She stared at him and blinked a couple of times, trying to process what he'd said. His eyebrows were furrowed in concern. She felt her forehead, but couldn't tell a difference. Although, now that he'd mentioned it, she did feel a little dizzy. She sat down on the bed. "I'm fine," she insisted. He sat next to her but didn't look convinced. "Can I see the ring?" she asked. He smiled and nodded then handed her the box.

She gasped at the beauty of the antique ring. An oversized diamond shimmered in the center, orbited by smaller diamonds. A pattern of diamonds and emeralds lined the golden band all the way around. There wasn't a spot on it that didn't sparkle. She slipped it on her finger. The unfamiliar weight felt warm and secure. She would never take it off. "Where did you get it?"

"It was my mother's," he said. "It's been passed down for several generations." Annabelle had never seen a ring so beautiful. It fit her taste perfectly. *Wait until Margaret sees it,* she thought. But the excitement of that faded when she realized Margaret wouldn't see it. She hadn't missed her friend much since she'd left, she had been too distracted, but now she wanted nothing more than to tell Margaret everything. She wanted Margaret to meet Ezra, to be at their wedding. She wished her family could as well. How could she marry a man her father had never met? But it had to be this way if she stayed with Ezra. As painful as it was, she chose him.

"It's beautiful," she said. He smiled but then returned to looking concerned. He put the back of his hand on her forehead and bit his lip.

"Annabelle, are you sure you're feeling well? It seems like you're running a fever."

The room did feel hot, and the dizziness hadn't really gone away when she sat back down. And her eyes felt heavy. With a rush of guilt, she remembered Hogget and Hazel being sick.

"Ezra! It's not me that's sick. It's Hazel and Hogget! Thank goodness you're here, you can take them back." The words sounded funny coming out of her mouth, like they were in slow motion. "But maybe I need to lie down too."

"I know about them. Harold's sick too. We're all going back tomorrow."

"But how can we?" Annabelle lay back down, struggling to keep her eyes open.

"Shhh. It'll be okay. With you guys sick too, how can they accuse you of being responsible for causing the illness? Why would you infect yourselves? I'll make it work out, I promise." He lay next to her and put his arm around her. She snuggled into his embrace—being close to him always made her feel better. And they would be close for the rest of their lives.

"I love you," she whispered.

"I love you too," he said. "Now try and get some rest."

Her bliss didn't lull her to sleep, however. Ezra's words echoed in her mind: *I want to have a family with you.* Annabelle couldn't give Ezra a family. The Colony had made her infertile. She had to tell him. What if it was a deal breaker for him? However, it seemed too difficult to form the words and finally sleep overtook her.

Chapter Thirty-Five
Annabelle

The sound of the oars lapping the water soothed Annabelle. It made her thoughts float far away, daydreaming. It was nice to leave her ill body behind for a bit and be up in the clouds, thinking about Ezra. Thinking about her *fiancé*, Ezra. The memory of the proposal seemed enhanced, as if the fever had burned it deeper into her mind. She could close her eyes and relive it over and over, relishing every detail. It was the only relief she got from her body's complaints.

She would recover, though. She was sure of it. Laying in Ezra's lap, she felt safe, his arms wrapped around her, squeezing her slightly with each row. She knew he would take care of everything.

The gentle rocking of the boat stopped suddenly, rousing Annabelle fully awake. She pried her eyes open to see why they'd stopped. How long had they been on the water? Her mind felt clearer, and she gazed up at Ezra. He looked out at the water, motionless, his face frozen in concentration. What was he looking at?

When she tried to sit, he glanced down at her. He rested his hand gently on her cheek and gave her the most loving look she'd ever received. She tried not to think about everything he saw her go through during her night of illness. The fact that he looked at her with devoted love proved that he would never leave.

"What are you looking at?" She tried to sit up again. He looked surprised to hear her speak, and quickly shushed her. "It's okay," she said, trying to reassure him, "I feel a little better." He shook his head this time and put his finger to his lips then pointed toward the water. She realized that he'd shushed her because of whatever he was looking at. She nodded and he helped her sit up.

She looked over the boat's edge and didn't see anything except a peaceful day. The clear sky reflected its beautiful blue onto the water. The mountains in the distance glistened white and the air smelled salty and sweet.

Just when she thought he had stopped to enjoy the view she saw it. Something huge jumped out of the water. It was black on the top and white on the bottom, with smooth skin and a large tail. An orca whale! It was more majestic than she ever imagined. She leaned forward and placed a hand over her heart, overwhelmed with awe. She never thought she'd get to witness such magnificent creatures. She blinked back tears. "Incredible," she whispered.

When she looked directly at the water she wondered how she'd missed them before. They were swimming everywhere she looked. They seemed to take up the whole Sound, some even swam directly under their boat. Every second or so one would arc through the air and hit the water with a roaring splash. Others jumped playfully, chasing each other. The water all around erupted with geysers as they came to the surface for air.

"How many?" she whispered. It seemed like there were at least a hundred, but maybe more? Three hundred?

"I don't know," Ezra whispered back, "I think close to four hundred. This is one of the larger pods that travels through here."

Just then one popped its head up next to their boat. Annabelle jumped at the sight of it. The animal seemed to smile at her, and she relaxed. Ezra's hands rested on her shoulders, keeping her steady. Annabelle stared at the animal, her heart racing with anticipation. This orca could easily topple their boat over. However, looking at its face she got the sense that she had no such intention. The orca bobbed up and down, her eyes darted between Annabelle and Ezra. She seemed to be saying "hello." Her eyes were as black as her back and looked small compared to the large white oval that adorned each side of her head. Annabelle could see intelligence in those eyes. This animal studied her and Ezra the same way they watched her.

The orca opened her mouth to expose a big pink tongue. An uncountable number of perfectly white, pointy teeth lined her mouth. She stuck her tongue out at them and then as quickly as she had appeared, she was gone.

She and Ezra both let out a breath. "Wow," she whispered. He squeezed her shoulder in agreement.

They watched as the animals swam by. Curtis had stopped his boat as well and looked as transfixed as she felt. In his boat Ernie was also awake and watching, along with Hazel. Hogget, Calvin, and Harold, however, were still out cold. Speeda stood on the other end of their boat, calmly watching the whales.

Annabelle understood why they had stopped. It wasn't just to watch, but also to show these animals respect. This was their water, and even though Annabelle felt like an intruder, they didn't seem to mind sharing the space and carried on in their playfulness uninhibited. They seemed to leap through the air for the pure joy of it. Sometimes they swam upside down exposing their belly to the sky, sometimes they jumped backward and landed on their side. They filled her with such a sense of bliss she forgot all about her sickness. They were the pure expression of joy and by witnessing them she got to keep a little part of that joy forever.

Slowly their numbers dwindled. "Do they always travel in such large groups?" she asked Ezra. She wondered if this was just a seasonal gathering.

"They're all one family," he said, his face peaceful. She knew he reveled in their joy as well. She understood why he had his tattoos now. "Pretty incredible, huh?" He looked down at her and she nodded, smiling back. "The young stay by their mother's side their whole life. They are highly social animals."

"I'm so grateful I got to see them."

"Me too. They mean a lot to me." He gazed into Annabelle's eyes. She felt honored that she could keep his attention even though the orcas were still in view. "I've always loved how they stay with their family forever. That's what I want for us and our family."

Annabelle lowered her head. The rapture she had felt from seeing the orcas began to fade as guilt edged its way into her mind. Family. Ezra wanted a family. She had to tell him the truth.

"Ezra, I can't have babies," she blurted out. He tilted his head to the side and pursed his lips. His eyes lost their glossy, daydream quality. Annabelle's heart sank. Maybe she shouldn't have said anything.

"What do you mean?" he asked.

"I mean, I'm infertile," she said, looking down. "The Colony made me infertile, made all women that way at birth."

"Oh." He looked away for a second. Then he turned back to her, nodding. He lifted her head up, forcing her to look at him. "Annabelle, I want you. Exactly as you are. If that means we can't have babies, then so be it." He stroked her cheek with his thumb. "Even if it is just the two of us forever, that is better than a life without you."

Annabelle tried to smile but her guilt had opened a door and let the sickness back in. Her eyes felt heavy now. Her body shouted at her.

"I'm sorry," she whispered.

"Shh," he said. "I'm serious. It doesn't matter to me."

She wanted to believe him, but her doubts wouldn't let her. As the years passed, would he come to resent her that she couldn't give him a family? She wanted more than anything for him to be happy. What if, in the end, she was the reason that he wouldn't find true happiness?

***

Curtis

Curtis waited anxiously for Ezra to return with good news. They'd made it back to Seattle, and Curtis waited with the sick at the boathouse. Hazel and Harold both sat up now and seemed lucid, although still weak. Ernie, Annabelle and Hogget weren't getting worse, but not really better either. They all lay in a row, and Curtis attempted to get them to sit up and drink water. Calvin was the only one still unconscious, and his fever hadn't broken yet. He seemed dangerously dehydrated, and Curtis wasn't sure what they could do for him.

Of all the ill will Curtis had wished on his brother, death certainly hadn't been included in it. His stomach twisted in knots every time Calvin failed to respond. What if Calvin died? What would Curtis do? So much of his identity had been wrapped up in Calvin that it almost felt like a part of himself would die with him. He'd never realized how much he really cared about his brother until he faced the possibility that he might lose him.

He also fretted about what Ezra would say when he came back. Would they really be welcomed back with open arms just because they were sick now? Ezra had insisted they would.

"Don't you see, them being sick is our ticket back," Ezra had said. "It proves you're all innocent."

Curtis paced back and forth in front of the others. He couldn't do anything more for them. He finally decided to sit outside and wait for Ezra. He rested elbows on knees and held his head between his hands.

He took a deep, pained breath while he faced the truth. Hadn't he wished for this? It almost seemed like he himself had brought on the illness by sheer will power alone. It had been effective at getting his group out of Seattle, just like he wanted. It also targeted the Seattle Clan, possibly giving them a message to not mess with the Colony. But, he knew he wasn't responsible for it. He'd never come up with a plan at all.

Before the illness, he couldn't find anyone who expressed contempt for the Colony, making him wonder if Ovid had told them anything at all. Everyone's kindness had started to seem genuine and he had to face the fact that, maybe, the Colony was wrong. Their ignorance couldn't have been intentional and Ovid was definitely a conspiracy theorist. But the Colony *was* wrong about a lot of things, knowingly or not. Because of their ignorance, Curtis had started to doubt if outsiders were a threat. When he couldn't find any reason to hurt anyone, he'd stopped plotting.

It devastated him to admit that everything he'd learned growing up was wrong. He felt betrayed by the Colony. He felt foolish. He winced, thinking about the things he'd almost done. He didn't understand the Colony's motivations, or what they were ignorant of, but he was sure that the Seattle people were innocent.

While he had hesitated making his plan, it seemed like someone else found a way to get his group to leave. And he thought he had a pretty good idea who. This thought drove fear deep into his stomach. What else was this person capable of? What would they do when they saw his group return?

Everything was a mess—he felt lost and confused. The only thing he was sure of was that he didn't want Calvin to die.

Finally, as the sun started to set, Ezra appeared, along with Wataru and three other men. They marched toward him, looks of determination on their faces. Were they here to help them, or help dispose of them? Curtis didn't stand until they were right in front of him. He found himself staring at their legs and forced his eyes up to Ezra's. Ezra wasn't smiling, but he looked hopeful. Curtis stood.

"Well?" he asked.

"Let's get moving," Ezra said. "We can put them in quarantine."

It seemed like forever before they reached the sick room. Curtis was surprised to find no patients left in the room.

They lay Calvin on an empty mat and Curtis stepped back, wondering what was next.

"What happened to all the sick people?" he asked Ezra.

Ezra shrugged. "They all got better." He'd carried Annabelle the whole way and gently placed her on a mat.

She looked much better off than Calvin, and Curtis thought she would recover quickly. "It was just a bad case of food poisoning. Your group must have eaten something tainted from the kitchen before you left."

"But I thought two people died?"

"Turns out it was just one." Ezra looked at the ground. "Marble Sims, and she'd been sick for weeks, so we don't know if it was this illness that killed her." He wrinkled his eyebrows. "Still unfortunate of course."

"I'm sorry to hear that," Curtis said automatically. He still didn't feel relief. Looking at Calvin's face, ashen and pale, he worried it might be too late.

Minnie entered. Half her hair had escaped from her ponytail and she had dark circles under her eyes. "So, you're back," she said to Curtis when she bent over Calvin. It sounded like an accusation. Curtis usually would be annoyed by her; but at the moment, she was the only one who could help Calvin.

"He needs fluids. That's about all we can do for him." Minnie stood and locked eyes with Curtis. Her face was hard to read, but she sounded sincere.

"Thank you," he said. She moved on to Annabelle.

Minnie made her way around the room, tending to everyone. Calvin and Hogget needed more coaxing to drink Minnie's tea, and the others seemed to improve just from resting. Curtis sat silently by Calvin's side. He watched as people brought in food and supplies, trying to gage their mood, but they all kept their distance. They were helpful now but would these people run them out of town the next time an outbreak struck?

He found himself dozing. He stood, trying to keep himself awake. But it didn't really matter—there wasn't anything he could do for Calvin now. He studied his brother's face. It looked less pale. He crouched down and placed his hand on Calvin's forehead. Relief flooded through him. His fever had finally broken. Curtis sat back down feeling dizzy with emotion. He felt like crying. Calvin was going to recover. He wanted to share the good news with someone but when he looked around the room he saw that everyone was asleep. Even Ezra was sound asleep next to Annabelle with her cradled in his arms.

Curtis wanted to sleep too, but he didn't think he would sleep well here. He decided to retire to the guest quarters instead.

His room was still in shambles, just the way they'd left it. He made no attempt to tidy anything and headed straight for the bed. He was almost asleep when he heard his door open.

"Curtis?" It was Poppy. Energy flooded through his body as his heat rate accelerated. Poppy had this effect on him, but this time, it was more than just his attraction to her. She might be dangerous.

"Poppy?" he said and sat up. She closed the door behind her but didn't turn the light on, instead, she approached the bed. Moonlight from the window illuminated her outline, but he couldn't see her face or if she carried anything. It excited and terrified him at the same time.

She pulled his blanket back and Curtis thought she wanted him to get up, but then she got under the covers next to him. Her huckleberry and lavender scent enticed him and he couldn't believe she sat next to him in bed.

"Kiss me, Curtis," she commanded. He wanted to, but there was a quiver in her voice and a raspiness that she didn't usually have. Had she been crying? It took all his strength, but he scooted away from her.

"What's going on?" he asked, but he suspected what it must've been. She'd seen Annabelle and Ezra together. "This is about Ezra, isn't it?" he said, when she didn't respond.

She burst into tears. "Did you see the ring on her finger? Why did he bring her back here? I thought it was pretty clear she wasn't welcome here anymore. And where did he get that ring? I didn't even know he had one." She buried her face in her hands and sobbed. *She's a mess. Even more messed up than me.*

He had his theories about the sickness, and he wanted confirmation. How would he pull the truth out of her?

"It doesn't even matter anymore anyway," she said in between sobs. "Dad's heir has been born, so now I'm worthless. He doesn't even care about me ending up with Ezra anymore. Having his own son was what he always wanted."

"Shhh, you aren't worthless." Curtis rubbed her arm.

She tried to kiss him.

"Poppy, wait." He gently pushed her back. "You're not worthless, trust me," he said. She didn't say anything. She didn't cry or try to kiss him, but she didn't leave either. She just stared at him, her eyes wide. Even though she was far from it, she looked innocent. "I want to kiss you so bad, you have no idea. But not like this," he said.

She narrowed her eyes and sighed. "Well, it's too bad your brother is the sick one then," she said. This actually made Curtis smile. She was back to her old manipulative self. Her words didn't hurt him though. After seeing her vulnerability she had lost some power over him.

"Yes, well, that's too bad," he said, matching her tone. "He just loves muffins so much, you see."

Her eyes grew wider and he knew that she hadn't been expecting that. "What are you talking about?"

"You know exactly what I'm talking about."

"Please don't tell," she whispered. "I'll do anything, please."

How bizarre to be sitting next to someone who tried to kill me yesterday. "I understand why you did it to us but, God Poppy, why did you poison your own mother?" This was hard for Curtis to wrap his mind around. It had almost made him remove her from his list of suspects.

"I didn't mean to! Someone took her a piece of pie; she wasn't supposed to get sick." Poppy started crying again.

So she poisoned the pie and the muffins, what else is she capable of? Who else was she hoping to harm? "And what about Hazel and Hogget, you were just going to let them die out there with us?"

"I didn't know they were going with you! I thought they were just seeing you off. Honestly, when I heard they had left I was so worried. I…" She wiped her tears aggressively as if they were annoying her. "My plan was flawed. Okay, I really messed up. I know that now."

"You realize you are admitting to trying to kill me," he said. He needed to hear himself say it too.

He was a little impressed at how effective her plan had been, flawed or not. Hadn't it done exactly what he had wanted? It got them exiled. It also sent a message to the Seattle Clan: don't mess with us. If he'd known what was really going on, he could've figured out a way to get everyone back to the Colony.

"That isn't true. You know I only had one target in mind. But how else could I target her without it being obvious?"

"Do you realize how crazy you are?"

"I panicked after you guys left, really." She stared at the ceiling. "I even thought about going after you myself. I knew everyone here would be fine but then I started to think about your survival rate out there alone. I realized that maybe what I'd done was wrong. As painful as it was to see Ezra run off after you, I was glad he did because I knew he'd save you."

Curtis shook his head. Could she seriously be that delusional? Did she really believe that a tiny amount of regret could wash away her guilt?

"Admit it," Poppy said, "you're just as crazy as I am. I've seen through you since day one. You're so jealous of your brother that you put on an act for everyone." She looked at him now.

She was more right than she realized. Hadn't he even pondered killing Ovid? Maybe he even would have done it if Minnie hadn't walked in when she did. Poppy was a killer, and so was he. He didn't like that fact, but it was the truth.

Having Poppy understand him felt liberating. He didn't have to put on an act for her—she already had him figured out.

"I won't tell if you won't," he said. She smiled mischeviously at him and he tucked a loose hair behind her ear. Locking eyes with her made his heart race. Her smile grew, and he smiled back.

"But wait a minute," she said. "Why didn't you eat one of my muffins?" She sounded offended.

Curtis laughed. "Are you serious?" He pulled her to him. "I'm not much of a sweets person," he whispered into her neck.

She lifted her face to his and he finally let her kiss him. He gave into the kiss, becoming intoxicated by her huckleberry scent. Who was he to pass judgement? Maybe it was better to be messed up with Poppy than to be messed up alone.

Chapter Thirty-Six
Annabelle

"I think I might want to be a shepherd," Annabelle told Ezra. It was morning, and he had let her sleep in, like he had every day since she'd been sick. She'd been staying in his room ever since their return, two weeks prior. It had made her uneasy to travel through the building, just one floor below Raymond and his family, but in his room she felt comfortable.

Annabelle hadn't been in any rush to get better because it meant she got to have her own private nurse tending to her day and night: Ezra. She also delayed her recovery because of her apprehension about being back in Seattle. She couldn't believe they would be welcomed back so easily. She hadn't ventured into the cafeteria yet, and once she'd recovered, she spent her time at the pasture with Hogget.

Hogget had been very ill and had taken the longest to recover but as soon as he could walk steadily, he insisted on spending the days with his sheep. It appeared Hogget knew what was best and after a day with his flock he came home stronger and more energetic.

"Annabelle, the shepherd," Ezra said. "I can see it." He set a breakfast picnic basket on the bed and sat at the edge, grinning at her. He hadn't ever said how happy he was they were able to come back to Seattle, but she knew he felt it. It thrilled her he didn't have to leave anymore.

She wanted him to be happy and hoped everything would return to normal, but it was tainted now. She'd seen how quickly Raymond could turn on someone. She felt like everyone constantly scrutinized her. In a way, it reminded her of the Colony, one slip up and it went in your parenthood file. She no longer felt free in Seattle like before. Hopefully, that would change with time.

"You'll have to take a day off from your flock today. The baby ceremony is at noon and everyone has to attend." Ezra handed her a plate of food from the basket. Then poured her some tea.

"Oh," Annabelle said, staring down at her food. She hadn't realized that she had to go. He had told her a few times that the ceremony was for welcoming Raymond's son into the clan and giving everyone a chance to meet him. "But don't the sheep have to be let out to pasture?" It was a lame excuse but all she could come up with.

"I guarantee that Hogget has already done it." He took a sip of tea and studied her for a moment. "What are you worried about?"

Annabelle held her tea, soaking in the warmth. "After everything that happened, I'm still a little apprehensive about facing everyone." She looked at him now.

He nodded. "I get that, but you can't hide forever. The way to feel accepted is to get to know people, show them that you're worth keeping around. I've been putting feelers out and honestly everyone feels embarrassed about what happened. They feel like they overreacted. And they feel terrible that you guys got sick too. The others are finding a place with us. Harold and Calvin have been out with the fishermen every day, and Curtis has become our newest chef. If they let Curtis in the kitchen, it shows they trust you." Of course Ezra wanted them to stay in Seattle, and that meant she was going to have to come out of hiding.

"Do you really think they'll ever fully accept us, knowing we're from the Colony?"

"They don't care about where you're from," Ezra said. "Their reaction was just panic over the sickness."

"But you cared," Annabelle said.

Ezra blew out a slow breath. He grabbed her hand. "That was my own hang up, and I'm sorry. I was wrong, and it wasn't fair of me to judge you like that. But I don't think anyone else cares about it. They all accepted Ovid, and they love him!" He kissed her hand. "They'll love you too."

"Okay, you're right. I have to face them someday, might as well be today." She smiled at him and took a sip of tea, soaking in warmth from his words and the hot drink.

Ezra's face lit up. "It'll be fun. People love these gatherings. They'll all be in a good mood," he said, finishing his pitch even though he didn't have to. "And I borrowed a dress from Hazel for you. People like to dress up for these things." He raised his eyebrows and grinned. She grinned back, the thought of dressing up sounded delightful.

Two hours later they walked outside the campus toward the ceremony site. When they reached the forest's edge, Ezra stopped and presented his arm to her.

"My lady," he said. "You're so beautiful."

She beamed at him and took his arm. "Thank you," she said. She felt it too. It was amazing what a dress could do for her mental state. The dress wasn't even that fancy. It was just a blue woolen dress, with a halter top and a knee length skirt. But she felt glamorous in it. When she first put it on she wanted to do a twirl, and as if Ezra could read her mind, he asked her to spin around for him.

Ezra cleaned up as well. He styled his hair and wore a new blue shirt she'd never seen before and black slacks.

They walked through the woods, and she felt like they were on the way to a ball. They came to a fork in the path and turned left instead of going straight toward the boat launch. Not knowing where they were going added to the excitement. But she didn't have to wait long before the path through the trees ended abruptly at a clearing.

Calling the space a clearing didn't give it justice. It looked more like an outdoor banquet hall. Annabelle's eyes were drawn to the flowers everywhere. Centerpieces of pastel roses, irises and orchids sat on top of the large round tables. All along the perimeter flowers of all types bloomed. At the end of the clearing, flowers covered a bassinet. Four white pillars towered over the bassinet, flanked by more potted flowers. Pink rose petals covered the buffet table and an elaborate cake looked like a blooming rose itself. The elegant scene reminded Annabelle of a wedding reception but with a little more whimsy.

"It's breathtaking," she said to Ezra.

"We have Ovid to thank for that."

People mingled, laughter filled the air, and someone played a guitar. Ezra ushered her to a table near the front, exchanging greetings all the way there. Harold, Calvin, Wataru and his family sat at their table, along with a couple of people she had seen before but didn't know well.

"Hello," she said, making eye contact with the others and sat down.

"I'll get us some drinks," Ezra said and disappeared into the crowd.

"You look lovely," Harold said.

"Thanks, you clean up nice yourself." He looked better than she had seen him since leaving the Colony. He was clean shaven and his white button up shirt looked new. Annabelle let her eyes wander over the tables, looking for the others from the Colony. A few tables over sat Hazel, Hogget, Ernie and Curtis. She waved at Hazel when she caught her eye. Then she motioned to her dress and mouthed "thank you." Hazel smiled and nodded.

Ezra returned a few minutes later with two glasses of an orange beverage and placed one in front of Annabelle.

"It's so good to see you all are well," a woman to her right said. Annabelle turned to her. "We were so worried when you came back."

"Thank you," Annabelle said. "I do feel better." She held her hand out to the women, "What was your name again? I'm Annabelle." The woman looked at her kindly as they shook hands.

"I'm Tabitha," she said. Tabitha's light brown hair spilled around her shoulders, and she looked to be in her late twenties.

"Nice to meet you." Annabelle wanted to say something else. Something charming and witty but nothing came to her, so instead she just smiled. Tabitha didn't seem to mind and even though they didn't say anything else Annabelle felt more at ease. Maybe Ezra was right, people were willing to accept them.

Soon silence fell over the crowd and Annabelle saw Raymond and Rose, with babe in arms, standing in front of the pillars.

"Welcome and thank you all for joining us in welcoming the newest member into our community." Raymond spoke proudly. He stood tall and his tailored gray shirt and trousers showed his slenderness. "We have so much to be grateful for. I can't express how happy I am to see us all healthy once again and that we have survived this latest trial. My son has come to join us at a great time. We're thriving and growing, and I'm confident he'll witness much prosperity in his lifetime." He put his arm around Rose and gazed down at the baby in her arms. "So please, enjoy the festivities. To start us out, Poppy would like to sing." Poppy approached them, looked at her baby brother and placed a gentle kiss on his forehead before turning to the group.

She looked stunning. Her hair was in an elaborate french twist, with a few curly tendrils framing her face. She wore a white sundress, which fit her looser than what she wore daily, and it made her look elegant.

Poppy began to sing sweetly and full of emotion. "Sleep baby sleep, and dream of a new world for us. Sweet dreams for a sweet future, you are our next. The joy for a new generation, the joy for tomorrow, the joy for today, the joy to replace our sorrow. Sleep baby sleep and dream of a new world for us…" Her voice projected across the clearing, transfixing everyone.

Annabelle felt moved by the performance and noticed Tabitha wipe a few tears from her face. Annabelle found her hand making it's way to Gran's necklace. Hearing Poppy sing about generations suddenly made her heart ache, thinking of Gran. She had Ezra back, but would never discover the key's secret. She'd thought she could let the mystery go, but now, a weight seemed to wrap around her shoulders. She was going to let Gran down. She tried to shrug off the feeling and focus on the ceremony.

A few other performances followed but nothing came close to what Poppy sang. Having shared the experience of the ceremony with the Seattle Clan made Annabelle feel more comfortable. By welcoming the baby with them, she felt like she was one of them. Perhaps this bonding experience was just what her group needed to be fully accepted. She glanced around at the others, smiling, feeling at home, dancing to the guitar music. Yes, this could work.

The rest of her group mingled and seemed to have a good time. Curtis followed Poppy around but at one point, Poppy turned and grabbed Curtis' hand. Annabelle leaned forward, could they be a couple? Selfishly, this made her relieved because it meant that Poppy wouldn't be an issue for Ezra and her. Harold and Calvin must have made a lot of friends through fishing because she barely had a chance to speak to them. And of course, Ernie had long ago found his place with Hazel. Was she the only one who hadn't ventured out? She sat back in her chair, feeling foolish.

She understood why everyone had been so scared when the illness struck, and why Raymond had been so frantic— after all his pregnant wife was sick. If she worked hard to earn these people's trust, she knew she would be fully accepted. Once accepted, she doubted that there could be a repeat experience of before. She gazed down at her ring and moved her finger around to make all the gems sparkle in the light. This was going to be her life. With Ezra, it would be a happy life. *Sorry Gran. I hope you can forgive me.*

She felt someone grasp her shoulder. "Congratulations on your engagement," they said. Annabelle looked up to find Rose holding the baby.

Annabelle stood, she wasn't sure if that was what she was supposed to do, but it felt like the respectful thing. "Thank you.

And congratulations to you," she said and finally got a glimpse of the baby. He slept soundly, wrapped up in a white blanket. He had a head of thick dark hair and a squished up face with chubby red cheeks, but he was adorable. "He's so precious," she said sincerely.

"Let me hold the little bugger," Ezra said and held his arms out. Rose smiled and gently transferred him into Ezra's arms. The baby turned his head back and forth a couple times, and settled into Ezra's arms but didn't wake up. Ezra rocked him back and forth. He did it so naturally Annabelle wondered if he even realized he was doing it.

"Hey there, little Ray," he said. It occurred to Annabelle that she hadn't ever asked what the baby's name was. It didn't surprise her that he had been named after his dad. "I'm your Uncle Ezra," he went on. Watching him filled Annabelle with pride. Ezra was good at being an uncle, and Ray would be lucky to have him.

Ray started making rapid facial expressions in his sleep. "Oh, look at that!" Ezra said, entranced. Ray's face finally settled down, but he stopped with a smile and his tongue sticking out ever so slightly. "Oh, look at his little tongue," Ezra pointed out. He looked to Rose for confirmation of the incredible discovery. Rose smiled and put her hand on Ezra's back while she looked down at her baby's face.

Annabelle's heart swelled. She loved seeing a man melt in the presence of a baby. Most men she knew shied away from babies, afraid they would break them. But not Ezra, he doted on Ray. It was very sweet. But as the seconds ticked by the sweetness of the moment shifted to a tragedy for Ezra. The one man who treasured a baby was one who would never have his own—if he stayed with her. Her smile disappeared, and she watched him with her eyebrows drawn. It pained her to watch now.

Before long, Rose took her son back and moved on to the next table. However, Annabelle's pain at the thought of never having a baby didn't leave her as easily. She pushed the food around on her plate. She had told Ezra about her infertility on the boat, and they hadn't discussed it again. She feared bringing it up now, but also worried about the regret he'd feel later if he changed his mind. And what about herself? She'd always wanted to have kids—it had never been a question. And it wasn't just about gaining status in the Colony, she truly wanted to be a mother and have a family. She wanted to know what it was like to love someone the way a mother does. To watch her children learn and grow and witness the world through their innocent eyes. She didn't want to miss out on that part of the human experience. But she could only have children within the Colony.

She looked at Ezra, he was still beaming from holding the baby. He chatted with the man next to him, laughing and joking. She loved him so much but what would happen to their love if they couldn't let it grow? If they both truly wanted children, would not being able to have them create a void in their happiness?

If only there was a way to have him and to have kids. But of course, there wasn't. Or, was there? She got a fluttery feeling in her chest as she formulated a plan. Maybe there was a way, and now that she'd entertained the possibility, she couldn't imagine trying for anything less. Her hand found its way to Gran's key again. Maybe she could still uncover its secret as well.

She looked up and locked eyes with Harold. "I have to go back to the Colony," she said. Harold stared in astonishment but didn't say anything.

"What?" Ezra said, turning away from his other conversation. "What did you say?"

She continued looking at Harold. "I have to go back." Then she looked at Ezra. "Ezra, it's the only way I can have children. I can't get pregnant here."

Ezra held up a hand to stop her from going on. "Annabelle, I told you that didn't matter—"

"But it does matter." She pushed his hand down. She couldn't live a life filled with regret and wouldn't condemn Ezra to that life either. "I want kids too, and I can't have them here."

"But how will you have kids in the Colony? How will you get approval?" Calvin asked. Annabelle tapped her lip with a finger. He brought up a good point. For the first time in her life, she felt outraged that the decision to have a baby was in the hands of someone else. She wanted to have a baby someday and no one else should have to give her permission first. She grimaced, thinking about all the couples she'd denied parenthood. She wished she could take it back and grant permission to everyone seeking it.

Calvin was right—there was no way she could get approval. She would have to be married first but Ezra couldn't go back with her.

Ezra put his arm around her and kissed her on the head. "Annabelle, seriously, you don't have to do this." She felt the pressure growing inside of her. There had to be a way. She would find a way. She had to, for Gran, and for their future. If she wanted to have a fulfilled life with Ezra, she had to fight to get it.

"I'll go with you," Harold said.

"You will?" Annabelle turned back to him. His face was serious and his eyes intense. He meant it.

"We can say we bonded over the ordeal we faced on the mission," Harold said. Annabelle nodded, it could work. "We know what they want to hear."

"Yes, and I know how to pass the approval process. I bet we could pull it off." She focused all her concentration on Harold. On this plan. The whole ceremony could have disappeared and she wouldn't have noticed. All the details were coming together in her mind. They could make this happen. They would make this happen.

It wouldn't be easy. They would face a mountain of questions and would have to hide behind lies the whole time they were in the Colony. If they got caught they might face more serious punishment than banishment. She swallowed. Was it worth the risk? Pretending to love Harold would be a challenge and she'd be away from Ezra.

"Whoa, wait a minute. What are you guys saying?" Ezra was trying to interrupt her tunnel vision, trying to stop her wheels from turning. "Wouldn't you guys have to get married?" With this question, she finally turned to look at him. He wore a frown and had worry in his eyes.

The easy thing would be to stay with him and forget the whole plan. They would be happy, she was sure of it. But what if a dark cloud hovered over them? She didn't think she could forgive herself if she didn't at least try. If things started to go wrong in the Colony they could always escape and return to Seattle. She would know she did everything possible, and then be able to make peace with not having children. But if she didn't at least try. . .

"Ezra, I have to do this." She grabbed his hands. "For us. I can't let us live a life that will be full of regret in the future." She searched his eyes, trying to transmit the importance of this. "Trust me, we can pull this off."

"Annabelle, I don't want to lose you. It's not worth the risk. I want you more than I want kids, trust me."

"You say that now, but how do you know you won't regret it in the future? I don't want to set us up for failure. We have to at least try this," Annabelle said. "Please."

"But when would you go? How long would you be gone?" He squeezed her hands.

"We wouldn't be able to go until next spring," Harold said. "Plenty of time for you two to get married first."

Annabelle raised her eyebrows. "See? It can work. And we have lots of time to figure out the details."

He sighed, and Annabelle knew that he wasn't going to fight her. She smiled, filled with hope, and the pressure that had built inside of her changed to excitement. This would work, it had to work, and then she and Ezra could live a perfect life.

Ezra wasn't looking at her though, he stared at the table. Annabelle stood. "Dance with me?" She pulled him up and led him to the grass where a few others were dancing.

Annabelle wrapped her arms around his neck. "Ezra, I love you. I want to be with you forever. You can trust me." She searched his eyes and understood his reservations. She wouldn't want him to go if the roles were reversed. "I'll leave if it gets too dangerous, and we'll escape as soon as I'm pregnant. I bet it will only take a few months. And then I'll be back with you and we can start our family. Please let me at least try."

"We would have lots of details to work out first," he said.

"Does that mean you're saying yes?"

"And I'll be out of my mind worrying about you."

"Are you saying yes?" Annabelle gripped his shoulders.

"And I don't like that you'll be marrying Harold."

"I understand that," she said. "Believe me, you don't have to worry about me and Harold though."

"I know. I trust you." He pulled her in close, wrapping his arms all the way around her. "But that doesn't mean I will like it."

Annabelle rested her head against his chest. It would be so hard to be apart from him. She had set out on the mission hoping to find adventure but never expected to fall in love. Now that she had it, she wouldn't settle for an incomplete life. She wanted it all. Wanted to give Ezra it all.

"Can we at least discuss it?" she asked.

He let out a slow breath. "Let's enjoy the party first."

Annabelle waited anxiously for the party to end. She couldn't get her mind off her plan, and the hope that Ezra would agree. People started leaving and she waited for Ezra to say he was ready to go. He lingered, seeming to avoid the discussion that loomed.

When only a few others remained, he came to her, but avoided eye contact. "Let's meet in my library. Harold, can you join us?"

"Of course," Harold said and stood. Harold seemed as enthusiastic as Annabelle about returning to the Colony and it occurred to her that there was something going on with him that she didn't know about.

The three walked silently to Ezra's library. After flipping on the lights, Ezra turned to his bookcases.

Ezra's still stalling. At least he's willing to discuss it though. She and Harold sat at the table and she turned to him. "Harold, I really appreciate that you're willing to go. But I have to admit, it surprises me. I thought you wanted to travel," she said.

"I did." He rubbed his hand through his hair. "Clara visited me in a dream... she demanded I go back and expose the Colony. And she's right. The people there have a right to know they're being lied to."

Ezra sat next to Annabelle, holding a notebook. "You want to expose the Colony?" he asked. "How exactly would you do that?"

"Honestly, I have no idea. But I think this might be the perfect opportunity. It'll be easier to keep our story straight if it's just the two of us."

Annabelle considered his words. He was right, but his plan was more dangerous than hers. "I'll help you find a way," she said. Dangerous or not, she would do everything she could.

Ezra sighed and Annabelle studied his stern expression. *I bet he can't argue with Harold's motivations. Maybe he's cracking.*

Ezra pulled a map from the notebook and spread it out on the table. *Cascadia* was written across the top in large, loopy letters. "*If* we do this, what's the plan?"

Harold pointed at the map. "I think we could take the same route back, but as we approach the Colony we stay away from the main path. We don't want to be spotted before we're ready."

"I'd come with you," Ezra said.

"Yes, you can come on the trek across the mountains, but we'd have to part ways before getting to the Colony," Harold said.

"And how long will it take to . . . accomplish all this?" Ezra leaned back and crossed his arms.

Annabelle turned to him. "I think we could get approval and be pregnant in three months max."

"And how exactly would that work?" Ezra narrowed his eyes.

Annabelle grinned at him. "Don't worry. Since my eggs have been removed, conception takes place in a lab. You'll even be the father, of course. We'll just swap Harold's sperm sample with yours."

"But if I can't go near the Colony, how would you get my, um, sample?" Ezra shook his head. "This is the strangest conversation I've ever had."

"We'll have to rendezvous when it's close to conception time. Maybe a couple months after we part ways," Annabelle said.

Ezra studied the map. "I've always wanted to explore the area just south of the Colony. Perhaps I could go there while I'm waiting."

Harold nodded. "That could work."

Annabelle took Ezra's hand and he finally looked at her. "What do you think?" she asked, and held her breath.

"I don't like it," Ezra said. "But I can see your mind's set on it. I feel better knowing I'll be nearby and that it'll only be for three months." He held her gaze and Annabelle knew he was going to say yes. Her heart pounded while she waited.

Finally, he nodded. "What can I do to help?"

Acknowledgements

Writing The Edge of Cascadia wouldn't have been possible without the help of so many people and all their amazing support. Thanks to all my family and friends who read early drafts and got me going in the right direction. Thanks to Suzie for listening to me speak about my book for hours and hours and always showing interest and encouraging me.

Thanks to my husband for designing the perfect cover. Thanks for always helping me brainstorm, for reading chapters and rewrites, and supporting me through the ups and downs. I never would have been able to finish without your endless support.

Thanks to my parents and Mark for your support and enthusiasm. Your input has been so valuable.

Thanks to everyone at Sage's Tower Publishing for making my publishing dream come true. This all wouldn't have been possible without you. Thanks to the Sage's Tower beta readers who took the time to read my book and give me such awesome feedback. You shaped my book and made it so much better. Thanks to Lori for helping me polish the book and make it shine.

And special thanks to Amy and Nicole for believing in my book and working so hard to get it published.

And finally, thanks to you, new reader. I hope you enjoyed my book!

Author Bio

S.A. Sebuchi grew up in Washington and discovered a love for writing at a young age. She attended the University of Washington in Seattle where she received a BA in Comparative History of Ideas. She lives on 5 acres in the woods with her husband and two children. She loves reading, writing, and living inside her imagination.

CPSIA information can be obtained
at www.ICGtesting.com
Printed in the USA
BVHW081820290721
613187BV00009B/643